STAR TREK™

NEW VISIONS

PHOTOMONTAGE AND STORY BY:
JOHN BYRNE

EDITS BY:
CHRIS RYALL

COLLECTION EDITS BY:
JUSTIN EISINGER
AND ALONZO SIMON

COLLECTION DESIGN BY:
GILBERTO LAZCANO

STAR TREK CREATED BY:
GENE RODDENBERRY

Special thanks to Risa Kessler and John Van Citters of CBS Consumer Products for their invaluable assistance.

ISBN: 978-1-63140-367-5

18 17 16 15   1 2 3 4

Ted Adams, CEO & Publisher
Greg Goldstein, President & COO
Robbie Robbins, EVP/Sr. Graphic Artist
Chris Ryall, Chief Creative Officer/Editor-in-Chief
Matthew Ruzicka, CPA, Chief Financial Officer
Alan Payne, VP of Sales
Dirk Wood, VP of Marketing
Lorelei Bunjes, VP of Digital Services
Jeff Webber, VP of Digital Publishing & Business Development

www.IDWPUBLISHING.com
IDW founded by Ted Adams, Alex Garner, Kris Oprisko, and Robbie Robbins

Facebook: facebook.com/idwpublishing
Twitter: @idwpublishing
YouTube: youtube.com/idwpublishing
Instagram: instagram.com/idwpublishing
deviantART: idwpublishing.deviantart.com
Pinterest: pinterest.com/idwpublishing/idw-staff-faves

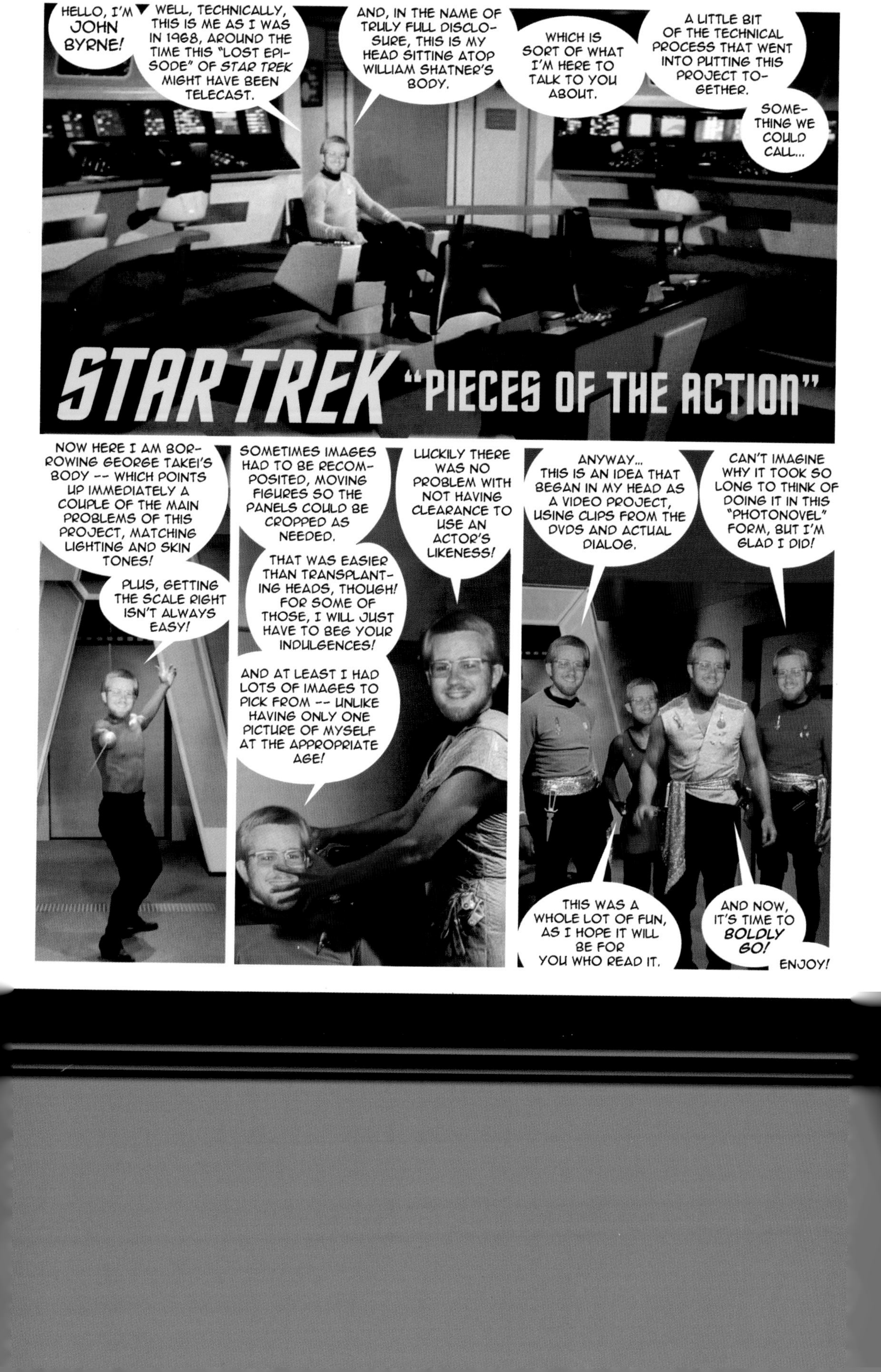
HELLO, I'M JOHN BYRNE!
WELL, TECHNICALLY, THIS IS ME AS I WAS IN 1968, AROUND THE TIME THIS "LOST EPISODE" OF STAR TREK MIGHT HAVE BEEN TELECAST.
AND, IN THE NAME OF TRULY FULL DISCLOSURE, THIS IS MY HEAD SITTING ATOP WILLIAM SHATNER'S BODY.
WHICH IS SORT OF WHAT I'M HERE TO TALK TO YOU ABOUT.
A LITTLE BIT OF THE TECHNICAL PROCESS THAT WENT INTO PUTTING THIS PROJECT TOGETHER.
SOMETHING WE COULD CALL...
STAR TREK "PIECES OF THE ACTION"
NOW HERE I AM BORROWING GEORGE TAKEI'S BODY -- WHICH POINTS UP IMMEDIATELY A COUPLE OF THE MAIN PROBLEMS OF THIS PROJECT, MATCHING LIGHTING AND SKIN TONES!
PLUS, GETTING THE SCALE RIGHT ISN'T ALWAYS EASY!
SOMETIMES IMAGES HAD TO BE RECOMPOSITED, MOVING FIGURES SO THE PANELS COULD BE CROPPED AS NEEDED.
THAT WAS EASIER THAN TRANSPLANTING HEADS, THOUGH! FOR SOME OF THOSE, I WILL JUST HAVE TO BEG YOUR INDULGENCES!
AND AT LEAST I HAD LOTS OF IMAGES TO PICK FROM -- UNLIKE HAVING ONLY ONE PICTURE OF MYSELF AT THE APPROPRIATE AGE!
LUCKILY THERE WAS NO PROBLEM WITH NOT HAVING CLEARANCE TO USE AN ACTOR'S LIKENESS!
ANYWAY... THIS IS AN IDEA THAT BEGAN IN MY HEAD AS A VIDEO PROJECT, USING CLIPS FROM THE DVDS AND ACTUAL DIALOG.
CAN'T IMAGINE WHY IT TOOK SO LONG TO THINK OF DOING IT IN THIS "PHOTONOVEL" FORM, BUT I'M GLAD I DID!
THIS WAS A WHOLE LOT OF FUN, AS I HOPE IT WILL BE FOR YOU WHO READ IT.
AND NOW, IT'S TIME TO BOLDLY GO!
ENJOY!

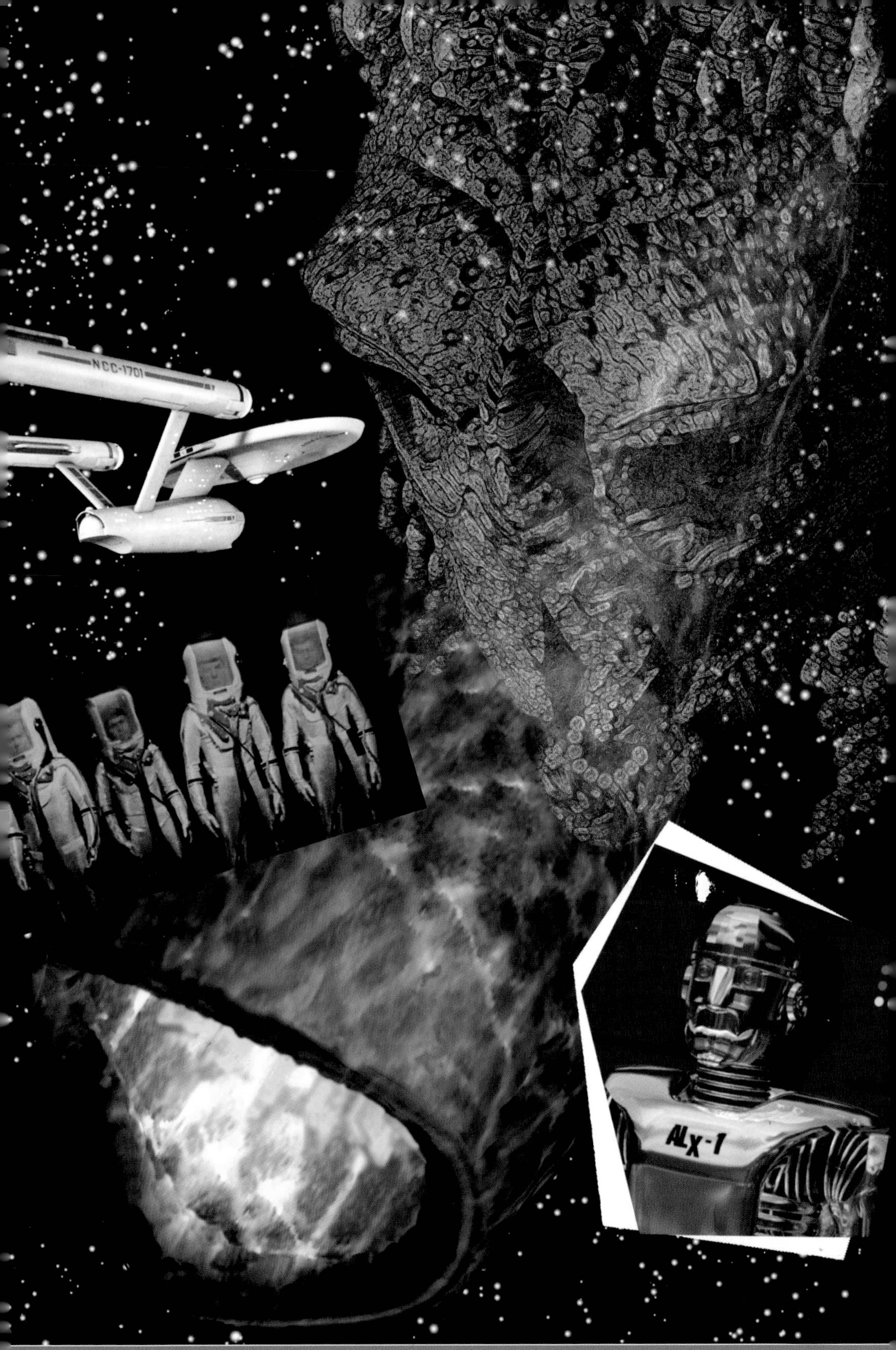
NCC-1701
ALX-1

CRY VENGEANCE

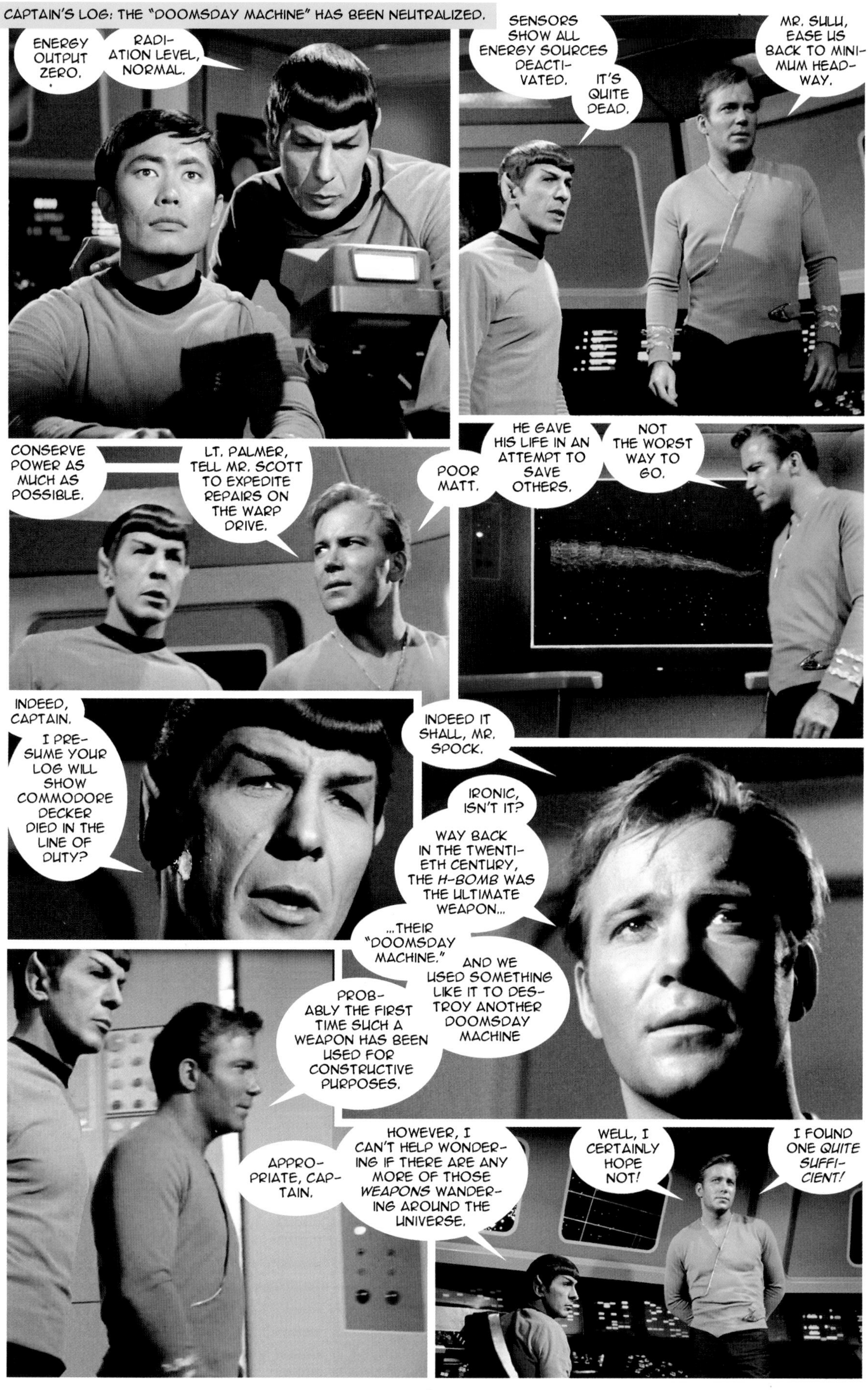
CAPTAIN'S LOG: THE "DOOMSDAY MACHINE" HAS BEEN NEUTRALIZED.
ENERGY OUTPUT ZERO.
RADIATION LEVEL, NORMAL.
SENSORS SHOW ALL ENERGY SOURCES DEACTIVATED.
IT'S QUITE DEAD.
MR. SULU, EASE US BACK TO MINIMUM HEADWAY.
CONSERVE POWER AS MUCH AS POSSIBLE.
LT. PALMER, TELL MR. SCOTT TO EXPEDITE REPAIRS ON THE WARP DRIVE.
POOR MATT.
HE GAVE HIS LIFE IN AN ATTEMPT TO SAVE OTHERS.
NOT THE WORST WAY TO GO.
INDEED, CAPTAIN.
I PRESUME YOUR LOG WILL SHOW COMMODORE DECKER DIED IN THE LINE OF DUTY?
INDEED IT SHALL, MR. SPOCK.
IRONIC, ISN'T IT?
WAY BACK IN THE TWENTIETH CENTURY, THE *H-BOMB* WAS THE ULTIMATE WEAPON...
...THEIR "DOOMSDAY MACHINE."
AND WE USED SOMETHING LIKE IT TO DESTROY ANOTHER DOOMSDAY MACHINE
PROBABLY THE FIRST TIME SUCH A WEAPON HAS BEEN USED FOR CONSTRUCTIVE PURPOSES.
APPROPRIATE, CAPTAIN.
HOWEVER, I CAN'T HELP WONDERING IF THERE ARE ANY MORE OF THOSE *WEAPONS* WANDERING AROUND THE UNIVERSE.
WELL, I CERTAINLY HOPE NOT!
I FOUND ONE *QUITE SUFFICIENT!*

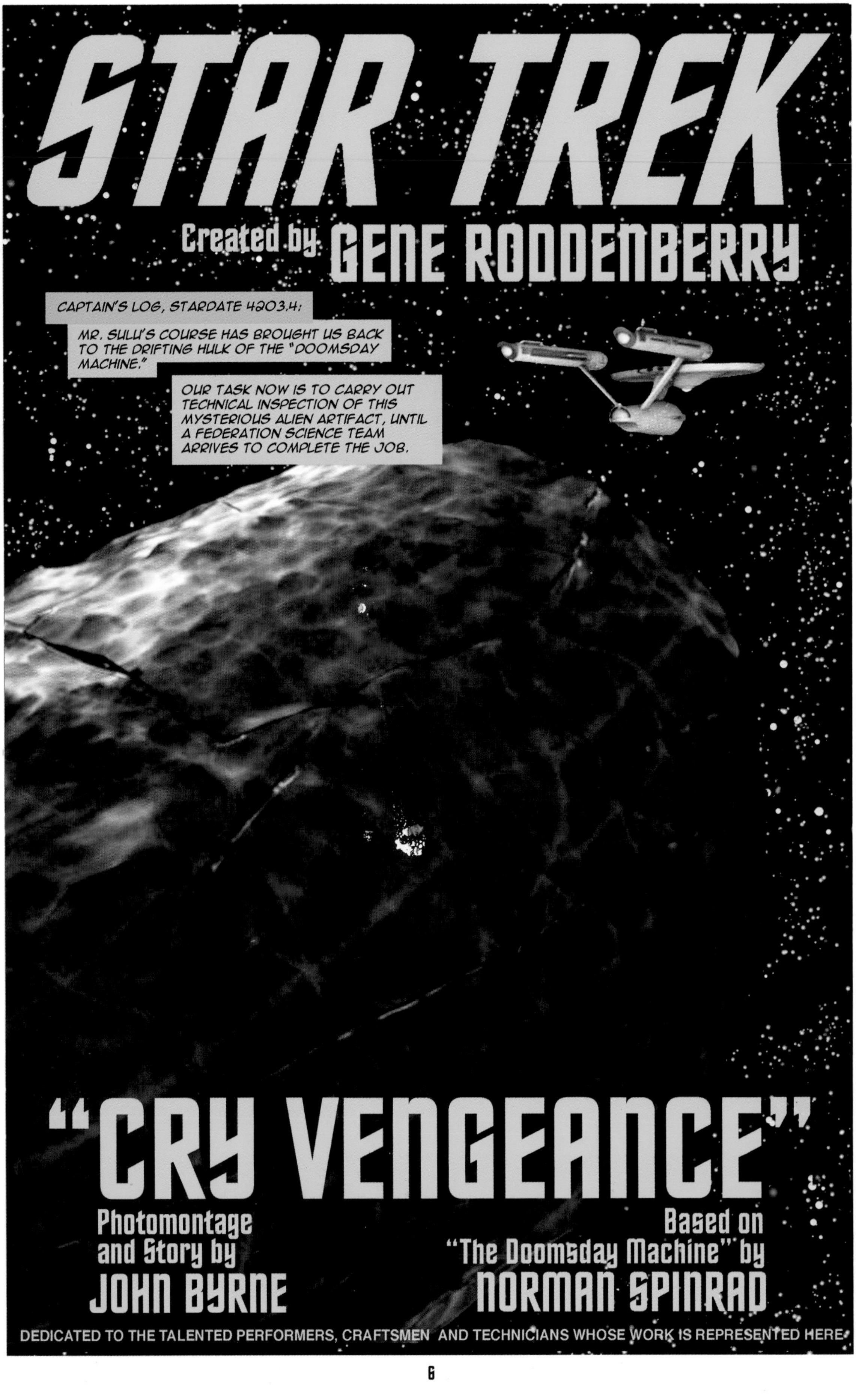
STAR TREK
Created by GENE RODDENBERRY
CAPTAIN'S LOG, STARDATE 4203.4:
MR. SULU'S COURSE HAS BROUGHT US BACK TO THE DRIFTING HULK OF THE "DOOMSDAY MACHINE."
OUR TASK NOW IS TO CARRY OUT TECHNICAL INSPECTION OF THIS MYSTERIOUS ALIEN ARTIFACT, UNTIL A FEDERATION SCIENCE TEAM ARRIVES TO COMPLETE THE JOB.
"CRY VENGEANCE"
Photomontage and Story by JOHN BYRNE
Based on "The Doomsday Machine" by NORMAN SPINRAD
DEDICATED TO THE TALENTED PERFORMERS, CRAFTSMEN AND TECHNICIANS WHOSE WORK IS REPRESENTED HERE

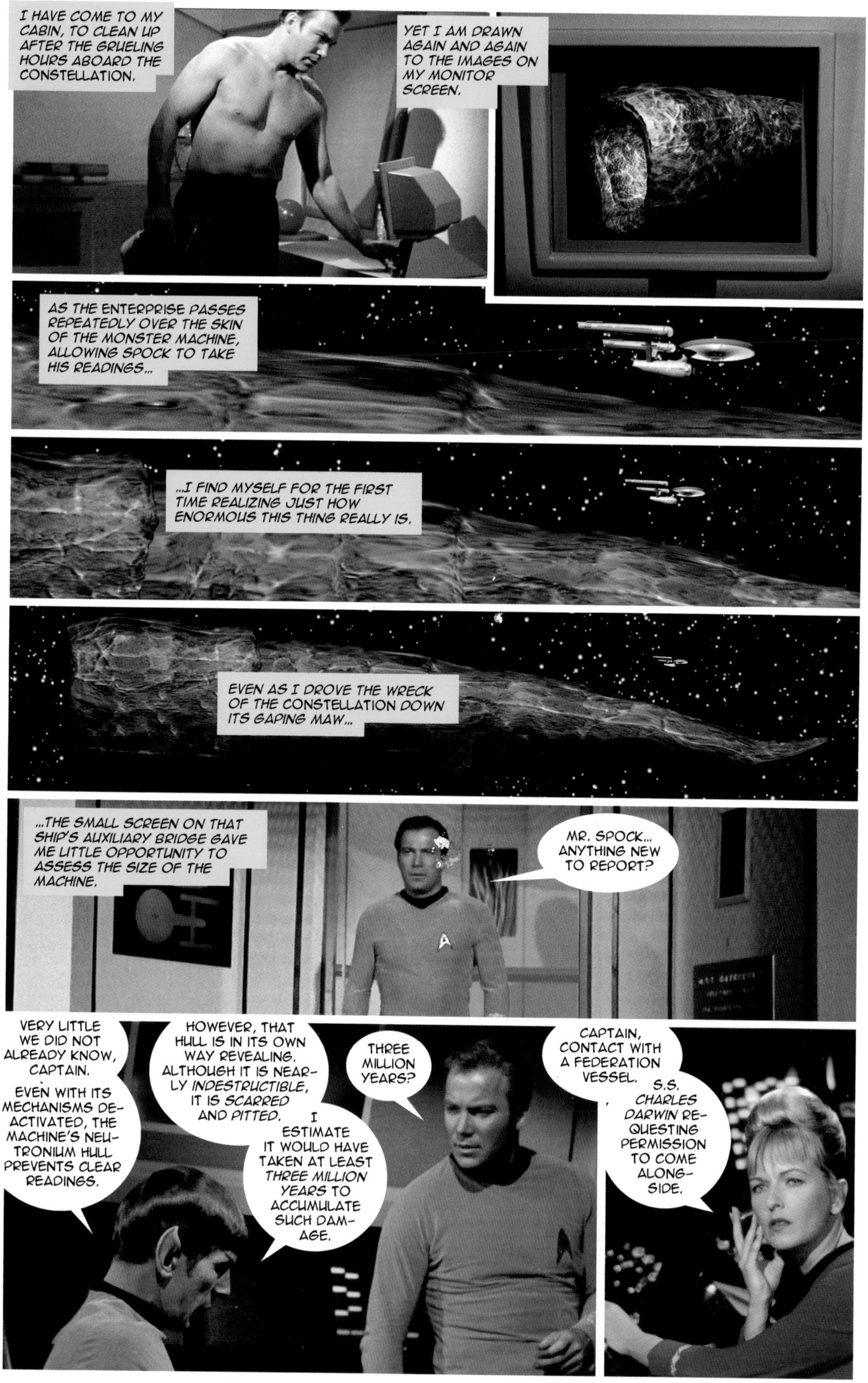
I HAVE COME TO MY CABIN, TO CLEAN UP AFTER THE GRUELING HOURS ABOARD THE CONSTELLATION.
YET I AM DRAWN AGAIN AND AGAIN TO THE IMAGES ON MY MONITOR SCREEN.
AS THE ENTERPRISE PASSES REPEATEDLY OVER THE SKIN OF THE MONSTER MACHINE, ALLOWING SPOCK TO TAKE HIS READINGS...
...I FIND MYSELF FOR THE FIRST TIME REALIZING JUST HOW ENORMOUS THIS THING REALLY IS.
EVEN AS I DROVE THE WRECK OF THE CONSTELLATION DOWN ITS GAPING MAW...
...THE SMALL SCREEN ON THAT SHIP'S AUXILIARY BRIDGE GAVE ME LITTLE OPPORTUNITY TO ASSESS THE SIZE OF THE MACHINE.
MR. SPOCK... ANYTHING NEW TO REPORT?
VERY LITTLE WE DID NOT ALREADY KNOW, CAPTAIN.
EVEN WITH ITS MECHANISMS DE-ACTIVATED, THE MACHINE'S NEU-TRONIUM HULL PREVENTS CLEAR READINGS.
HOWEVER, THAT HULL IS IN ITS OWN WAY REVEALING. ALTHOUGH IT IS NEAR-LY INDESTRUCTIBLE, IT IS SCARRED AND PITTED.
I ESTIMATE IT WOULD HAVE TAKEN AT LEAST THREE MILLION YEARS TO ACCUMULATE SUCH DAM-AGE.
THREE MILLION YEARS?
CAPTAIN, CONTACT WITH A FEDERATION VESSEL.
S.S. CHARLES DARWIN RE-QUESTING PERMISSION TO COME ALONG-SIDE.

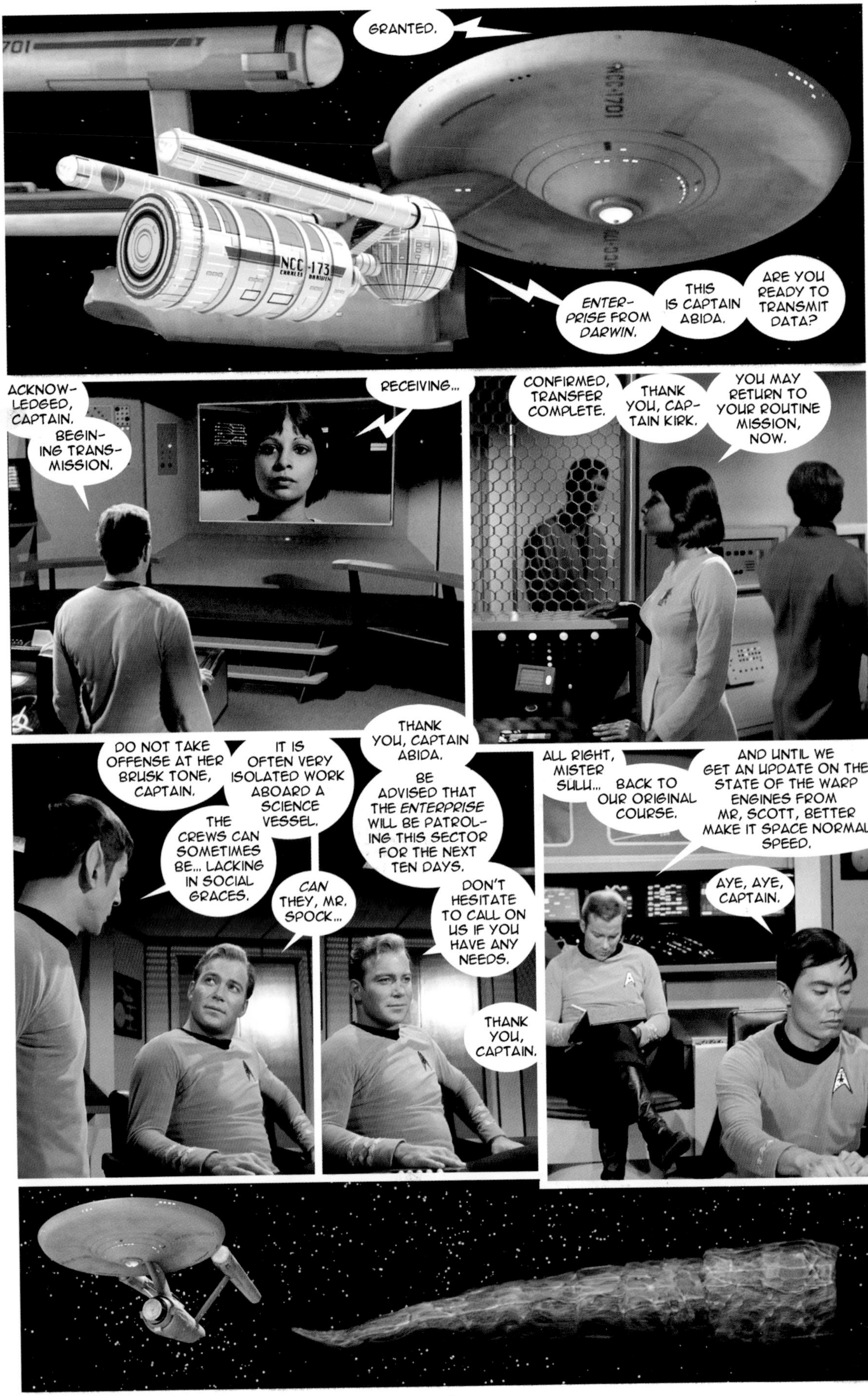
GRANTED.
ENTERPRISE FROM DARWIN.
THIS IS CAPTAIN ABIDA.
ARE YOU READY TO TRANSMIT DATA?
ACKNOWLEDGED, CAPTAIN.
BEGINING TRANSMISSION.
RECEIVING...
CONFIRMED, TRANSFER COMPLETE.
THANK YOU, CAPTAIN KIRK.
YOU MAY RETURN TO YOUR ROUTINE MISSION, NOW.
DO NOT TAKE OFFENSE AT HER BRUSK TONE, CAPTAIN.
IT IS OFTEN VERY ISOLATED WORK ABOARD A SCIENCE VESSEL.
THE CREWS CAN SOMETIMES BE... LACKING IN SOCIAL GRACES.
CAN THEY, MR. SPOCK...
THANK YOU, CAPTAIN ABIDA.
BE ADVISED THAT THE *ENTERPRISE* WILL BE PATROLING THIS SECTOR FOR THE NEXT TEN DAYS.
DON'T HESITATE TO CALL ON US IF YOU HAVE ANY NEEDS.
THANK YOU, CAPTAIN.
ALL RIGHT, MISTER SULU...
BACK TO OUR ORIGINAL COURSE.
AND UNTIL WE GET AN UPDATE ON THE STATE OF THE WARP ENGINES FROM MR. SCOTT, BETTER MAKE IT SPACE NORMAL SPEED.
AYE, AYE, CAPTAIN.

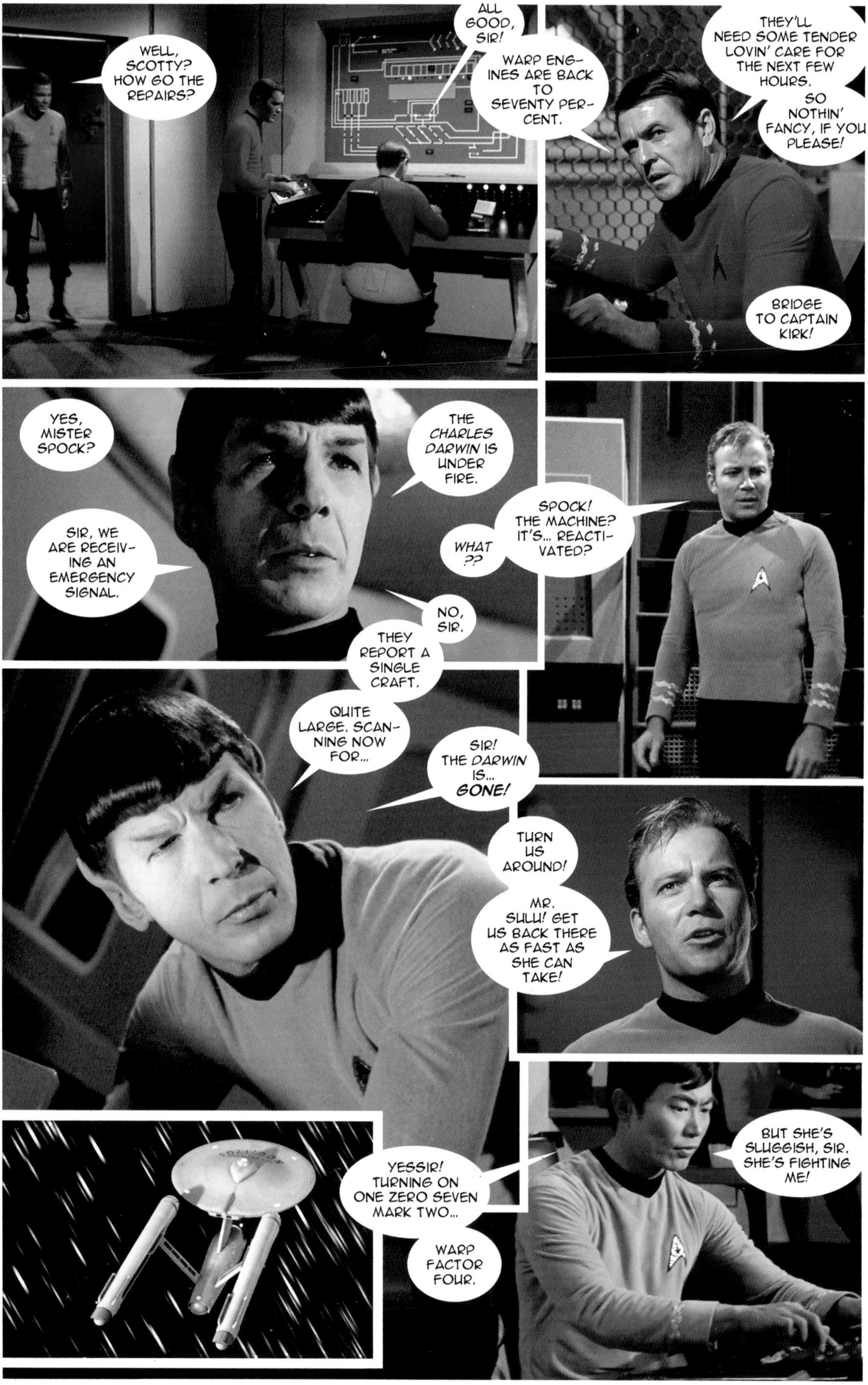
WELL, SCOTTY? HOW GO THE REPAIRS?
ALL GOOD, SIR!
WARP ENG-INES ARE BACK TO SEVENTY PER-CENT.
THEY'LL NEED SOME TENDER LOVIN' CARE FOR THE NEXT FEW HOURS.
SO NOTHIN' FANCY, IF YOU PLEASE!
BRIDGE TO CAPTAIN KIRK!
YES, MISTER SPOCK?
SIR, WE ARE RECEIV-ING AN EMERGENCY SIGNAL.
THE CHARLES DARWIN IS UNDER FIRE.
WHAT ??
SPOCK! THE MACHINE? IT'S... REACTI-VATED?
NO, SIR.
THEY REPORT A SINGLE CRAFT.
QUITE LARGE. SCAN-NING NOW FOR...
SIR! THE DARWIN IS... GONE!
TURN US AROUND!
MR. SULU! GET US BACK THERE AS FAST AS SHE CAN TAKE!
YESSIR! TURNING ON ONE ZERO SEVEN MARK TWO...
WARP FACTOR FOUR.
BUT SHE'S SLUGGISH, SIR. SHE'S FIGHTING ME!

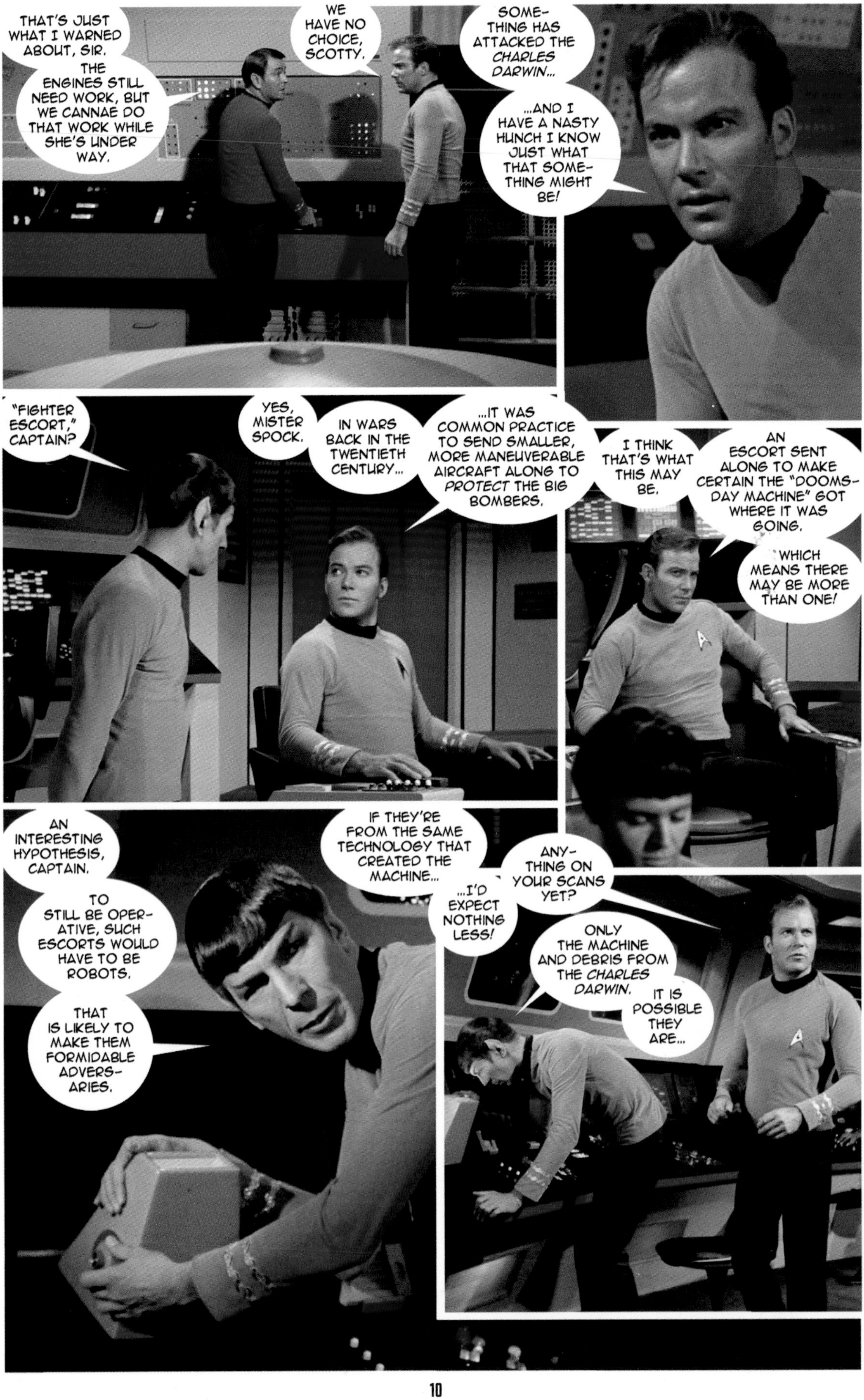
THAT'S JUST WHAT I WARNED ABOUT, SIR.
THE ENGINES STILL NEED WORK, BUT WE CANNAE DO THAT WORK WHILE SHE'S UNDER WAY.
WE HAVE NO CHOICE, SCOTTY.
SOMETHING HAS ATTACKED THE *CHARLES DARWIN*...
...AND I HAVE A NASTY HUNCH I KNOW JUST WHAT THAT SOMETHING MIGHT BE!
"FIGHTER ESCORT," CAPTAIN?
YES, MISTER SPOCK.
IN WARS BACK IN THE TWENTIETH CENTURY...
...IT WAS COMMON PRACTICE TO SEND SMALLER, MORE MANEUVERABLE AIRCRAFT ALONG TO *PROTECT* THE BIG BOMBERS.
I THINK THAT'S WHAT THIS MAY BE.
AN ESCORT SENT ALONG TO MAKE CERTAIN THE "DOOMSDAY MACHINE" GOT WHERE IT WAS GOING.
WHICH MEANS THERE MAY BE MORE THAN ONE!
AN INTERESTING HYPOTHESIS, CAPTAIN.
TO STILL BE OPERATIVE, SUCH ESCORTS WOULD HAVE TO BE ROBOTS.
THAT IS LIKELY TO MAKE THEM FORMIDABLE ADVERSARIES.
IF THEY'RE FROM THE SAME TECHNOLOGY THAT CREATED THE MACHINE...
...I'D EXPECT NOTHING LESS!
ANYTHING ON YOUR SCANS YET?
ONLY THE MACHINE AND DEBRIS FROM THE *CHARLES DARWIN*.
IT IS POSSIBLE THEY ARE...

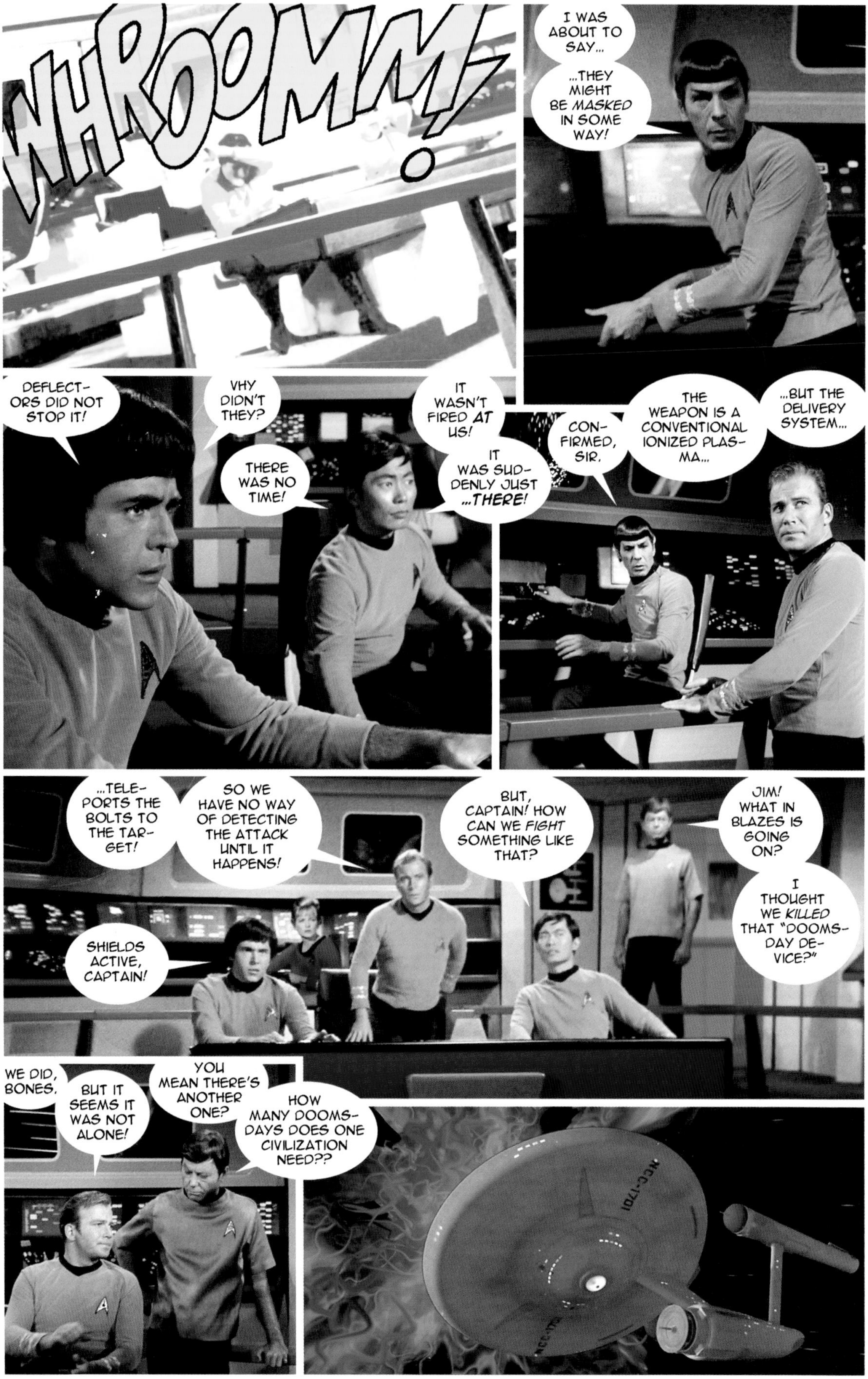
WHROOMM!
I WAS ABOUT TO SAY...
...THEY MIGHT BE MASKED IN SOME WAY!
DEFLECTORS DID NOT STOP IT!
VHY DIDN'T THEY?
THERE WAS NO TIME!
IT WASN'T FIRED AT US!
IT WAS SUDDENLY JUST ...THERE!
CONFIRMED, SIR.
THE WEAPON IS A CONVENTIONAL IONIZED PLASMA...
...BUT THE DELIVERY SYSTEM...
...TELEPORTS THE BOLTS TO THE TARGET!
SO WE HAVE NO WAY OF DETECTING THE ATTACK UNTIL IT HAPPENS!
BUT, CAPTAIN! HOW CAN WE FIGHT SOMETHING LIKE THAT?
JIM! WHAT IN BLAZES IS GOING ON?
I THOUGHT WE KILLED THAT "DOOMSDAY DEVICE?"
SHIELDS ACTIVE, CAPTAIN!
WE DID, BONES.
BUT IT SEEMS IT WAS NOT ALONE!
YOU MEAN THERE'S ANOTHER ONE?
HOW MANY DOOMSDAYS DOES ONE CIVILIZATION NEED??
NCC-1701

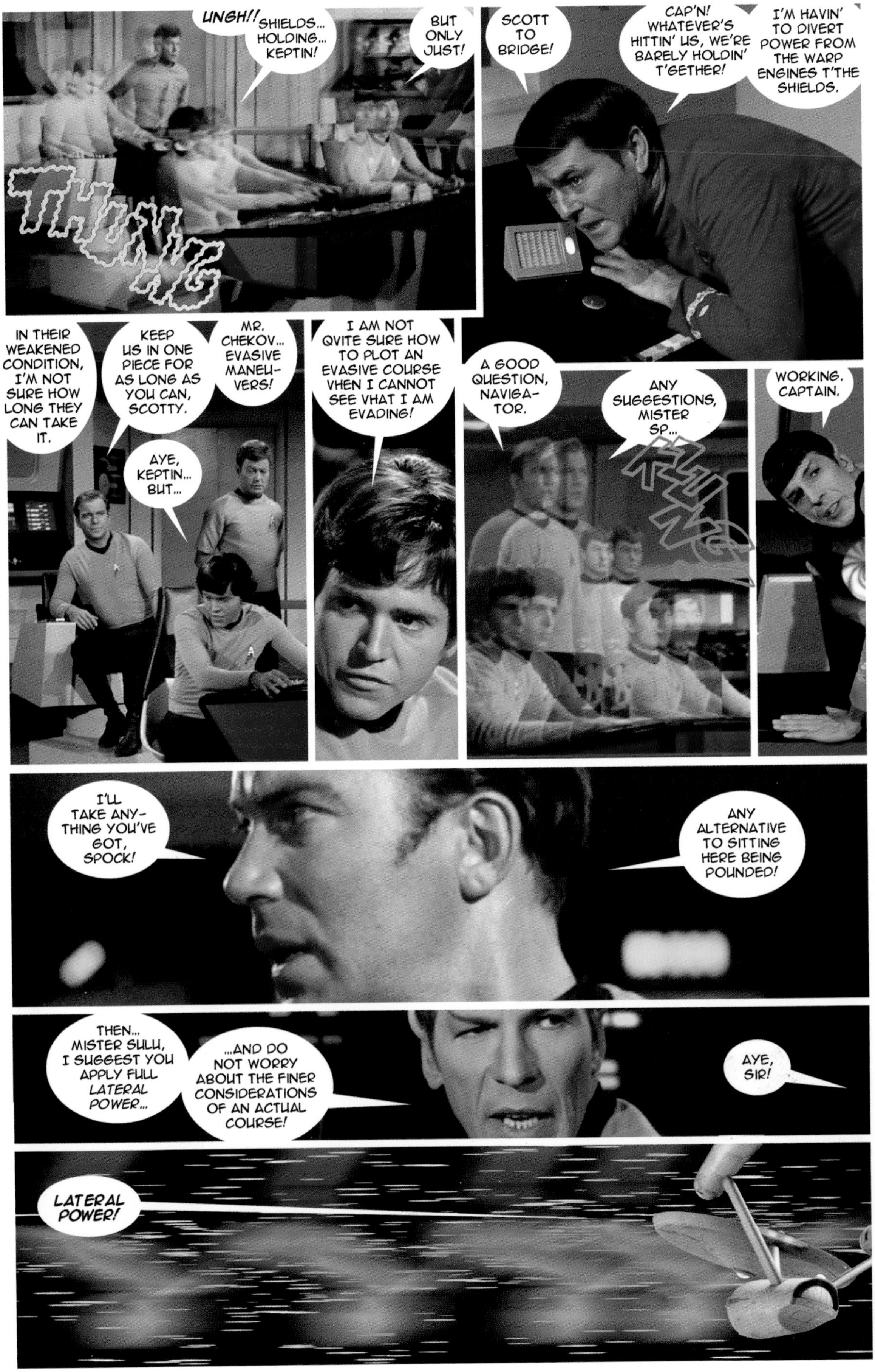
UNGH!!
SHIELDS... HOLDING... KEPTIN!
BUT ONLY JUST!
THUNG
SCOTT TO BRIDGE!
CAP'N! WHATEVER'S HITTIN' US, WE'RE BARELY HOLDIN' T'GETHER!
I'M HAVIN' TO DIVERT POWER FROM THE WARP ENGINES T'THE SHIELDS.
IN THEIR WEAKENED CONDITION, I'M NOT SURE HOW LONG THEY CAN TAKE IT.
KEEP US IN ONE PIECE FOR AS LONG AS YOU CAN, SCOTTY.
AYE, KEPTIN... BUT...
MR. CHEKOV... EVASIVE MANEU-VERS!
I AM NOT QVITE SURE HOW TO PLOT AN EVASIVE COURSE VHEN I CANNOT SEE VHAT I AM EVADING!
A GOOD QUESTION, NAVIGA-TOR.
ANY SUGGESTIONS, MISTER SP...
KLUNG
WORKING, CAPTAIN.
I'LL TAKE ANY-THING YOU'VE GOT, SPOCK!
ANY ALTERNATIVE TO SITTING HERE BEING POUNDED!
THEN... MISTER SULU, I SUGGEST YOU APPLY FULL LATERAL POWER...
...AND DO NOT WORRY ABOUT THE FINER CONSIDERATIONS OF AN ACTUAL COURSE!
AYE, SIR!
LATERAL POWER!

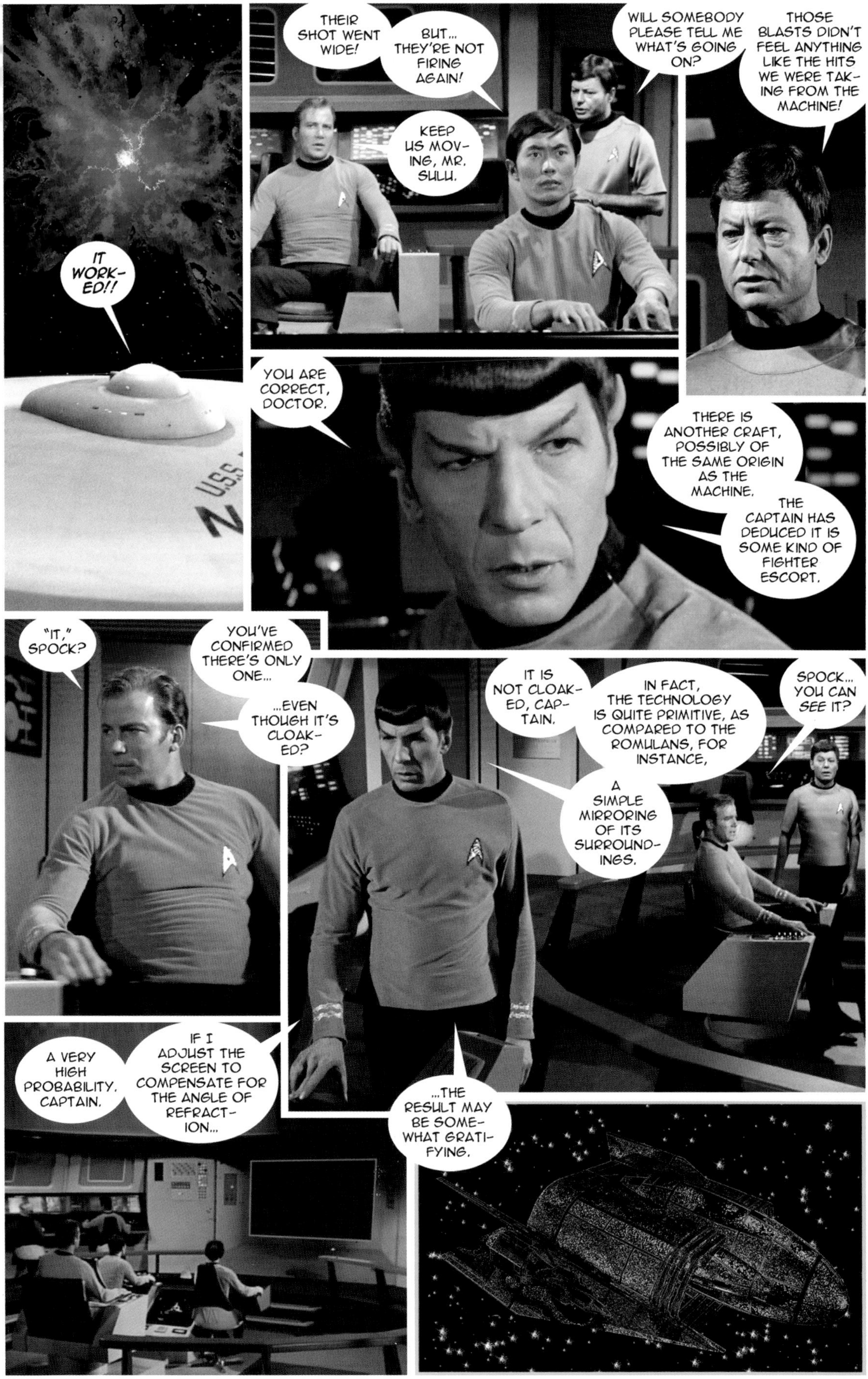
IT WORKED!!
THEIR SHOT WENT WIDE!
BUT... THEY'RE NOT FIRING AGAIN!
KEEP US MOVING, MR. SULU.
WILL SOMEBODY PLEASE TELL ME WHAT'S GOING ON?
THOSE BLASTS DIDN'T FEEL ANYTHING LIKE THE HITS WE WERE TAKING FROM THE MACHINE!
YOU ARE CORRECT, DOCTOR.
THERE IS ANOTHER CRAFT, POSSIBLY OF THE SAME ORIGIN AS THE MACHINE.
THE CAPTAIN HAS DEDUCED IT IS SOME KIND OF FIGHTER ESCORT.
"IT," SPOCK?
YOU'VE CONFIRMED THERE'S ONLY ONE...
...EVEN THOUGH IT'S CLOAKED?
IT IS NOT CLOAKED, CAPTAIN.
IN FACT, THE TECHNOLOGY IS QUITE PRIMITIVE, AS COMPARED TO THE ROMULANS, FOR INSTANCE,
A SIMPLE MIRRORING OF ITS SURROUNDINGS.
SPOCK... YOU CAN SEE IT?
A VERY HIGH PROBABILITY, CAPTAIN.
IF I ADJUST THE SCREEN TO COMPENSATE FOR THE ANGLE OF REFRACTION...
...THE RESULT MAY BE SOMEWHAT GRATIFYING.

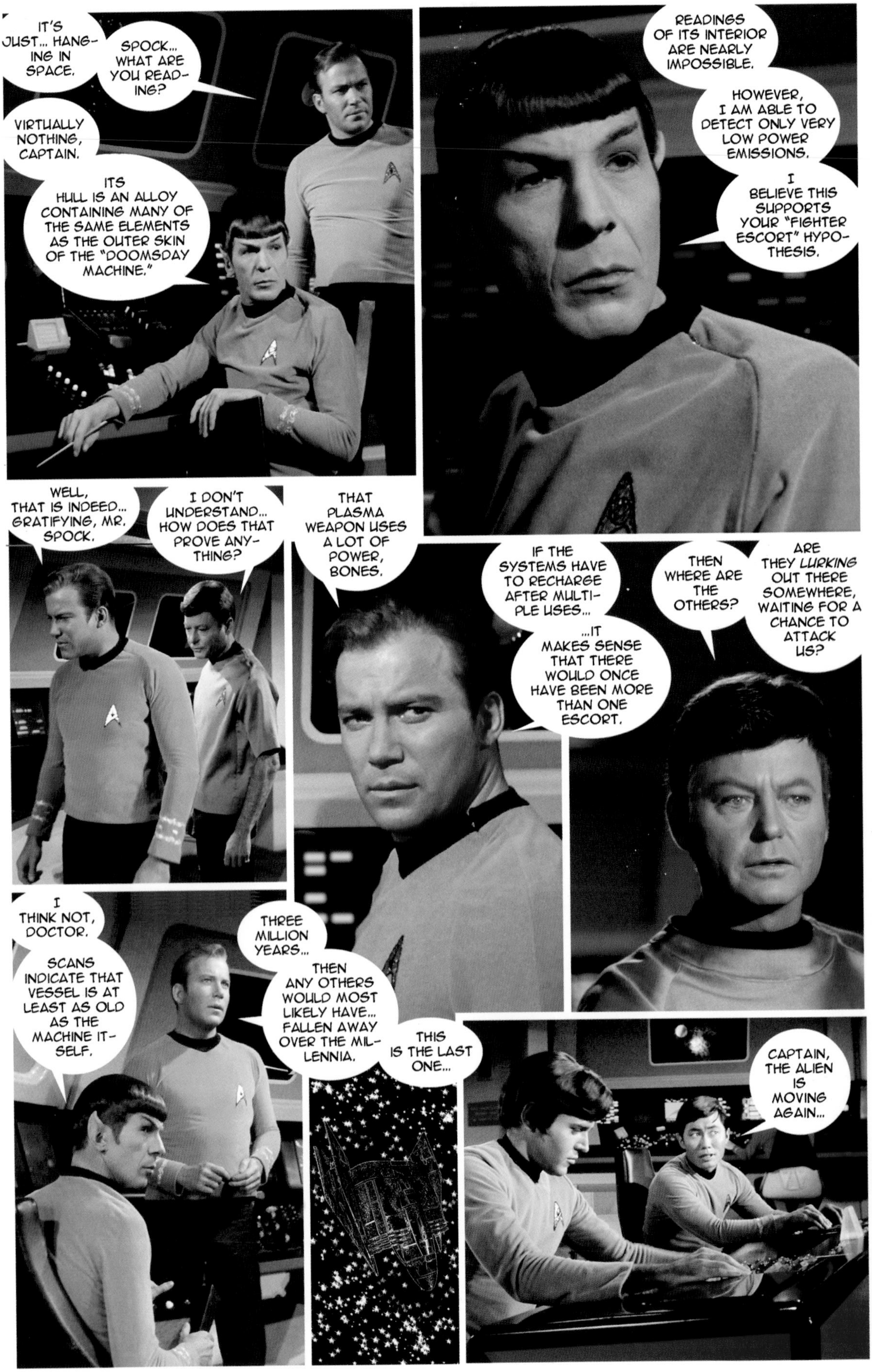
IT'S JUST... HANGING IN SPACE.
SPOCK... WHAT ARE YOU READING?
VIRTUALLY NOTHING, CAPTAIN.
ITS HULL IS AN ALLOY CONTAINING MANY OF THE SAME ELEMENTS AS THE OUTER SKIN OF THE "DOOMSDAY MACHINE."
READINGS OF ITS INTERIOR ARE NEARLY IMPOSSIBLE.
HOWEVER, I AM ABLE TO DETECT ONLY VERY LOW POWER EMISSIONS.
I BELIEVE THIS SUPPORTS YOUR "FIGHTER ESCORT" HYPOTHESIS.
WELL, THAT IS INDEED... GRATIFYING, MR. SPOCK.
I DON'T UNDERSTAND... HOW DOES THAT PROVE ANYTHING?
THAT PLASMA WEAPON USES A LOT OF POWER, BONES.
IF THE SYSTEMS HAVE TO RECHARGE AFTER MULTIPLE USES...
...IT MAKES SENSE THAT THERE WOULD ONCE HAVE BEEN MORE THAN ONE ESCORT.
THEN WHERE ARE THE OTHERS?
ARE THEY *LURKING* OUT THERE SOMEWHERE, WAITING FOR A CHANCE TO ATTACK US?
I THINK NOT, DOCTOR.
SCANS INDICATE THAT VESSEL IS AT LEAST AS OLD AS THE MACHINE ITSELF.
THREE MILLION YEARS...
THEN ANY OTHERS WOULD MOST LIKELY HAVE... FALLEN AWAY OVER THE MILLENNIA.
THIS IS THE LAST ONE...
CAPTAIN, THE ALIEN IS MOVING AGAIN...

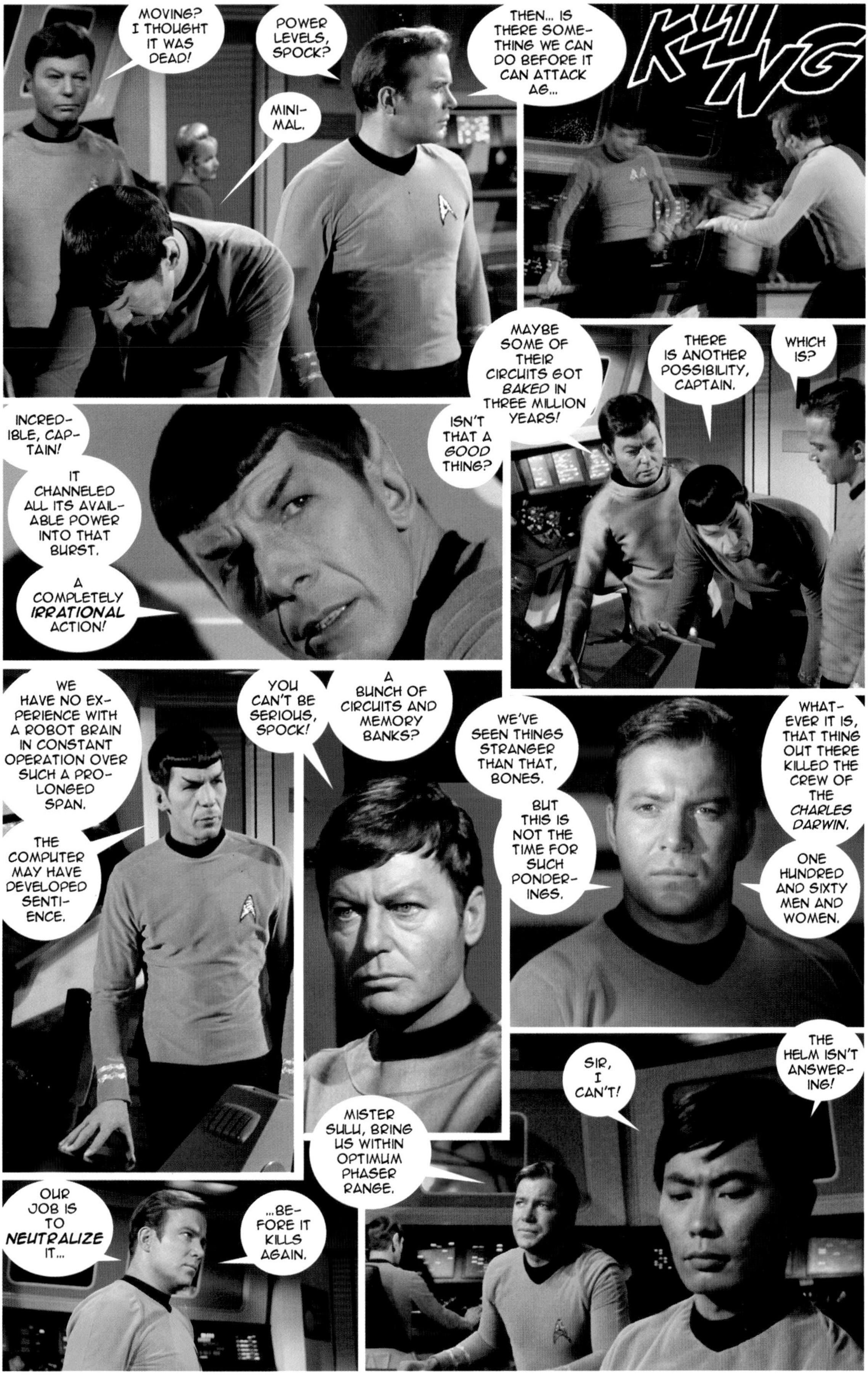
MOVING? I THOUGHT IT WAS DEAD!
POWER LEVELS, SPOCK?
MINI-MAL.
THEN... IS THERE SOME-THING WE CAN DO BEFORE IT CAN ATTACK AG...
K'LUNG
INCRED-IBLE, CAP-TAIN!
IT CHANNELED ALL ITS AVAIL-ABLE POWER INTO THAT BURST.
A COMPLETELY IRRATIONAL ACTION!
ISN'T THAT A GOOD THING?
MAYBE SOME OF THEIR CIRCUITS GOT BAKED IN THREE MILLION YEARS!
THERE IS ANOTHER POSSIBILITY, CAPTAIN.
WHICH IS?
WE HAVE NO EX-PERIENCE WITH A ROBOT BRAIN IN CONSTANT OPERATION OVER SUCH A PRO-LONGED SPAN.
THE COMPUTER MAY HAVE DEVELOPED SENTI-ENCE.
YOU CAN'T BE SERIOUS, SPOCK!
A BUNCH OF CIRCUITS AND MEMORY BANKS?
WE'VE SEEN THINGS STRANGER THAN THAT, BONES.
BUT THIS IS NOT THE TIME FOR SUCH PONDER-INGS.
WHAT-EVER IT IS, THAT THING OUT THERE KILLED THE CREW OF THE CHARLES DARWIN.
ONE HUNDRED AND SIXTY MEN AND WOMEN.
OUR JOB IS TO NEUTRALIZE IT...
...BE-FORE IT KILLS AGAIN.
MISTER SULU, BRING US WITHIN OPTIMUM PHASER RANGE.
SIR, I CAN'T!
THE HELM ISN'T ANSWER-ING!

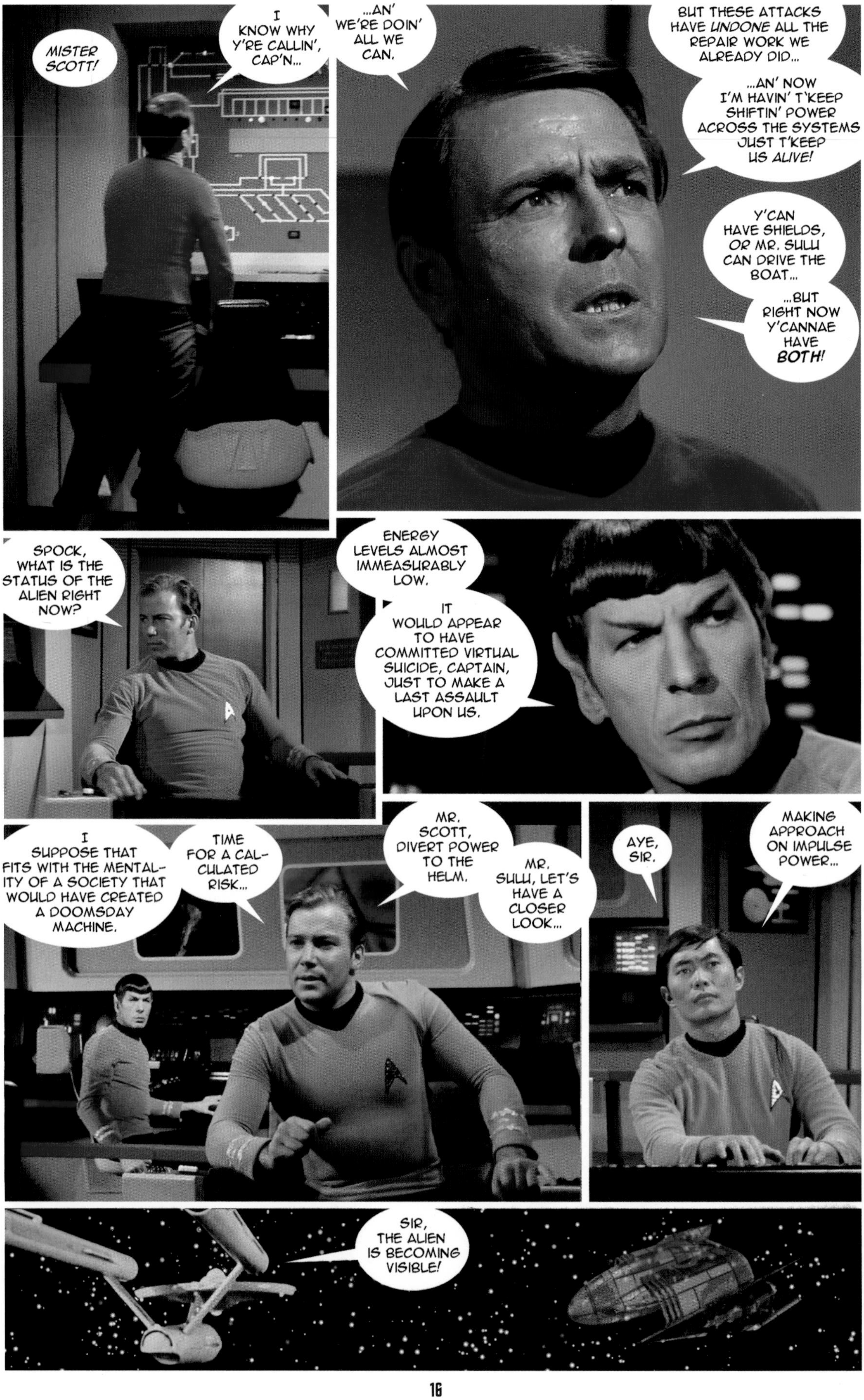
MISTER SCOTT!
I KNOW WHY Y'RE CALLIN', CAP'N...
...AN' WE'RE DOIN' ALL WE CAN.
BUT THESE ATTACKS HAVE UNDONE ALL THE REPAIR WORK WE ALREADY DID...
...AN' NOW I'M HAVIN' T'KEEP SHIFTIN' POWER ACROSS THE SYSTEMS JUST T'KEEP US ALIVE!
Y'CAN HAVE SHIELDS, OR MR. SULU CAN DRIVE THE BOAT...
...BUT RIGHT NOW Y'CANNAE HAVE BOTH!
SPOCK, WHAT IS THE STATUS OF THE ALIEN RIGHT NOW?
ENERGY LEVELS ALMOST IMMEASURABLY LOW.
IT WOULD APPEAR TO HAVE COMMITTED VIRTUAL SUICIDE, CAPTAIN, JUST TO MAKE A LAST ASSAULT UPON US.
I SUPPOSE THAT FITS WITH THE MENTALITY OF A SOCIETY THAT WOULD HAVE CREATED A DOOMSDAY MACHINE.
TIME FOR A CALCULATED RISK...
MR. SCOTT, DIVERT POWER TO THE HELM.
MR. SULU, LET'S HAVE A CLOSER LOOK...
AYE, SIR.
MAKING APPROACH ON IMPULSE POWER...
SIR, THE ALIEN IS BECOMING VISIBLE!

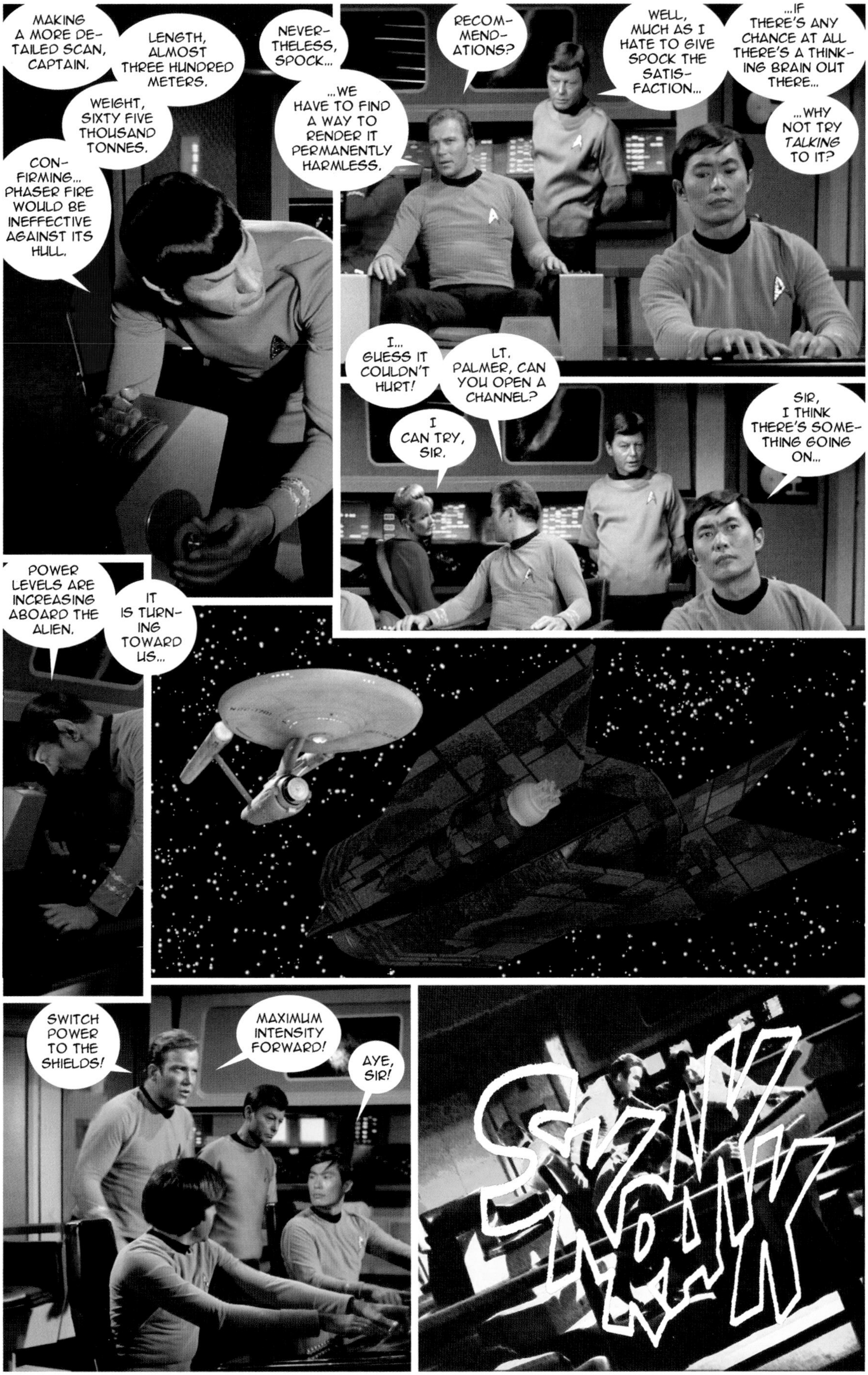
MAKING A MORE DE-TAILED SCAN, CAPTAIN.
LENGTH, ALMOST THREE HUNDRED METERS.
WEIGHT, SIXTY FIVE THOUSAND TONNES.
CON-FIRMING... PHASER FIRE WOULD BE INEFFECTIVE AGAINST ITS HULL.
NEVER-THELESS, SPOCK...
...WE HAVE TO FIND A WAY TO RENDER IT PERMANENTLY HARMLESS.
RECOM-MEND-ATIONS?
WELL, MUCH AS I HATE TO GIVE SPOCK THE SATIS-FACTION...
...IF THERE'S ANY CHANCE AT ALL THERE'S A THINK-ING BRAIN OUT THERE...
...WHY NOT TRY *TALKING* TO IT?
I... GUESS IT COULDN'T HURT!
LT. PALMER, CAN YOU OPEN A CHANNEL?
I CAN TRY, SIR.
SIR, I THINK THERE'S SOME-THING GOING ON...
POWER LEVELS ARE INCREASING ABOARD THE ALIEN.
IT IS TURN-ING TOWARD US...
SWITCH POWER TO THE SHIELDS!
MAXIMUM INTENSITY FORWARD!
AYE, SIR!

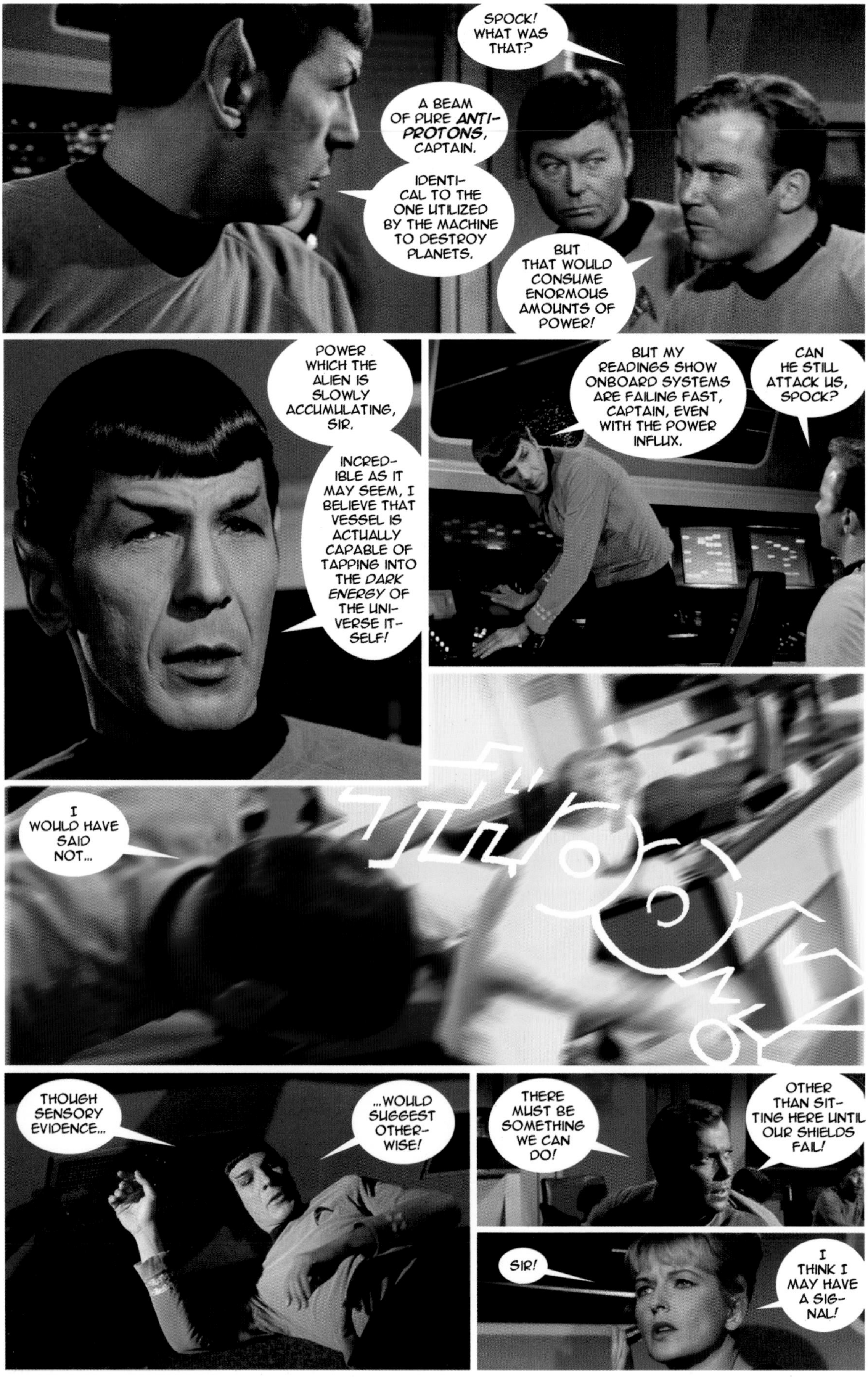
SPOCK! WHAT WAS THAT?
A BEAM OF PURE ANTI-PROTONS, CAPTAIN.
IDENTI-CAL TO THE ONE UTILIZED BY THE MACHINE TO DESTROY PLANETS.
BUT THAT WOULD CONSUME ENORMOUS AMOUNTS OF POWER!
POWER WHICH THE ALIEN IS SLOWLY ACCUMULATING, SIR.
INCRED-IBLE AS IT MAY SEEM, I BELIEVE THAT VESSEL IS ACTUALLY CAPABLE OF TAPPING INTO THE DARK ENERGY OF THE UNI-VERSE IT-SELF!
BUT MY READINGS SHOW ONBOARD SYSTEMS ARE FAILING FAST, CAPTAIN, EVEN WITH THE POWER INFLUX.
CAN HE STILL ATTACK US, SPOCK?
I WOULD HAVE SAID NOT...
THOUGH SENSORY EVIDENCE...
...WOULD SUGGEST OTHER-WISE!
THERE MUST BE SOMETHING WE CAN DO!
OTHER THAN SIT-TING HERE UNTIL OUR SHIELDS FAIL!
SIR!
I THINK I MAY HAVE A SIG-NAL!

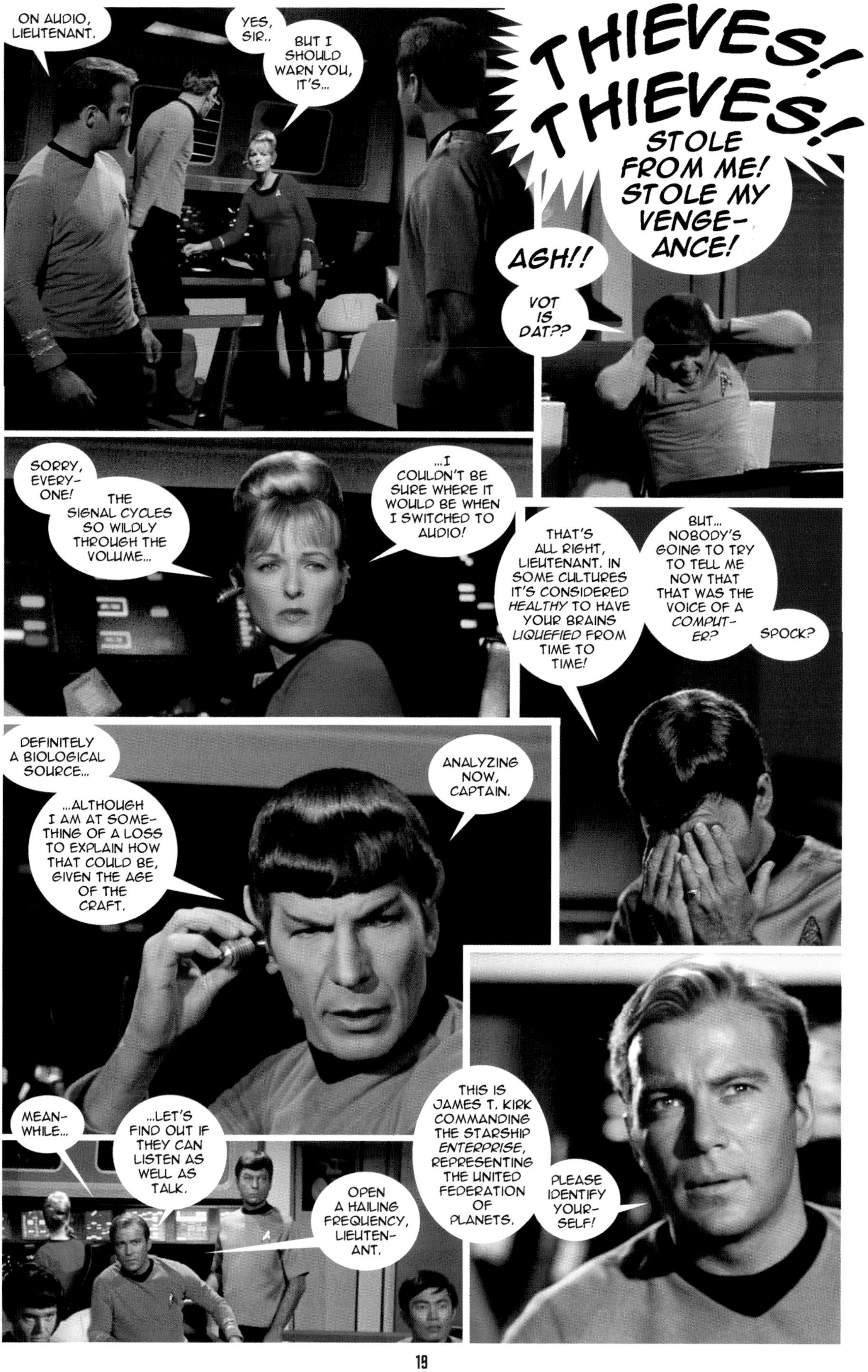
ON AUDIO, LIEUTENANT.
YES, SIR..
BUT I SHOULD WARN YOU, IT'S...
THIEVES! THIEVES!
STOLE FROM ME! STOLE MY VENGE-ANCE!
AGH!!
VOT IS DAT??
SORRY, EVERY-ONE!
THE SIGNAL CYCLES SO WILDLY THROUGH THE VOLUME...
...I COULDN'T BE SURE WHERE IT WOULD BE WHEN I SWITCHED TO AUDIO!
THAT'S ALL RIGHT, LIEUTENANT. IN SOME CULTURES IT'S CONSIDERED *HEALTHY* TO HAVE YOUR BRAINS *LIQUEFIED* FROM TIME TO TIME!
BUT... NOBODY'S GOING TO TRY TO TELL ME NOW THAT THAT WAS THE VOICE OF A *COMPUT-ER*?
SPOCK?
ANALYZING NOW, CAPTAIN.
DEFINITELY A BIOLOGICAL SOURCE...
...ALTHOUGH I AM AT SOME-THING OF A LOSS TO EXPLAIN HOW THAT COULD BE, GIVEN THE AGE OF THE CRAFT.
MEAN-WHILE...
...LET'S FIND OUT IF THEY CAN LISTEN AS WELL AS TALK.
OPEN A HAILING FREQUENCY, LIEUTEN-ANT.
THIS IS JAMES T. KIRK COMMANDING THE STARSHIP *ENTERPRISE*, REPRESENTING THE UNITED FEDERATION OF PLANETS.
PLEASE IDENTIFY YOUR-SELF!

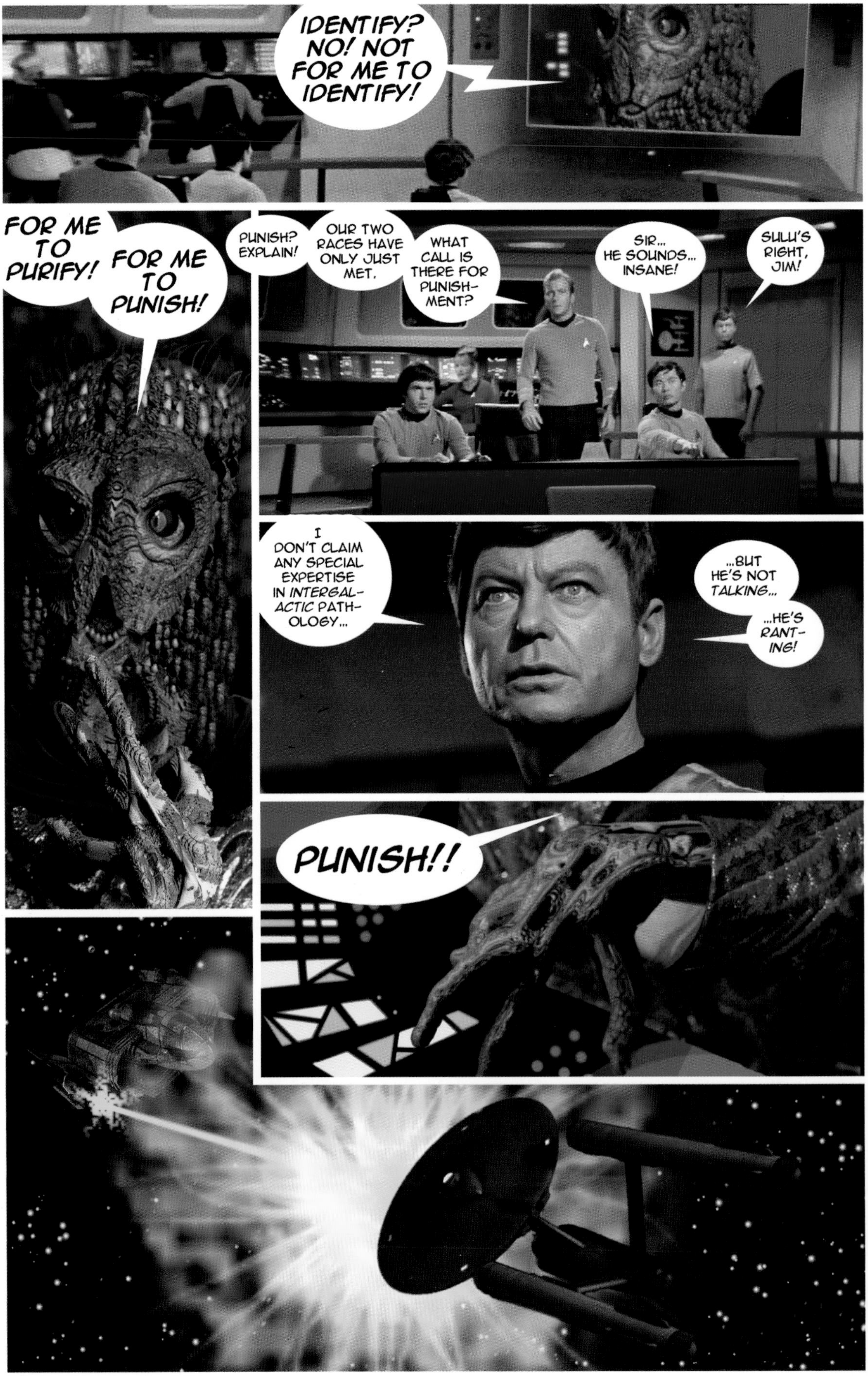
IDENTIFY? NO! NOT FOR ME TO IDENTIFY!
FOR ME TO PURIFY!
FOR ME TO PUNISH!
PUNISH? EXPLAIN!
OUR TWO RACES HAVE ONLY JUST MET.
WHAT CALL IS THERE FOR PUNISH-MENT?
SIR... HE SOUNDS... INSANE!
SULU'S RIGHT, JIM!
I DON'T CLAIM ANY SPECIAL EXPERTISE IN INTERGAL-ACTIC PATH-OLOGY...
...BUT HE'S NOT TALKING...
...HE'S RANT-ING!
PUNISH!!

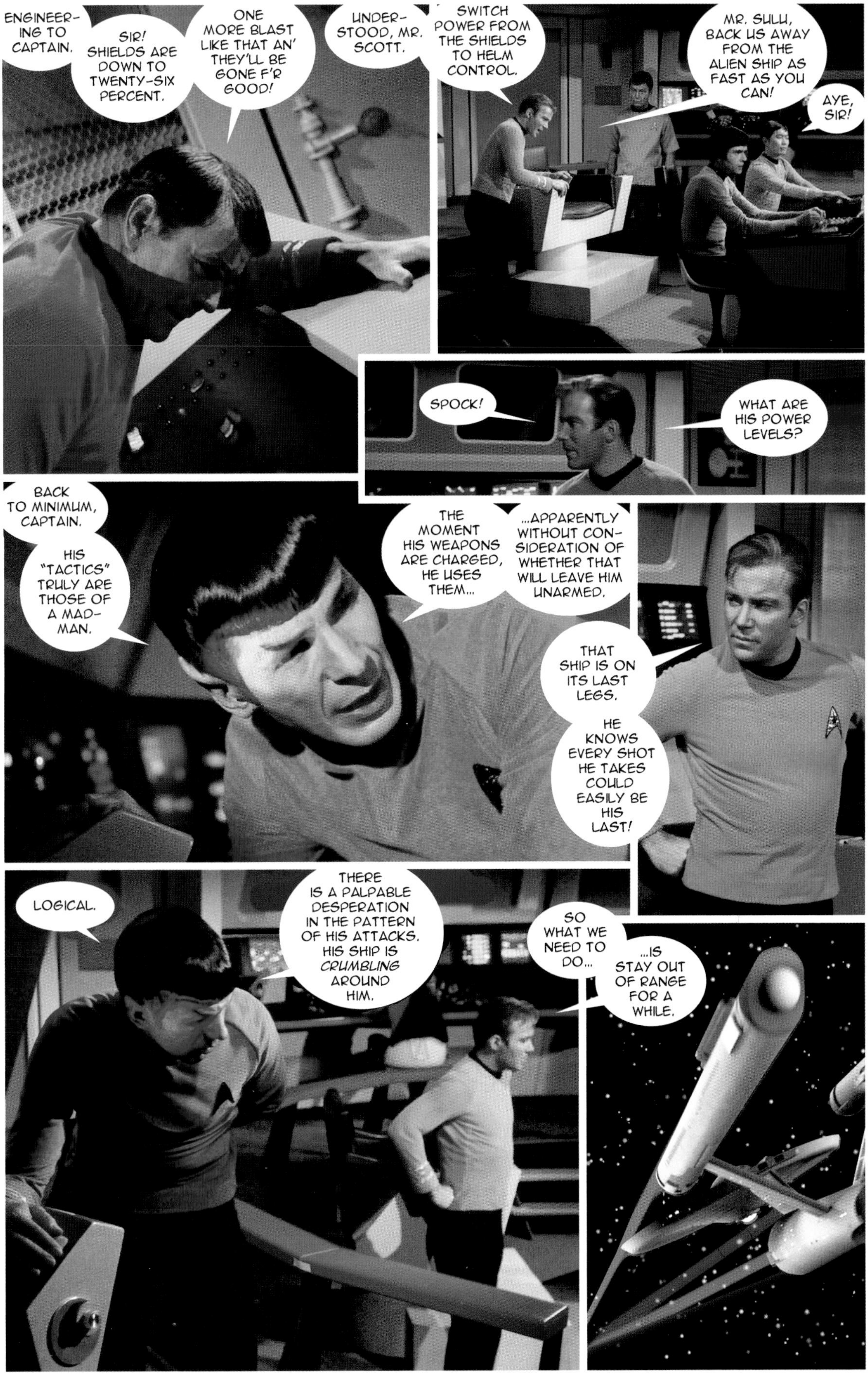

ENGINEERING TO CAPTAIN.
SIR! SHIELDS ARE DOWN TO TWENTY-SIX PERCENT.
ONE MORE BLAST LIKE THAT AN' THEY'LL BE GONE F'R GOOD!
UNDERSTOOD, MR. SCOTT.
SWITCH POWER FROM THE SHIELDS TO HELM CONTROL.
MR. SULU, BACK US AWAY FROM THE ALIEN SHIP AS FAST AS YOU CAN!
AYE, SIR!
SPOCK!
WHAT ARE HIS POWER LEVELS?
BACK TO MINIMUM, CAPTAIN.
HIS "TACTICS" TRULY ARE THOSE OF A MADMAN.
THE MOMENT HIS WEAPONS ARE CHARGED, HE USES THEM...
...APPARENTLY WITHOUT CONSIDERATION OF WHETHER THAT WILL LEAVE HIM UNARMED.
THAT SHIP IS ON ITS LAST LEGS.
HE KNOWS EVERY SHOT HE TAKES COULD EASILY BE HIS LAST!
LOGICAL.
THERE IS A PALPABLE DESPERATION IN THE PATTERN OF HIS ATTACKS. HIS SHIP IS *CRUMBLING* AROUND HIM.
SO WHAT WE NEED TO DO...
...IS STAY OUT OF RANGE FOR A WHILE.

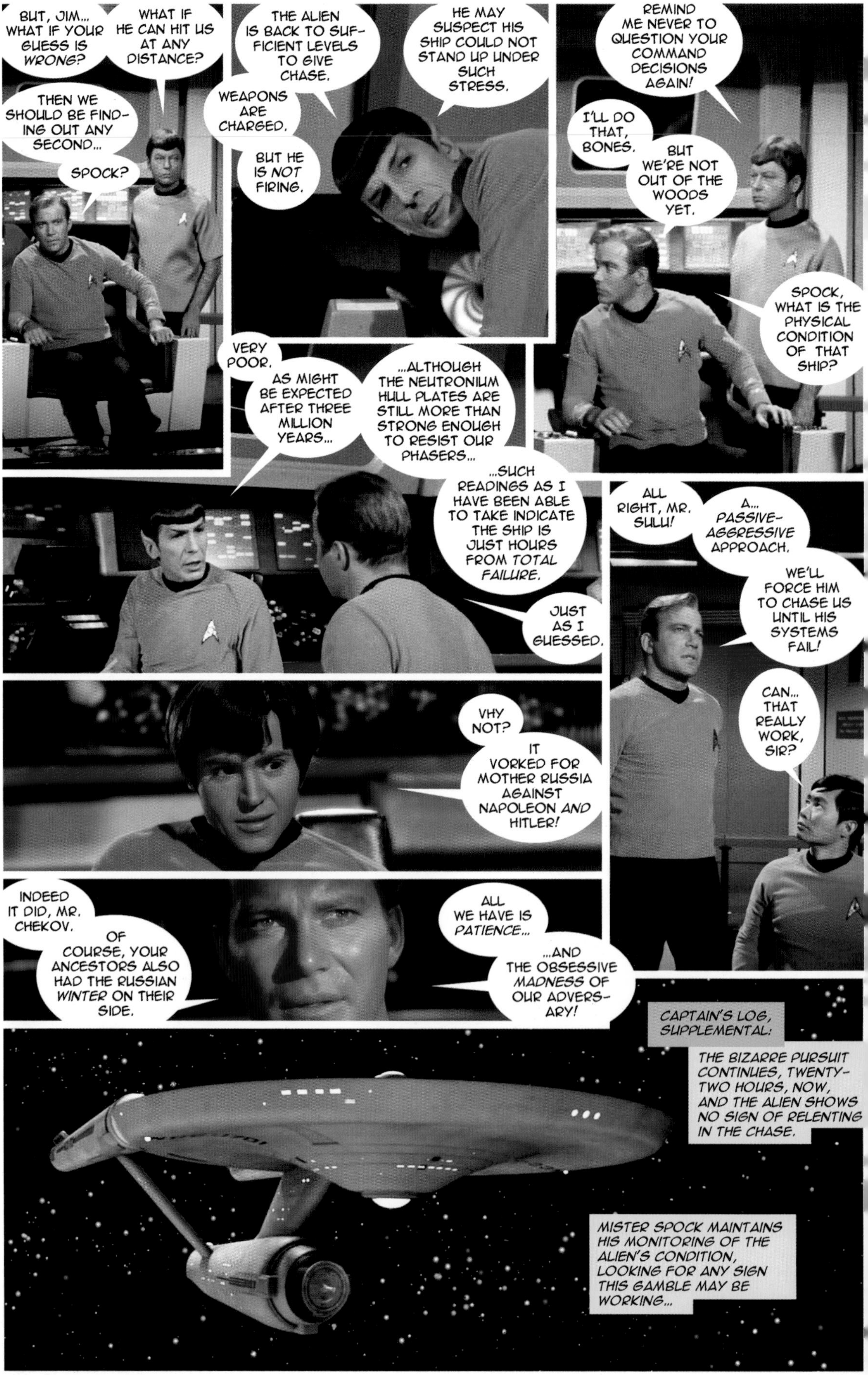

BUT, JIM... WHAT IF YOUR GUESS IS WRONG?
WHAT IF HE CAN HIT US AT ANY DISTANCE?
THEN WE SHOULD BE FINDING OUT ANY SECOND...
SPOCK?
THE ALIEN IS BACK TO SUFFICIENT LEVELS TO GIVE CHASE.
WEAPONS ARE CHARGED.
BUT HE IS NOT FIRING.
HE MAY SUSPECT HIS SHIP COULD NOT STAND UP UNDER SUCH STRESS.
REMIND ME NEVER TO QUESTION YOUR COMMAND DECISIONS AGAIN!
I'LL DO THAT, BONES.
BUT WE'RE NOT OUT OF THE WOODS YET.
SPOCK, WHAT IS THE PHYSICAL CONDITION OF THAT SHIP?
VERY POOR.
AS MIGHT BE EXPECTED AFTER THREE MILLION YEARS...
...ALTHOUGH THE NEUTRONIUM HULL PLATES ARE STILL MORE THAN STRONG ENOUGH TO RESIST OUR PHASERS...
...SUCH READINGS AS I HAVE BEEN ABLE TO TAKE INDICATE THE SHIP IS JUST HOURS FROM TOTAL FAILURE.
JUST AS I GUESSED.
ALL RIGHT, MR. SULU!
A... PASSIVE-AGGRESSIVE APPROACH.
WE'LL FORCE HIM TO CHASE US UNTIL HIS SYSTEMS FAIL!
CAN... THAT REALLY WORK, SIR?
VHY NOT?
IT VORKED FOR MOTHER RUSSIA AGAINST NAPOLEON AND HITLER!
INDEED IT DID, MR. CHEKOV.
OF COURSE, YOUR ANCESTORS ALSO HAD THE RUSSIAN WINTER ON THEIR SIDE.
ALL WE HAVE IS PATIENCE...
...AND THE OBSESSIVE MADNESS OF OUR ADVERSARY!
CAPTAIN'S LOG, SUPPLEMENTAL:
THE BIZARRE PURSUIT CONTINUES, TWENTY-TWO HOURS, NOW, AND THE ALIEN SHOWS NO SIGN OF RELENTING IN THE CHASE.
MISTER SPOCK MAINTAINS HIS MONITORING OF THE ALIEN'S CONDITION, LOOKING FOR ANY SIGN THIS GAMBLE MAY BE WORKING...

MEANWHILE, I HAVE TAKEN ENGINEER SCOTT'S REPORT ON OUR PRESENT CONDITION.

AYE, SIR, EVERYTHING IS BACK TO ABOUT SIXTY PERCENT, AN HOLDIN'.

IT'D BE A GOOD BIT BETTER F'R US IF WE COULD SHUT THE ENGINES DOWN F'R A WHILE!

THEN I COULD HAVE THEM UP TO ONE HUNDRED PERCENT IN A COUPLE OF HOURS.

NOT AN OPTION, SCOTTY.

AT LEAST, NOT UNTIL WE FIGURE OUT SOME WAY TO STOP THAT MADMAN OUT THERE.

AYE, AND THAT'S ANOTHER THING!

DO YE REALLY THINK THAT ALIEN WAS FLYIN' ESCORT ON THE MACHINE F'R THREE MILLION YEARS?

THREE MILLION YEARS, ALL ALONE OUT THERE IN THE INTERGALACTIC VOID.

ANY SANE CREATURE WOULD GO MAD AN' BACK A HUNDRED THOUSAND TIMES OVER!

AN' WHY WOULD HE KEEP FLYIN' WITH THE MACHINE, AFTER ITS JOB WAS DONE?

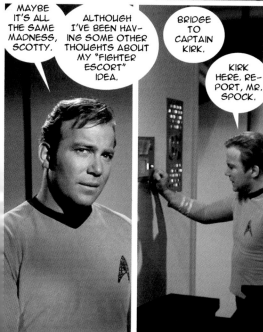

MAYBE IT'S ALL THE SAME MADNESS, SCOTTY.

ALTHOUGH I'VE BEEN HAVING SOME OTHER THOUGHTS ABOUT MY "FIGHTER ESCORT" IDEA.

BRIDGE TO CAPTAIN KIRK.

KIRK HERE. REPORT, MR. SPOCK.

STRUCTURAL STRESS LEVELS ABOARD THE ALIEN SHIP APPEAR TO BE AT MAXIMUM, CAPTAIN.

I DO NOT BELIEVE IT CAN TOLERATE MORE THAN A FEW MINUTES LONGER.

I'LL BE RIGHT THERE.

STATUS, SPOCK?

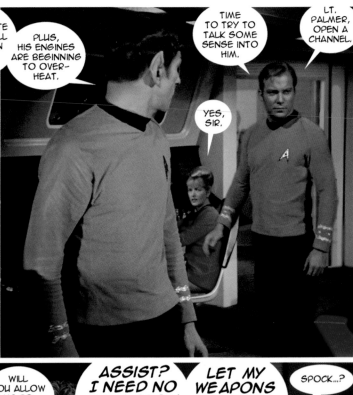

ESTIMATING COMPLETE LOSS OF HULL INTEGRITY IN THIRTEEN MINUTES.

PLUS, HIS ENGINES ARE BEGINNING TO OVERHEAT.

TIME TO TRY TO TALK SOME SENSE INTO HIM.

LT. PALMER, OPEN A CHANNEL.

YES, SIR.

ATTENTION, COMMANDER OF SHIP PURSUING US. THIS IS CAPTAIN KIRK.

OUR SCANS SHOW YOUR VESSEL IS ABOUT TO UNDERGO CATASTROPHIC FAILURE.

WILL YOU ALLOW US TO ASSIST YOU?

ASSIST? I NEED NO HELP FROM SUCH AS YOU!

LET MY WEAPONS ANSWER FOR ME!

SPOCK....?

HE IS STILL BEYOND THE RANGE OF HIS WEAPONS, CAPTAIN.

BUT HE IS NONETHELESS PREPARING TO FIRE.

AT THIS POINT I CAN NO LONGER PREDICT WHAT WILL....

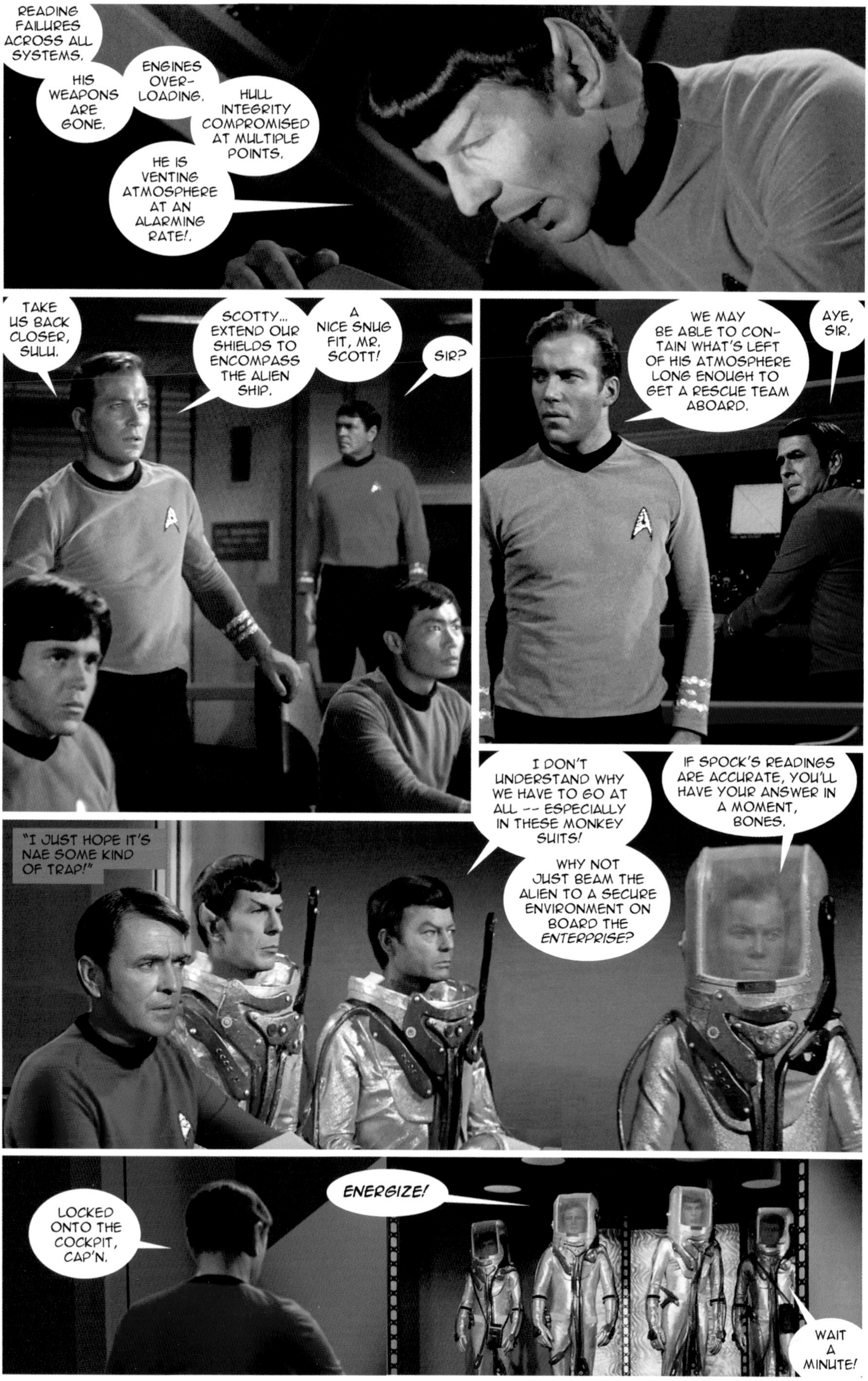
READING FAILURES ACROSS ALL SYSTEMS.
HIS WEAPONS ARE GONE.
ENGINES OVER-LOADING.
HULL INTEGRITY COMPROMISED AT MULTIPLE POINTS.
HE IS VENTING ATMOSPHERE AT AN ALARMING RATE!.
TAKE US BACK CLOSER, SULU.
SCOTTY... EXTEND OUR SHIELDS TO ENCOMPASS THE ALIEN SHIP.
A NICE SNUG FIT, MR. SCOTT!
SIR?
WE MAY BE ABLE TO CON-TAIN WHAT'S LEFT OF HIS ATMOSPHERE LONG ENOUGH TO GET A RESCUE TEAM ABOARD.
AYE, SIR.
"I JUST HOPE IT'S NAE SOME KIND OF TRAP!"
I DON'T UNDERSTAND WHY WE HAVE TO GO AT ALL -- ESPECIALLY IN THESE MONKEY SUITS!
WHY NOT JUST BEAM THE ALIEN TO A SECURE ENVIRONMENT ON BOARD THE *ENTERPRISE*?
IF SPOCK'S READINGS ARE ACCURATE, YOU'LL HAVE YOUR ANSWER IN A MOMENT, BONES.
LOCKED ONTO THE COCKPIT, CAP'N.
ENERGIZE!
WAIT A MINUTE!

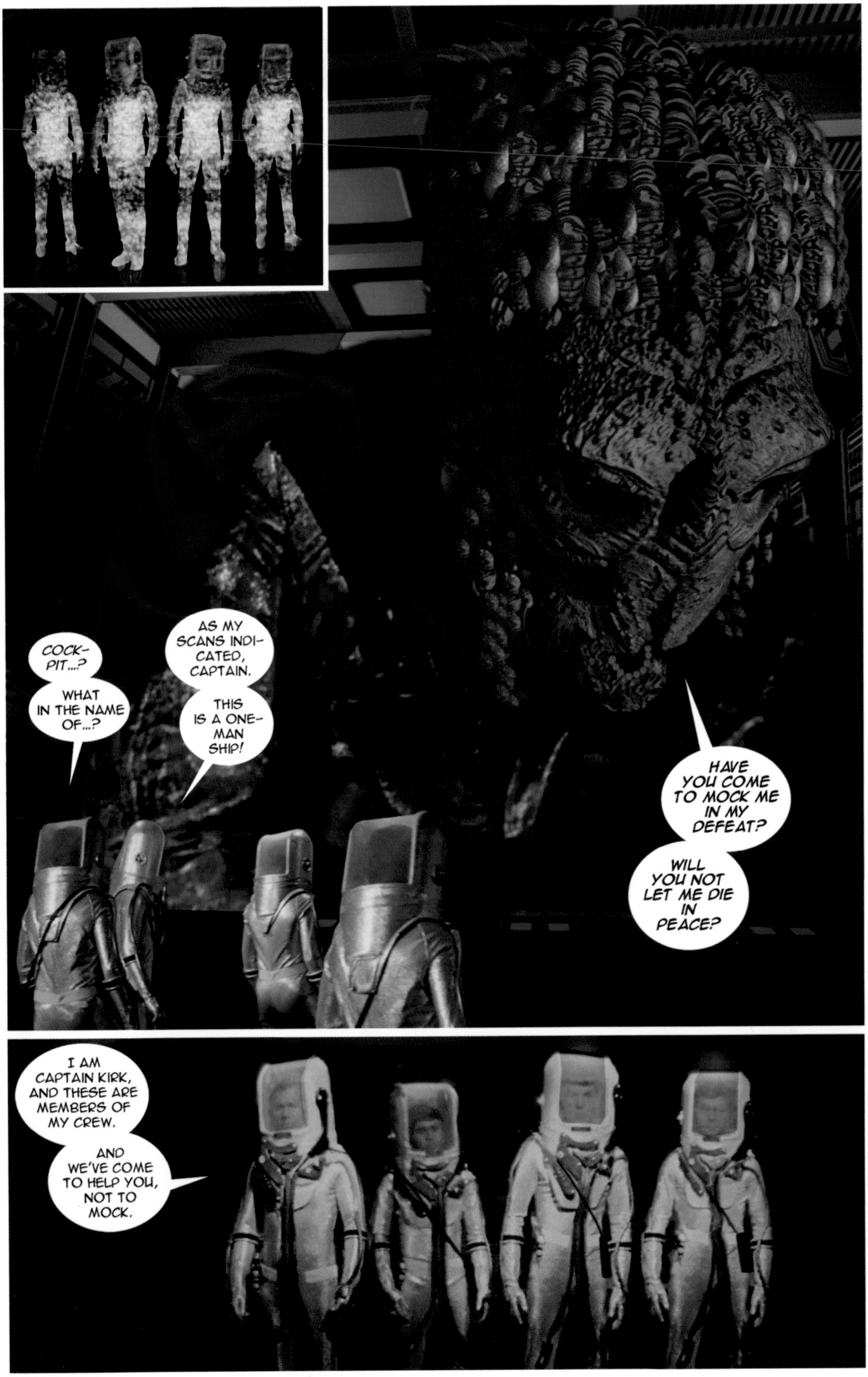
COCK-PIT...?
WHAT IN THE NAME OF...?
AS MY SCANS INDI-CATED, CAPTAIN.
THIS IS A ONE-MAN SHIP!
HAVE YOU COME TO MOCK ME IN MY DEFEAT?
WILL YOU NOT LET ME DIE IN PEACE?
I AM CAPTAIN KIRK, AND THESE ARE MEMBERS OF MY CREW.
AND WE'VE COME TO HELP YOU, NOT TO MOCK.

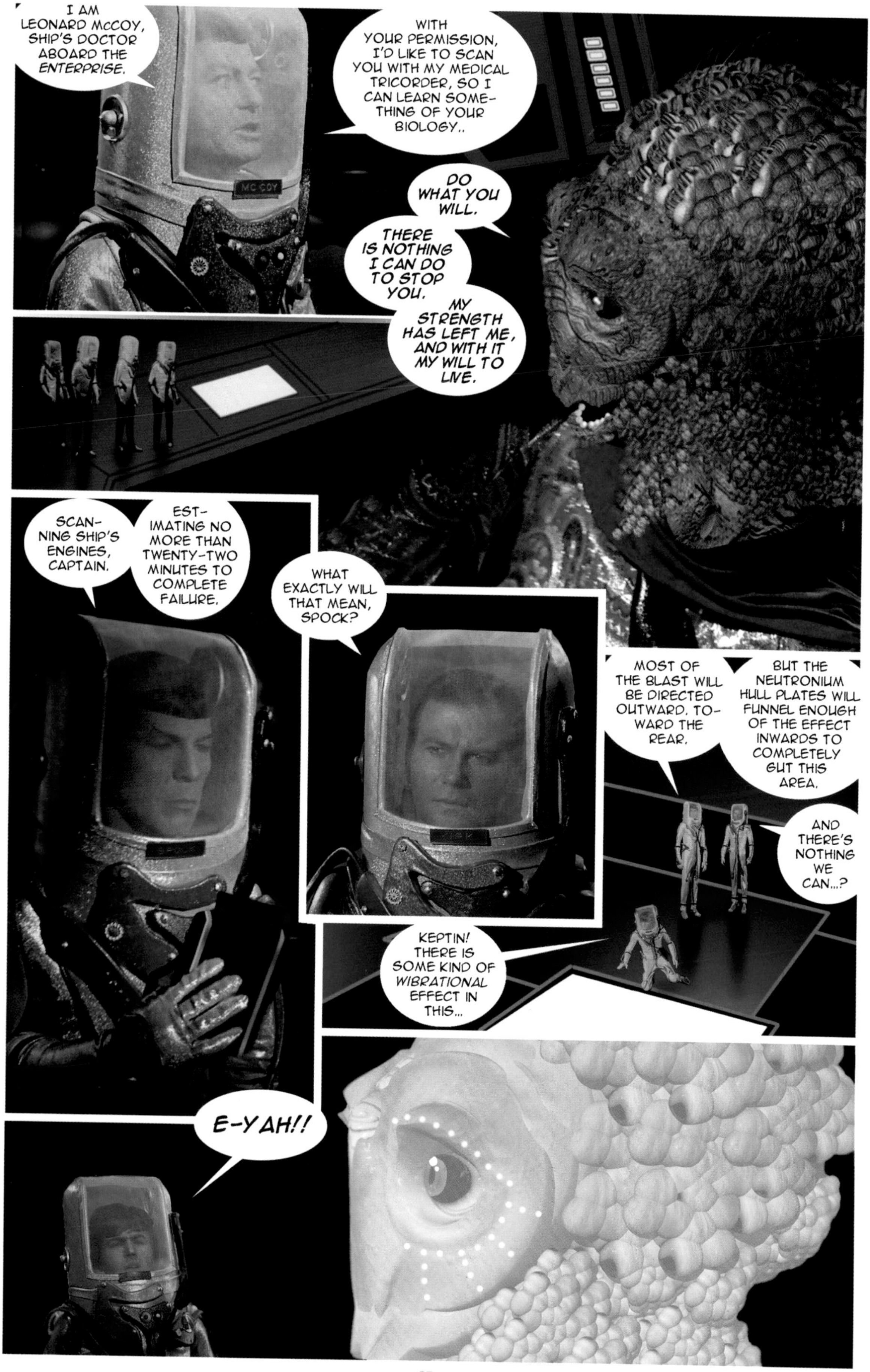

I AM LEONARD McCOY, SHIP'S DOCTOR ABOARD THE *ENTERPRISE*.
WITH YOUR PERMISSION, I'D LIKE TO SCAN YOU WITH MY MEDICAL TRICORDER, SO I CAN LEARN SOMETHING OF YOUR BIOLOGY..
MC COY
DO WHAT YOU WILL.
THERE IS NOTHING I CAN DO TO STOP YOU.
MY STRENGTH HAS LEFT ME, AND WITH IT MY WILL TO LIVE.
SCANNING SHIP'S ENGINES, CAPTAIN.
ESTIMATING NO MORE THAN TWENTY-TWO MINUTES TO COMPLETE FAILURE.
WHAT EXACTLY WILL THAT MEAN, SPOCK?
MOST OF THE BLAST WILL BE DIRECTED OUTWARD, TOWARD THE REAR.
BUT THE NEUTRONIUM HULL PLATES WILL FUNNEL ENOUGH OF THE EFFECT INWARDS TO COMPLETELY GUT THIS AREA.
AND THERE'S NOTHING WE CAN...?
KEPTIN! THERE IS SOME KIND OF *WIBRATIONAL* EFFECT IN THIS...
E-YAH!!

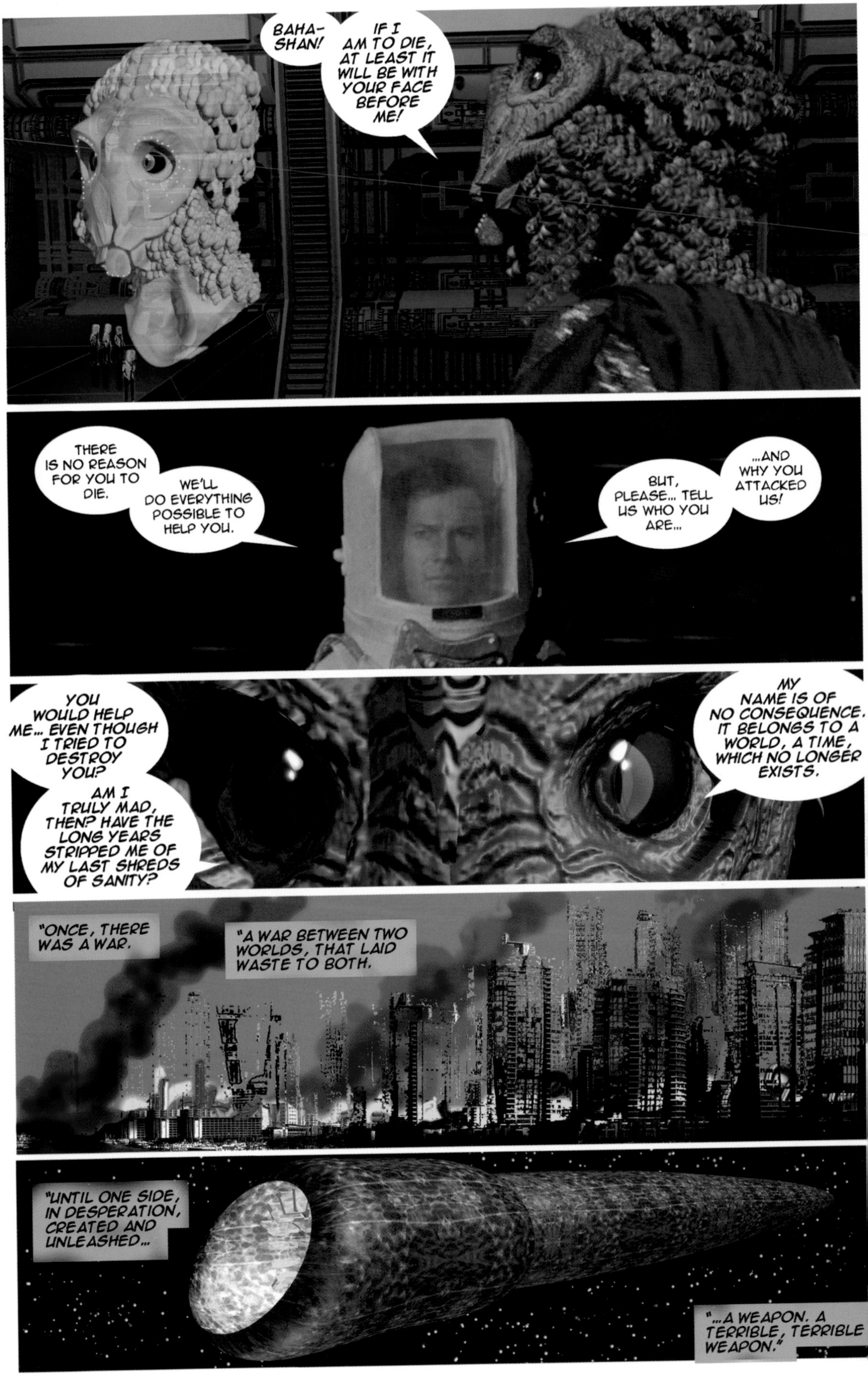

BAHA-SHAN!
IF I AM TO DIE, AT LEAST IT WILL BE WITH YOUR FACE BEFORE ME!
THERE IS NO REASON FOR YOU TO DIE.
WE'LL DO EVERYTHING POSSIBLE TO HELP YOU.
BUT, PLEASE... TELL US WHO YOU ARE...
...AND WHY YOU ATTACKED US!
YOU WOULD HELP ME... EVEN THOUGH I TRIED TO DESTROY YOU?
AM I TRULY MAD, THEN? HAVE THE LONG YEARS STRIPPED ME OF MY LAST SHREDS OF SANITY?
MY NAME IS OF NO CONSEQUENCE. IT BELONGS TO A WORLD, A TIME, WHICH NO LONGER EXISTS.
"ONCE, THERE WAS A WAR.
"A WAR BETWEEN TWO WORLDS, THAT LAID WASTE TO BOTH.
"UNTIL ONE SIDE, IN DESPERATION, CREATED AND UNLEASHED...
"...A WEAPON. A TERRIBLE, TERRIBLE WEAPON."

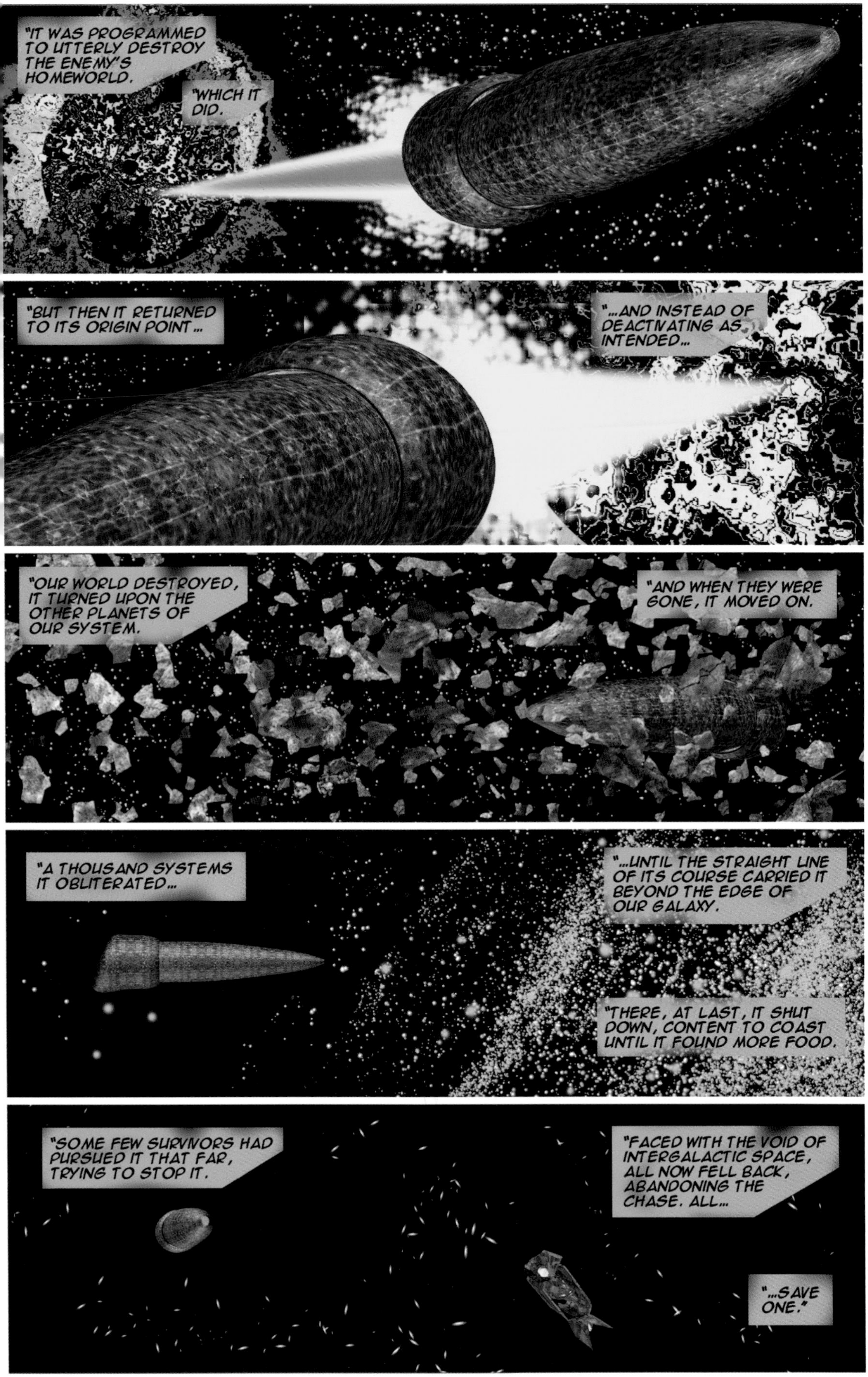
"IT WAS PROGRAMMED TO UTTERLY DESTROY THE ENEMY'S HOMEWORLD.
"WHICH IT DID.
"BUT THEN IT RETURNED TO ITS ORIGIN POINT...
"...AND INSTEAD OF DEACTIVATING AS INTENDED...
"OUR WORLD DESTROYED, IT TURNED UPON THE OTHER PLANETS OF OUR SYSTEM.
"AND WHEN THEY WERE GONE, IT MOVED ON.
"A THOUSAND SYSTEMS IT OBLITERATED...
"...UNTIL THE STRAIGHT LINE OF ITS COURSE CARRIED IT BEYOND THE EDGE OF OUR GALAXY.
"THERE, AT LAST, IT SHUT DOWN, CONTENT TO COAST UNTIL IT FOUND MORE FOOD.
"SOME FEW SURVIVORS HAD PURSUED IT THAT FAR, TRYING TO STOP IT.
"FACED WITH THE VOID OF INTERGALACTIC SPACE, ALL NOW FELL BACK, ABANDONING THE CHASE. ALL...
"...SAVE ONE."

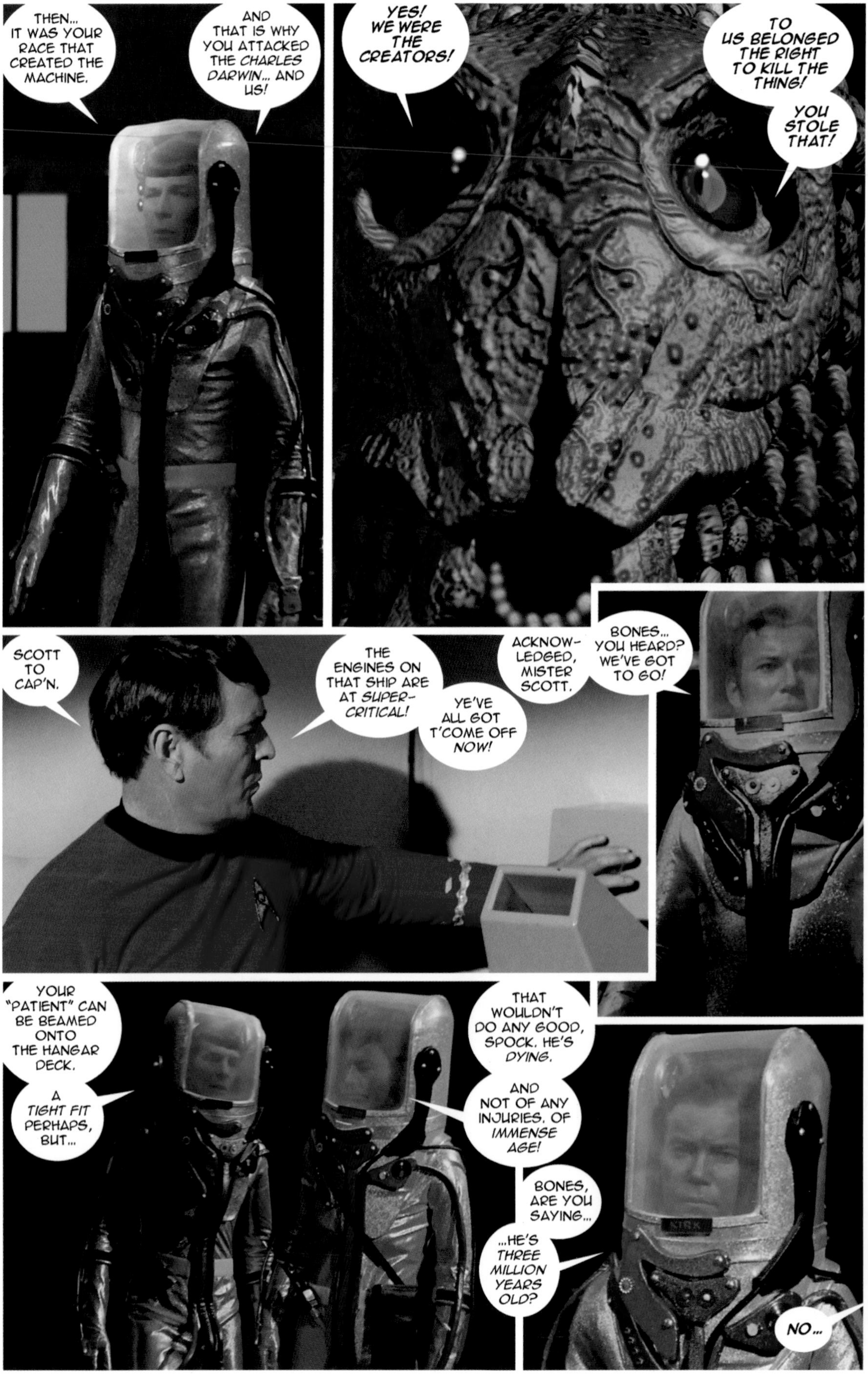

THEN... IT WAS YOUR RACE THAT CREATED THE MACHINE.
AND THAT IS WHY YOU ATTACKED THE *CHARLES DARWIN*... AND US!
YES! WE WERE THE CREATORS!
TO US BELONGED THE RIGHT TO KILL THE THING!
YOU STOLE THAT!
SCOTT TO CAP'N.
THE ENGINES ON THAT SHIP ARE AT *SUPER-CRITICAL!*
YE'VE ALL GOT T'COME OFF *NOW!*
ACKNOW-LEDGED, MISTER SCOTT.
BONES... YOU HEARD? WE'VE GOT TO GO!
YOUR "PATIENT" CAN BE BEAMED ONTO THE HANGAR DECK.
A *TIGHT FIT* PERHAPS, BUT...
THAT WOULDN'T DO ANY GOOD, SPOCK. HE'S *DYING.*
AND NOT OF ANY INJURIES. OF *IMMENSE AGE!*
BONES, ARE YOU SAYING...
...HE'S *THREE MILLION YEARS OLD?*
NO...

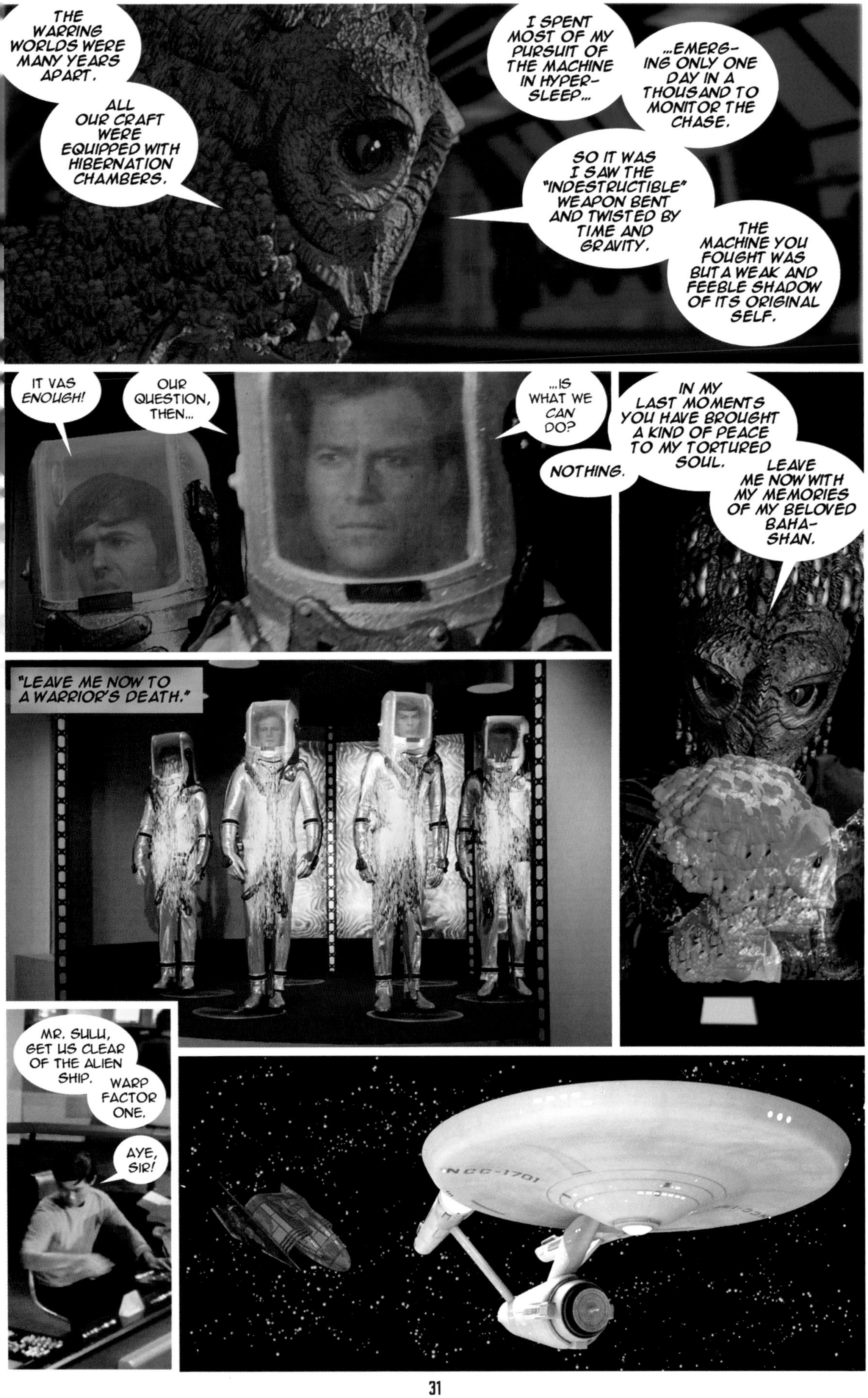
THE WARRING WORLDS WERE MANY YEARS APART.
ALL OUR CRAFT WERE EQUIPPED WITH HIBERNATION CHAMBERS.
I SPENT MOST OF MY PURSUIT OF THE MACHINE IN HYPER-SLEEP...
...EMERG-ING ONLY ONE DAY IN A THOUSAND TO MONITOR THE CHASE.
SO IT WAS I SAW THE "INDESTRUCTIBLE" WEAPON BENT AND TWISTED BY TIME AND GRAVITY.
THE MACHINE YOU FOUGHT WAS BUT A WEAK AND FEEBLE SHADOW OF ITS ORIGINAL SELF.
IT VAS ENOUGH!
OUR QUESTION, THEN...
...IS WHAT WE CAN DO?
NOTHING.
IN MY LAST MOMENTS YOU HAVE BROUGHT A KIND OF PEACE TO MY TORTURED SOUL.
LEAVE ME NOW WITH MY MEMORIES OF MY BELOVED BAHA-SHAN.
"LEAVE ME NOW TO A WARRIOR'S DEATH."
MR. SULU, GET US CLEAR OF THE ALIEN SHIP.
WARP FACTOR ONE.
AYE, SIR!
NCC-1701

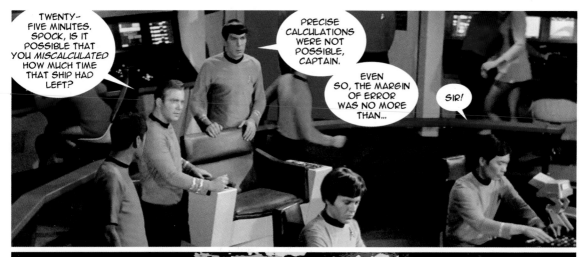

TWENTY-FIVE MINUTES, SPOCK, IS IT POSSIBLE THAT YOU *MISCALCULATED* HOW MUCH TIME THAT SHIP HAD LEFT?

PRECISE CALCULATIONS WERE NOT POSSIBLE, CAPTAIN.

EVEN SO, THE MARGIN OF ERROR WAS NO MORE THAN...

SIR!

LOOKS LIKE YOU WERE RIGHT ABOUT US NEEDING SOME DISTANCE!

BUT THERE'S ONE OTHER ITEM.

I'M A DOCTOR, NOT A MATHEMATICIAN, BUT IF THAT ALIEN WAS OUT OF STASIS EVEN JUST ONE DAY IN A THOUSAND...

...DOESN'T THAT ADD UP TO...?

THREE THOUSAND YEARS.

WE CANNOT, OF COURSE, KNOW WHAT THAT REPRESENTS, RELATIVE TO THE NATURAL LIFESPAN OF HIS SPECIES.

STUDIES HAVE SUGGESTED EXTENDED PERIODS IN STASIS CAN EVEN *PROLONG* LIFE.

BUT EVEN IF IT WAS *NORMAL* FOR HIM, IT STILL MEANS HE WAS ALONE FOR THIRTY CENTURIES.

ALONE WITH NOTHING BUT HIS RAGE AND FURY... AND GUILT.

NO WONDER HE WENT MAD.

AT LEAST AT THE END, HE HAD A MOMENT OF CLARITY.

AND... PERHAPS, A MOMENT TO *FORGIVE HIM-SELF*..

THE END

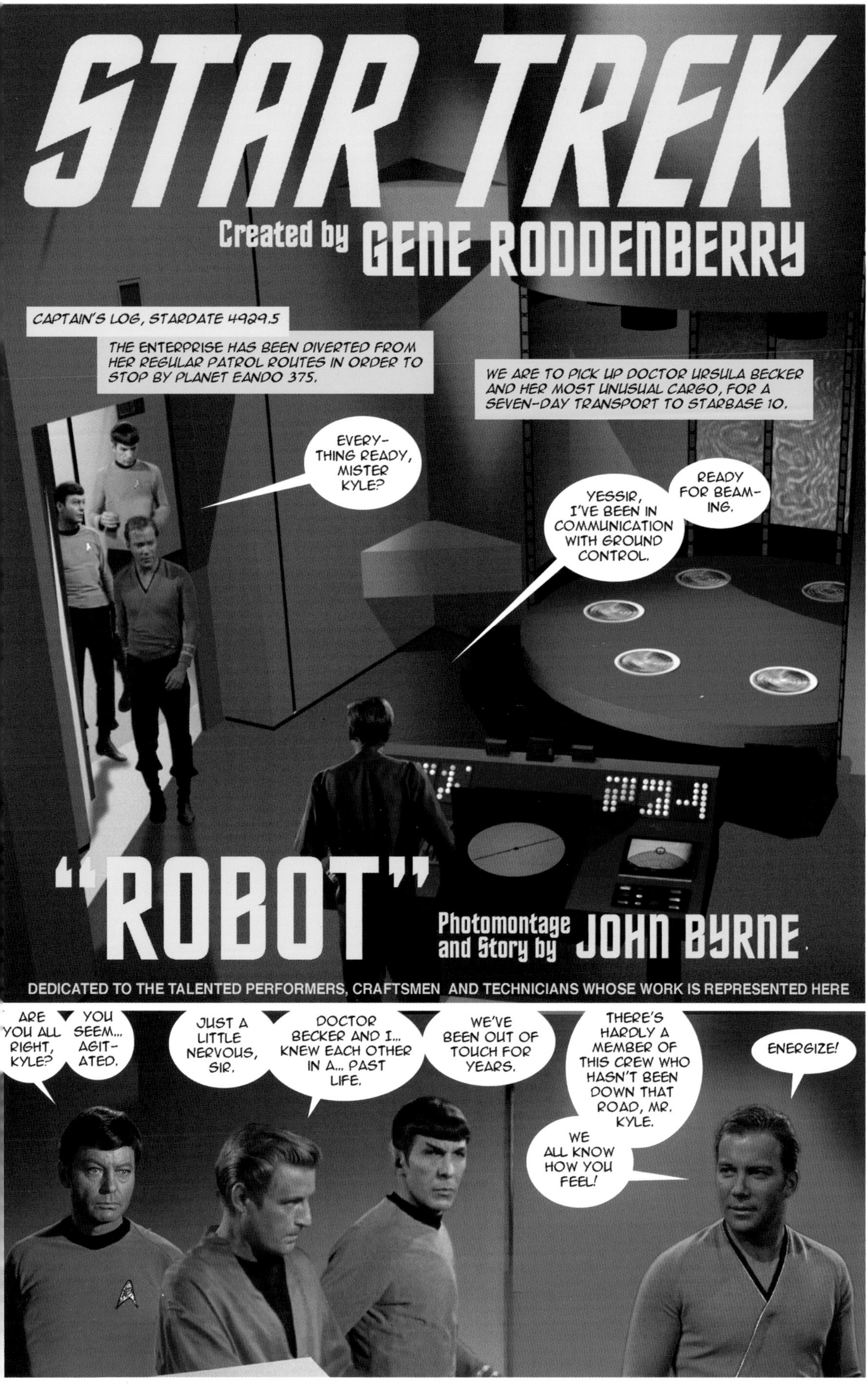
STAR TREK
Created by GENE RODDENBERRY
CAPTAIN'S LOG, STARDATE 4929.5
THE ENTERPRISE HAS BEEN DIVERTED FROM HER REGULAR PATROL ROUTES IN ORDER TO STOP BY PLANET EANDO 375.
WE ARE TO PICK UP DOCTOR URSULA BECKER AND HER MOST UNUSUAL CARGO, FOR A SEVEN-DAY TRANSPORT TO STARBASE 10.
EVERYTHING READY, MISTER KYLE?
YESSIR, I'VE BEEN IN COMMUNICATION WITH GROUND CONTROL.
READY FOR BEAMING.
"ROBOT"
Photomontage and Story by JOHN BYRNE
DEDICATED TO THE TALENTED PERFORMERS, CRAFTSMEN AND TECHNICIANS WHOSE WORK IS REPRESENTED HERE
ARE YOU ALL RIGHT, KYLE?
YOU SEEM... AGITATED.
JUST A LITTLE NERVOUS, SIR.
DOCTOR BECKER AND I... KNEW EACH OTHER IN A... PAST LIFE.
WE'VE BEEN OUT OF TOUCH FOR YEARS.
THERE'S HARDLY A MEMBER OF THIS CREW WHO HASN'T BEEN DOWN THAT ROAD, MR. KYLE.
WE ALL KNOW HOW YOU FEEL!
ENERGIZE!

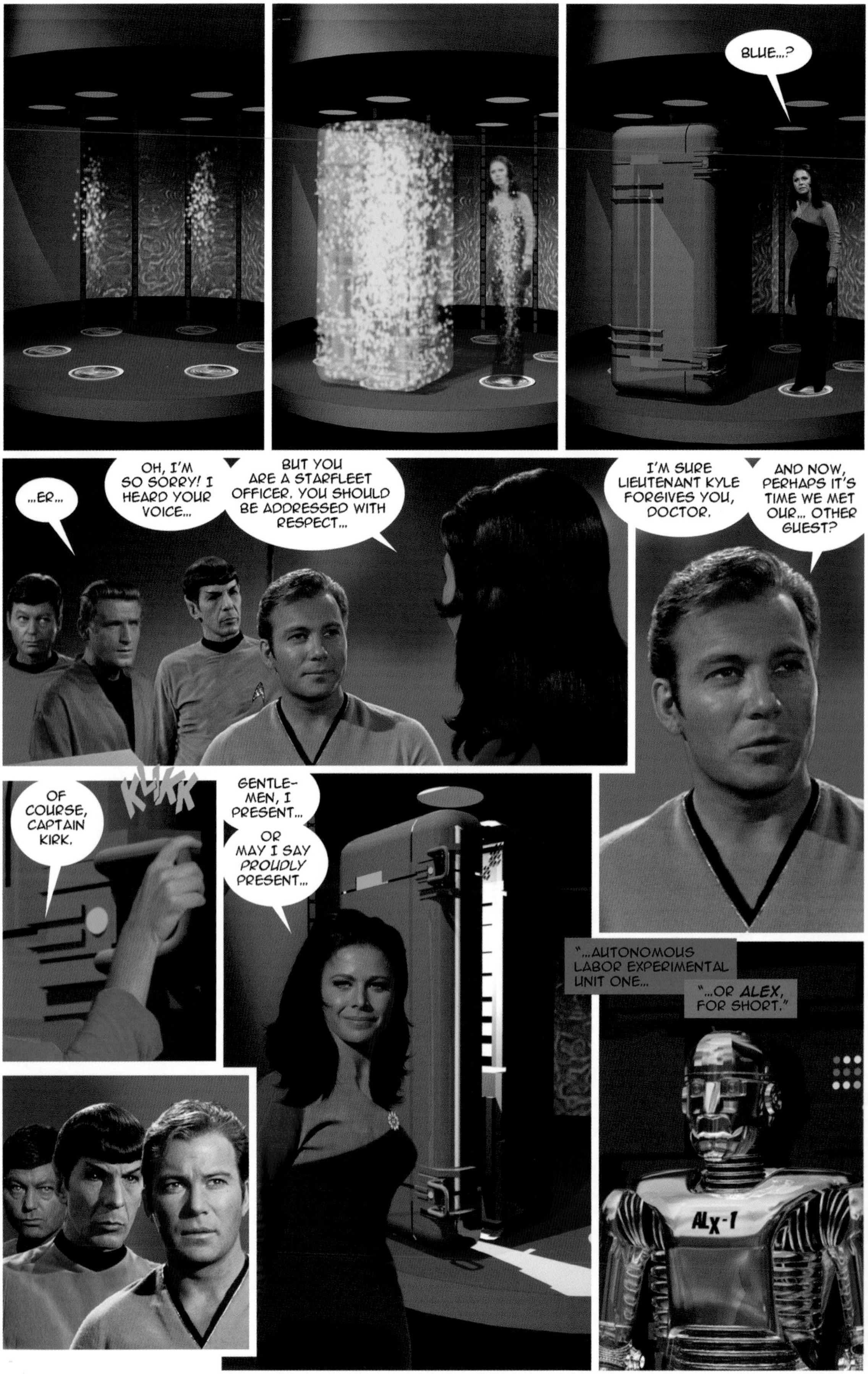
BLUE...?
...ER...
OH, I'M SO SORRY! I HEARD YOUR VOICE...
BUT YOU ARE A STARFLEET OFFICER. YOU SHOULD BE ADDRESSED WITH RESPECT...
I'M SURE LIEUTENANT KYLE FORGIVES YOU, DOCTOR.
AND NOW, PERHAPS IT'S TIME WE MET OUR... OTHER GUEST?
OF COURSE, CAPTAIN KIRK.
KLIKK
GENTLE-MEN, I PRESENT...
OR MAY I SAY *PROUDLY* PRESENT...
"...AUTONOMOUS LABOR EXPERIMENTAL UNIT ONE...
"...OR *ALEX*, FOR SHORT."
ALX-1

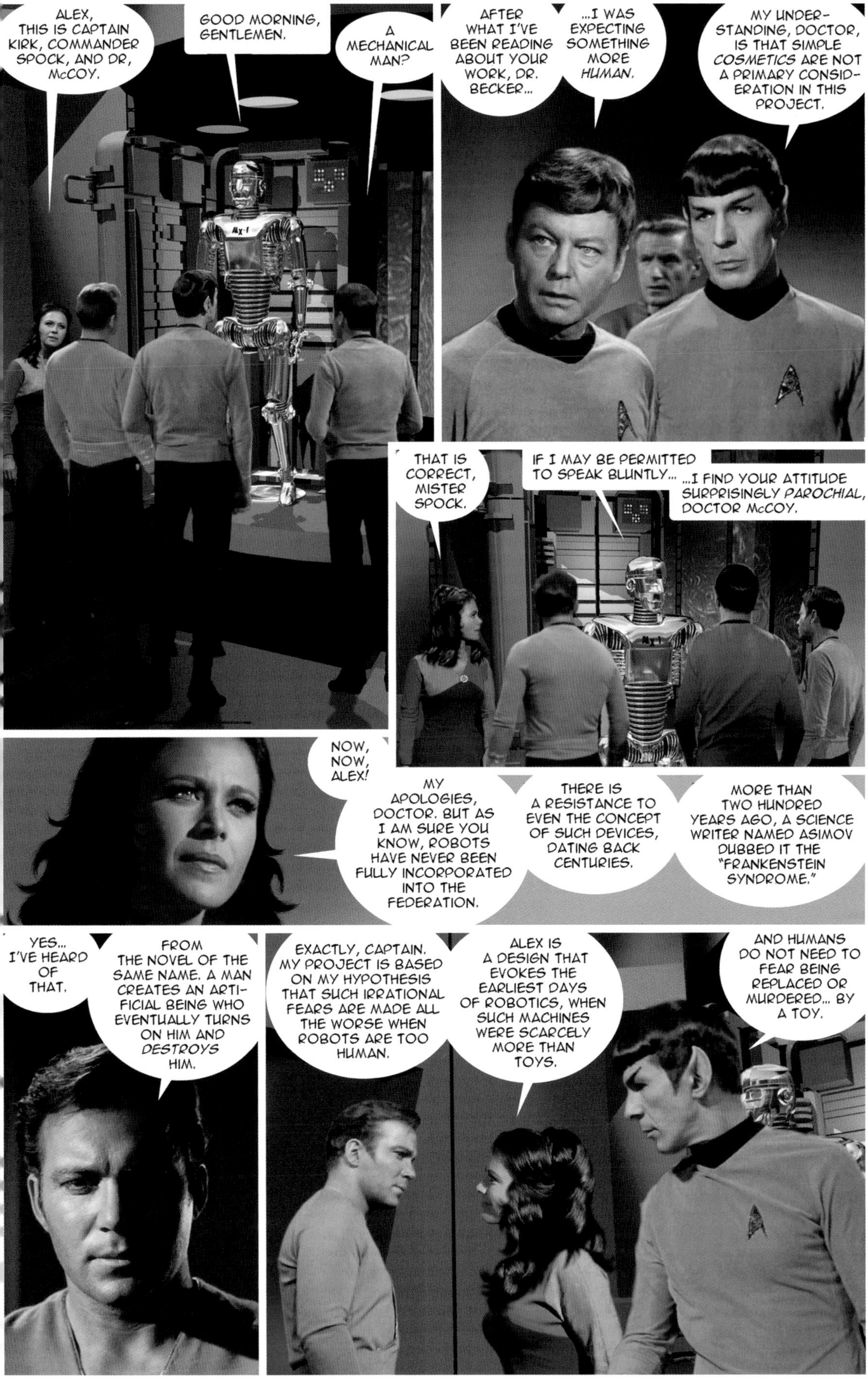
ALEX, THIS IS CAPTAIN KIRK, COMMANDER SPOCK, AND DR. McCOY.
GOOD MORNING, GENTLEMEN.
A MECHANICAL MAN?
AFTER WHAT I'VE BEEN READING ABOUT YOUR WORK, DR. BECKER...
...I WAS EXPECTING SOMETHING MORE *HUMAN*.
MY UNDERSTANDING, DOCTOR, IS THAT SIMPLE *COSMETICS* ARE NOT A PRIMARY CONSIDERATION IN THIS PROJECT.
THAT IS CORRECT, MISTER SPOCK.
IF I MAY BE PERMITTED TO SPEAK BLUNTLY...
...I FIND YOUR ATTITUDE SURPRISINGLY *PAROCHIAL*, DOCTOR McCOY.
NOW, NOW, ALEX!
MY APOLOGIES, DOCTOR. BUT AS I AM SURE YOU KNOW, ROBOTS HAVE NEVER BEEN FULLY INCORPORATED INTO THE FEDERATION.
THERE IS A RESISTANCE TO EVEN THE CONCEPT OF SUCH DEVICES, DATING BACK CENTURIES.
MORE THAN TWO HUNDRED YEARS AGO, A SCIENCE WRITER NAMED ASIMOV DUBBED IT THE "FRANKENSTEIN SYNDROME."
YES... I'VE HEARD OF THAT.
FROM THE NOVEL OF THE SAME NAME. A MAN CREATES AN ARTIFICIAL BEING WHO EVENTUALLY TURNS ON HIM AND *DESTROYS* HIM.
EXACTLY, CAPTAIN. MY PROJECT IS BASED ON MY HYPOTHESIS THAT SUCH IRRATIONAL FEARS ARE MADE ALL THE WORSE WHEN ROBOTS ARE TOO HUMAN.
ALEX IS A DESIGN THAT EVOKES THE EARLIEST DAYS OF ROBOTICS, WHEN SUCH MACHINES WERE SCARCELY MORE THAN TOYS.
AND HUMANS DO NOT NEED TO FEAR BEING REPLACED OR MURDERED... BY A TOY.

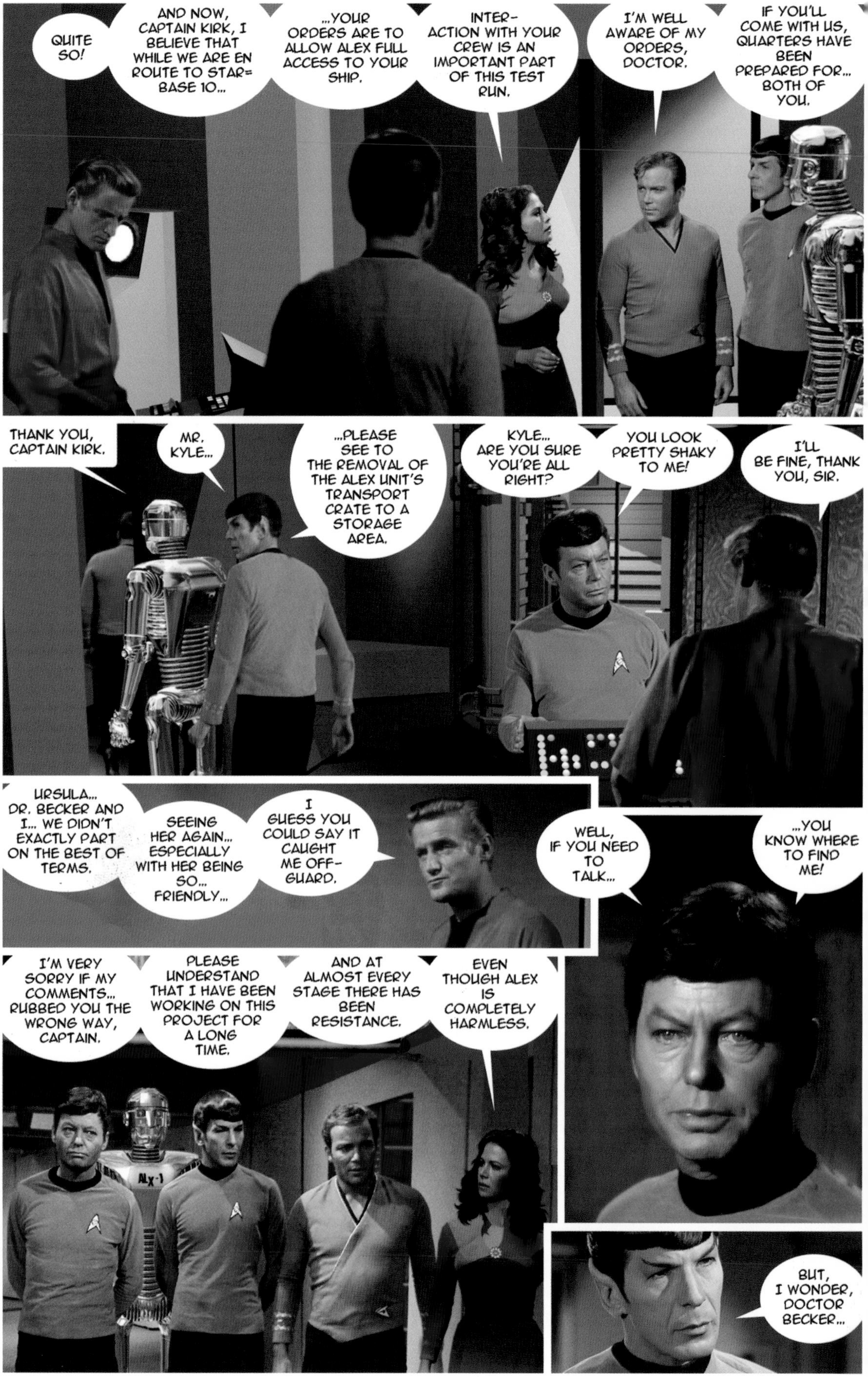
QUITE SO!
AND NOW, CAPTAIN KIRK, I BELIEVE THAT WHILE WE ARE EN ROUTE TO STAR= BASE 10...
...YOUR ORDERS ARE TO ALLOW ALEX FULL ACCESS TO YOUR SHIP.
INTER- ACTION WITH YOUR CREW IS AN IMPORTANT PART OF THIS TEST RUN.
I'M WELL AWARE OF MY ORDERS, DOCTOR.
IF YOU'LL COME WITH US, QUARTERS HAVE BEEN PREPARED FOR... BOTH OF YOU.
THANK YOU, CAPTAIN KIRK.
MR. KYLE...
...PLEASE SEE TO THE REMOVAL OF THE ALEX UNIT'S TRANSPORT CRATE TO A STORAGE AREA.
KYLE... ARE YOU SURE YOU'RE ALL RIGHT?
YOU LOOK PRETTY SHAKY TO ME!
I'LL BE FINE, THANK YOU, SIR.
URSULA... DR. BECKER AND I... WE DIDN'T EXACTLY PART ON THE BEST OF TERMS.
SEEING HER AGAIN... ESPECIALLY WITH HER BEING SO... FRIENDLY...
I GUESS YOU COULD SAY IT CAUGHT ME OFF- GUARD.
WELL, IF YOU NEED TO TALK...
...YOU KNOW WHERE TO FIND ME!
I'M VERY SORRY IF MY COMMENTS... RUBBED YOU THE WRONG WAY, CAPTAIN.
PLEASE UNDERSTAND THAT I HAVE BEEN WORKING ON THIS PROJECT FOR A LONG TIME.
AND AT ALMOST EVERY STAGE THERE HAS BEEN RESISTANCE.
EVEN THOUGH ALEX IS COMPLETELY HARMLESS.
ALX-1
BUT, I WONDER, DOCTOR BECKER...

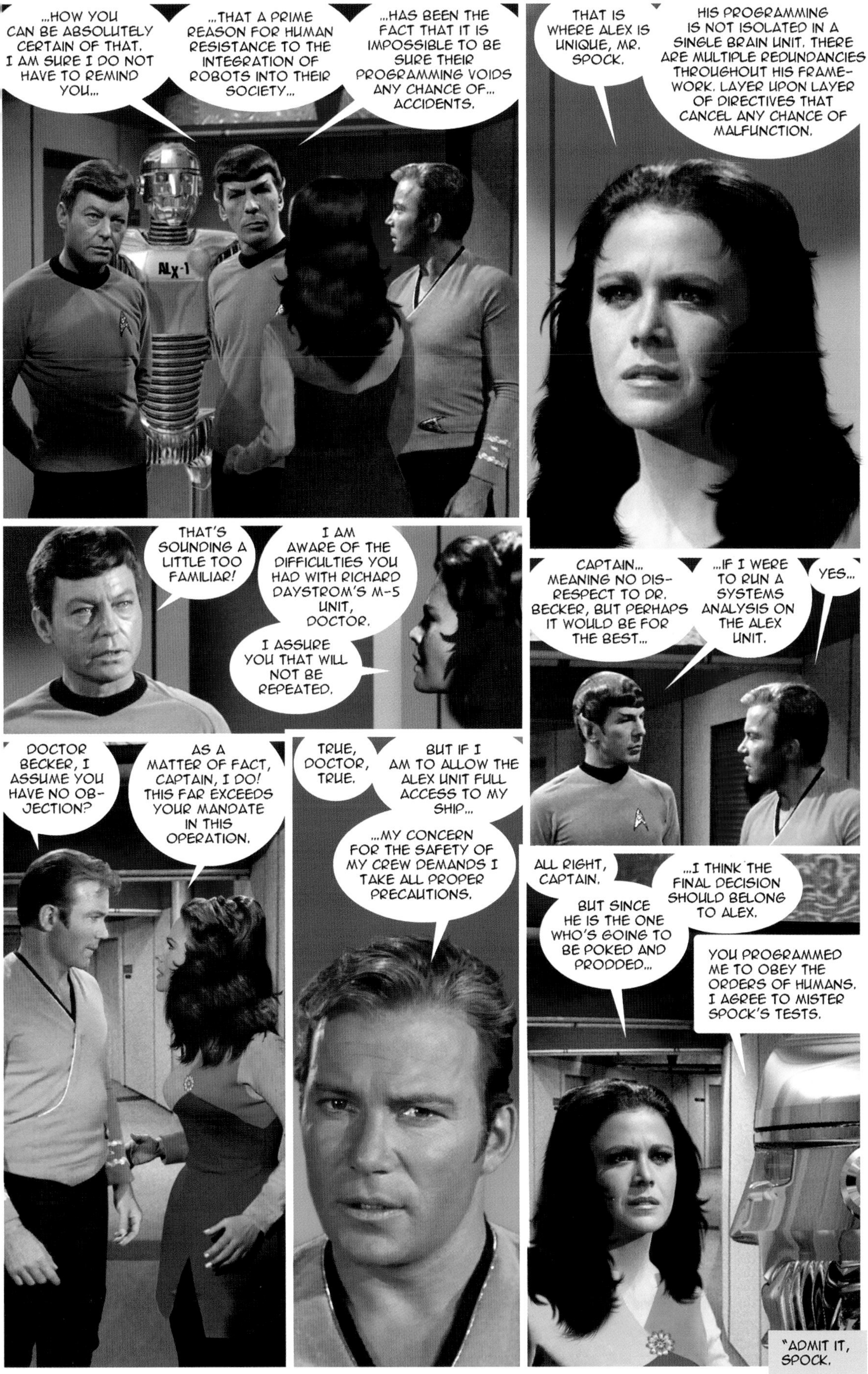
...HOW YOU CAN BE ABSOLUTELY CERTAIN OF THAT. I AM SURE I DO NOT HAVE TO REMIND YOU...
...THAT A PRIME REASON FOR HUMAN RESISTANCE TO THE INTEGRATION OF ROBOTS INTO THEIR SOCIETY...
...HAS BEEN THE FACT THAT IT IS IMPOSSIBLE TO BE SURE THEIR PROGRAMMING VOIDS ANY CHANCE OF... ACCIDENTS.
ALX-1
THAT IS WHERE ALEX IS UNIQUE, MR. SPOCK.
HIS PROGRAMMING IS NOT ISOLATED IN A SINGLE BRAIN UNIT. THERE ARE MULTIPLE REDUNDANCIES THROUGHOUT HIS FRAMEWORK. LAYER UPON LAYER OF DIRECTIVES THAT CANCEL ANY CHANCE OF MALFUNCTION.
THAT'S SOUNDING A LITTLE TOO FAMILIAR!
I AM AWARE OF THE DIFFICULTIES YOU HAD WITH RICHARD DAYSTROM'S M-5 UNIT, DOCTOR.
I ASSURE YOU THAT WILL NOT BE REPEATED.
CAPTAIN... MEANING NO DISRESPECT TO DR. BECKER, BUT PERHAPS IT WOULD BE FOR THE BEST...
...IF I WERE TO RUN A SYSTEMS ANALYSIS ON THE ALEX UNIT.
YES...
DOCTOR BECKER, I ASSUME YOU HAVE NO OBJECTION?
AS A MATTER OF FACT, CAPTAIN, I DO! THIS FAR EXCEEDS YOUR MANDATE IN THIS OPERATION.
TRUE, DOCTOR, TRUE.
BUT IF I AM TO ALLOW THE ALEX UNIT FULL ACCESS TO MY SHIP...
...MY CONCERN FOR THE SAFETY OF MY CREW DEMANDS I TAKE ALL PROPER PRECAUTIONS.
ALL RIGHT, CAPTAIN.
BUT SINCE HE IS THE ONE WHO'S GOING TO BE POKED AND PRODDED...
...I THINK THE FINAL DECISION SHOULD BELONG TO ALEX.
YOU PROGRAMMED ME TO OBEY THE ORDERS OF HUMANS. I AGREE TO MISTER SPOCK'S TESTS.
"ADMIT IT, SPOCK.

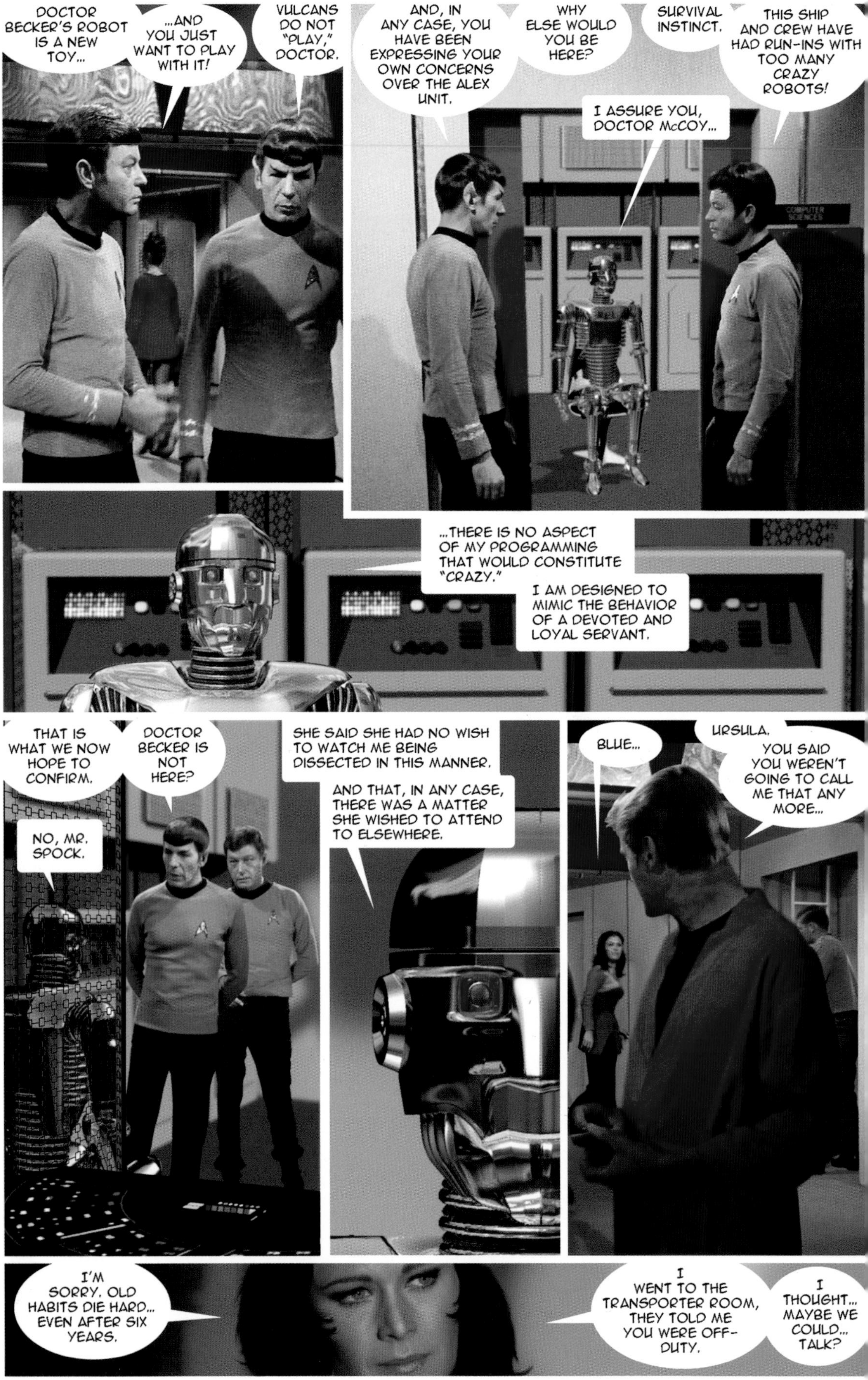
DOCTOR BECKER'S ROBOT IS A NEW TOY...
...AND YOU JUST WANT TO PLAY WITH IT!
VULCANS DO NOT "PLAY," DOCTOR.
AND, IN ANY CASE, YOU HAVE BEEN EXPRESSING YOUR OWN CONCERNS OVER THE ALEX UNIT.
WHY ELSE WOULD YOU BE HERE?
SURVIVAL INSTINCT.
THIS SHIP AND CREW HAVE HAD RUN-INS WITH TOO MANY CRAZY ROBOTS!
I ASSURE YOU, DOCTOR McCOY...
COMPUTER SCIENCES
...THERE IS NO ASPECT OF MY PROGRAMMING THAT WOULD CONSTITUTE "CRAZY."
I AM DESIGNED TO MIMIC THE BEHAVIOR OF A DEVOTED AND LOYAL SERVANT.
THAT IS WHAT WE NOW HOPE TO CONFIRM.
DOCTOR BECKER IS NOT HERE?
NO, MR. SPOCK.
SHE SAID SHE HAD NO WISH TO WATCH ME BEING DISSECTED IN THIS MANNER.
AND THAT, IN ANY CASE, THERE WAS A MATTER SHE WISHED TO ATTEND TO ELSEWHERE.
BLUE...
URSULA.
YOU SAID YOU WEREN'T GOING TO CALL ME THAT ANY MORE...
I'M SORRY. OLD HABITS DIE HARD... EVEN AFTER SIX YEARS.
I WENT TO THE TRANSPORTER ROOM, THEY TOLD ME YOU WERE OFF-DUTY.
I THOUGHT... MAYBE WE COULD... TALK?

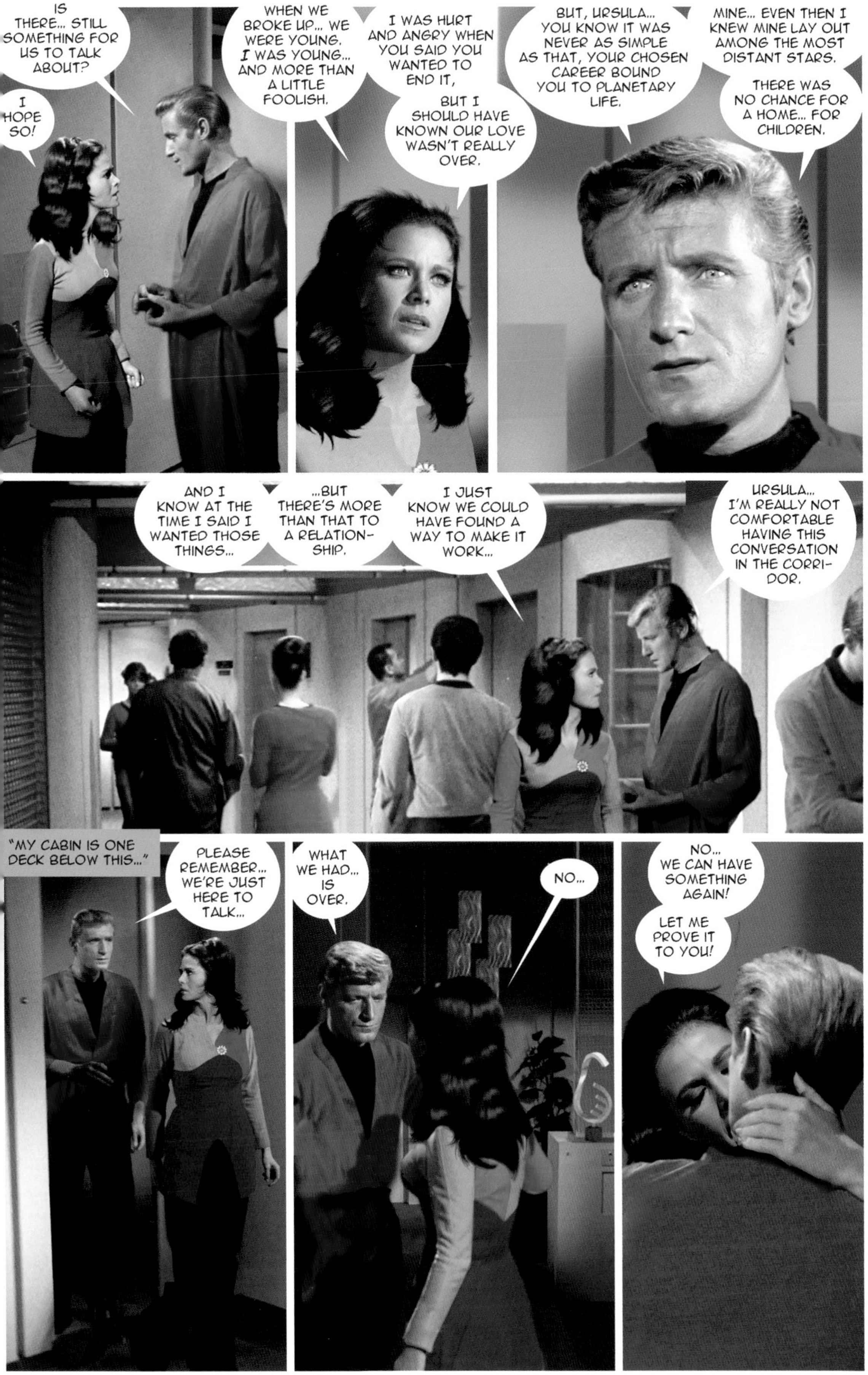
IS THERE... STILL SOMETHING FOR US TO TALK ABOUT?
I HOPE SO!
WHEN WE BROKE UP... WE WERE YOUNG. I WAS YOUNG... AND MORE THAN A LITTLE FOOLISH.
I WAS HURT AND ANGRY WHEN YOU SAID YOU WANTED TO END IT,
BUT I SHOULD HAVE KNOWN OUR LOVE WASN'T REALLY OVER.
BUT, URSULA... YOU KNOW IT WAS NEVER AS SIMPLE AS THAT. YOUR CHOSEN CAREER BOUND YOU TO PLANETARY LIFE.
MINE... EVEN THEN I KNEW MINE LAY OUT AMONG THE MOST DISTANT STARS.
THERE WAS NO CHANCE FOR A HOME... FOR CHILDREN.
AND I KNOW AT THE TIME I SAID I WANTED THOSE THINGS...
...BUT THERE'S MORE THAN THAT TO A RELATION-SHIP.
I JUST KNOW WE COULD HAVE FOUND A WAY TO MAKE IT WORK...
URSULA... I'M REALLY NOT COMFORTABLE HAVING THIS CONVERSATION IN THE CORRI-DOR.
"MY CABIN IS ONE DECK BELOW THIS..."
PLEASE REMEMBER... WE'RE JUST HERE TO TALK...
WHAT WE HAD... IS OVER.
NO...
NO... WE CAN HAVE SOMETHING AGAIN!
LET ME PROVE IT TO YOU!

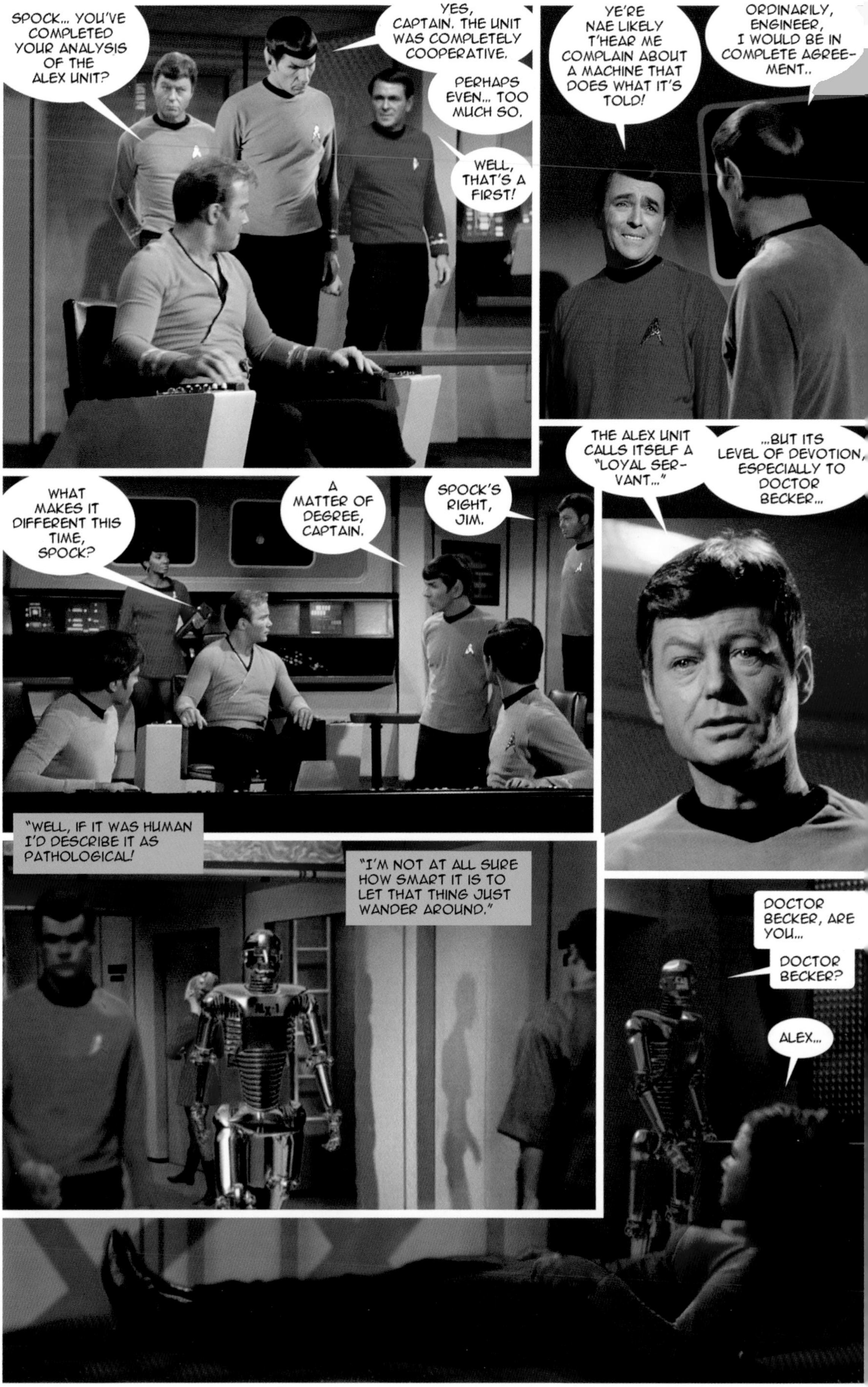

SPOCK... YOU'VE COMPLETED YOUR ANALYSIS OF THE ALEX UNIT?
YES, CAPTAIN. THE UNIT WAS COMPLETELY COOPERATIVE.
PERHAPS EVEN... TOO MUCH SO.
WELL, THAT'S A FIRST!
YE'RE NAE LIKELY T'HEAR ME COMPLAIN ABOUT A MACHINE THAT DOES WHAT IT'S TOLD!
ORDINARILY, ENGINEER, I WOULD BE IN COMPLETE AGREE-MENT..
WHAT MAKES IT DIFFERENT THIS TIME, SPOCK?
A MATTER OF DEGREE, CAPTAIN.
SPOCK'S RIGHT, JIM.
THE ALEX UNIT CALLS ITSELF A "LOYAL SER-VANT..."
...BUT ITS LEVEL OF DEVOTION, ESPECIALLY TO DOCTOR BECKER...
"WELL, IF IT WAS HUMAN I'D DESCRIBE IT AS PATHOLOGICAL!
"I'M NOT AT ALL SURE HOW SMART IT IS TO LET THAT THING JUST WANDER AROUND."
DOCTOR BECKER, ARE YOU...
DOCTOR BECKER?
ALEX...

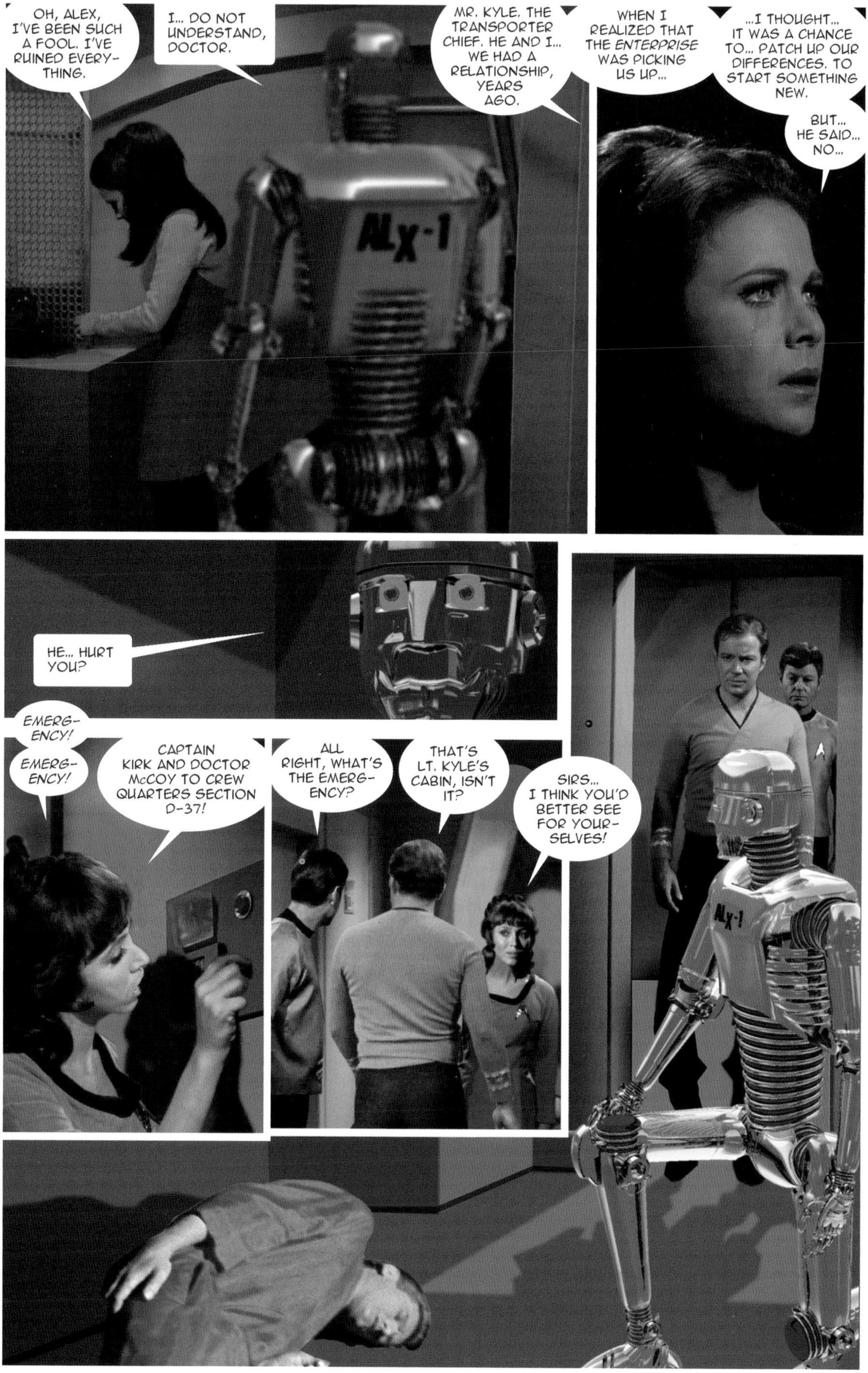

OH, ALEX, I'VE BEEN SUCH A FOOL. I'VE RUINED EVERY-THING.
I... DO NOT UNDERSTAND, DOCTOR.
MR. KYLE. THE TRANSPORTER CHIEF. HE AND I... WE HAD A RELATIONSHIP, YEARS AGO.
WHEN I REALIZED THAT THE *ENTERPRISE* WAS PICKING US UP...
...I THOUGHT... IT WAS A CHANCE TO... PATCH UP OUR DIFFERENCES. TO START SOMETHING NEW.
BUT... HE SAID... NO...
ALX-1
HE... HURT YOU?
EMERG-ENCY!
EMERG-ENCY!
CAPTAIN KIRK AND DOCTOR McCOY TO CREW QUARTERS SECTION D-37!
ALL RIGHT, WHAT'S THE EMERG-ENCY?
THAT'S LT. KYLE'S CABIN, ISN'T IT?
SIRS... I THINK YOU'D BETTER SEE FOR YOUR-SELVES!
ALX-1

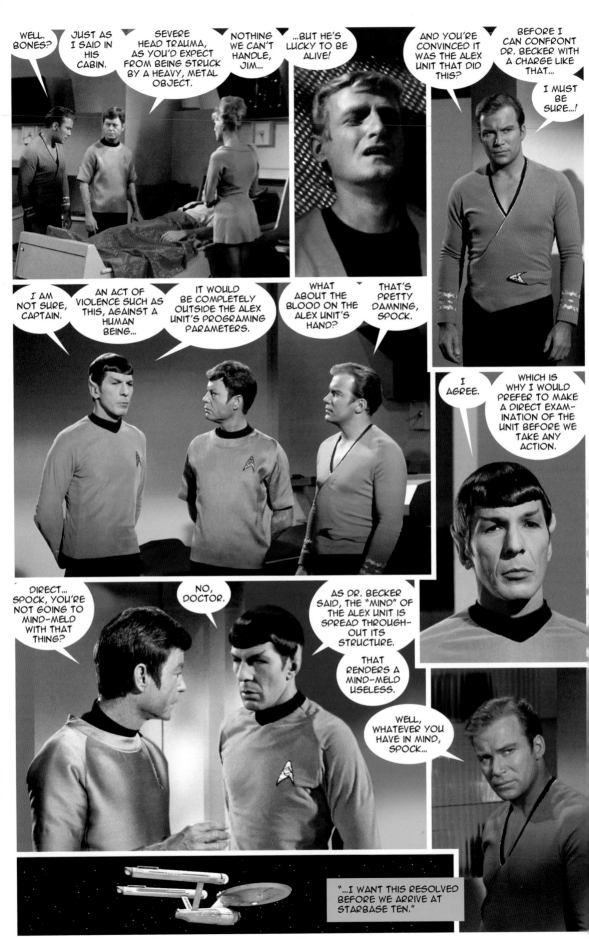

WELL, BONES?

JUST AS I SAID IN HIS CABIN.

SEVERE HEAD TRAUMA, AS YOU'D EXPECT FROM BEING STRUCK BY A HEAVY, METAL OBJECT.

NOTHING WE CAN'T HANDLE, JIM...

...BUT HE'S LUCKY TO BE ALIVE!

AND YOU'RE CONVINCED IT WAS THE ALEX UNIT THAT DID THIS?

BEFORE I CAN CONFRONT DR. BECKER WITH A CHARGE LIKE THAT...

I MUST BE SURE...!

I AM NOT SURE, CAPTAIN.

AN ACT OF VIOLENCE SUCH AS THIS, AGAINST A HUMAN BEING...

IT WOULD BE COMPLETELY OUTSIDE THE ALEX UNIT'S PROGRAMING PARAMETERS.

WHAT ABOUT THE BLOOD ON THE ALEX UNIT'S HAND?

THAT'S PRETTY DAMNING, SPOCK.

I AGREE.

WHICH IS WHY I WOULD PREFER TO MAKE A DIRECT EXAMINATION OF THE UNIT BEFORE WE TAKE ANY ACTION.

DIRECT... SPOCK, YOU'RE NOT GOING TO MIND-MELD WITH THAT THING?

NO, DOCTOR.

AS DR. BECKER SAID, THE "MIND" OF THE ALEX UNIT IS SPREAD THROUGHOUT ITS STRUCTURE.

THAT RENDERS A MIND-MELD USELESS.

WELL, WHATEVER YOU HAVE IN MIND, SPOCK...

"...I WANT THIS RESOLVED BEFORE WE ARRIVE AT STARBASE TEN."

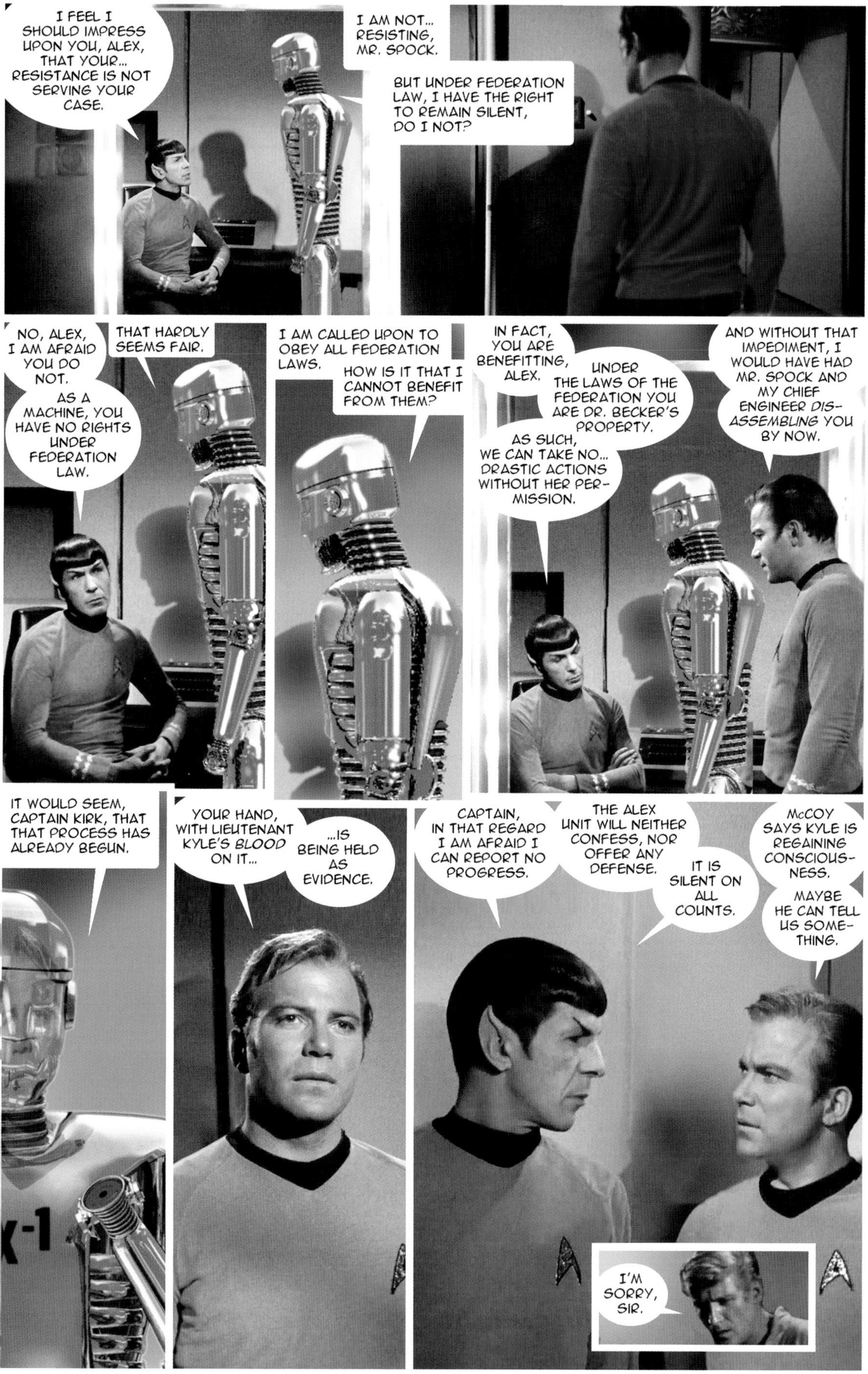
I FEEL I SHOULD IMPRESS UPON YOU, ALEX, THAT YOUR... RESISTANCE IS NOT SERVING YOUR CASE.
I AM NOT... RESISTING, MR. SPOCK.
BUT UNDER FEDERATION LAW, I HAVE THE RIGHT TO REMAIN SILENT, DO I NOT?
NO, ALEX, I AM AFRAID YOU DO NOT.
AS A MACHINE, YOU HAVE NO RIGHTS UNDER FEDERATION LAW.
THAT HARDLY SEEMS FAIR.
I AM CALLED UPON TO OBEY ALL FEDERATION LAWS.
HOW IS IT THAT I CANNOT BENEFIT FROM THEM?
IN FACT, YOU ARE BENEFITTING, ALEX.
UNDER THE LAWS OF THE FEDERATION YOU ARE DR. BECKER'S PROPERTY.
AS SUCH, WE CAN TAKE NO... DRASTIC ACTIONS WITHOUT HER PERMISSION.
AND WITHOUT THAT IMPEDIMENT, I WOULD HAVE HAD MR. SPOCK AND MY CHIEF ENGINEER *DIS-ASSEMBLING* YOU BY NOW.
IT WOULD SEEM, CAPTAIN KIRK, THAT THAT PROCESS HAS ALREADY BEGUN.
X-1
YOUR HAND, WITH LIEUTENANT KYLE'S *BLOOD* ON IT...
...IS BEING HELD AS EVIDENCE.
CAPTAIN, IN THAT REGARD I AM AFRAID I CAN REPORT NO PROGRESS.
THE ALEX UNIT WILL NEITHER CONFESS, NOR OFFER ANY DEFENSE.
IT IS SILENT ON ALL COUNTS.
McCOY SAYS KYLE IS REGAINING CONSCIOUS-NESS.
MAYBE HE CAN TELL US SOME-THING.
I'M SORRY, SIR.

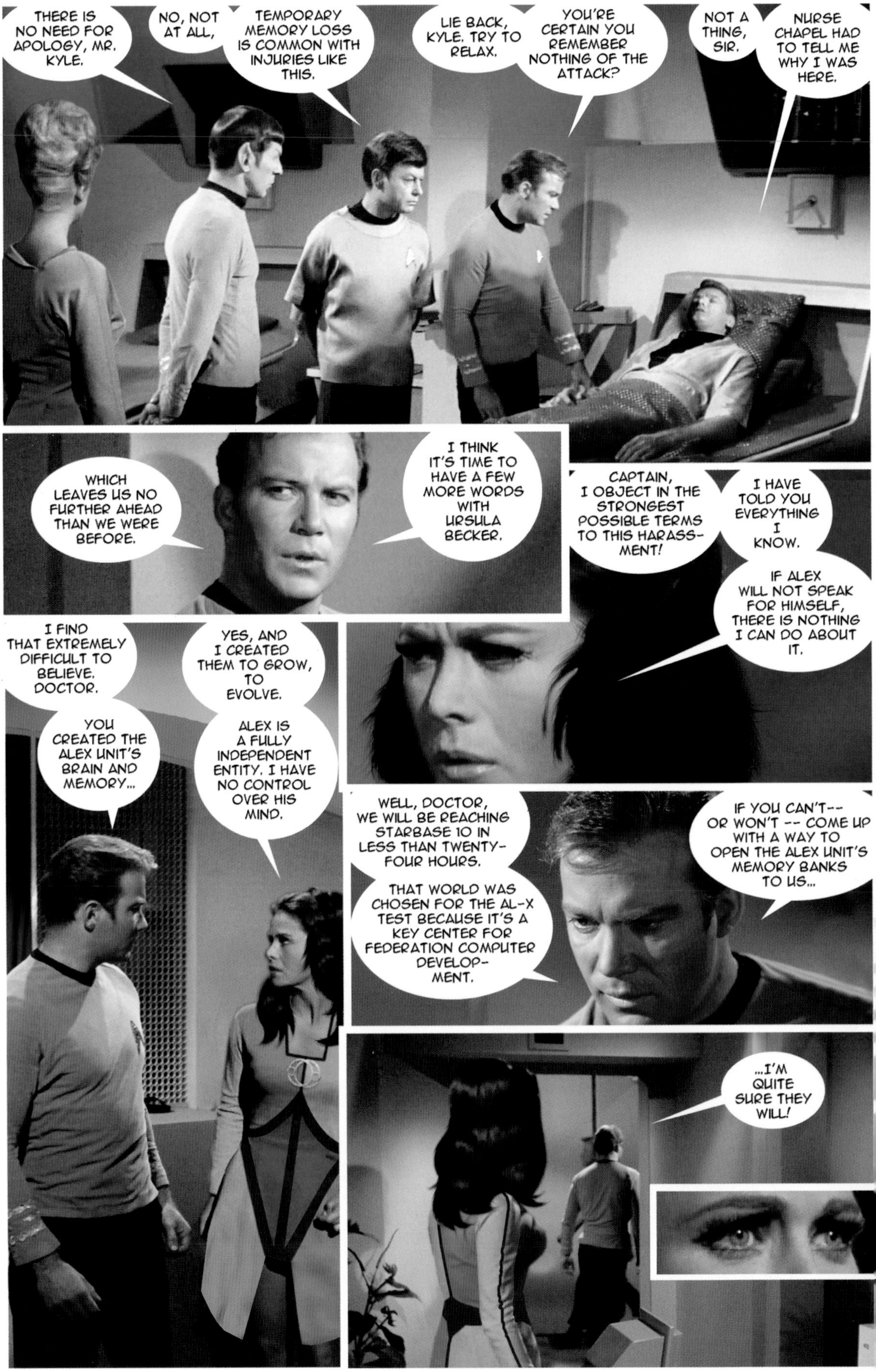

THERE IS NO NEED FOR APOLOGY, MR. KYLE.
NO, NOT AT ALL,
TEMPORARY MEMORY LOSS IS COMMON WITH INJURIES LIKE THIS.
LIE BACK, KYLE. TRY TO RELAX.
YOU'RE CERTAIN YOU REMEMBER NOTHING OF THE ATTACK?
NOT A THING, SIR.
NURSE CHAPEL HAD TO TELL ME WHY I WAS HERE.
WHICH LEAVES US NO FURTHER AHEAD THAN WE WERE BEFORE.
I THINK IT'S TIME TO HAVE A FEW MORE WORDS WITH URSULA BECKER.
CAPTAIN, I OBJECT IN THE STRONGEST POSSIBLE TERMS TO THIS HARASS-MENT!
I HAVE TOLD YOU EVERYTHING I KNOW.
IF ALEX WILL NOT SPEAK FOR HIMSELF, THERE IS NOTHING I CAN DO ABOUT IT.
I FIND THAT EXTREMELY DIFFICULT TO BELIEVE, DOCTOR.
YOU CREATED THE ALEX UNIT'S BRAIN AND MEMORY...
YES, AND I CREATED THEM TO GROW, TO EVOLVE.
ALEX IS A FULLY INDEPENDENT ENTITY. I HAVE NO CONTROL OVER HIS MIND.
WELL, DOCTOR, WE WILL BE REACHING STARBASE 10 IN LESS THAN TWENTY-FOUR HOURS.
THAT WORLD WAS CHOSEN FOR THE AL-X TEST BECAUSE IT'S A KEY CENTER FOR FEDERATION COMPUTER DEVELOP-MENT.
IF YOU CAN'T-- OR WON'T -- COME UP WITH A WAY TO OPEN THE ALEX UNIT'S MEMORY BANKS TO US...
...I'M QUITE SURE THEY WILL!

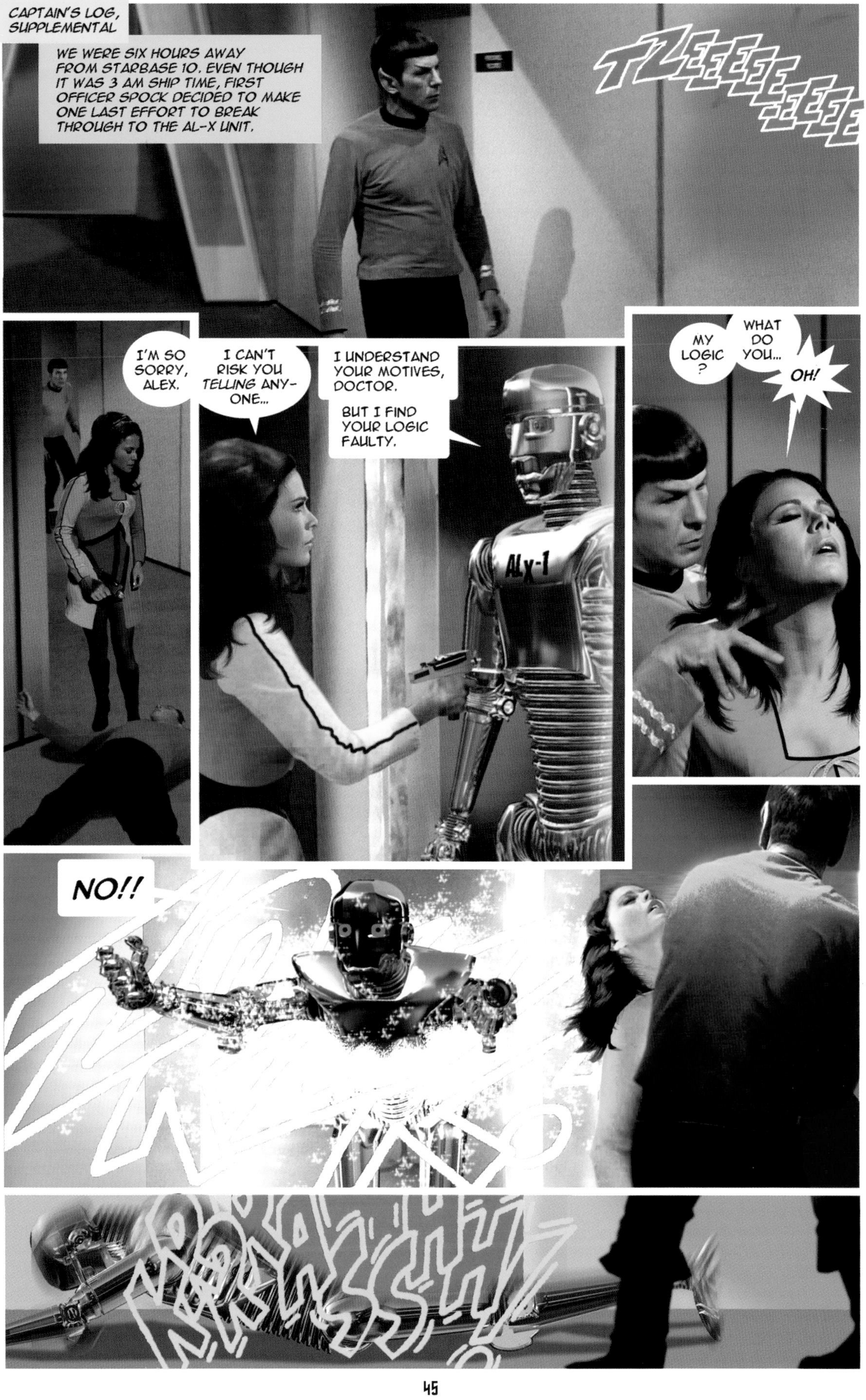
CAPTAIN'S LOG, SUPPLEMENTAL
WE WERE SIX HOURS AWAY FROM STARBASE 10. EVEN THOUGH IT WAS 3 AM SHIP TIME, FIRST OFFICER SPOCK DECIDED TO MAKE ONE LAST EFFORT TO BREAK THROUGH TO THE AL-X UNIT.
TZEEEEEEEEEEEE
I'M SO SORRY, ALEX.
I CAN'T RISK YOU TELLING ANY-ONE...
I UNDERSTAND YOUR MOTIVES, DOCTOR.
BUT I FIND YOUR LOGIC FAULTY.
ALx-1
MY LOGIC ?
WHAT DO YOU...
OH!
NO!!

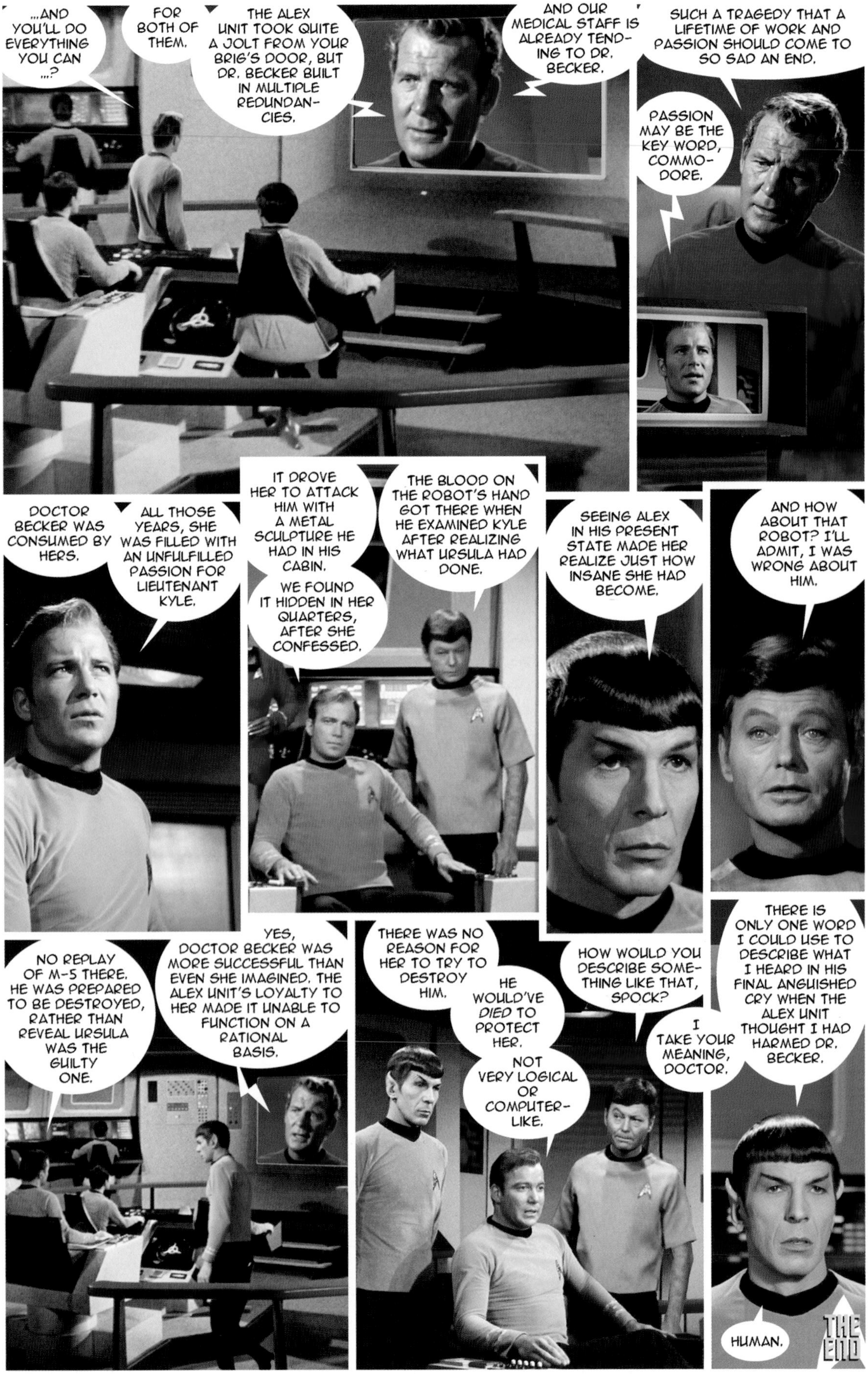
...AND YOU'LL DO EVERYTHING YOU CAN ...?
FOR BOTH OF THEM.
THE ALEX UNIT TOOK QUITE A JOLT FROM YOUR BRIG'S DOOR, BUT DR. BECKER BUILT IN MULTIPLE REDUNDANCIES.
AND OUR MEDICAL STAFF IS ALREADY TENDING TO DR. BECKER.
SUCH A TRAGEDY THAT A LIFETIME OF WORK AND PASSION SHOULD COME TO SO SAD AN END.
PASSION MAY BE THE KEY WORD, COMMODORE.
DOCTOR BECKER WAS CONSUMED BY HERS.
ALL THOSE YEARS, SHE WAS FILLED WITH AN UNFULFILLED PASSION FOR LIEUTENANT KYLE.
IT DROVE HER TO ATTACK HIM WITH A METAL SCULPTURE HE HAD IN HIS CABIN.
WE FOUND IT HIDDEN IN HER QUARTERS, AFTER SHE CONFESSED.
THE BLOOD ON THE ROBOT'S HAND GOT THERE WHEN HE EXAMINED KYLE AFTER REALIZING WHAT URSULA HAD DONE.
SEEING ALEX IN HIS PRESENT STATE MADE HER REALIZE JUST HOW INSANE SHE HAD BECOME.
AND HOW ABOUT THAT ROBOT? I'LL ADMIT, I WAS WRONG ABOUT HIM.
NO REPLAY OF M-5 THERE. HE WAS PREPARED TO BE DESTROYED, RATHER THAN REVEAL URSULA WAS THE GUILTY ONE.
YES, DOCTOR BECKER WAS MORE SUCCESSFUL THAN EVEN SHE IMAGINED. THE ALEX UNIT'S LOYALTY TO HER MADE IT UNABLE TO FUNCTION ON A RATIONAL BASIS.
THERE WAS NO REASON FOR HER TO TRY TO DESTROY HIM.
HE WOULD'VE *DIED* TO PROTECT HER.
NOT VERY LOGICAL OR COMPUTER-LIKE.
HOW WOULD YOU DESCRIBE SOMETHING LIKE THAT, SPOCK?
I TAKE YOUR MEANING, DOCTOR.
THERE IS ONLY ONE WORD I COULD USE TO DESCRIBE WHAT I HEARD IN HIS FINAL ANGUISHED CRY WHEN THE ALEX UNIT THOUGHT I HAD HARMED DR. BECKER.
HUMAN.
THE END

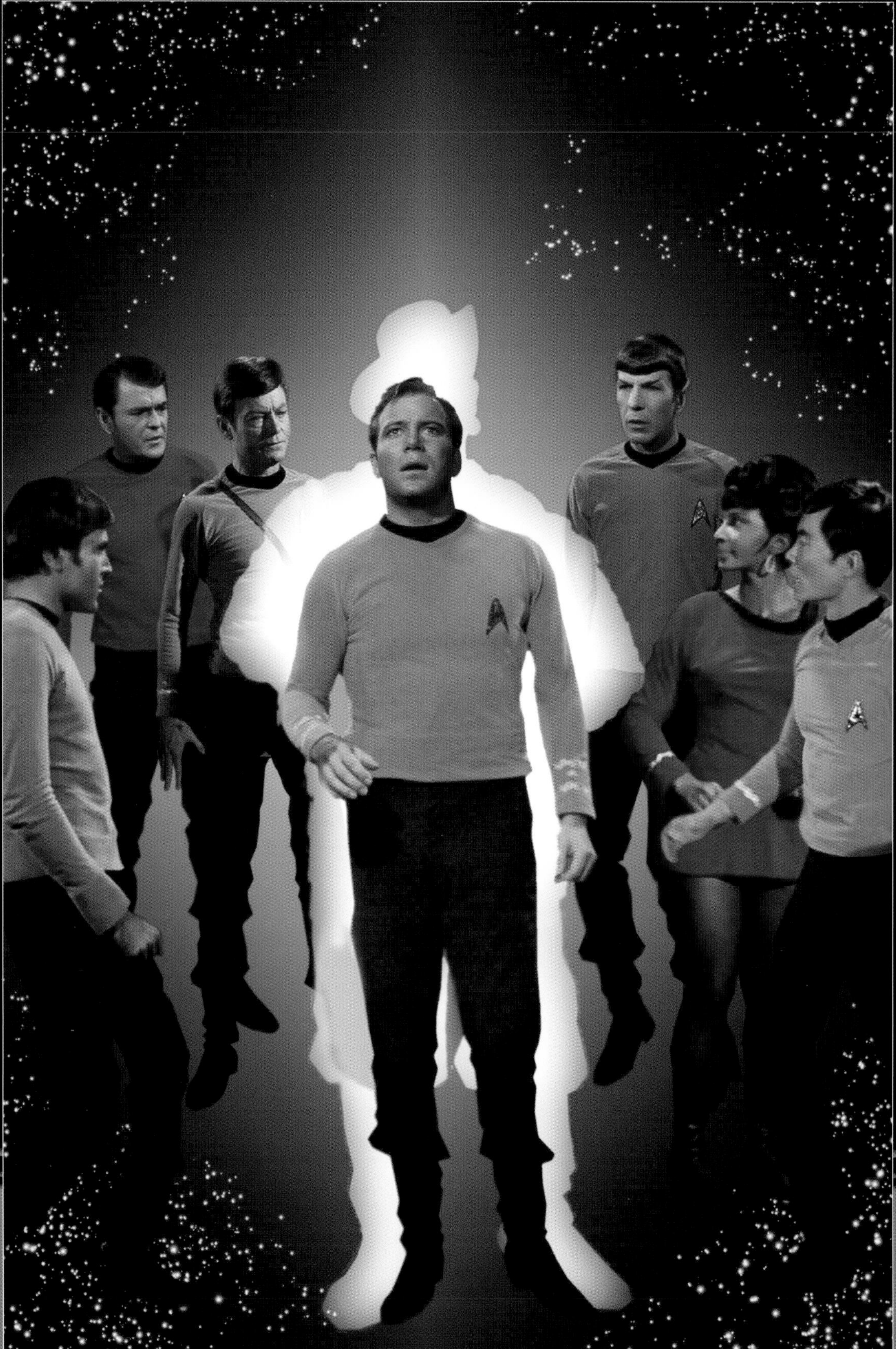

MADE OUT OF MUDD

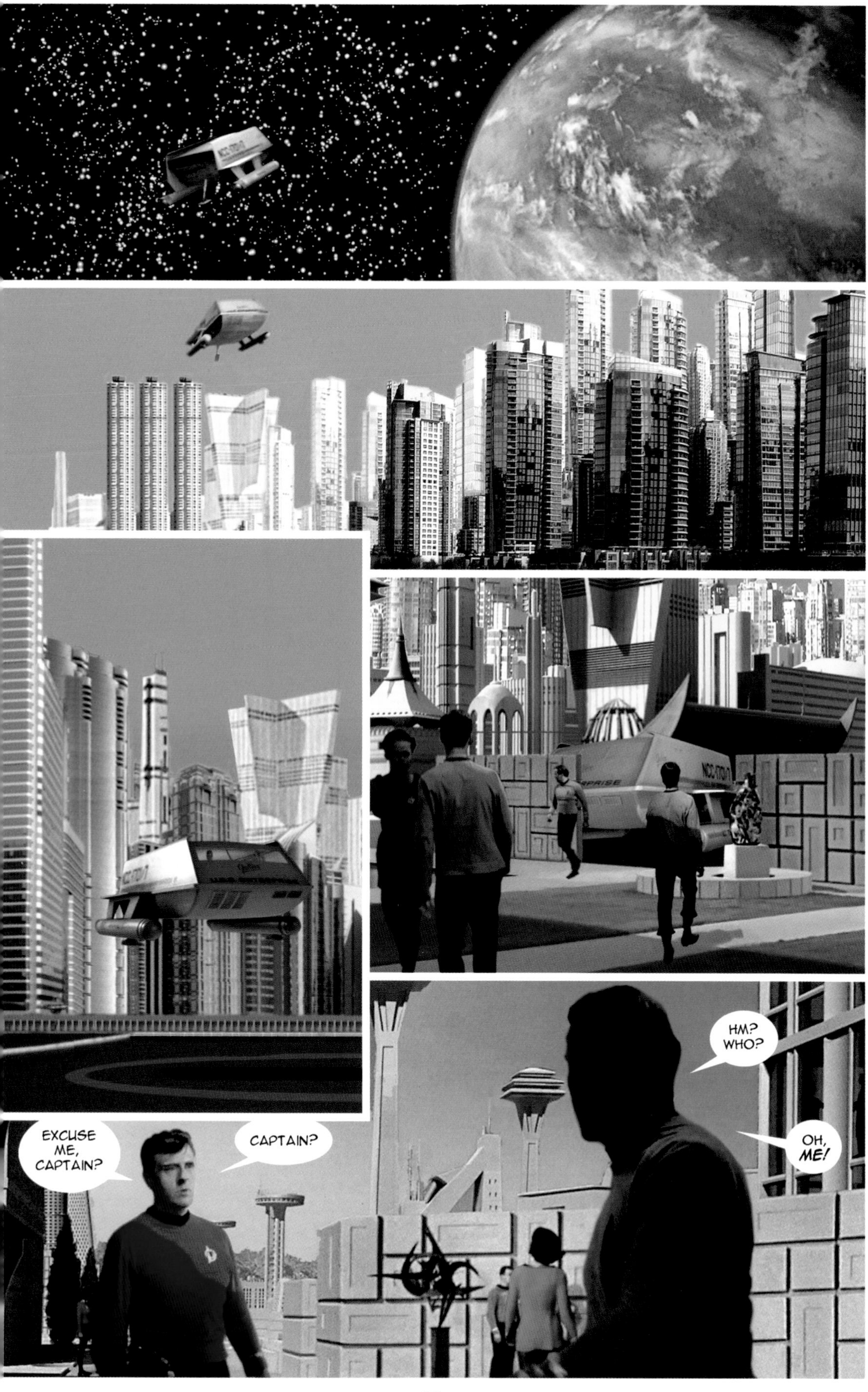
EXCUSE ME, CAPTAIN?
CAPTAIN?
HM? WHO?
OH, ME!

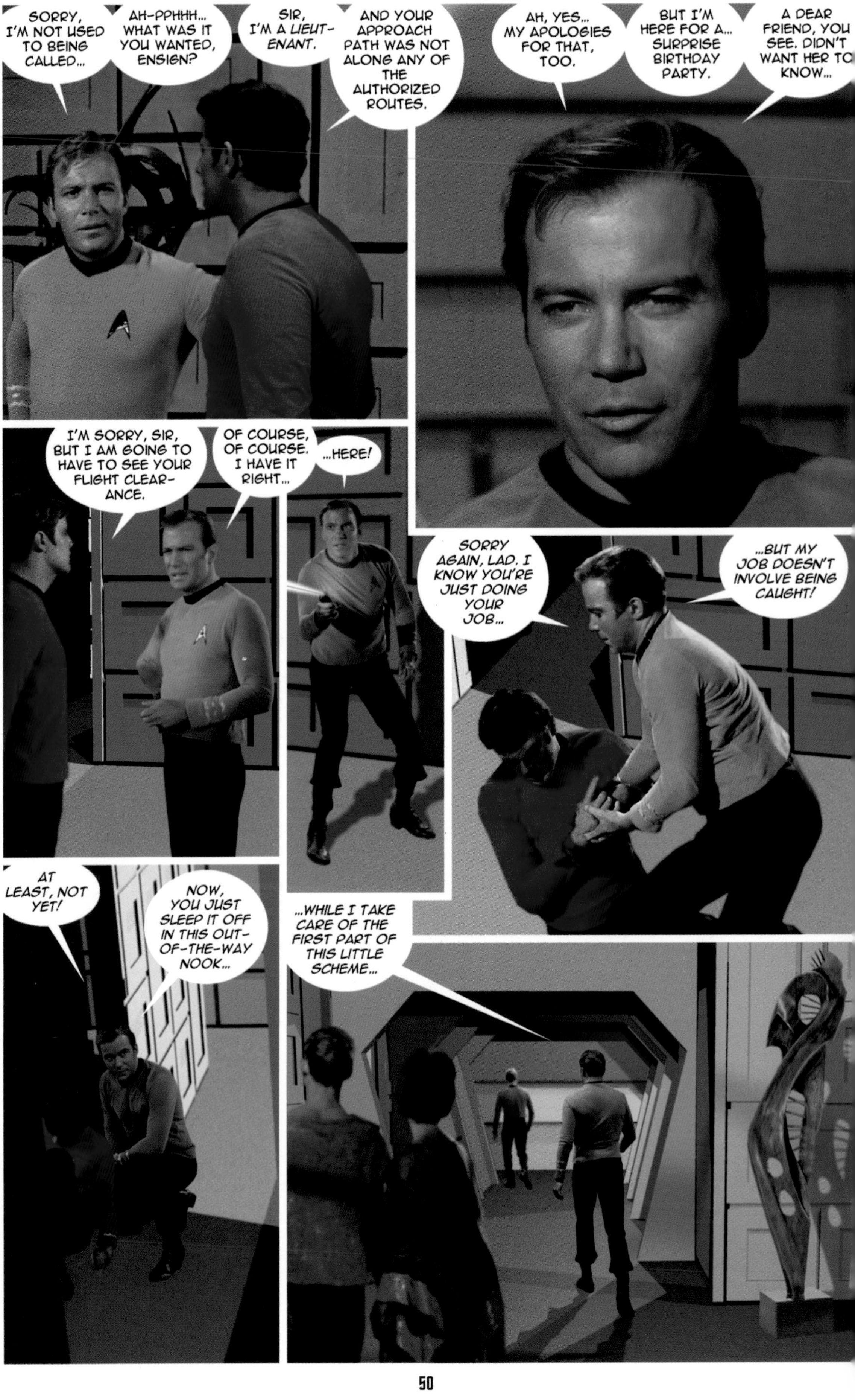
SORRY, I'M NOT USED TO BEING CALLED...
AH-PPHHH... WHAT WAS IT YOU WANTED, ENSIGN?
SIR, I'M A *LIEUT-ENANT*.
AND YOUR APPROACH PATH WAS NOT ALONG ANY OF THE AUTHORIZED ROUTES.
AH, YES... MY APOLOGIES FOR THAT, TOO.
BUT I'M HERE FOR A... SURPRISE BIRTHDAY PARTY.
A DEAR FRIEND, YOU SEE. DIDN'T WANT HER TO KNOW...
I'M SORRY, SIR, BUT I AM GOING TO HAVE TO SEE YOUR FLIGHT CLEAR-ANCE.
OF COURSE, OF COURSE. I HAVE IT RIGHT...
...HERE!
SORRY AGAIN, LAD. I KNOW YOU'RE JUST DOING YOUR JOB...
...BUT MY JOB DOESN'T INVOLVE BEING CAUGHT!
AT LEAST, NOT YET!
NOW, YOU JUST SLEEP IT OFF IN THIS OUT-OF-THE-WAY NOOK...
...WHILE I TAKE CARE OF THE FIRST PART OF THIS LITTLE SCHEME...

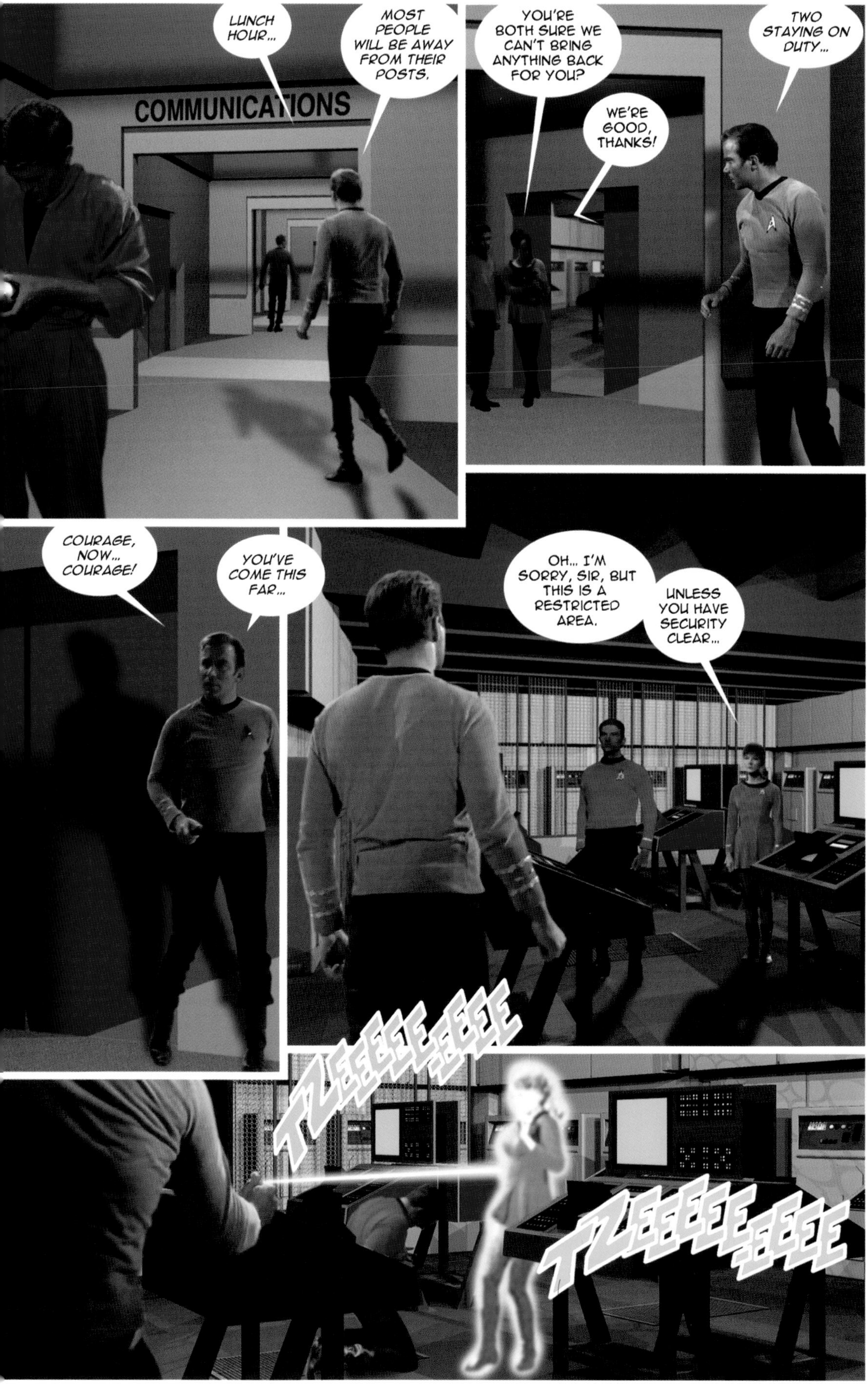
COMMUNICATIONS
LUNCH HOUR...
MOST PEOPLE WILL BE AWAY FROM THEIR POSTS.
YOU'RE BOTH SURE WE CAN'T BRING ANYTHING BACK FOR YOU?
WE'RE GOOD, THANKS!
TWO STAYING ON DUTY...
COURAGE, NOW... COURAGE!
YOU'VE COME THIS FAR...
OH... I'M SORRY, SIR, BUT THIS IS A RESTRICTED AREA.
UNLESS YOU HAVE SECURITY CLEAR...
TZEEEEEEEE
TZEEEEEEEEE

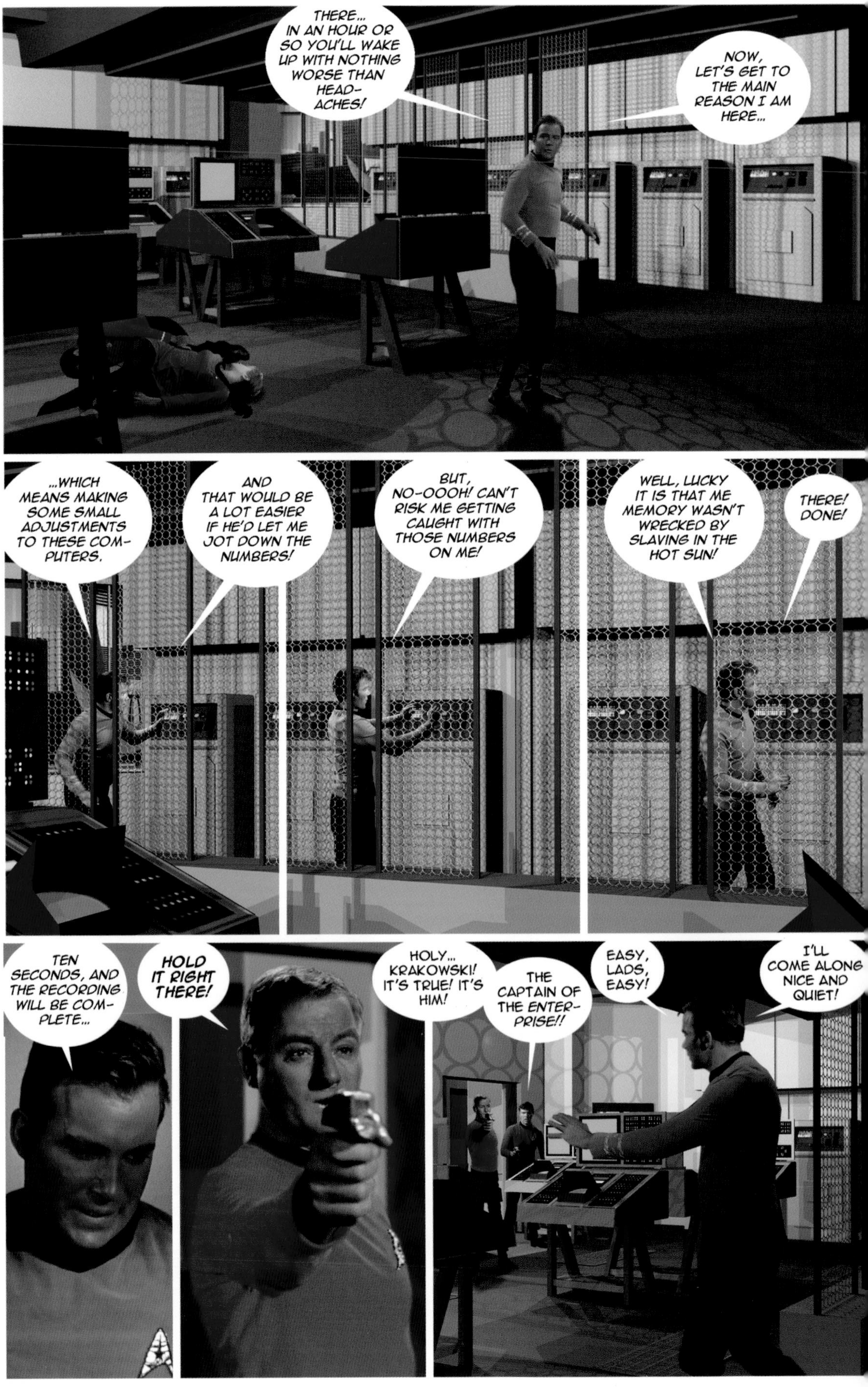
THERE... IN AN HOUR OR SO YOU'LL WAKE UP WITH NOTHING WORSE THAN HEAD-ACHES!
NOW, LET'S GET TO THE MAIN REASON I AM HERE...
...WHICH MEANS MAKING SOME SMALL ADJUSTMENTS TO THESE COM-PUTERS.
AND THAT WOULD BE A LOT EASIER IF HE'D LET ME JOT DOWN THE NUMBERS!
BUT, NO-OOOH! CAN'T RISK ME GETTING CAUGHT WITH THOSE NUMBERS ON ME!
WELL, LUCKY IT IS THAT ME MEMORY WASN'T WRECKED BY SLAVING IN THE HOT SUN!
THERE! DONE!
TEN SECONDS, AND THE RECORDING WILL BE COM-PLETE...
HOLD IT RIGHT THERE!
HOLY... KRAKOWSKI! IT'S TRUE! IT'S HIM!
THE CAPTAIN OF THE ENTER-PRISE!!
EASY, LADS, EASY!
I'LL COME ALONG NICE AND QUIET!

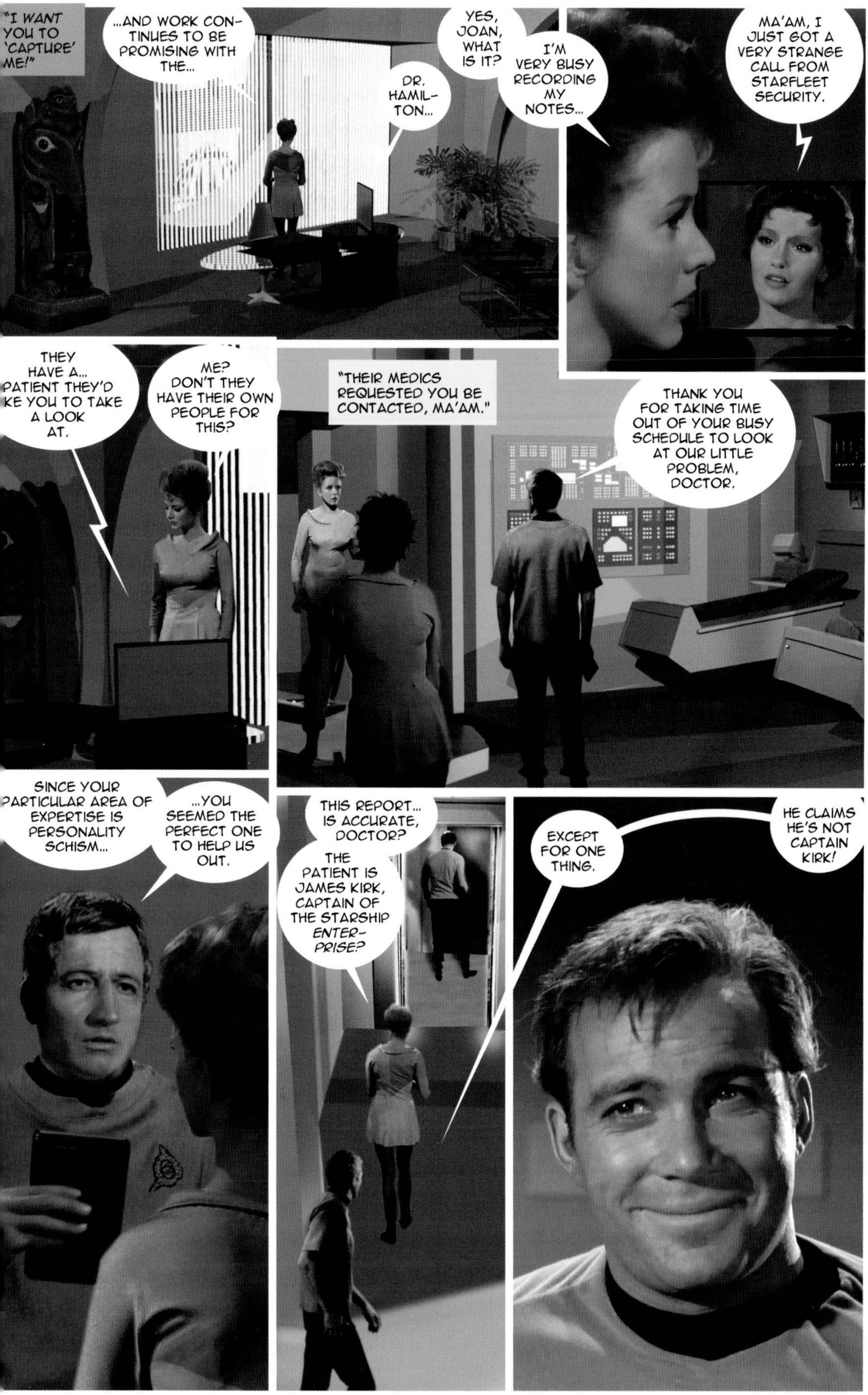
"I WANT YOU TO 'CAPTURE' ME!"
...AND WORK CONTINUES TO BE PROMISING WITH THE...
DR. HAMILTON...
YES, JOAN, WHAT IS IT?
I'M VERY BUSY RECORDING MY NOTES...
MA'AM, I JUST GOT A VERY STRANGE CALL FROM STARFLEET SECURITY.
THEY HAVE A... PATIENT THEY'D LIKE YOU TO TAKE A LOOK AT.
ME? DON'T THEY HAVE THEIR OWN PEOPLE FOR THIS?
"THEIR MEDICS REQUESTED YOU BE CONTACTED, MA'AM."
THANK YOU FOR TAKING TIME OUT OF YOUR BUSY SCHEDULE TO LOOK AT OUR LITTLE PROBLEM, DOCTOR.
SINCE YOUR PARTICULAR AREA OF EXPERTISE IS PERSONALITY SCHISM...
...YOU SEEMED THE PERFECT ONE TO HELP US OUT.
THIS REPORT... IS ACCURATE, DOCTOR?
THE PATIENT IS JAMES KIRK, CAPTAIN OF THE STARSHIP *ENTERPRISE*?
EXCEPT FOR ONE THING.
HE CLAIMS HE'S NOT CAPTAIN KIRK!

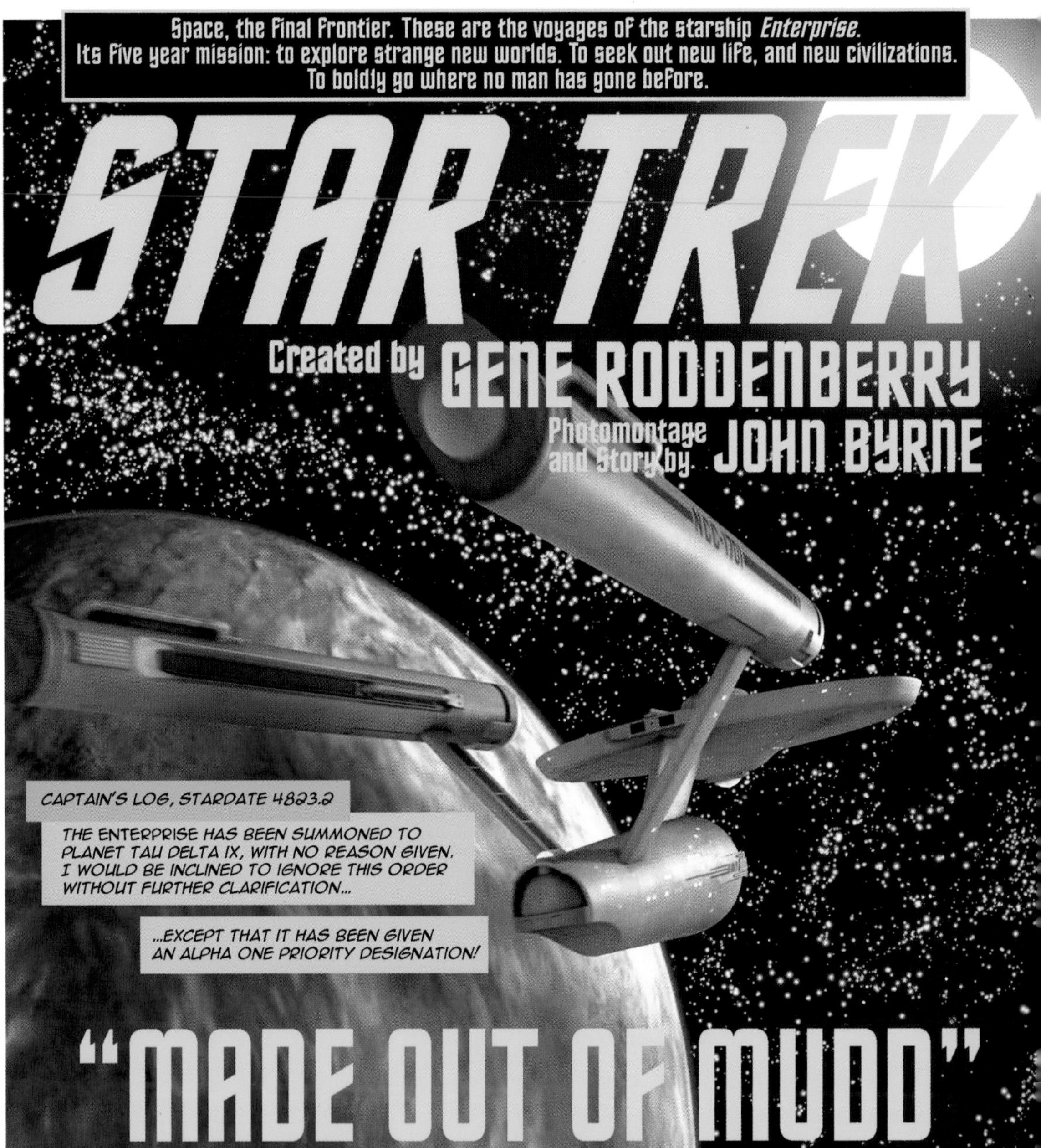

Space, the final frontier. These are the voyages of the starship *Enterprise*.
Its five year mission: to explore strange new worlds. To seek out new life, and new civilizations.
To boldly go where no man has gone before.
STAR TREK
Created by GENE RODDENBERRY
Photomontage and Story by JOHN BYRNE
NCC-1701
CAPTAIN'S LOG, STARDATE 4823.2
THE ENTERPRISE HAS BEEN SUMMONED TO PLANET TAU DELTA IX, WITH NO REASON GIVEN. I WOULD BE INCLINED TO IGNORE THIS ORDER WITHOUT FURTHER CLARIFICATION...
...EXCEPT THAT IT HAS BEEN GIVEN AN ALPHA ONE PRIORITY DESIGNATION!
"MADE OUT OF MUDD"
DEDICATED TO THE TALENTED PERFORMERS, CRAFTSMEN AND TECHNICIANS WHOSE WORK IS REPRESENTED HERE

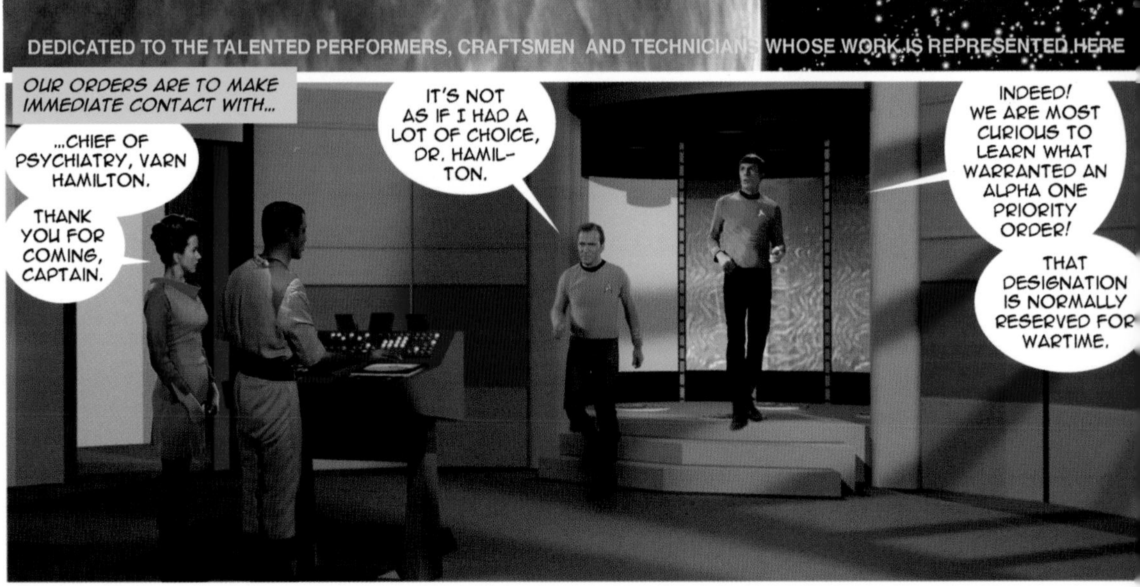

OUR ORDERS ARE TO MAKE IMMEDIATE CONTACT WITH...
...CHIEF OF PSYCHIATRY, VARN HAMILTON.
THANK YOU FOR COMING, CAPTAIN.
IT'S NOT AS IF I HAD A LOT OF CHOICE, DR. HAMIL-TON.
INDEED! WE ARE MOST CURIOUS TO LEARN WHAT WARRANTED AN ALPHA ONE PRIORITY ORDER!
THAT DESIGNATION IS NORMALLY RESERVED FOR WARTIME.

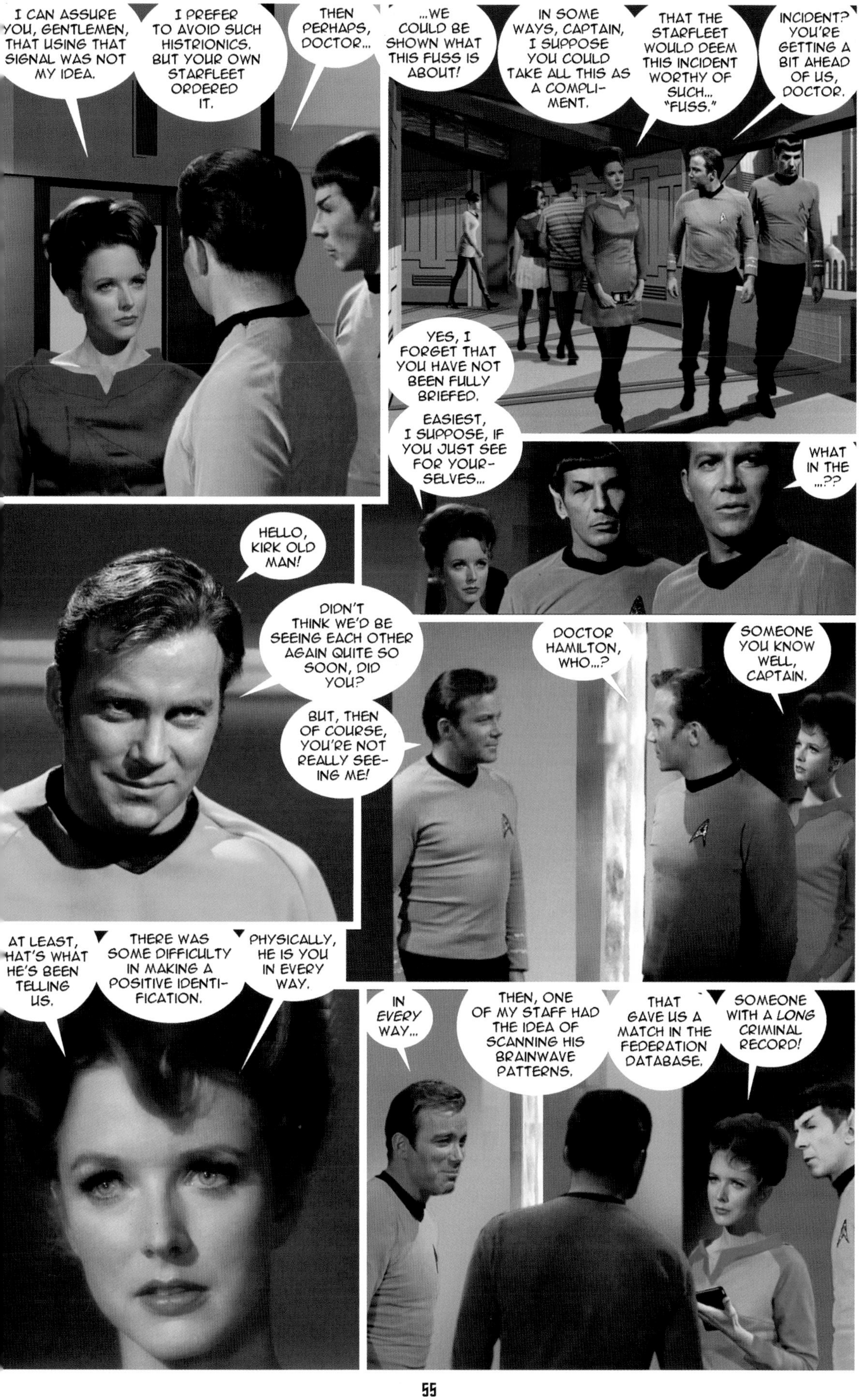
I CAN ASSURE YOU, GENTLEMEN, THAT USING THAT SIGNAL WAS NOT MY IDEA.
I PREFER TO AVOID SUCH HISTRIONICS. BUT YOUR OWN STARFLEET ORDERED IT.
THEN PERHAPS, DOCTOR...
...WE COULD BE SHOWN WHAT THIS FUSS IS ABOUT!
IN SOME WAYS, CAPTAIN, I SUPPOSE YOU COULD TAKE ALL THIS AS A COMPLIMENT.
THAT THE STARFLEET WOULD DEEM THIS INCIDENT WORTHY OF SUCH... "FUSS."
INCIDENT? YOU'RE GETTING A BIT AHEAD OF US, DOCTOR.
YES, I FORGET THAT YOU HAVE NOT BEEN FULLY BRIEFED.
EASIEST, I SUPPOSE, IF YOU JUST SEE FOR YOURSELVES...
WHAT IN THE ...??
HELLO, KIRK OLD MAN!
DIDN'T THINK WE'D BE SEEING EACH OTHER AGAIN QUITE SO SOON, DID YOU?
BUT, THEN OF COURSE, YOU'RE NOT REALLY SEEING ME!
DOCTOR HAMILTON, WHO...?
SOMEONE YOU KNOW WELL, CAPTAIN.
AT LEAST, HAT'S WHAT HE'S BEEN TELLING US.
THERE WAS SOME DIFFICULTY IN MAKING A POSITIVE IDENTIFICATION.
PHYSICALLY, HE IS YOU IN EVERY WAY.
IN *EVERY* WAY...
THEN, ONE OF MY STAFF HAD THE IDEA OF SCANNING HIS BRAINWAVE PATTERNS.
THAT GAVE US A MATCH IN THE FEDERATION DATABASE.
SOMEONE WITH A *LONG* CRIMINAL RECORD!

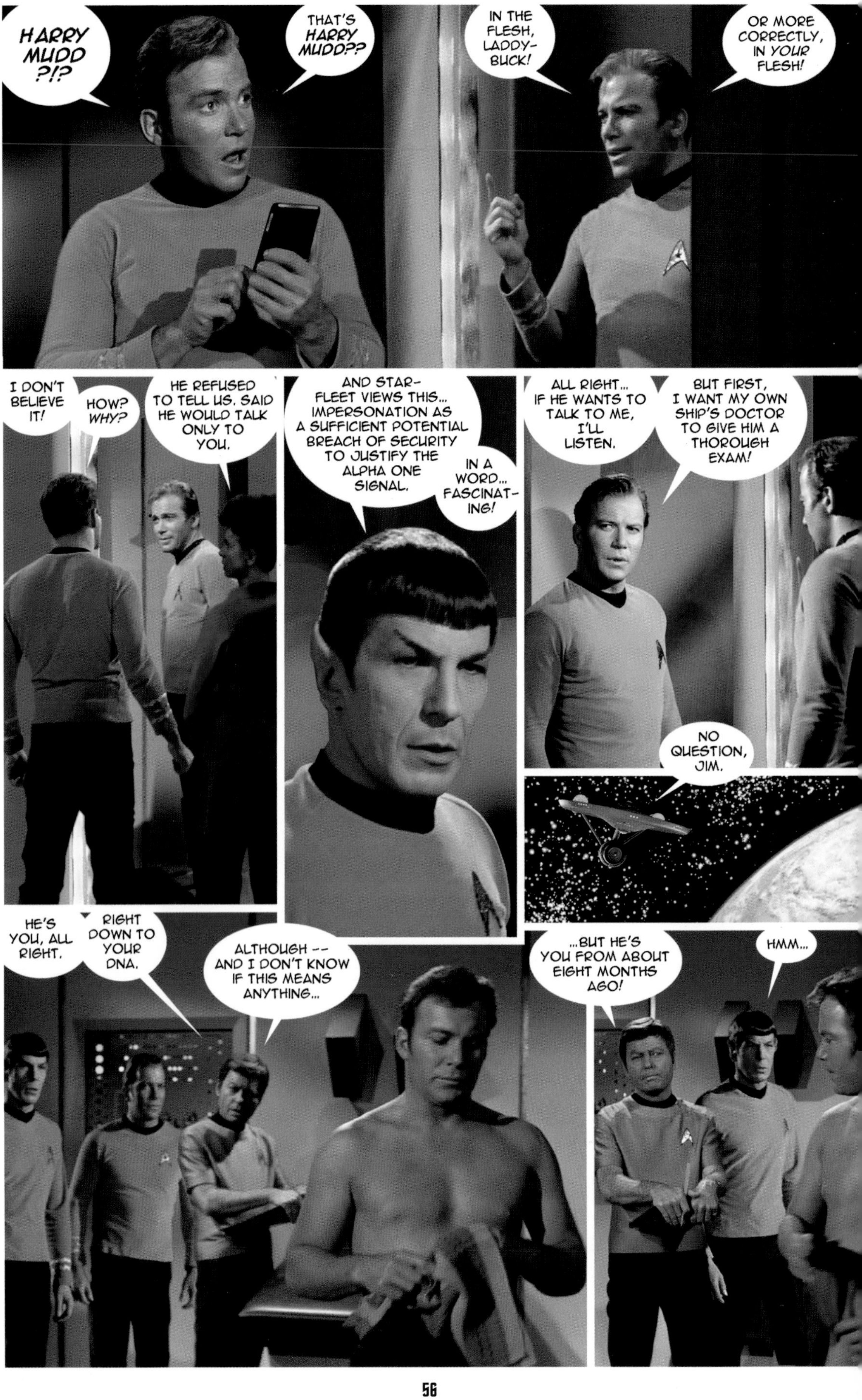
HARRY MUDD ?!?
THAT'S HARRY MUDD??
IN THE FLESH, LADDY-BUCK!
OR MORE CORRECTLY, IN YOUR FLESH!
I DON'T BELIEVE IT!
HOW? WHY?
HE REFUSED TO TELL US. SAID HE WOULD TALK ONLY TO YOU.
AND STAR-FLEET VIEWS THIS... IMPERSONATION AS A SUFFICIENT POTENTIAL BREACH OF SECURITY TO JUSTIFY THE ALPHA ONE SIGNAL.
IN A WORD... FASCINAT-ING!
ALL RIGHT... IF HE WANTS TO TALK TO ME, I'LL LISTEN.
BUT FIRST, I WANT MY OWN SHIP'S DOCTOR TO GIVE HIM A THOROUGH EXAM!
NO QUESTION, JIM.
HE'S YOU, ALL RIGHT.
RIGHT DOWN TO YOUR DNA.
ALTHOUGH -- AND I DON'T KNOW IF THIS MEANS ANYTHING...
...BUT HE'S YOU FROM ABOUT EIGHT MONTHS AGO!
HMM...

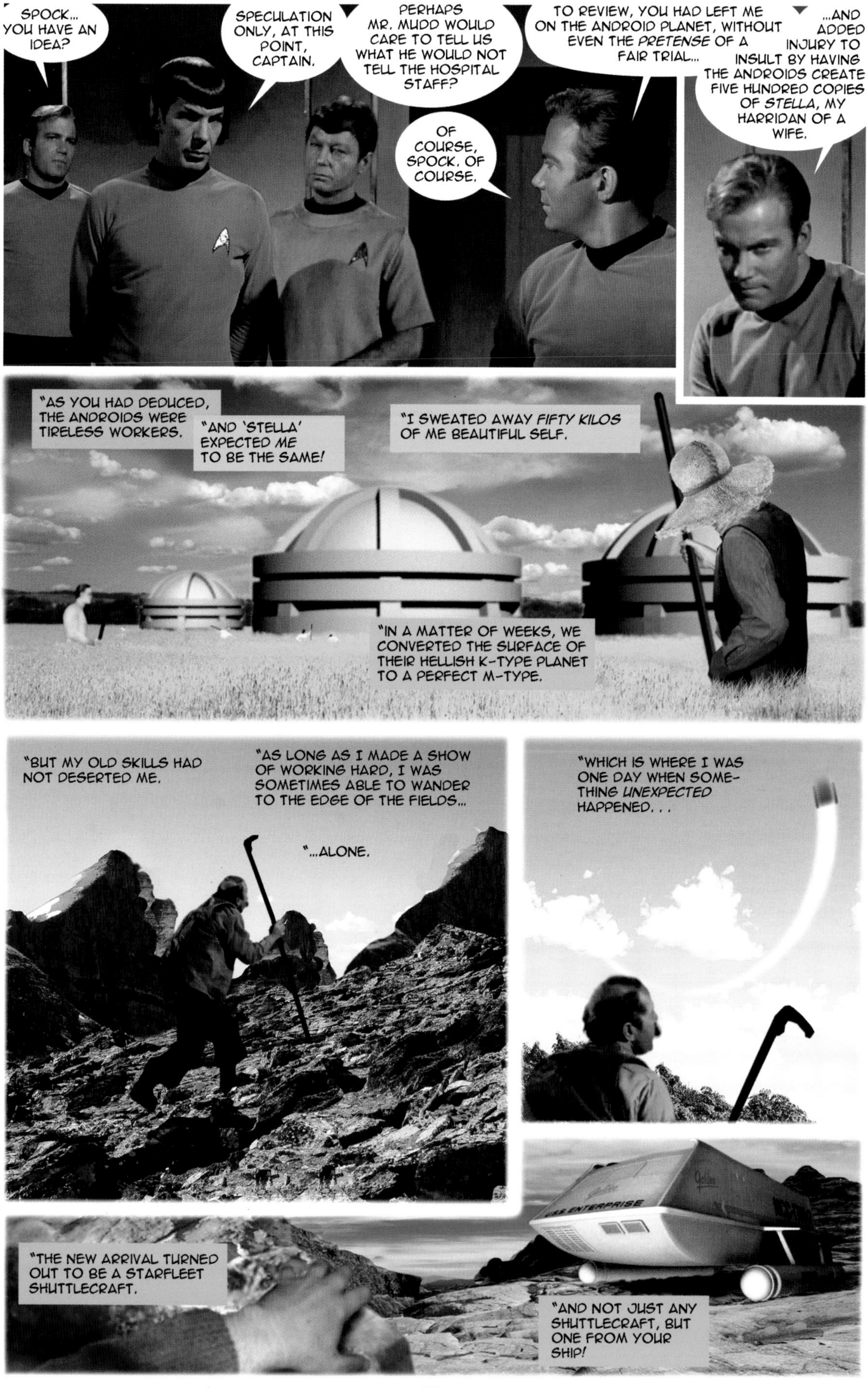
SPOCK... YOU HAVE AN IDEA?
SPECULATION ONLY, AT THIS POINT, CAPTAIN.
PERHAPS MR. MUDD WOULD CARE TO TELL US WHAT HE WOULD NOT TELL THE HOSPITAL STAFF?
OF COURSE, SPOCK. OF COURSE.
TO REVIEW, YOU HAD LEFT ME ON THE ANDROID PLANET, WITHOUT EVEN THE *PRETENSE* OF A FAIR TRIAL...
...AND ADDED INJURY TO INSULT BY HAVING THE ANDROIDS CREATE FIVE HUNDRED COPIES OF *STELLA*, MY HARRIDAN OF A WIFE.
"AS YOU HAD DEDUCED, THE ANDROIDS WERE TIRELESS WORKERS.
"AND 'STELLA' EXPECTED *ME* TO BE THE SAME!
"I SWEATED AWAY *FIFTY KILOS* OF ME BEAUTIFUL SELF.
"IN A MATTER OF WEEKS, WE CONVERTED THE SURFACE OF THEIR HELLISH K-TYPE PLANET TO A PERFECT M-TYPE.
"BUT MY OLD SKILLS HAD NOT DESERTED ME.
"AS LONG AS I MADE A SHOW OF WORKING HARD, I WAS SOMETIMES ABLE TO WANDER TO THE EDGE OF THE FIELDS...
"...ALONE.
"WHICH IS WHERE I WAS ONE DAY WHEN SOMETHING *UNEXPECTED* HAPPENED. . .
U.S.S. ENTERPRISE
"THE NEW ARRIVAL TURNED OUT TO BE A STARFLEET SHUTTLECRAFT.
"AND NOT JUST ANY SHUTTLECRAFT, BUT ONE FROM YOUR SHIP!

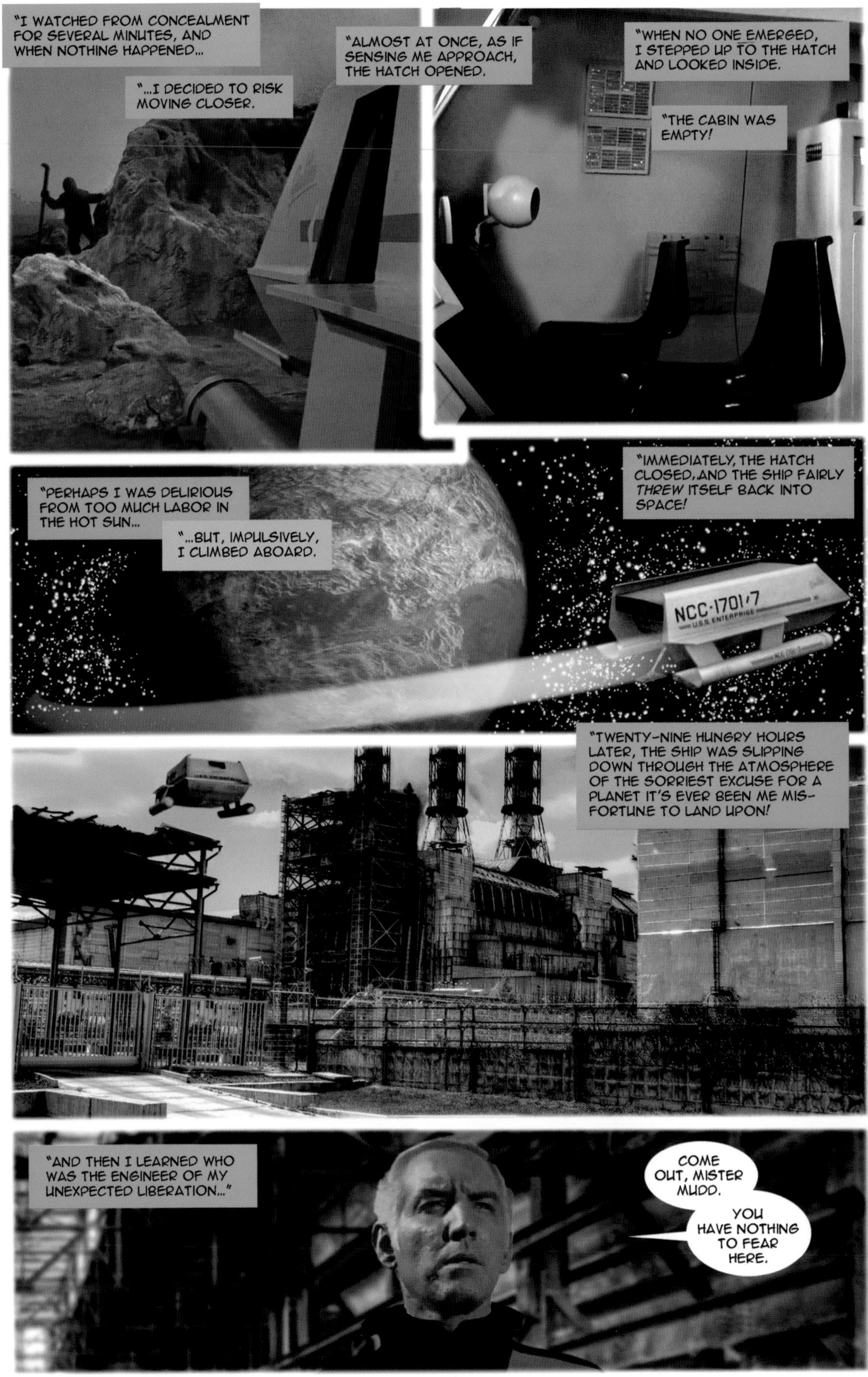
"I WATCHED FROM CONCEALMENT FOR SEVERAL MINUTES, AND WHEN NOTHING HAPPENED...
"...I DECIDED TO RISK MOVING CLOSER.
"ALMOST AT ONCE, AS IF SENSING ME APPROACH, THE HATCH OPENED.
"WHEN NO ONE EMERGED, I STEPPED UP TO THE HATCH AND LOOKED INSIDE.
"THE CABIN WAS EMPTY!
"PERHAPS I WAS DELIRIOUS FROM TOO MUCH LABOR IN THE HOT SUN...
"...BUT, IMPULSIVELY, I CLIMBED ABOARD.
"IMMEDIATELY, THE HATCH CLOSED, AND THE SHIP FAIRLY *THREW* ITSELF BACK INTO SPACE!
NCC-1701/7
U.S.S. ENTERPRISE
"TWENTY-NINE HUNGRY HOURS LATER, THE SHIP WAS SLIPPING DOWN THROUGH THE ATMOSPHERE OF THE SORRIEST EXCUSE FOR A PLANET IT'S EVER BEEN ME MIS-FORTUNE TO LAND UPON!
"AND THEN I LEARNED WHO WAS THE ENGINEER OF MY UNEXPECTED LIBERATION..."
COME OUT, MISTER MUDD.
YOU HAVE NOTHING TO FEAR HERE.

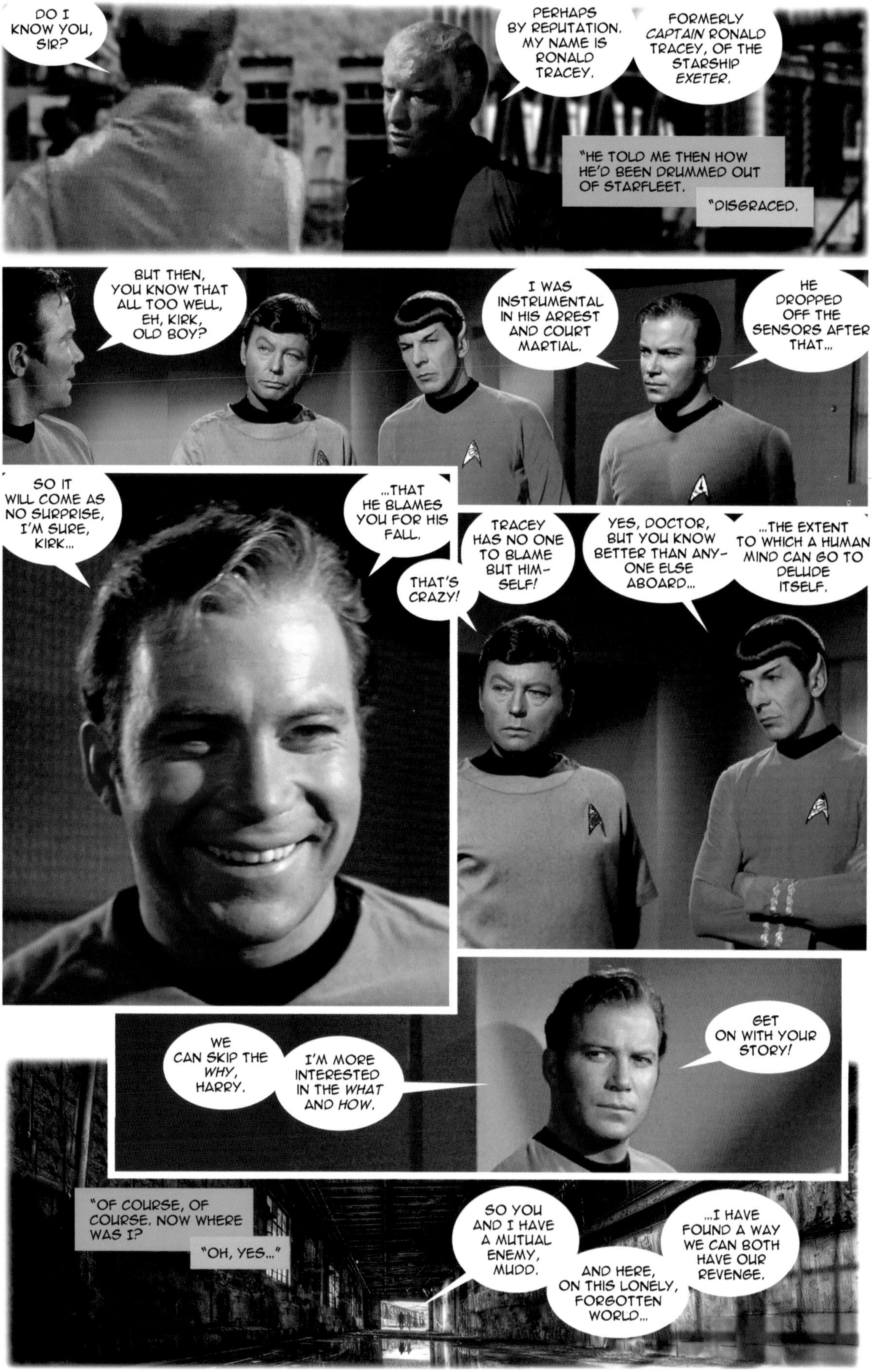
DO I KNOW YOU, SIR?
PERHAPS BY REPUTATION. MY NAME IS RONALD TRACEY.
FORMERLY CAPTAIN RONALD TRACEY, OF THE STARSHIP EXETER.
"HE TOLD ME THEN HOW HE'D BEEN DRUMMED OUT OF STARFLEET.
"DISGRACED.
BUT THEN, YOU KNOW THAT ALL TOO WELL, EH, KIRK, OLD BOY?
I WAS INSTRUMENTAL IN HIS ARREST AND COURT MARTIAL.
HE DROPPED OFF THE SENSORS AFTER THAT...
SO IT WILL COME AS NO SURPRISE, I'M SURE, KIRK...
...THAT HE BLAMES YOU FOR HIS FALL.
THAT'S CRAZY!
TRACEY HAS NO ONE TO BLAME BUT HIMSELF!
YES, DOCTOR, BUT YOU KNOW BETTER THAN ANYONE ELSE ABOARD...
...THE EXTENT TO WHICH A HUMAN MIND CAN GO TO DELUDE ITSELF.
WE CAN SKIP THE WHY, HARRY.
I'M MORE INTERESTED IN THE WHAT AND HOW.
GET ON WITH YOUR STORY!
"OF COURSE, OF COURSE. NOW WHERE WAS I?
"OH, YES..."
SO YOU AND I HAVE A MUTUAL ENEMY, MUDD.
AND HERE, ON THIS LONELY, FORGOTTEN WORLD...
...I HAVE FOUND A WAY WE CAN BOTH HAVE OUR REVENGE.

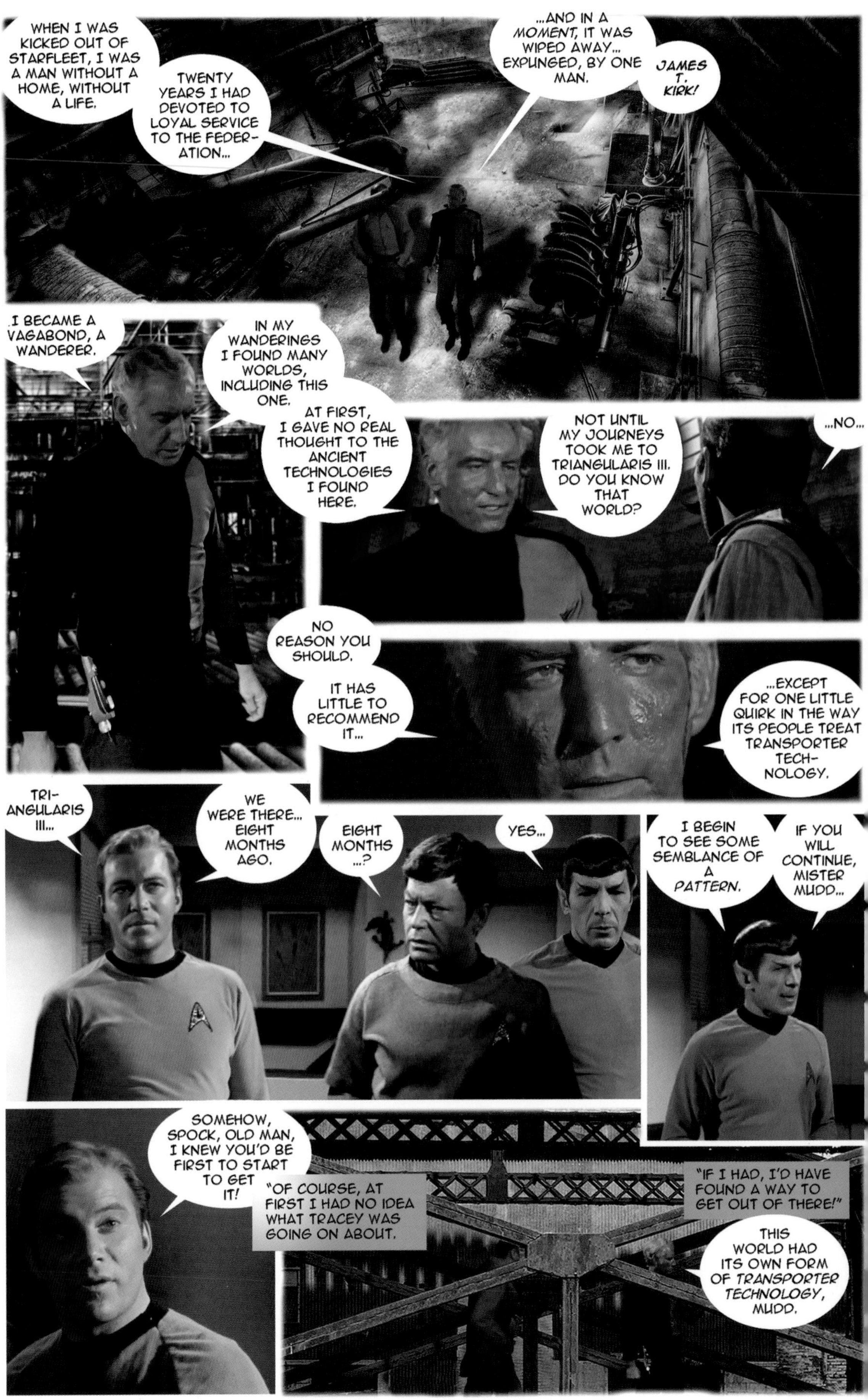
WHEN I WAS KICKED OUT OF STARFLEET, I WAS A MAN WITHOUT A HOME, WITHOUT A LIFE.
TWENTY YEARS I HAD DEVOTED TO LOYAL SERVICE TO THE FEDER-ATION...
...AND IN A MOMENT, IT WAS WIPED AWAY... EXPUNGED, BY ONE MAN.
JAMES T. KIRK!
.I BECAME A VAGABOND, A WANDERER.
IN MY WANDERINGS I FOUND MANY WORLDS, INCLUDING THIS ONE.
AT FIRST, I GAVE NO REAL THOUGHT TO THE ANCIENT TECHNOLOGIES I FOUND HERE.
NOT UNTIL MY JOURNEYS TOOK ME TO TRIANGULARIS III. DO YOU KNOW THAT WORLD?
...NO...
NO REASON YOU SHOULD.
IT HAS LITTLE TO RECOMMEND IT...
...EXCEPT FOR ONE LITTLE QUIRK IN THE WAY ITS PEOPLE TREAT TRANSPORTER TECH-NOLOGY.
TRI-ANGULARIS III...
WE WERE THERE... EIGHT MONTHS AGO.
EIGHT MONTHS ...?
YES...
I BEGIN TO SEE SOME SEMBLANCE OF A PATTERN.
IF YOU WILL CONTINUE, MISTER MUDD...
SOMEHOW, SPOCK, OLD MAN, I KNEW YOU'D BE FIRST TO START TO GET IT!
"OF COURSE, AT FIRST I HAD NO IDEA WHAT TRACEY WAS GOING ON ABOUT.
"IF I HAD, I'D HAVE FOUND A WAY TO GET OUT OF THERE!"
THIS WORLD HAD ITS OWN FORM OF TRANSPORTER TECHNOLOGY, MUDD.

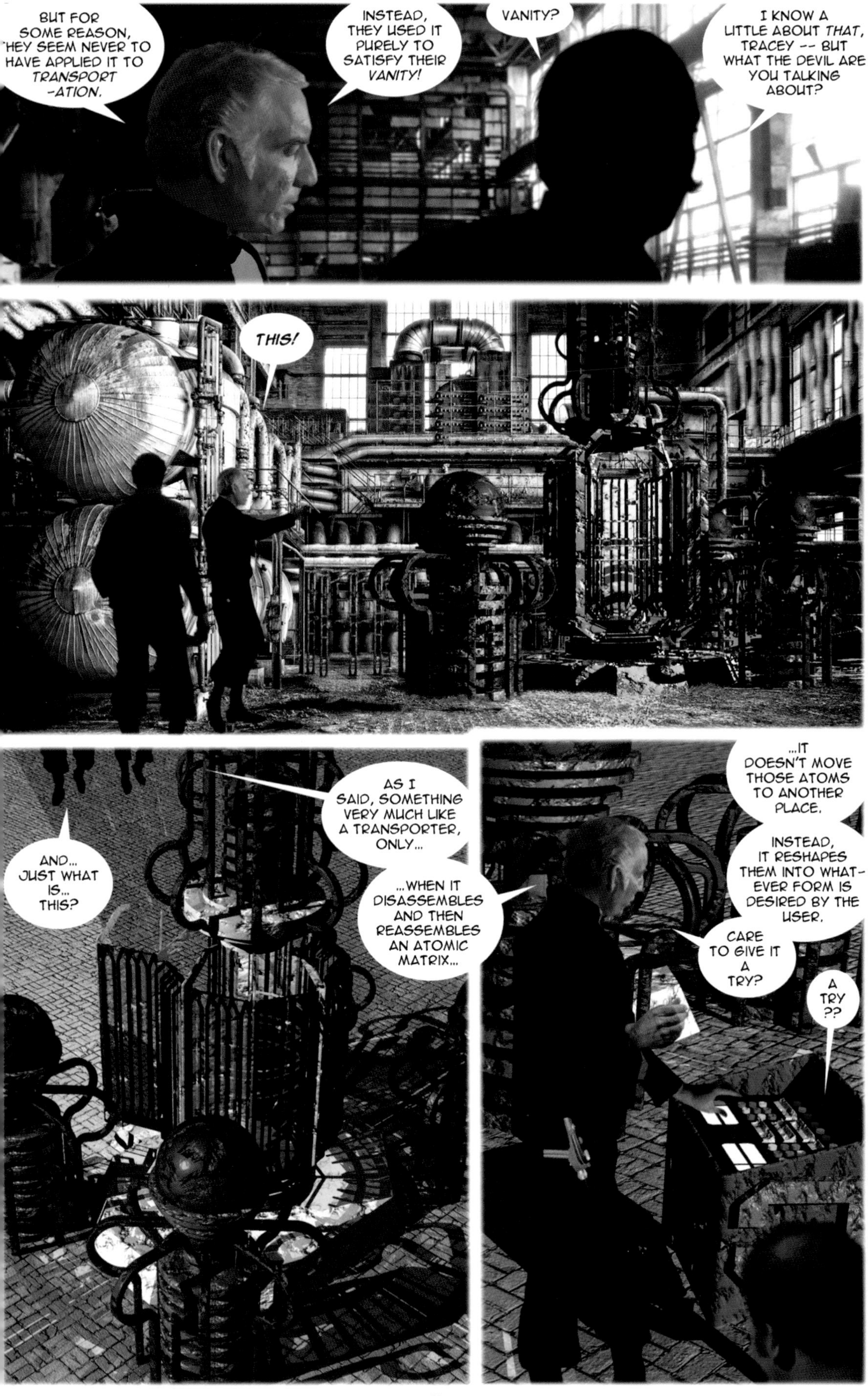
BUT FOR SOME REASON, THEY SEEM NEVER TO HAVE APPLIED IT TO *TRANSPORT -ATION.*
INSTEAD, THEY USED IT PURELY TO SATISFY THEIR *VANITY!*
VANITY?
I KNOW A LITTLE ABOUT *THAT,* TRACEY -- BUT WHAT THE DEVIL ARE YOU TALKING ABOUT?
THIS!
AND... JUST WHAT IS... THIS?
AS I SAID, SOMETHING VERY MUCH LIKE A TRANSPORTER, ONLY...
...WHEN IT DISASSEMBLES AND THEN REASSEMBLES AN ATOMIC MATRIX...
...IT DOESN'T MOVE THOSE ATOMS TO ANOTHER PLACE.
INSTEAD, IT RESHAPES THEM INTO WHAT-EVER FORM IS DESIRED BY THE USER.
CARE TO GIVE IT A TRY?
A TRY ??

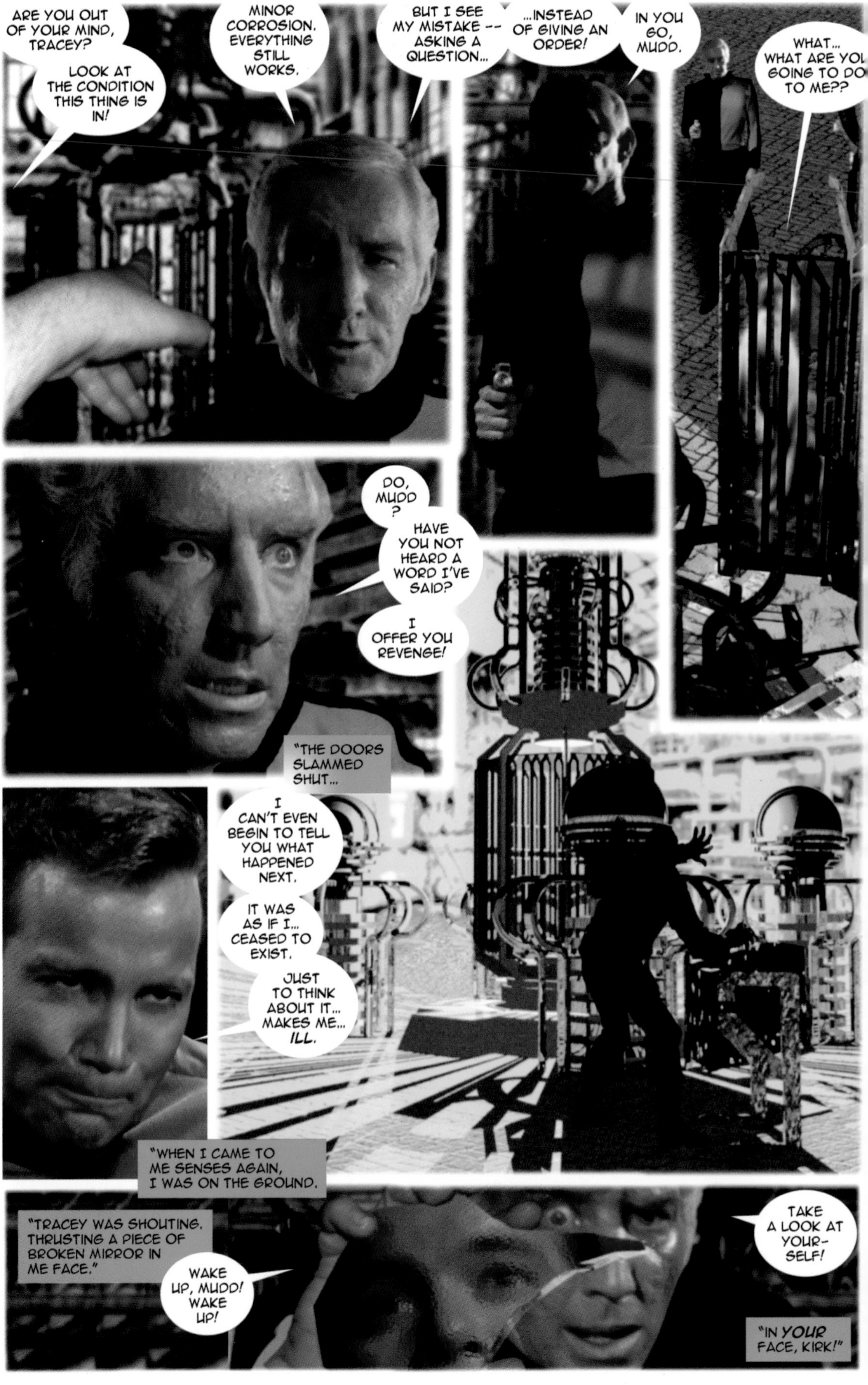

ARE YOU OUT OF YOUR MIND, TRACEY?
LOOK AT THE CONDITION THIS THING IS IN!
MINOR CORROSION. EVERYTHING STILL WORKS.
BUT I SEE MY MISTAKE -- ASKING A QUESTION...
...INSTEAD OF GIVING AN ORDER!
IN YOU GO, MUDD.
WHAT... WHAT ARE YOU GOING TO DO TO ME??
DO, MUDD?
HAVE YOU NOT HEARD A WORD I'VE SAID?
I OFFER YOU REVENGE!
"THE DOORS SLAMMED SHUT...
I CAN'T EVEN BEGIN TO TELL YOU WHAT HAPPENED NEXT.
IT WAS AS IF I... CEASED TO EXIST.
JUST TO THINK ABOUT IT... MAKES ME... ILL.
"WHEN I CAME TO ME SENSES AGAIN, I WAS ON THE GROUND.
"TRACEY WAS SHOUTING, THRUSTING A PIECE OF BROKEN MIRROR IN ME FACE."
WAKE UP, MUDD! WAKE UP!
TAKE A LOOK AT YOURSELF!
"IN YOUR FACE, KIRK!"

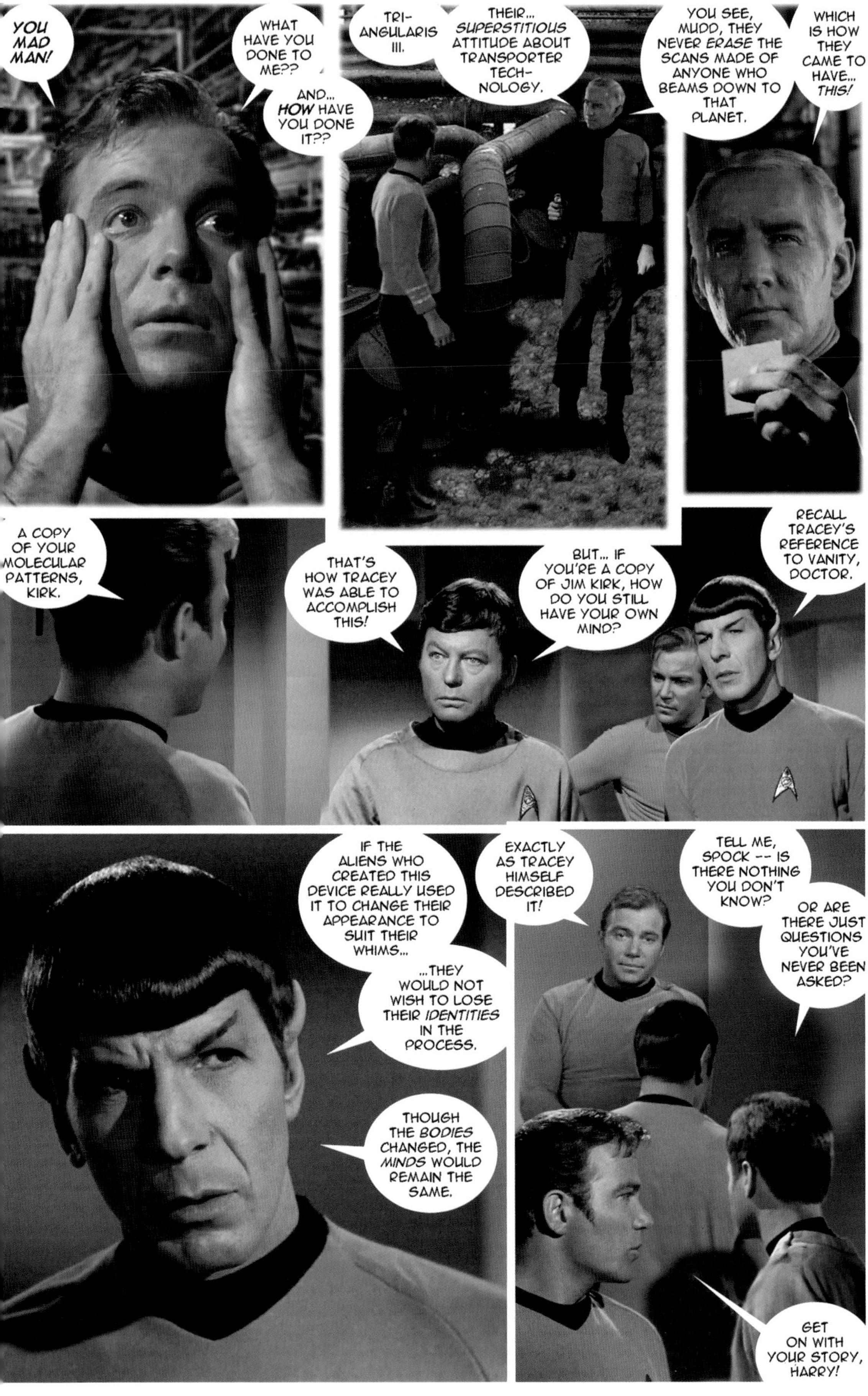
YOU MAD MAN!
WHAT HAVE YOU DONE TO ME??
AND... HOW HAVE YOU DONE IT??
TRI-ANGULARIS III.
THEIR... SUPERSTITIOUS ATTITUDE ABOUT TRANSPORTER TECH-NOLOGY.
YOU SEE, MUDD, THEY NEVER ERASE THE SCANS MADE OF ANYONE WHO BEAMS DOWN TO THAT PLANET.
WHICH IS HOW THEY CAME TO HAVE... THIS!
A COPY OF YOUR MOLECULAR PATTERNS, KIRK.
THAT'S HOW TRACEY WAS ABLE TO ACCOMPLISH THIS!
BUT... IF YOU'RE A COPY OF JIM KIRK, HOW DO YOU STILL HAVE YOUR OWN MIND?
RECALL TRACEY'S REFERENCE TO VANITY, DOCTOR.
IF THE ALIENS WHO CREATED THIS DEVICE REALLY USED IT TO CHANGE THEIR APPEARANCE TO SUIT THEIR WHIMS...
...THEY WOULD NOT WISH TO LOSE THEIR IDENTITIES IN THE PROCESS.
THOUGH THE BODIES CHANGED, THE MINDS WOULD REMAIN THE SAME.
EXACTLY AS TRACEY HIMSELF DESCRIBED IT!
TELL ME, SPOCK -- IS THERE NOTHING YOU DON'T KNOW?
OR ARE THERE JUST QUESTIONS YOU'VE NEVER BEEN ASKED?
GET ON WITH YOUR STORY, HARRY!

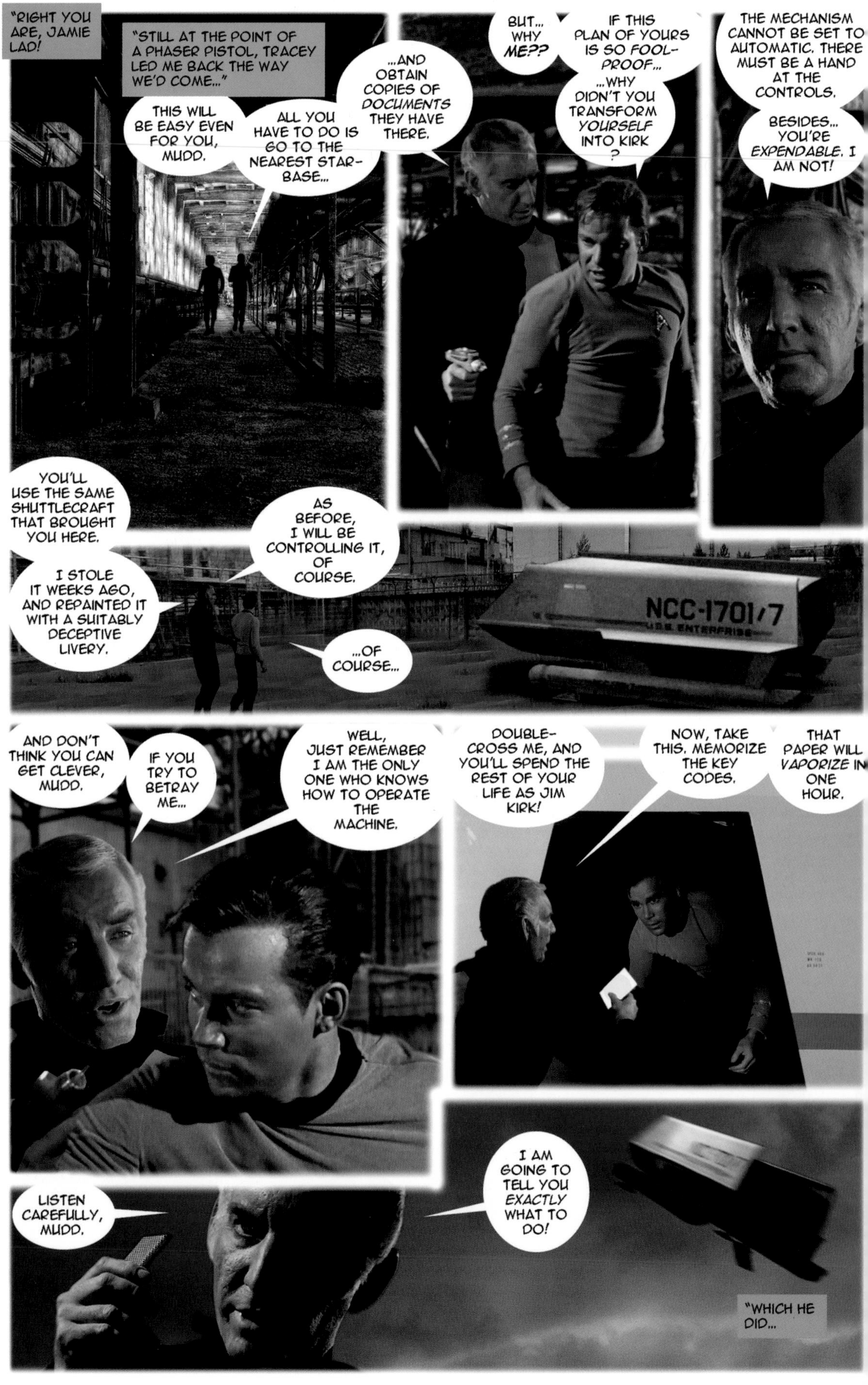
"RIGHT YOU ARE, JAMIE LAD!
"STILL AT THE POINT OF A PHASER PISTOL, TRACEY LED ME BACK THE WAY WE'D COME..."
THIS WILL BE EASY EVEN FOR YOU, MUDD.
ALL YOU HAVE TO DO IS GO TO THE NEAREST STAR-BASE...
...AND OBTAIN COPIES OF DOCUMENTS THEY HAVE THERE.
BUT... WHY ME??
IF THIS PLAN OF YOURS IS SO FOOL-PROOF...
...WHY DIDN'T YOU TRANSFORM YOURSELF INTO KIRK?
THE MECHANISM CANNOT BE SET TO AUTOMATIC. THERE MUST BE A HAND AT THE CONTROLS.
BESIDES... YOU'RE EXPENDABLE. I AM NOT!
YOU'LL USE THE SAME SHUTTLECRAFT THAT BROUGHT YOU HERE.
AS BEFORE, I WILL BE CONTROLLING IT, OF COURSE.
I STOLE IT WEEKS AGO, AND REPAINTED IT WITH A SUITABLY DECEPTIVE LIVERY.
...OF COURSE...
NCC-1701/7
U.S.S. ENTERPRISE
AND DON'T THINK YOU CAN GET CLEVER, MUDD.
IF YOU TRY TO BETRAY ME...
WELL, JUST REMEMBER I AM THE ONLY ONE WHO KNOWS HOW TO OPERATE THE MACHINE.
DOUBLE-CROSS ME, AND YOU'LL SPEND THE REST OF YOUR LIFE AS JIM KIRK!
NOW, TAKE THIS. MEMORIZE THE KEY CODES.
THAT PAPER WILL VAPORIZE IN ONE HOUR.
LISTEN CAREFULLY, MUDD.
I AM GOING TO TELL YOU EXACTLY WHAT TO DO!
"WHICH HE DID...

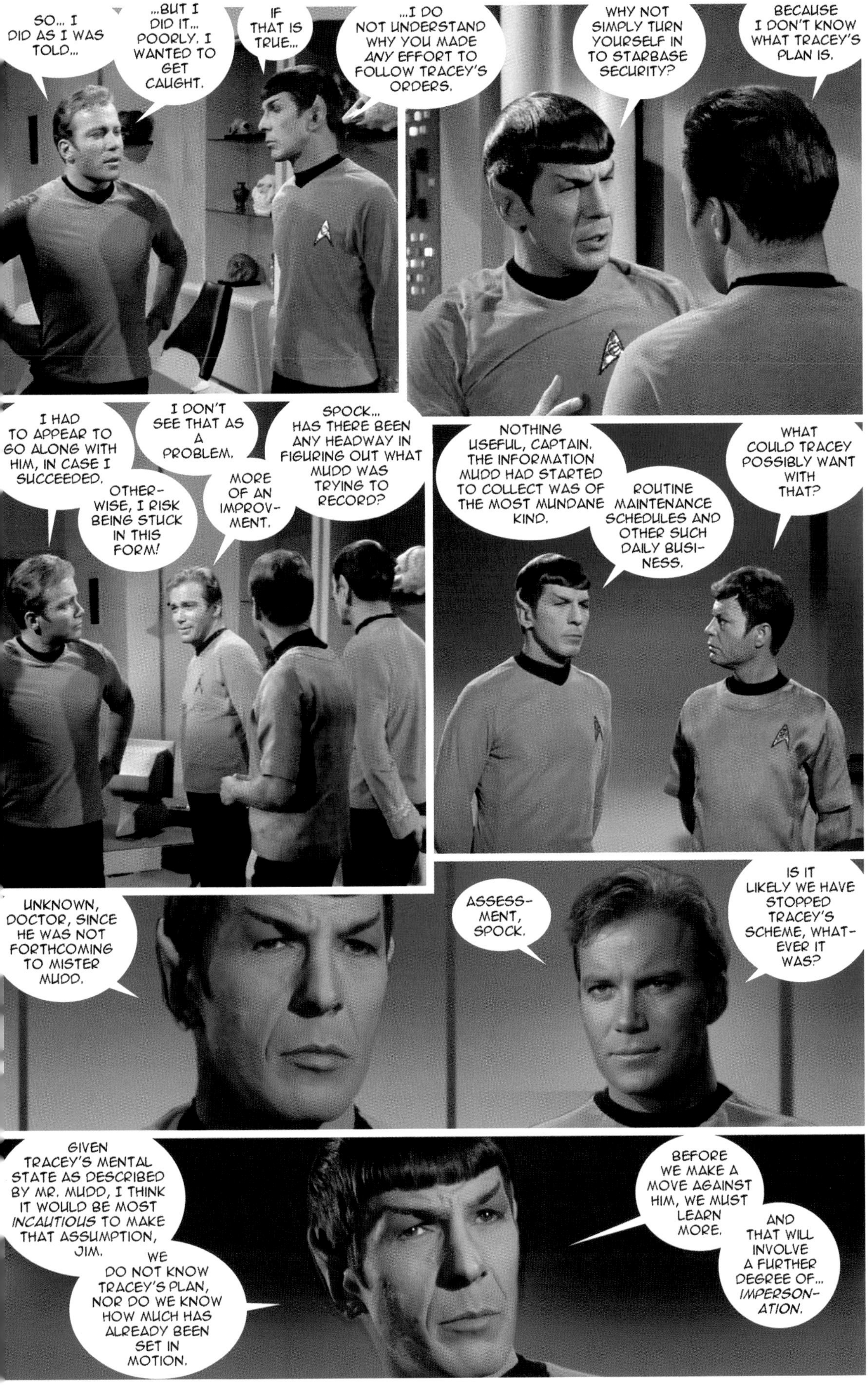
SO... I DID AS I WAS TOLD...
...BUT I DID IT... POORLY. I WANTED TO GET CAUGHT.
IF THAT IS TRUE...
...I DO NOT UNDERSTAND WHY YOU MADE *ANY* EFFORT TO FOLLOW TRACEY'S ORDERS.
WHY NOT SIMPLY TURN YOURSELF IN TO STARBASE SECURITY?
BECAUSE I DON'T KNOW WHAT TRACEY'S PLAN IS.
I HAD TO APPEAR TO GO ALONG WITH HIM, IN CASE I SUCCEEDED.
OTHER-WISE, I RISK BEING STUCK IN THIS FORM!
I DON'T SEE THAT AS A PROBLEM.
MORE OF AN IMPROV-MENT.
SPOCK... HAS THERE BEEN ANY HEADWAY IN FIGURING OUT WHAT MUDD WAS TRYING TO RECORD?
NOTHING USEFUL, CAPTAIN. THE INFORMATION MUDD HAD STARTED TO COLLECT WAS OF THE MOST MUNDANE KIND.
ROUTINE MAINTENANCE SCHEDULES AND OTHER SUCH DAILY BUSI-NESS.
WHAT COULD TRACEY POSSIBLY WANT WITH THAT?
UNKNOWN, DOCTOR, SINCE HE WAS NOT FORTHCOMING TO MISTER MUDD.
ASSESS-MENT, SPOCK.
IS IT LIKELY WE HAVE STOPPED TRACEY'S SCHEME, WHAT-EVER IT WAS?
GIVEN TRACEY'S MENTAL STATE AS DESCRIBED BY MR. MUDD, I THINK IT WOULD BE MOST *INCAUTIOUS* TO MAKE THAT ASSUMPTION, JIM.
WE DO NOT KNOW TRACEY'S PLAN, NOR DO WE KNOW HOW MUCH HAS ALREADY BEEN SET IN MOTION.
BEFORE WE MAKE A MOVE AGAINST HIM, WE MUST LEARN MORE.
AND THAT WILL INVOLVE A FURTHER DEGREE OF... *IMPERSON-ATION.*

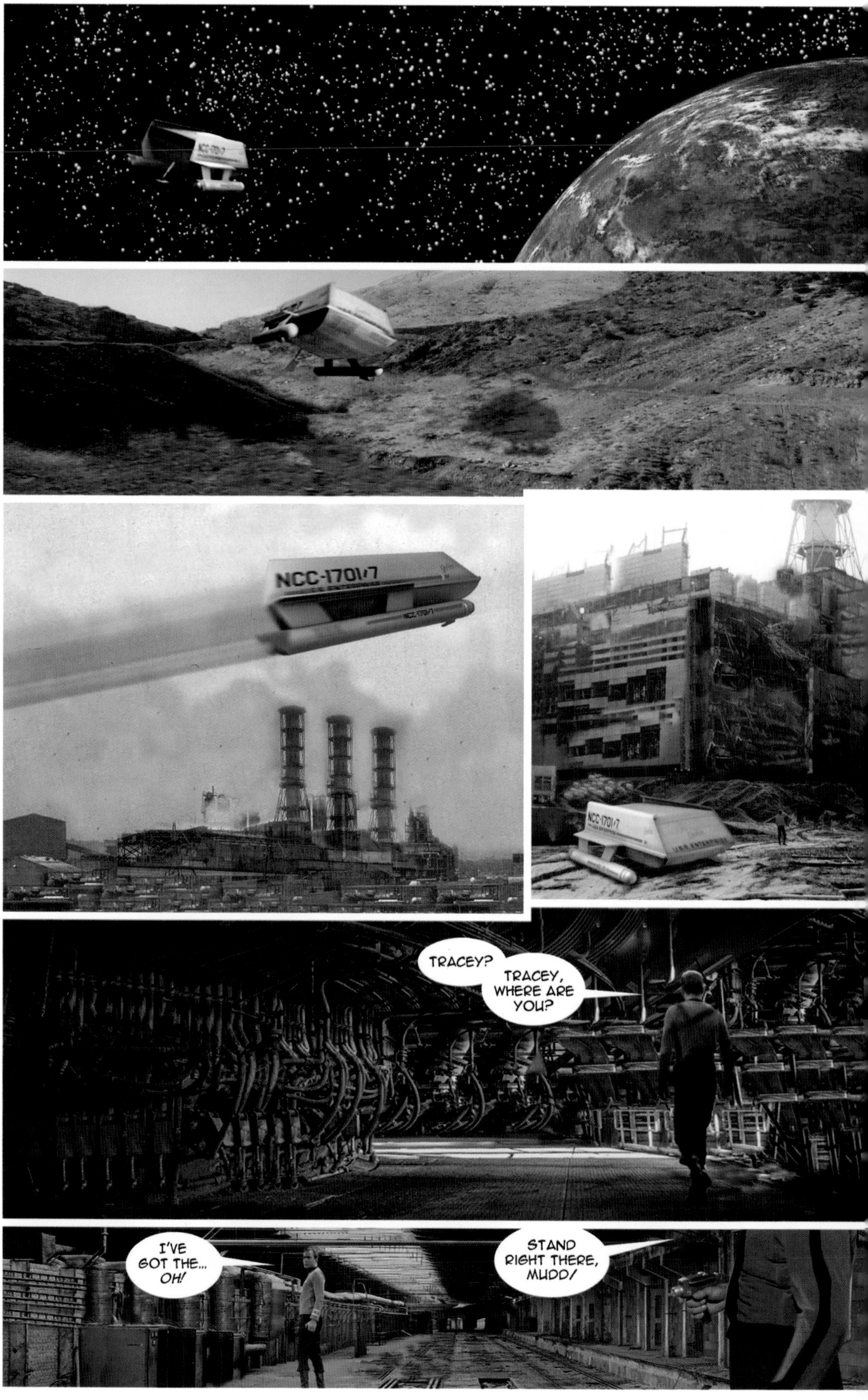
NCC-1701/7
NCC-1701/7
TRACEY?
TRACEY, WHERE ARE YOU?
I'VE GOT THE... OH!
STAND RIGHT THERE, MUDD!

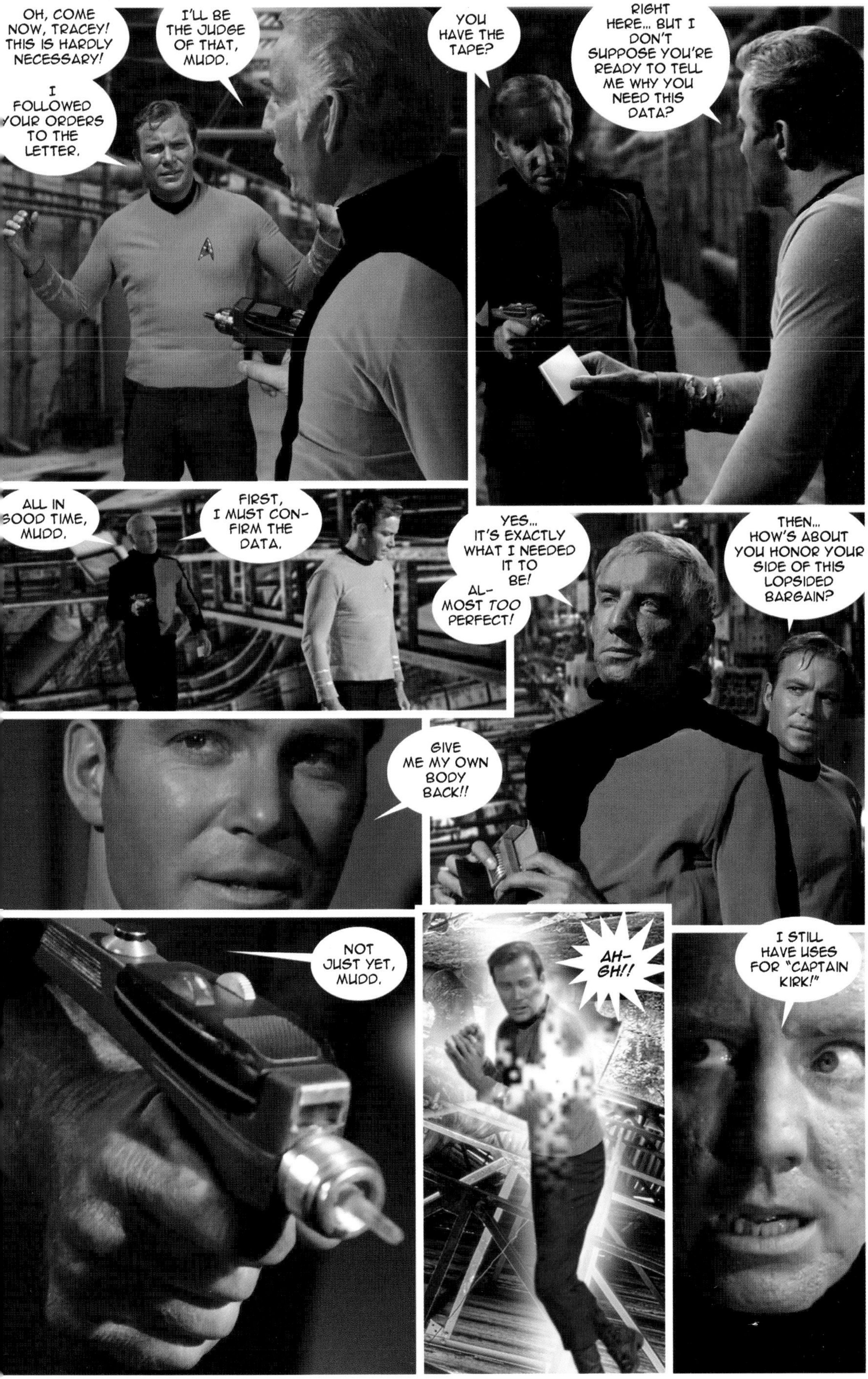
OH, COME NOW, TRACEY! THIS IS HARDLY NECESSARY!
I FOLLOWED YOUR ORDERS TO THE LETTER.
I'LL BE THE JUDGE OF THAT, MUDD.
YOU HAVE THE TAPE?
RIGHT HERE... BUT I DON'T SUPPOSE YOU'RE READY TO TELL ME WHY YOU NEED THIS DATA?
ALL IN GOOD TIME, MUDD.
FIRST, I MUST CONFIRM THE DATA.
YES... IT'S EXACTLY WHAT I NEEDED IT TO BE!
ALMOST *TOO* PERFECT!
THEN... HOW'S ABOUT YOU HONOR YOUR SIDE OF THIS LOPSIDED BARGAIN?
GIVE ME MY OWN BODY BACK!!
NOT JUST YET, MUDD.
AH-GH!!
I STILL HAVE USES FOR "CAPTAIN KIRK!"

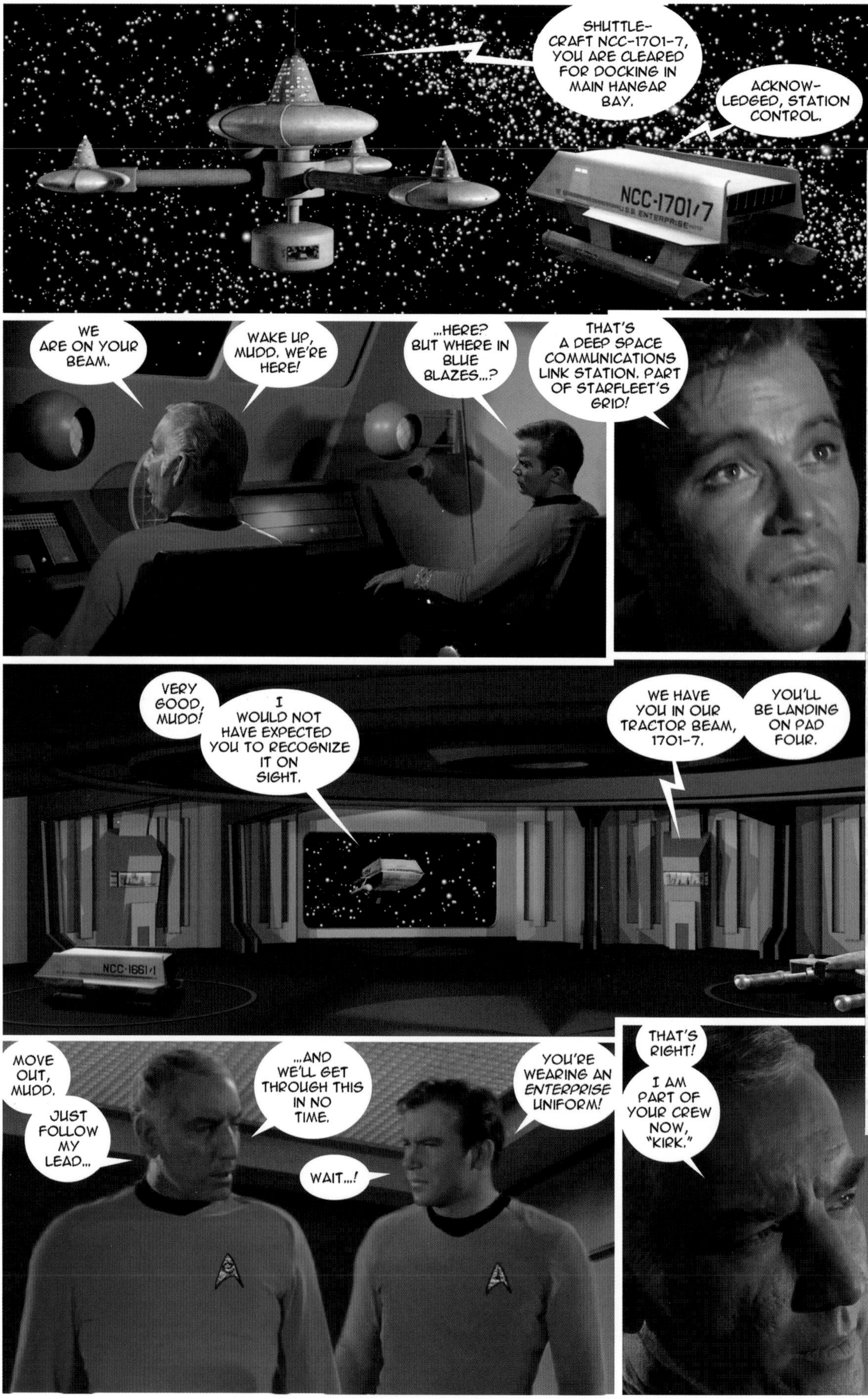
SHUTTLE-CRAFT NCC-1701-7, YOU ARE CLEARED FOR DOCKING IN MAIN HANGAR BAY.
ACKNOW-LEDGED, STATION CONTROL.
NCC-1701/7
U.S.S. ENTERPRISE
WE ARE ON YOUR BEAM.
WAKE UP, MUDD. WE'RE HERE!
...HERE? BUT WHERE IN BLUE BLAZES...?
THAT'S A DEEP SPACE COMMUNICATIONS LINK STATION. PART OF STARFLEET'S GRID!
VERY GOOD, MUDD!
I WOULD NOT HAVE EXPECTED YOU TO RECOGNIZE IT ON SIGHT.
WE HAVE YOU IN OUR TRACTOR BEAM, 1701-7.
YOU'LL BE LANDING ON PAD FOUR.
NCC-1661/1
MOVE OUT, MUDD.
JUST FOLLOW MY LEAD...
...AND WE'LL GET THROUGH THIS IN NO TIME.
WAIT...!
YOU'RE WEARING AN *ENTERPRISE* UNIFORM!
THAT'S RIGHT!
I AM PART OF YOUR CREW NOW, "KIRK."

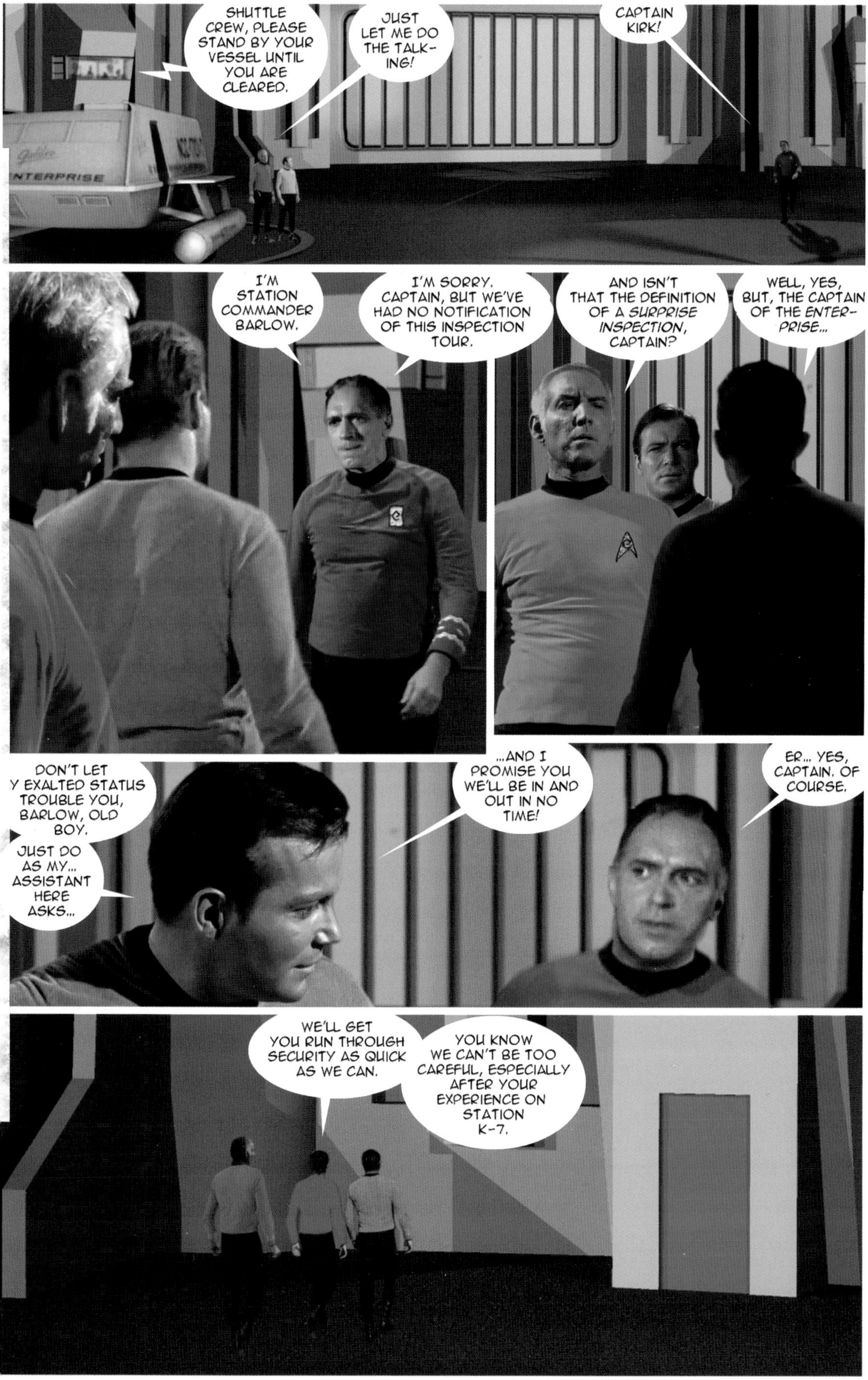
SHUTTLE CREW, PLEASE STAND BY YOUR VESSEL UNTIL YOU ARE CLEARED.
JUST LET ME DO THE TALK-ING!
CAPTAIN KIRK!
I'M STATION COMMANDER BARLOW.
I'M SORRY, CAPTAIN, BUT WE'VE HAD NO NOTIFICATION OF THIS INSPECTION TOUR.
AND ISN'T THAT THE DEFINITION OF A SURPRISE INSPECTION, CAPTAIN?
WELL, YES, BUT, THE CAPTAIN OF THE ENTER-PRISE...
DON'T LET Y EXALTED STATUS TROUBLE YOU, BARLOW, OLD BOY.
JUST DO AS MY... ASSISTANT HERE ASKS...
...AND I PROMISE YOU WE'LL BE IN AND OUT IN NO TIME!
ER... YES, CAPTAIN. OF COURSE.
WE'LL GET YOU RUN THROUGH SECURITY AS QUICK AS WE CAN.
YOU KNOW WE CAN'T BE TOO CAREFUL, ESPECIALLY AFTER YOUR EXPERIENCE ON STATION K-7.

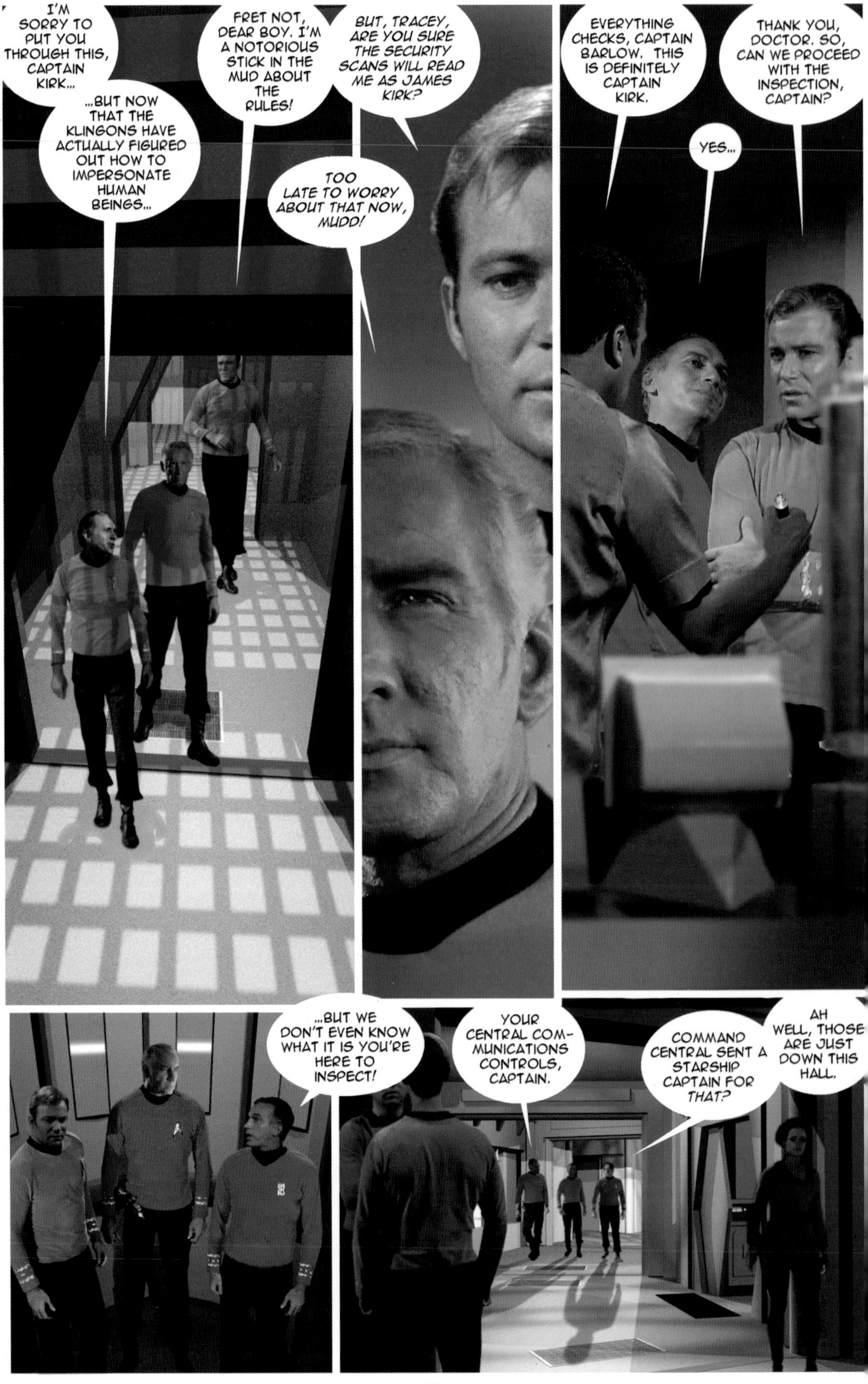
I'M SORRY TO PUT YOU THROUGH THIS, CAPTAIN KIRK...
...BUT NOW THAT THE KLINGONS HAVE ACTUALLY FIGURED OUT HOW TO IMPERSONATE HUMAN BEINGS...
FRET NOT, DEAR BOY. I'M A NOTORIOUS STICK IN THE MUD ABOUT THE RULES!
BUT, TRACEY, ARE YOU SURE THE SECURITY SCANS WILL READ ME AS JAMES KIRK?
TOO LATE TO WORRY ABOUT THAT NOW, MUDD!
EVERYTHING CHECKS, CAPTAIN BARLOW. THIS IS DEFINITELY CAPTAIN KIRK.
THANK YOU, DOCTOR. SO, CAN WE PROCEED WITH THE INSPECTION, CAPTAIN?
YES...
...BUT WE DON'T EVEN KNOW WHAT IT IS YOU'RE HERE TO INSPECT!
YOUR CENTRAL COMMUNICATIONS CONTROLS, CAPTAIN.
COMMAND CENTRAL SENT A STARSHIP CAPTAIN FOR THAT?
AH WELL, THOSE ARE JUST DOWN THIS HALL.

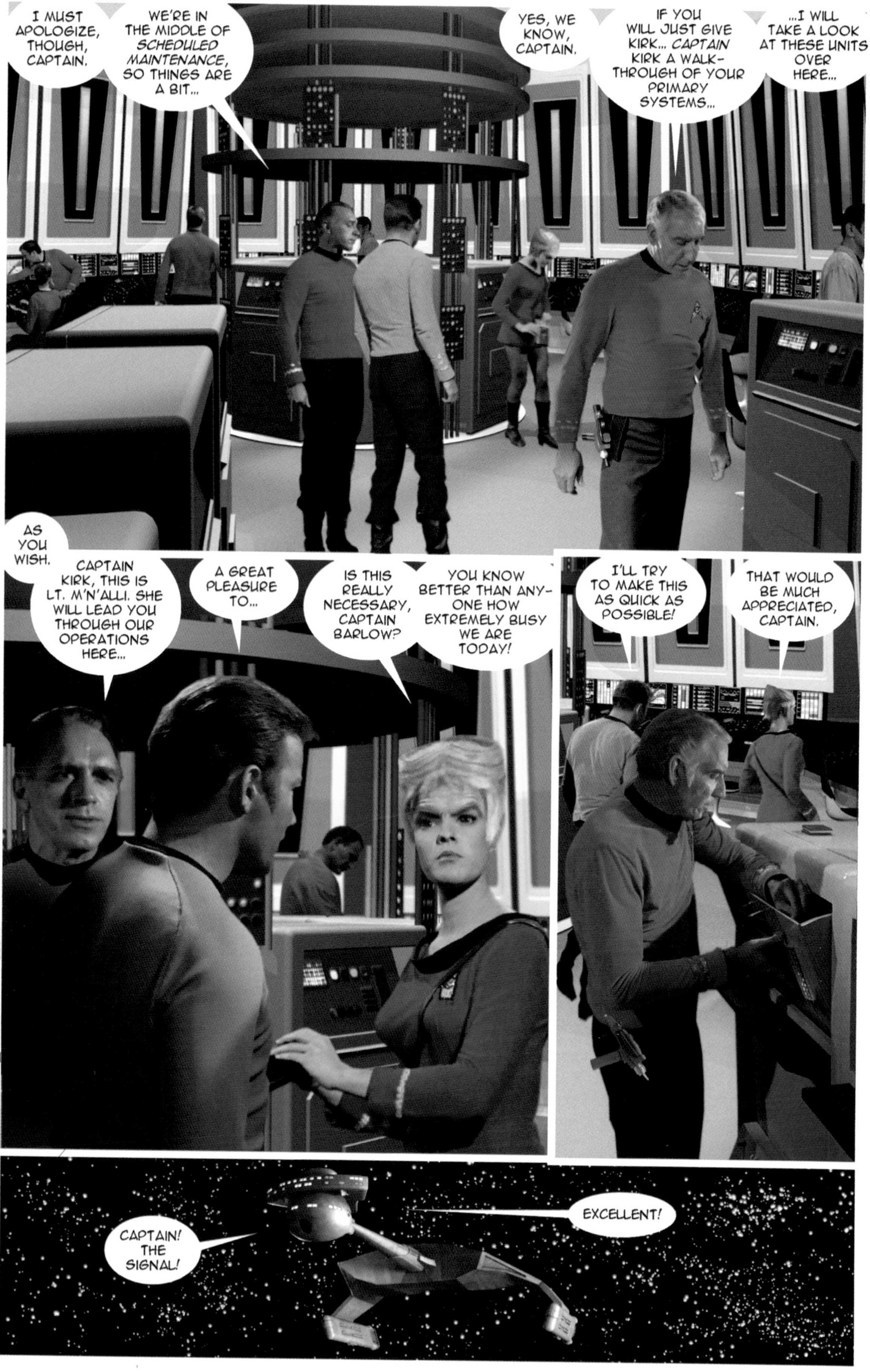
I MUST APOLOGIZE, THOUGH, CAPTAIN.
WE'RE IN THE MIDDLE OF *SCHEDULED MAINTENANCE*, SO THINGS ARE A BIT...
YES, WE KNOW, CAPTAIN.
IF YOU WILL JUST GIVE KIRK... *CAPTAIN* KIRK A WALK-THROUGH OF YOUR PRIMARY SYSTEMS...
...I WILL TAKE A LOOK AT THESE UNITS OVER HERE...
AS YOU WISH.
CAPTAIN KIRK, THIS IS LT. M'N'ALLI. SHE WILL LEAD YOU THROUGH OUR OPERATIONS HERE...
A GREAT PLEASURE TO...
IS THIS REALLY NECESSARY, CAPTAIN BARLOW?
YOU KNOW BETTER THAN ANY-ONE HOW EXTREMELY BUSY WE ARE TODAY!
I'LL TRY TO MAKE THIS AS QUICK AS POSSIBLE!
THAT WOULD BE MUCH APPRECIATED, CAPTAIN.
CAPTAIN! THE SIGNAL!
EXCELLENT!

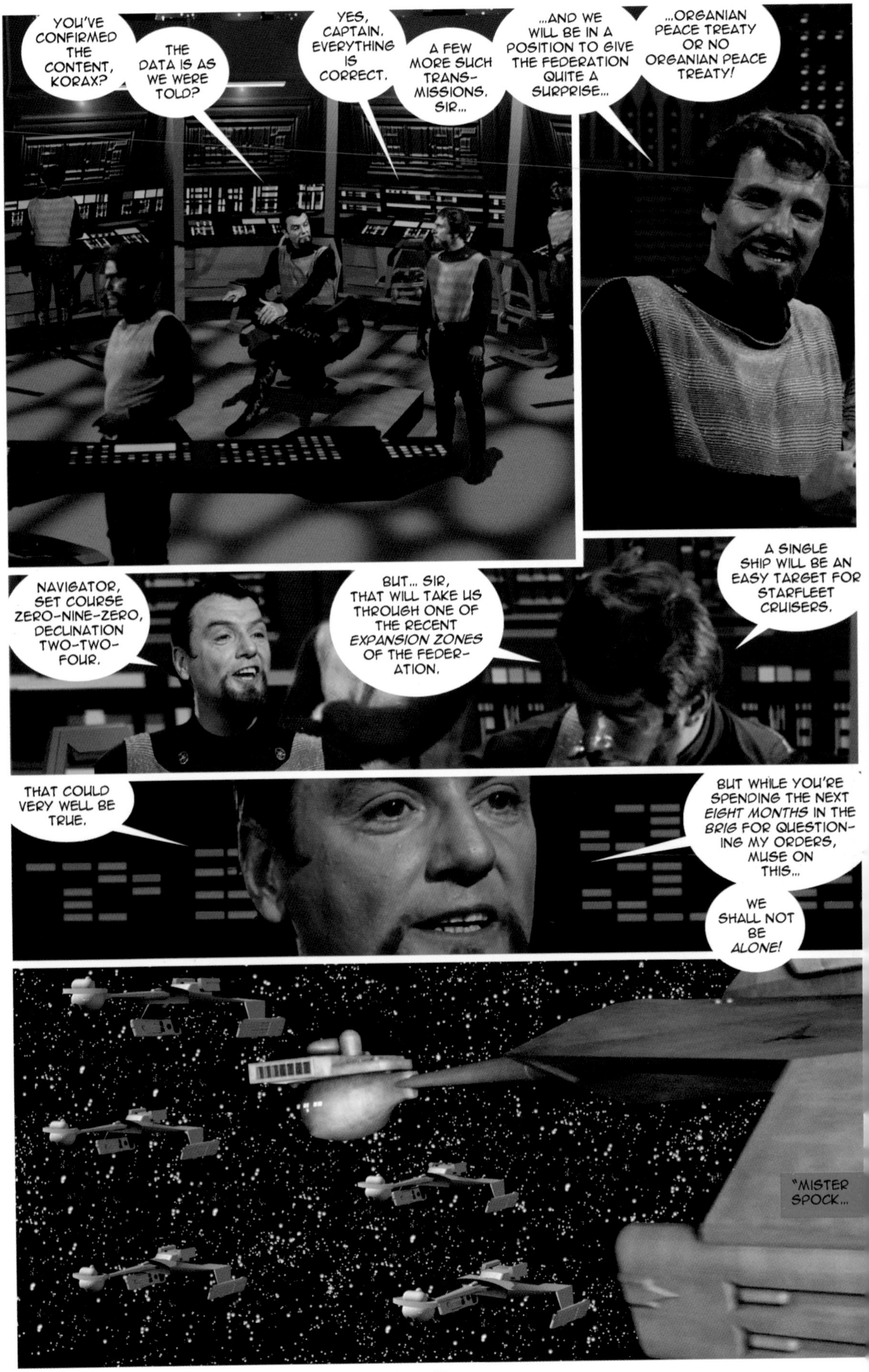

YOU'VE CONFIRMED THE CONTENT, KORAX?
THE DATA IS AS WE WERE TOLD?
YES, CAPTAIN. EVERYTHING IS CORRECT.
A FEW MORE SUCH TRANS-MISSIONS, SIR...
...AND WE WILL BE IN A POSITION TO GIVE THE FEDERATION QUITE A SURPRISE...
...ORGANIAN PEACE TREATY OR NO ORGANIAN PEACE TREATY!
NAVIGATOR, SET COURSE ZERO-NINE-ZERO, DECLINATION TWO-TWO-FOUR.
BUT... SIR, THAT WILL TAKE US THROUGH ONE OF THE RECENT *EXPANSION ZONES* OF THE FEDER-ATION.
A SINGLE SHIP WILL BE AN EASY TARGET FOR STARFLEET CRUISERS.
THAT COULD VERY WELL BE TRUE.
BUT WHILE YOU'RE SPENDING THE NEXT *EIGHT MONTHS* IN THE *BRIG* FOR QUESTION-ING MY ORDERS, MUSE ON THIS...
WE SHALL NOT BE *ALONE!*
"MISTER SPOCK...

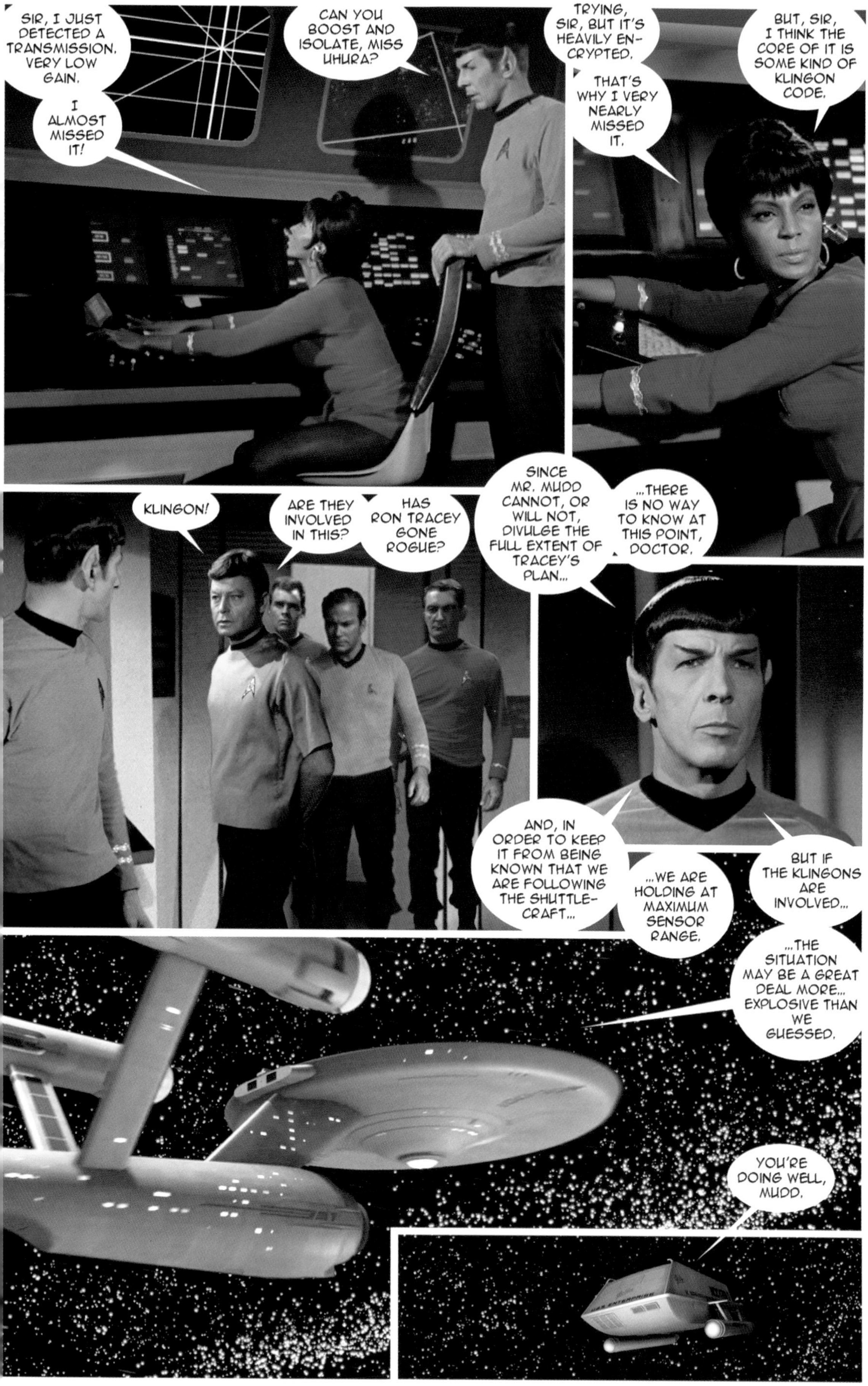
SIR, I JUST DETECTED A TRANSMISSION. VERY LOW GAIN.
I ALMOST MISSED IT!
CAN YOU BOOST AND ISOLATE, MISS UHURA?
TRYING, SIR, BUT IT'S HEAVILY EN-CRYPTED.
THAT'S WHY I VERY NEARLY MISSED IT.
BUT, SIR, I THINK THE CORE OF IT IS SOME KIND OF KLINGON CODE.
KLINGON!
ARE THEY INVOLVED IN THIS?
HAS RON TRACEY GONE ROGUE?
SINCE MR. MUDD CANNOT, OR WILL NOT, DIVULGE THE FULL EXTENT OF TRACEY'S PLAN...
...THERE IS NO WAY TO KNOW AT THIS POINT, DOCTOR.
AND, IN ORDER TO KEEP IT FROM BEING KNOWN THAT WE ARE FOLLOWING THE SHUTTLE-CRAFT...
...WE ARE HOLDING AT MAXIMUM SENSOR RANGE.
BUT IF THE KLINGONS ARE INVOLVED...
...THE SITUATION MAY BE A GREAT DEAL MORE... EXPLOSIVE THAN WE GUESSED.
YOU'RE DOING WELL, MUDD.

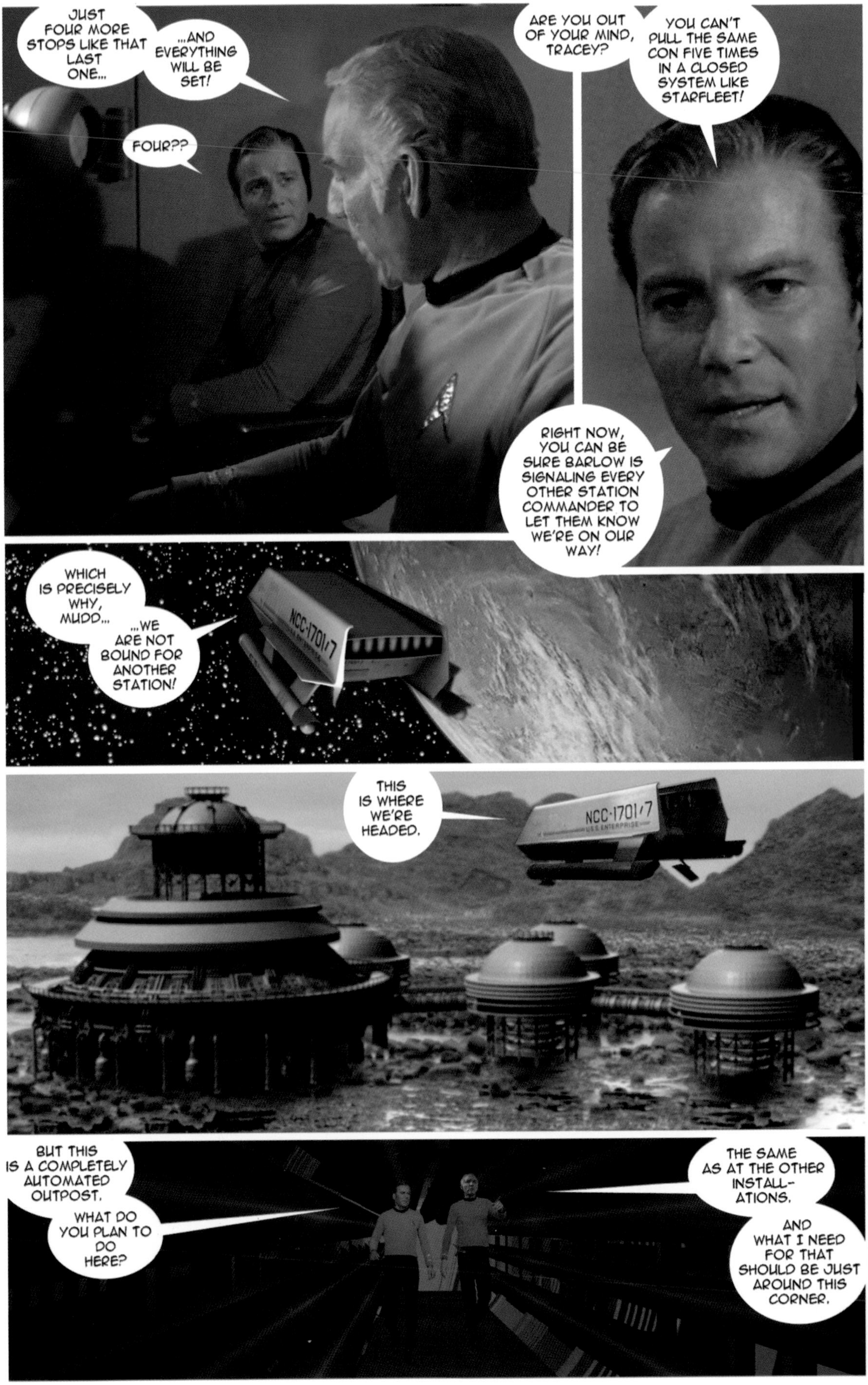
JUST FOUR MORE STOPS LIKE THAT LAST ONE...
...AND EVERYTHING WILL BE SET!
FOUR??
ARE YOU OUT OF YOUR MIND, TRACEY?
YOU CAN'T PULL THE SAME CON FIVE TIMES IN A CLOSED SYSTEM LIKE STARFLEET!
RIGHT NOW, YOU CAN BE SURE BARLOW IS SIGNALING EVERY OTHER STATION COMMANDER TO LET THEM KNOW WE'RE ON OUR WAY!
WHICH IS PRECISELY WHY, MUDD...
...WE ARE NOT BOUND FOR ANOTHER STATION!
NCC-1701/7
THIS IS WHERE WE'RE HEADED.
NCC-1701/7
U.S.S. ENTERPRISE
BUT THIS IS A COMPLETELY AUTOMATED OUTPOST.
WHAT DO YOU PLAN TO DO HERE?
THE SAME AS AT THE OTHER INSTALL-ATIONS.
AND WHAT I NEED FOR THAT SHOULD BE JUST AROUND THIS CORNER.

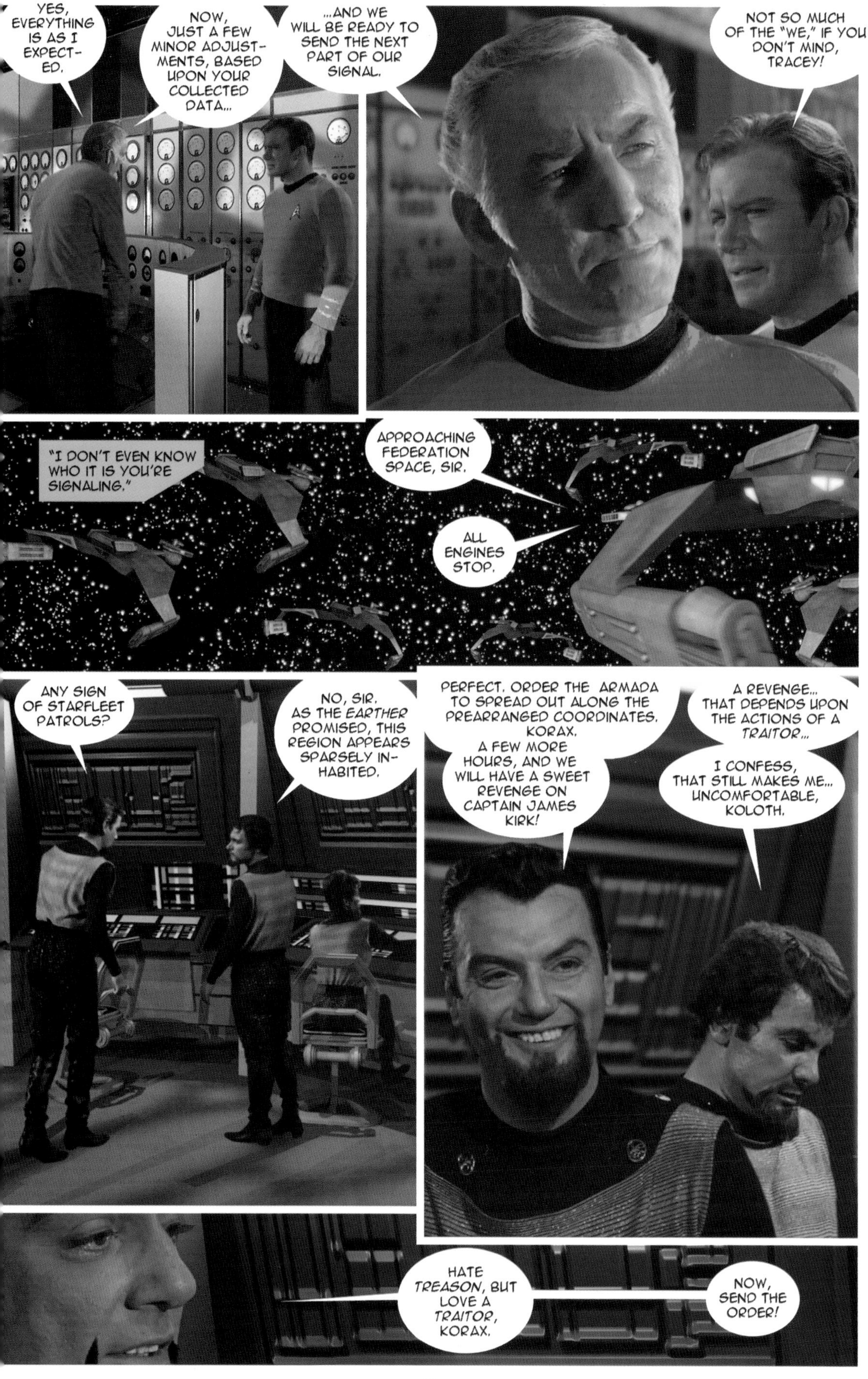
YES, EVERYTHING IS AS I EXPECTED.
NOW, JUST A FEW MINOR ADJUSTMENTS, BASED UPON YOUR COLLECTED DATA...
...AND WE WILL BE READY TO SEND THE NEXT PART OF OUR SIGNAL.
NOT SO MUCH OF THE "WE," IF YOU DON'T MIND, TRACEY!
"I DON'T EVEN KNOW WHO IT IS YOU'RE SIGNALING."
APPROACHING FEDERATION SPACE, SIR.
ALL ENGINES STOP.
ANY SIGN OF STARFLEET PATROLS?
NO, SIR. AS THE *EARTHER* PROMISED, THIS REGION APPEARS SPARSELY INHABITED.
PERFECT. ORDER THE ARMADA TO SPREAD OUT ALONG THE PREARRANGED COORDINATES, KORAX.
A FEW MORE HOURS, AND WE WILL HAVE A SWEET REVENGE ON CAPTAIN JAMES KIRK!
A REVENGE... THAT DEPENDS UPON THE ACTIONS OF A *TRAITOR*...
I CONFESS, THAT STILL MAKES ME... UNCOMFORTABLE, KOLOTH.
HATE *TREASON*, BUT LOVE A *TRAITOR*, KORAX.
NOW, SEND THE ORDER!

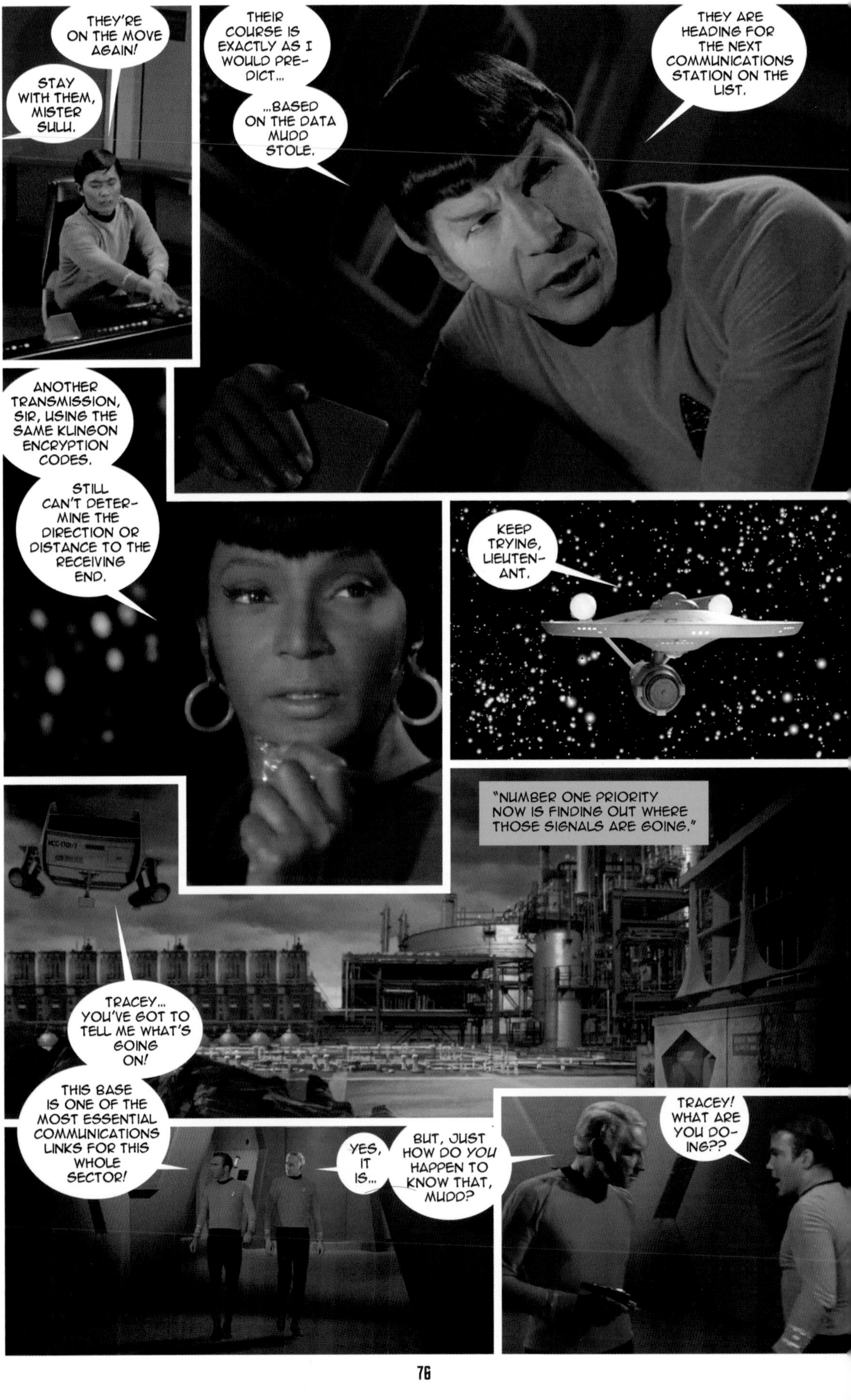
THEY'RE ON THE MOVE AGAIN!
STAY WITH THEM, MISTER SULU.
THEIR COURSE IS EXACTLY AS I WOULD PRE-DICT...
...BASED ON THE DATA MUDD STOLE.
THEY ARE HEADING FOR THE NEXT COMMUNICATIONS STATION ON THE LIST.
ANOTHER TRANSMISSION, SIR, USING THE SAME KLINGON ENCRYPTION CODES.
STILL CAN'T DETER-MINE THE DIRECTION OR DISTANCE TO THE RECEIVING END.
KEEP TRYING, LIEUTEN-ANT.
"NUMBER ONE PRIORITY NOW IS FINDING OUT WHERE THOSE SIGNALS ARE GOING."
TRACEY... YOU'VE GOT TO TELL ME WHAT'S GOING ON!
THIS BASE IS ONE OF THE MOST ESSENTIAL COMMUNICATIONS LINKS FOR THIS WHOLE SECTOR!
YES, IT IS...
BUT, JUST HOW DO *YOU* HAPPEN TO KNOW THAT, MUDD?
TRACEY! WHAT ARE YOU DO-ING??

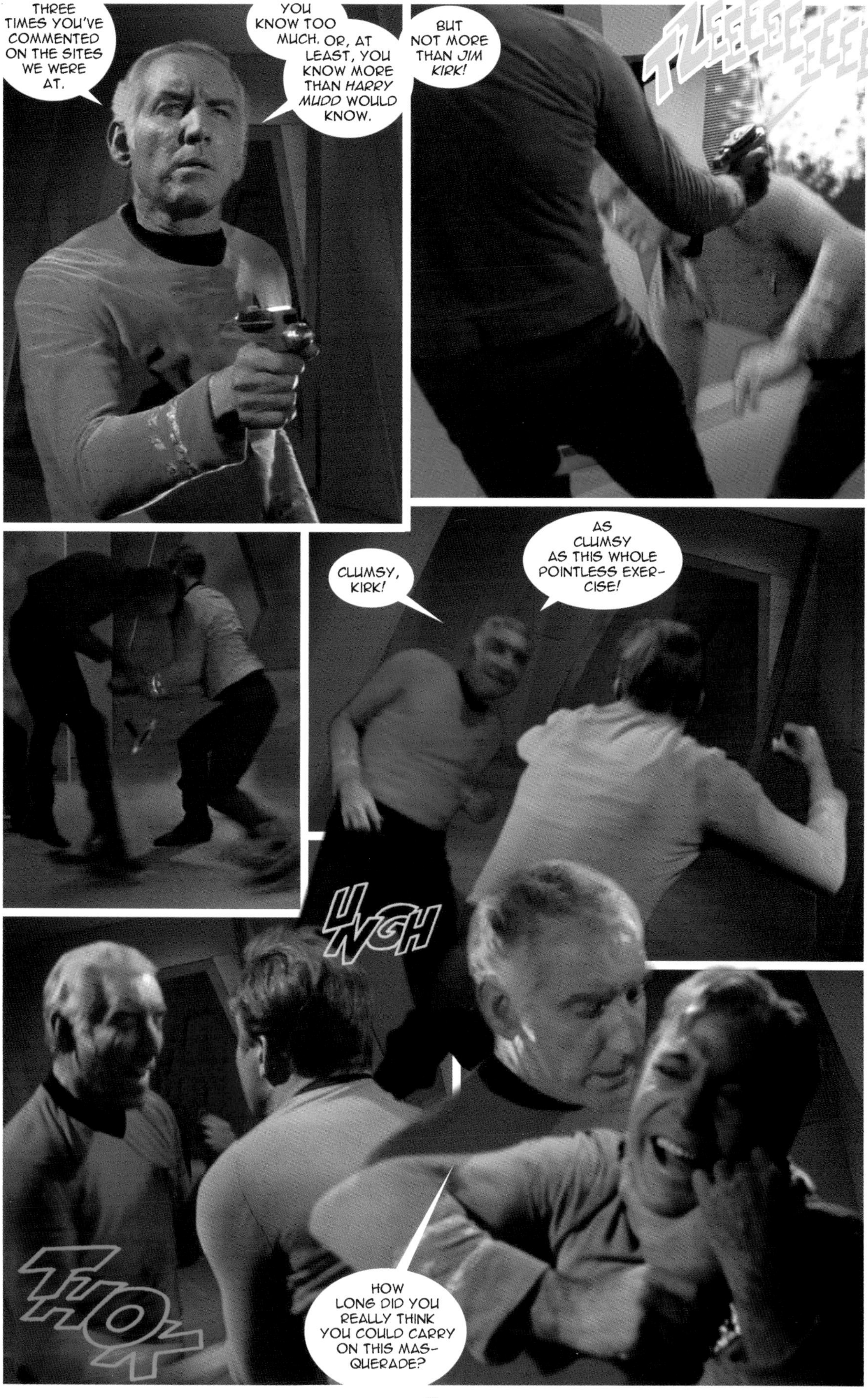

THREE TIMES YOU'VE COMMENTED ON THE SITES WE WERE AT.
YOU KNOW TOO MUCH. OR, AT LEAST, YOU KNOW MORE THAN *HARRY MUDD* WOULD KNOW.
BUT NOT MORE THAN *JIM KIRK*!
TZEEEEEEEEEE
CLUMSY, KIRK!
AS CLUMSY AS THIS WHOLE POINTLESS EXER-CISE!
UNGH
THOK
HOW LONG DID YOU REALLY THINK YOU COULD CARRY ON THIS MAS-QUERADE?

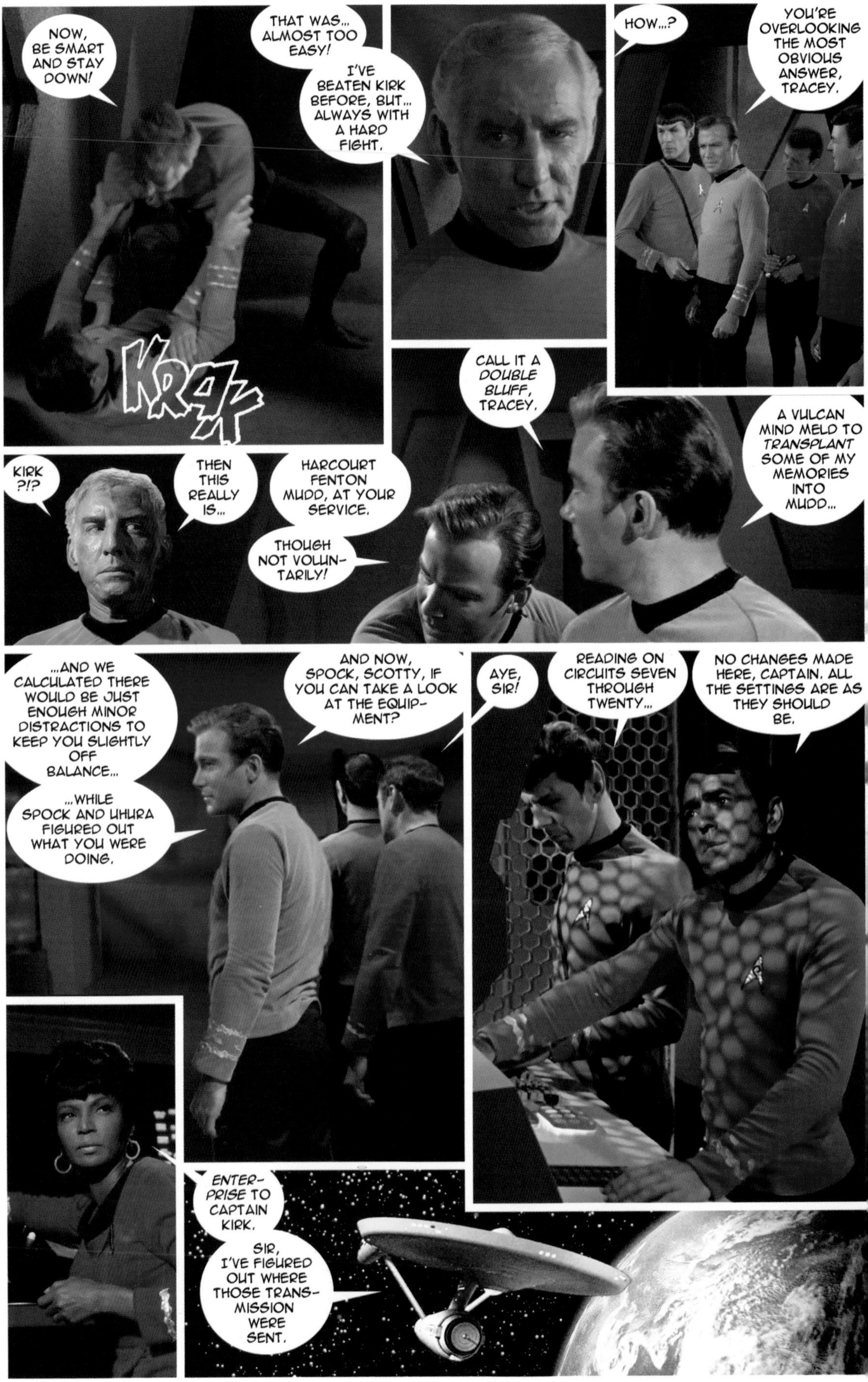
NOW, BE SMART AND STAY DOWN!
KRAK
THAT WAS... ALMOST TOO EASY!
I'VE BEATEN KIRK BEFORE, BUT... ALWAYS WITH A HARD FIGHT.
HOW...?
YOU'RE OVERLOOKING THE MOST OBVIOUS ANSWER, TRACEY.
KIRK ?!?
THEN THIS REALLY IS...
HARCOURT FENTON MUDD, AT YOUR SERVICE.
THOUGH NOT VOLUN-TARILY!
CALL IT A DOUBLE BLUFF, TRACEY.
A VULCAN MIND MELD TO TRANSPLANT SOME OF MY MEMORIES INTO MUDD...
...AND WE CALCULATED THERE WOULD BE JUST ENOUGH MINOR DISTRACTIONS TO KEEP YOU SLIGHTLY OFF BALANCE...
...WHILE SPOCK AND UHURA FIGURED OUT WHAT YOU WERE DOING.
AND NOW, SPOCK, SCOTTY, IF YOU CAN TAKE A LOOK AT THE EQUIP-MENT?
AYE, SIR!
READING ON CIRCUITS SEVEN THROUGH TWENTY...
NO CHANGES MADE HERE, CAPTAIN. ALL THE SETTINGS ARE AS THEY SHOULD BE.
ENTER-PRISE TO CAPTAIN KIRK.
SIR, I'VE FIGURED OUT WHERE THOSE TRANS-MISSION WERE SENT.

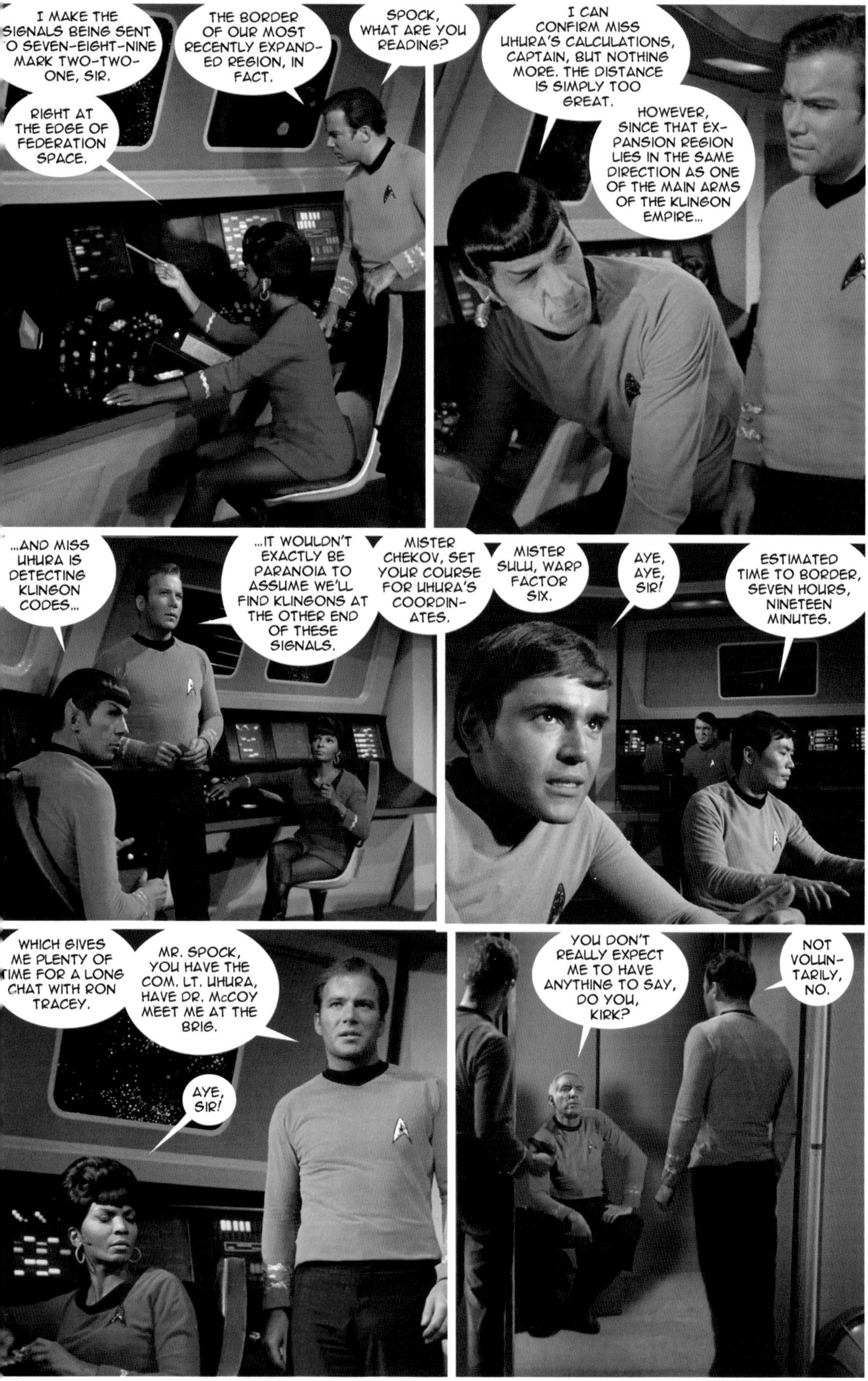
I MAKE THE SIGNALS BEING SENT TO SEVEN-EIGHT-NINE MARK TWO-TWO-ONE, SIR.
RIGHT AT THE EDGE OF FEDERATION SPACE.
THE BORDER OF OUR MOST RECENTLY EXPANDED REGION, IN FACT.
SPOCK, WHAT ARE YOU READING?
I CAN CONFIRM MISS UHURA'S CALCULATIONS, CAPTAIN, BUT NOTHING MORE. THE DISTANCE IS SIMPLY TOO GREAT.
HOWEVER, SINCE THAT EXPANSION REGION LIES IN THE SAME DIRECTION AS ONE OF THE MAIN ARMS OF THE KLINGON EMPIRE...
...AND MISS UHURA IS DETECTING KLINGON CODES...
...IT WOULDN'T EXACTLY BE PARANOIA TO ASSUME WE'LL FIND KLINGONS AT THE OTHER END OF THESE SIGNALS.
MISTER CHEKOV, SET YOUR COURSE FOR UHURA'S COORDINATES.
MISTER SULU, WARP FACTOR SIX.
AYE, AYE, SIR!
ESTIMATED TIME TO BORDER, SEVEN HOURS, NINETEEN MINUTES.
WHICH GIVES ME PLENTY OF TIME FOR A LONG CHAT WITH RON TRACEY.
MR. SPOCK, YOU HAVE THE COM. LT. UHURA, HAVE DR. McCOY MEET ME AT THE BRIG.
AYE, SIR!
YOU DON'T REALLY EXPECT ME TO HAVE ANYTHING TO SAY, DO YOU, KIRK?
NOT VOLUNTARILY, NO.

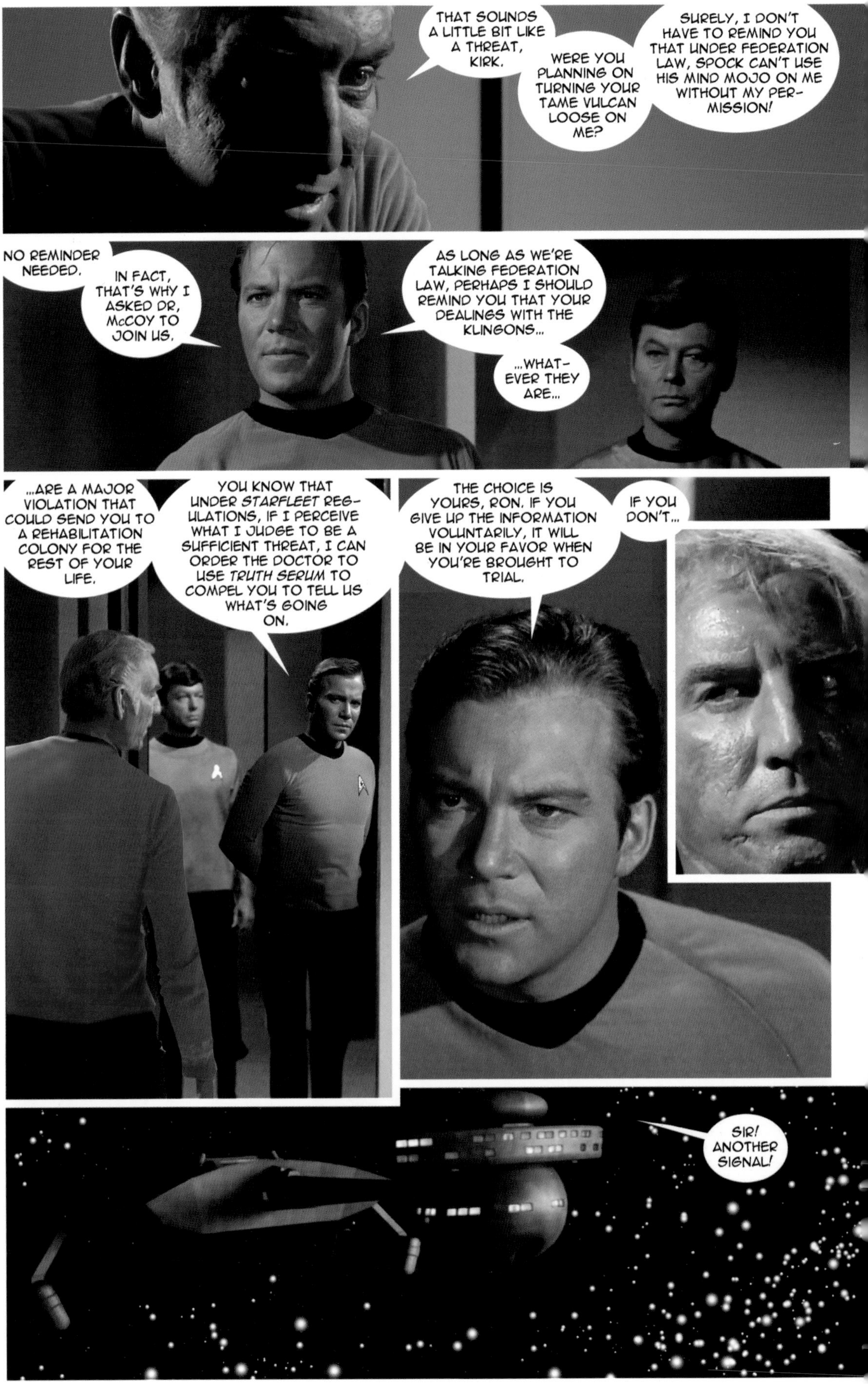
THAT SOUNDS A LITTLE BIT LIKE A THREAT, KIRK.
WERE YOU PLANNING ON TURNING YOUR TAME VULCAN LOOSE ON ME?
SURELY, I DON'T HAVE TO REMIND YOU THAT UNDER FEDERATION LAW, SPOCK CAN'T USE HIS MIND MOJO ON ME WITHOUT MY PER-MISSION!
NO REMINDER NEEDED.
IN FACT, THAT'S WHY I ASKED DR. McCOY TO JOIN US.
AS LONG AS WE'RE TALKING FEDERATION LAW, PERHAPS I SHOULD REMIND YOU THAT YOUR DEALINGS WITH THE KLINGONS...
...WHAT-EVER THEY ARE...
...ARE A MAJOR VIOLATION THAT COULD SEND YOU TO A REHABILITATION COLONY FOR THE REST OF YOUR LIFE.
YOU KNOW THAT UNDER *STARFLEET* REG-ULATIONS, IF I PERCEIVE WHAT I JUDGE TO BE A SUFFICIENT THREAT, I CAN ORDER THE DOCTOR TO USE *TRUTH SERUM* TO COMPEL YOU TO TELL US WHAT'S GOING ON.
THE CHOICE IS YOURS, RON. IF YOU GIVE UP THE INFORMATION VOLUNTARILY, IT WILL BE IN YOUR FAVOR WHEN YOU'RE BROUGHT TO TRIAL.
IF YOU DON'T...
SIR! ANOTHER SIGNAL!

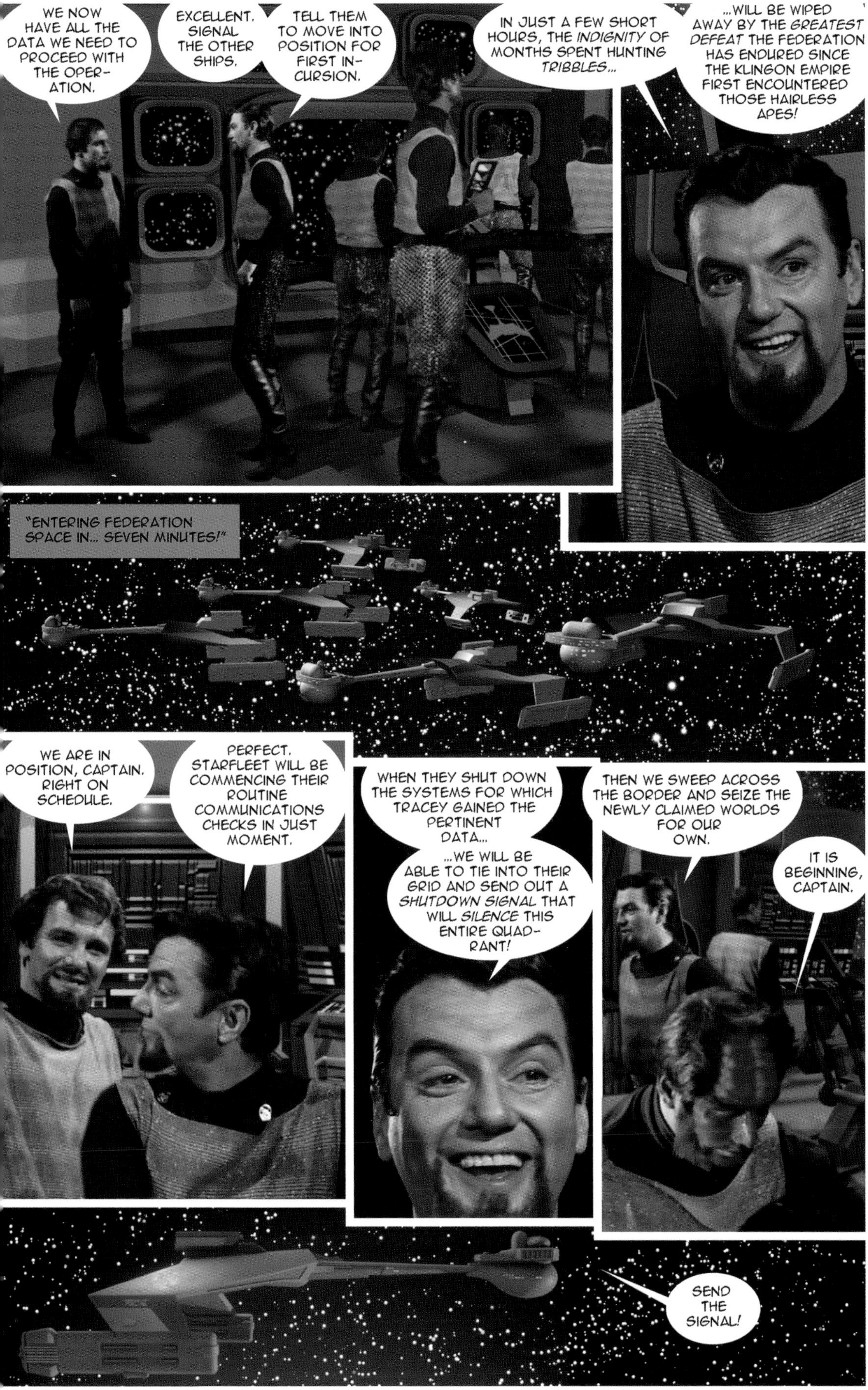
WE NOW HAVE ALL THE DATA WE NEED TO PROCEED WITH THE OPER-ATION.
EXCELLENT. SIGNAL THE OTHER SHIPS.
TELL THEM TO MOVE INTO POSITION FOR FIRST IN-CURSION.
IN JUST A FEW SHORT HOURS, THE *INDIGNITY* OF MONTHS SPENT HUNTING *TRIBBLES*...
...WILL BE WIPED AWAY BY THE *GREATEST DEFEAT* THE FEDERATION HAS ENDURED SINCE THE KLINGON EMPIRE FIRST ENCOUNTERED THOSE HAIRLESS APES!
"ENTERING FEDERATION SPACE IN... SEVEN MINUTES!"
WE ARE IN POSITION, CAPTAIN. RIGHT ON SCHEDULE.
PERFECT. STARFLEET WILL BE COMMENCING THEIR ROUTINE COMMUNICATIONS CHECKS IN JUST MOMENT.
WHEN THEY SHUT DOWN THE SYSTEMS FOR WHICH TRACEY GAINED THE PERTINENT DATA...
...WE WILL BE ABLE TO TIE INTO THEIR GRID AND SEND OUT A *SHUTDOWN SIGNAL* THAT WILL *SILENCE* THIS ENTIRE QUAD-RANT!
THEN WE SWEEP ACROSS THE BORDER AND SEIZE THE NEWLY CLAIMED WORLDS FOR OUR OWN.
IT IS BEGINNING, CAPTAIN.
SEND THE SIGNAL!

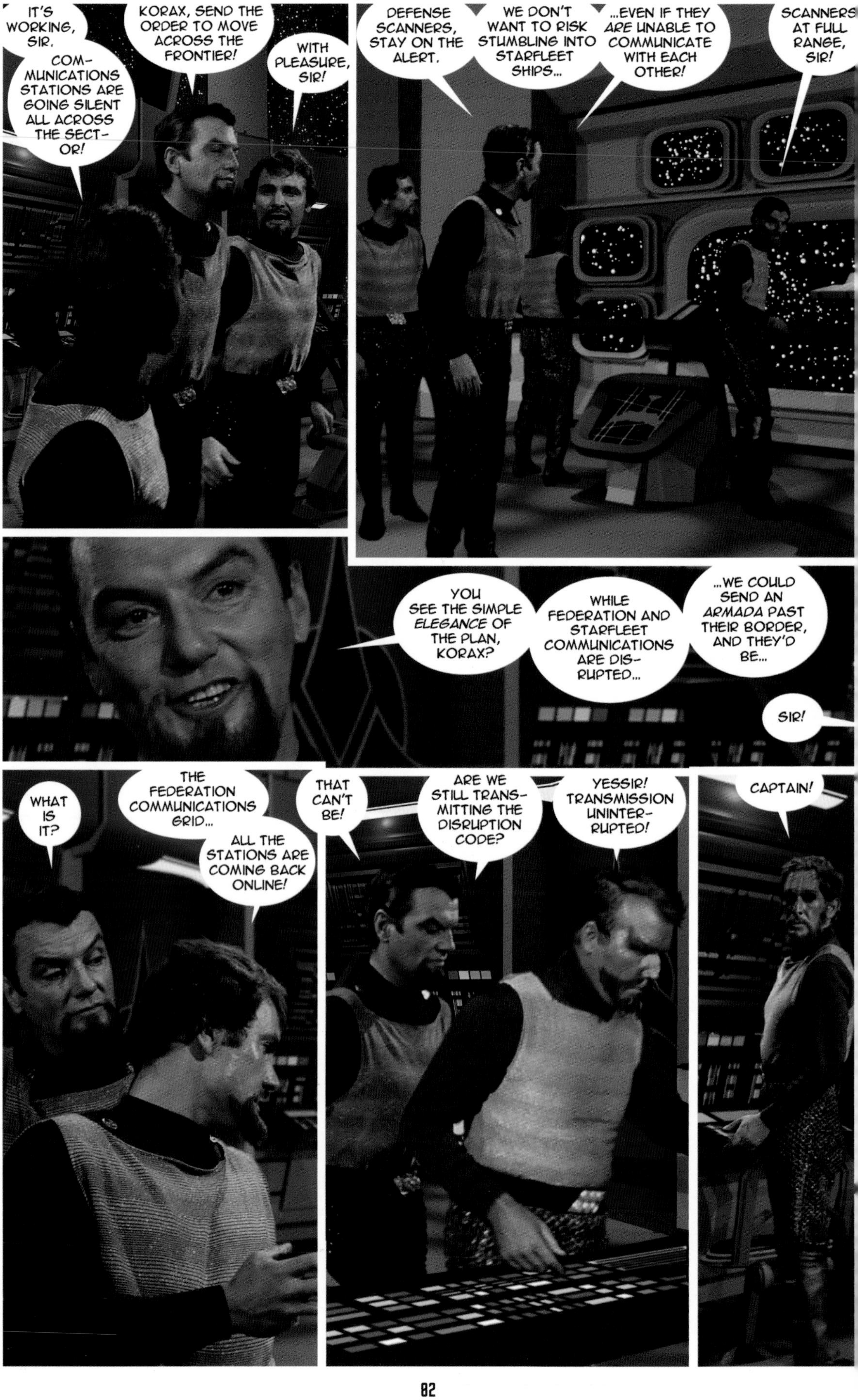
IT'S WORKING, SIR.
COM-MUNICATIONS STATIONS ARE GOING SILENT ALL ACROSS THE SECT-OR!
KORAX, SEND THE ORDER TO MOVE ACROSS THE FRONTIER!
WITH PLEASURE, SIR!
DEFENSE SCANNERS, STAY ON THE ALERT.
WE DON'T WANT TO RISK STUMBLING INTO STARFLEET SHIPS...
...EVEN IF THEY ARE UNABLE TO COMMUNICATE WITH EACH OTHER!
SCANNERS AT FULL RANGE, SIR!
YOU SEE THE SIMPLE ELEGANCE OF THE PLAN, KORAX?
WHILE FEDERATION AND STARFLEET COMMUNICATIONS ARE DIS-RUPTED...
...WE COULD SEND AN ARMADA PAST THEIR BORDER, AND THEY'D BE...
SIR!
WHAT IS IT?
THE FEDERATION COMMUNICATIONS GRID...
ALL THE STATIONS ARE COMING BACK ONLINE!
THAT CAN'T BE!
ARE WE STILL TRANS-MITTING THE DISRUPTION CODE?
YESSIR! TRANSMISSION UNINTER-RUPTED!
CAPTAIN!

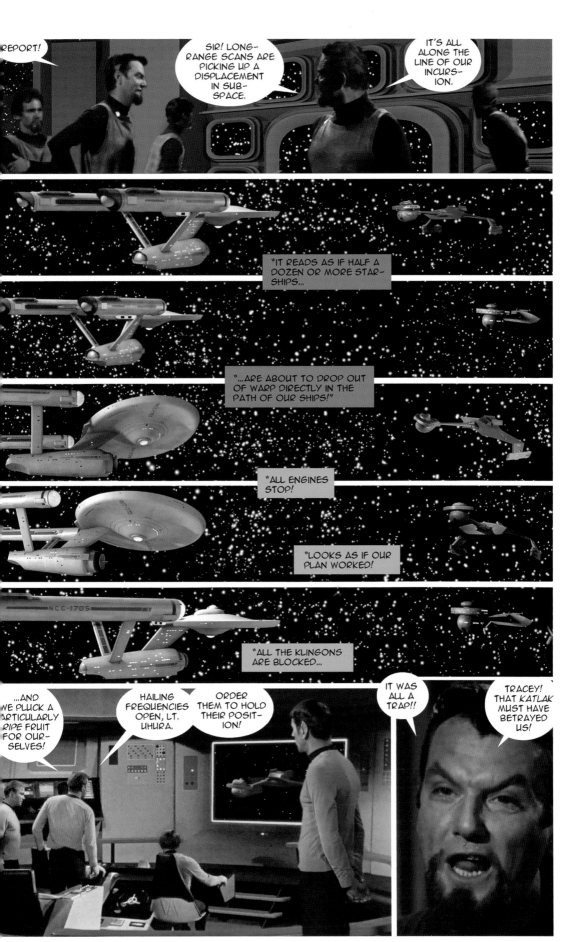

REPORT!

SIR! LONG-RANGE SCANS ARE PICKING UP A DISPLACEMENT IN SUB-SPACE.

IT'S ALL ALONG THE LINE OF OUR INCURSION.

"IT READS AS IF HALF A DOZEN OR MORE STAR-SHIPS...

"...ARE ABOUT TO DROP OUT OF WARP DIRECTLY IN THE PATH OF OUR SHIPS!"

"ALL ENGINES STOP!

"LOOKS AS IF OUR PLAN WORKED!

"ALL THE KLINGONS ARE BLOCKED...

...AND WE PLUCK A PARTICULARLY RIPE FRUIT FOR OUR-SELVES!

HAILING FREQUENCIES OPEN, LT. UHURA.

ORDER THEM TO HOLD THEIR POSIT-ION!

IT WAS ALL A TRAP!!

TRACEY! THAT KATLAK MUST HAVE BETRAYED US!

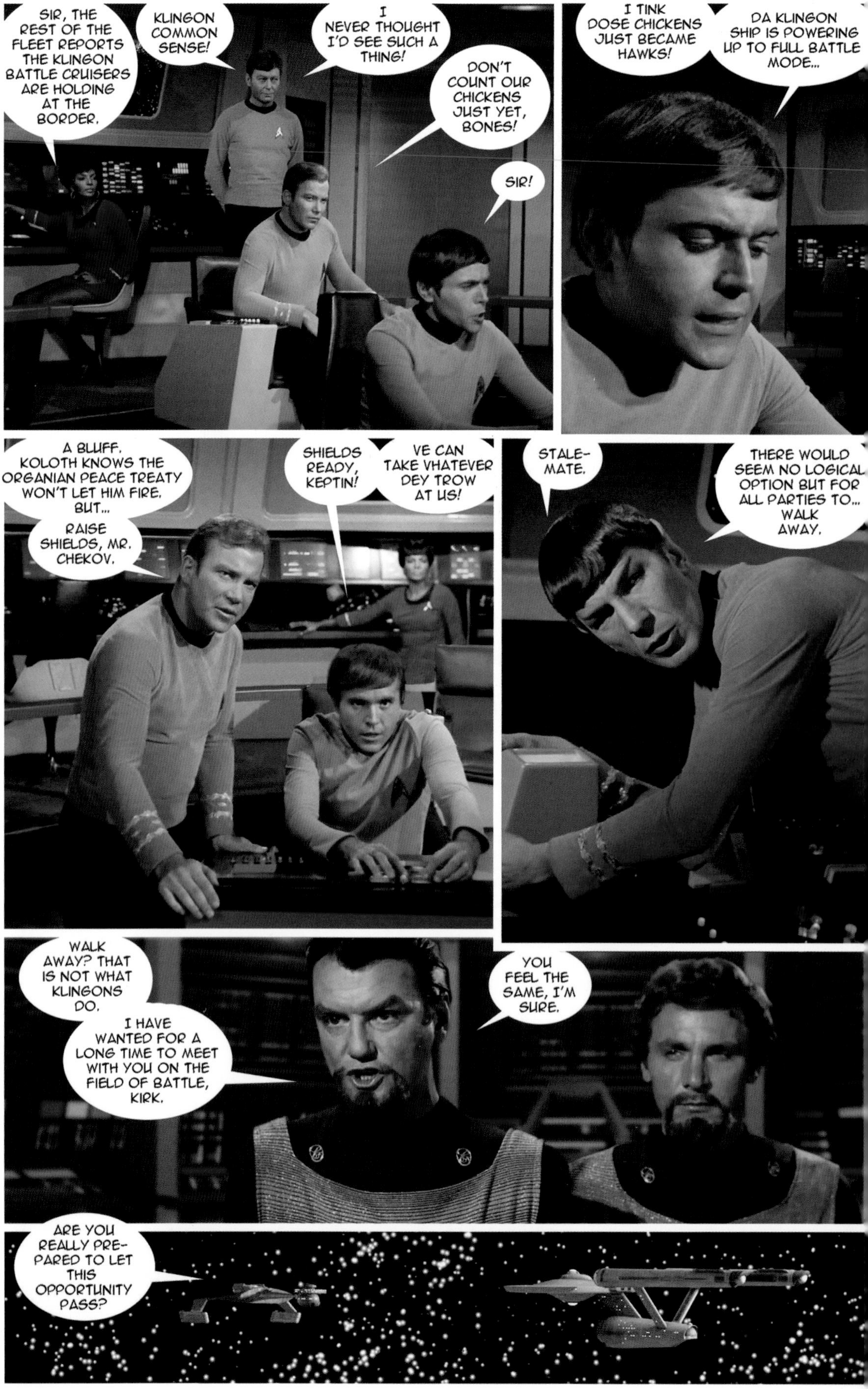
SIR, THE REST OF THE FLEET REPORTS THE KLINGON BATTLE CRUISERS ARE HOLDING AT THE BORDER.
KLINGON COMMON SENSE!
I NEVER THOUGHT I'D SEE SUCH A THING!
DON'T COUNT OUR CHICKENS JUST YET, BONES!
SIR!
I TINK DOSE CHICKENS JUST BECAME HAWKS!
DA KLINGON SHIP IS POWERING UP TO FULL BATTLE MODE...
A BLUFF. KOLOTH KNOWS THE ORGANIAN PEACE TREATY WON'T LET HIM FIRE. BUT...
RAISE SHIELDS, MR. CHEKOV.
SHIELDS READY, KEPTIN!
VE CAN TAKE VHATEVER DEY TROW AT US!
STALE-MATE.
THERE WOULD SEEM NO LOGICAL OPTION BUT FOR ALL PARTIES TO... WALK AWAY.
WALK AWAY? THAT IS NOT WHAT KLINGONS DO.
I HAVE WANTED FOR A LONG TIME TO MEET WITH YOU ON THE FIELD OF BATTLE, KIRK.
YOU FEEL THE SAME, I'M SURE.
ARE YOU REALLY PRE-PARED TO LET THIS OPPORTUNITY PASS?

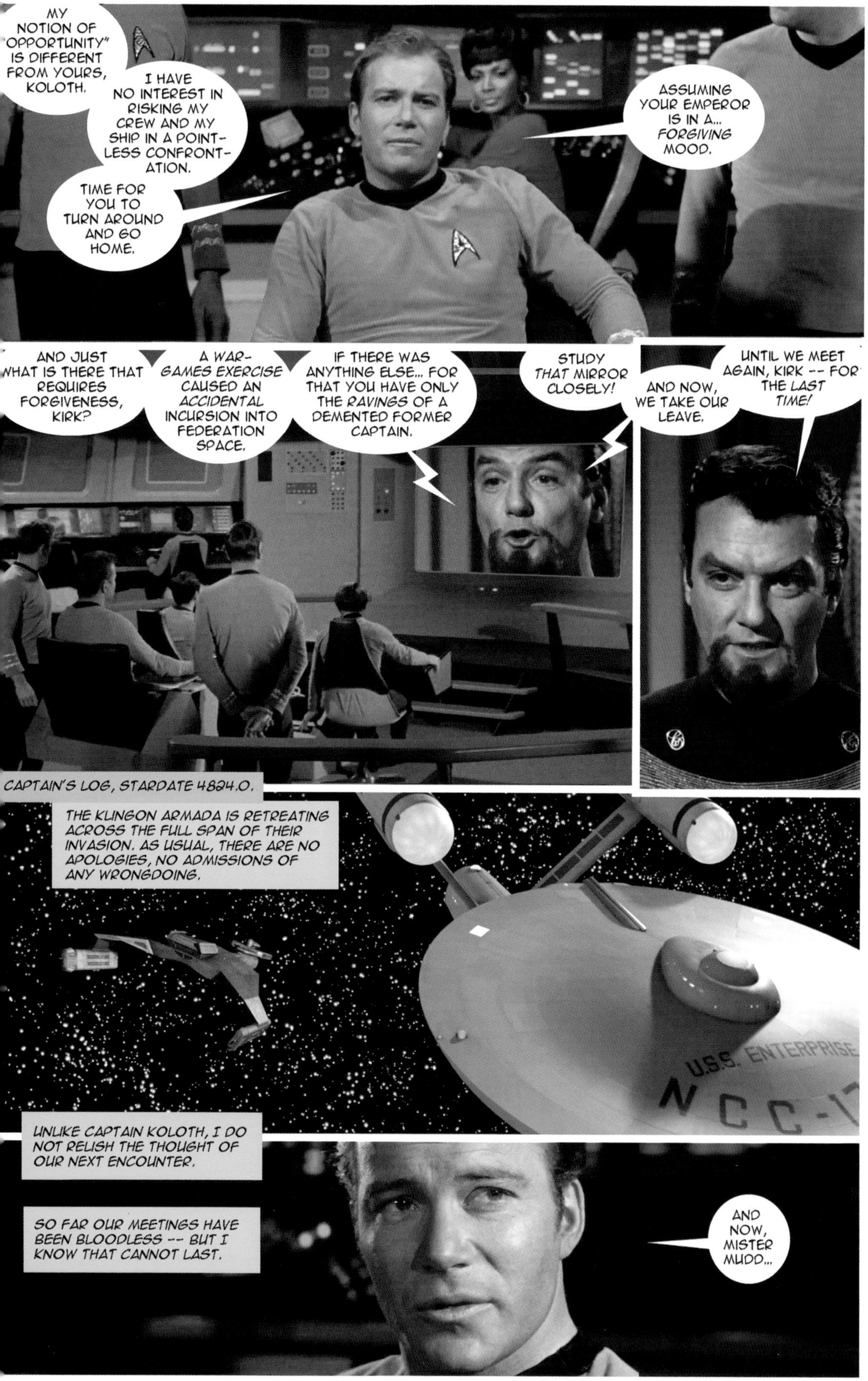

MY NOTION OF "OPPORTUNITY" IS DIFFERENT FROM YOURS, KOLOTH.
I HAVE NO INTEREST IN RISKING MY CREW AND MY SHIP IN A POINTLESS CONFRONTATION.
TIME FOR YOU TO TURN AROUND AND GO HOME.
ASSUMING YOUR EMPEROR IS IN A... FORGIVING MOOD.
AND JUST WHAT IS THERE THAT REQUIRES FORGIVENESS, KIRK?
A WAR-GAMES EXERCISE CAUSED AN ACCIDENTAL INCURSION INTO FEDERATION SPACE.
IF THERE WAS ANYTHING ELSE... FOR THAT YOU HAVE ONLY THE RAVINGS OF A DEMENTED FORMER CAPTAIN.
STUDY THAT MIRROR CLOSELY!
AND NOW, WE TAKE OUR LEAVE.
UNTIL WE MEET AGAIN, KIRK -- FOR THE LAST TIME!
CAPTAIN'S LOG, STARDATE 4824.0.
THE KLINGON ARMADA IS RETREATING ACROSS THE FULL SPAN OF THEIR INVASION. AS USUAL, THERE ARE NO APOLOGIES, NO ADMISSIONS OF ANY WRONGDOING.
U.S.S. ENTERPRISE
NCC-1
UNLIKE CAPTAIN KOLOTH, I DO NOT RELISH THE THOUGHT OF OUR NEXT ENCOUNTER.
SO FAR OUR MEETINGS HAVE BEEN BLOODLESS -- BUT I KNOW THAT CANNOT LAST.
AND NOW, MISTER MUDD...

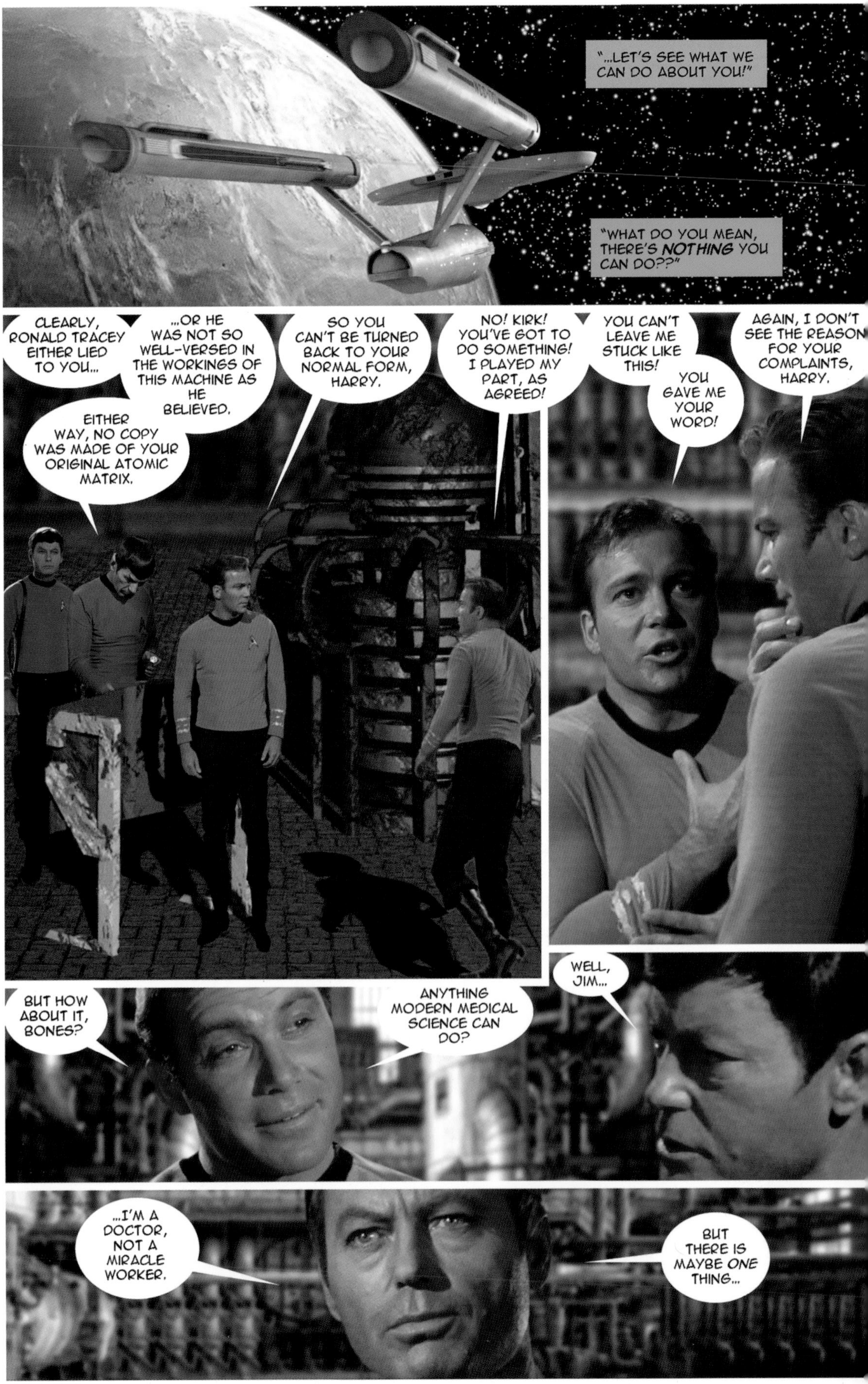
"...LET'S SEE WHAT WE CAN DO ABOUT YOU!"
"WHAT DO YOU MEAN, THERE'S *NOTHING* YOU CAN DO??"
CLEARLY, RONALD TRACEY EITHER LIED TO YOU...
...OR HE WAS NOT SO WELL-VERSED IN THE WORKINGS OF THIS MACHINE AS HE BELIEVED.
EITHER WAY, NO COPY WAS MADE OF YOUR ORIGINAL ATOMIC MATRIX.
SO YOU CAN'T BE TURNED BACK TO YOUR NORMAL FORM, HARRY.
NO! KIRK! YOU'VE GOT TO DO SOMETHING! I PLAYED MY PART, AS AGREED!
YOU CAN'T LEAVE ME STUCK LIKE THIS!
YOU GAVE ME YOUR WORD!
AGAIN, I DON'T SEE THE REASON FOR YOUR COMPLAINTS, HARRY.
BUT HOW ABOUT IT, BONES?
ANYTHING MODERN MEDICAL SCIENCE CAN DO?
WELL, JIM...
...I'M A DOCTOR, NOT A MIRACLE WORKER.
BUT THERE IS MAYBE *ONE* THING...

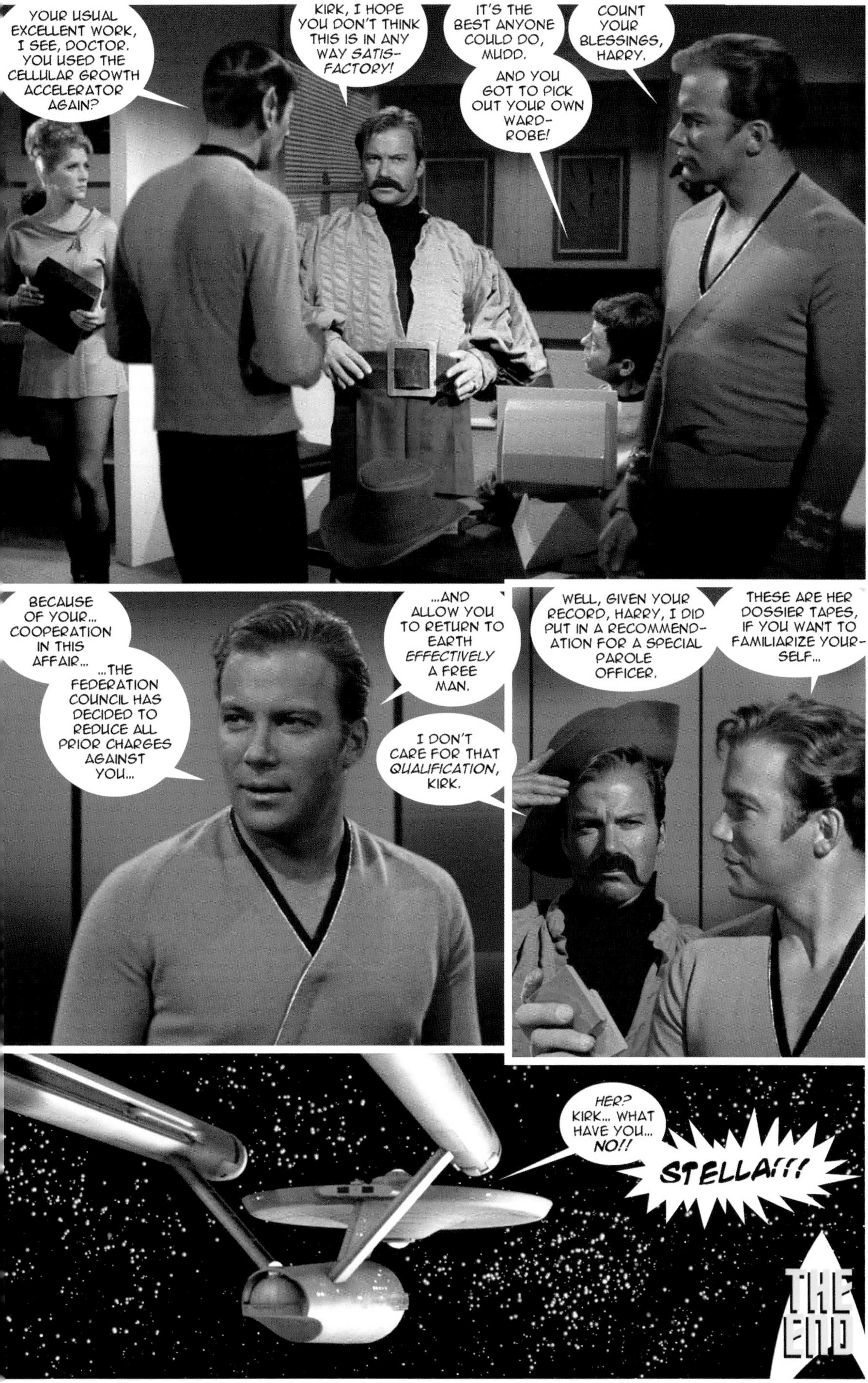

YOUR USUAL EXCELLENT WORK, I SEE, DOCTOR. YOU USED THE CELLULAR GROWTH ACCELERATOR AGAIN?
KIRK, I HOPE YOU DON'T THINK THIS IS IN ANY WAY *SATIS-FACTORY!*
IT'S THE BEST ANYONE COULD DO, MUDD.
AND YOU GOT TO PICK OUT YOUR OWN WARD-ROBE!
COUNT YOUR BLESSINGS, HARRY.
BECAUSE OF YOUR... COOPERATION IN THIS AFFAIR...
...THE FEDERATION COUNCIL HAS DECIDED TO REDUCE ALL PRIOR CHARGES AGAINST YOU...
...AND ALLOW YOU TO RETURN TO EARTH *EFFECTIVELY* A FREE MAN.
I DON'T CARE FOR THAT *QUALIFICATION*, KIRK.
WELL, GIVEN YOUR RECORD, HARRY, I DID PUT IN A RECOMMEND-ATION FOR A SPECIAL PAROLE OFFICER.
THESE ARE HER DOSSIER TAPES, IF YOU WANT TO FAMILIARIZE YOUR-SELF...
HER? KIRK... WHAT HAVE YOU... ***NO!!***
STELLA!!!
THE END

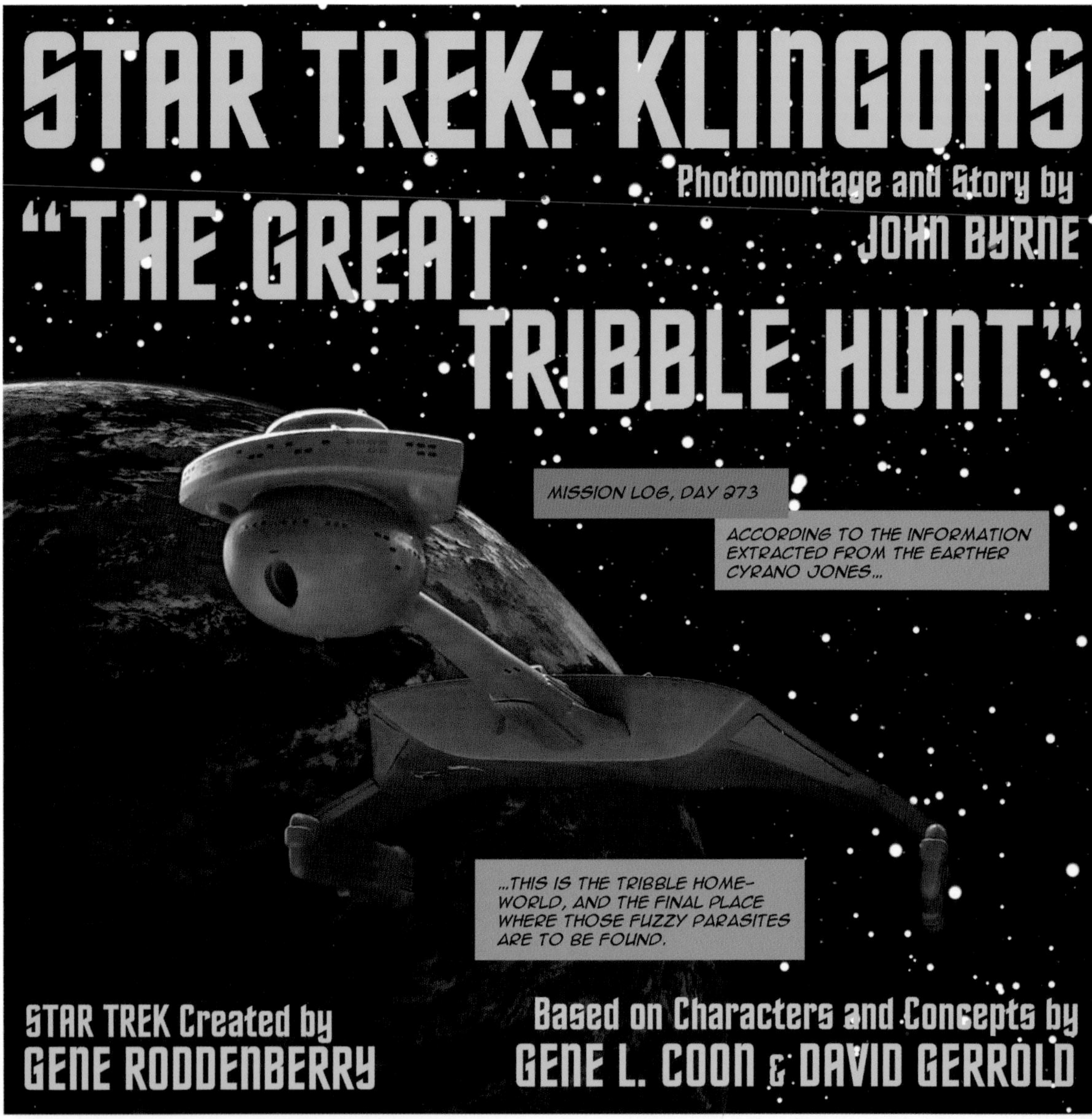
STAR TREK: KLINGONS
"THE GREAT TRIBBLE HUNT"
Photomontage and Story by
JOHN BYRNE
MISSION LOG, DAY 273
ACCORDING TO THE INFORMATION EXTRACTED FROM THE EARTHER CYRANO JONES...
...THIS IS THE TRIBBLE HOME-WORLD, AND THE FINAL PLACE WHERE THOSE FUZZY PARASITES ARE TO BE FOUND.
STAR TREK Created by
GENE RODDENBERRY
Based on Characters and Concepts by
GENE L. COON & DAVID GERROLD

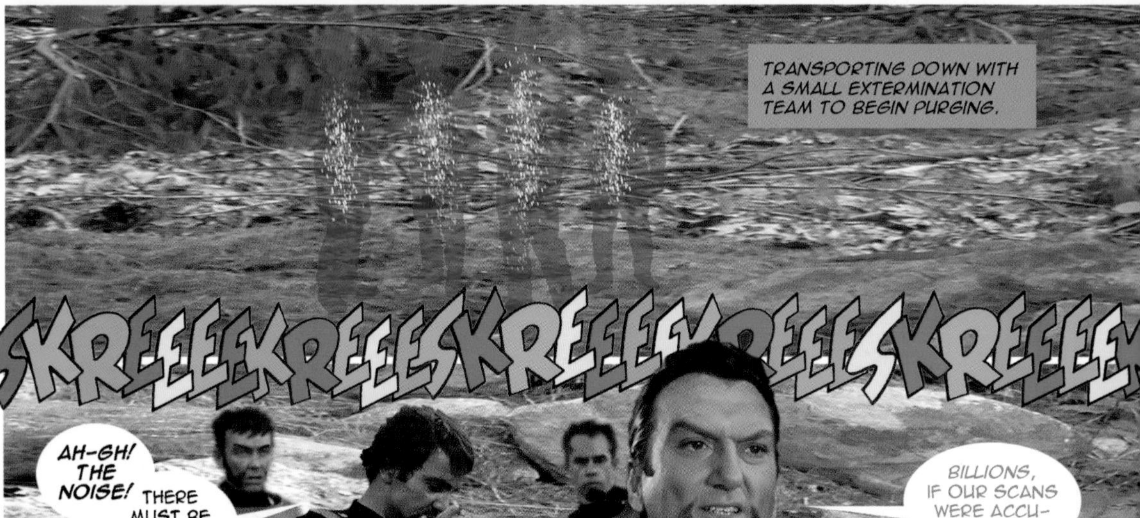
TRANSPORTING DOWN WITH A SMALL EXTERMINATION TEAM TO BEGIN PURGING.
SKREEEKREEESKREEEKREEESKREEE
AH-GH! THE NOISE!
THERE MUST BE MILLIONS OF THEM!!
BILLIONS, IF OUR SCANS WERE ACCU-RATE!

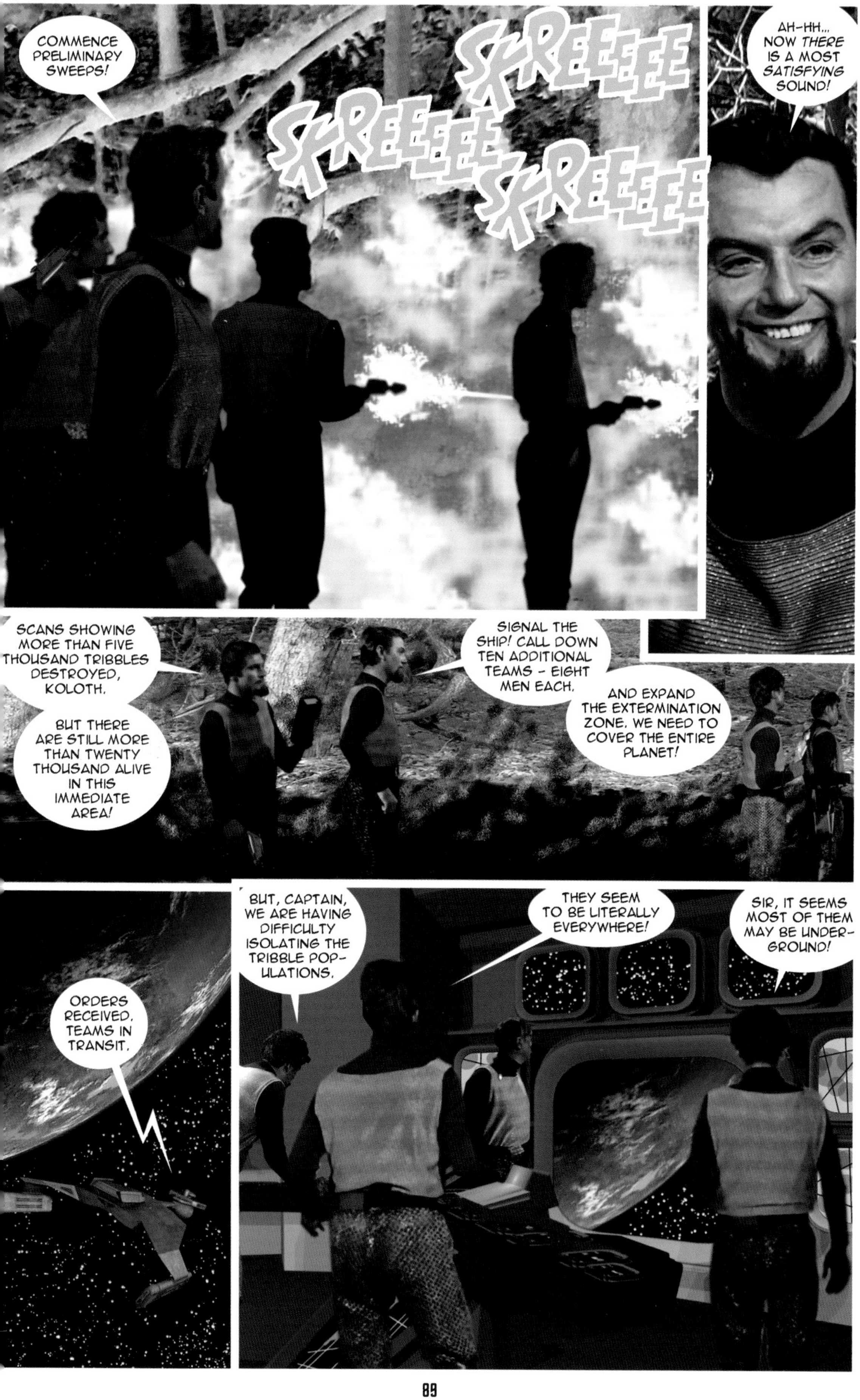
COMMENCE PRELIMINARY SWEEPS!
SKREEEEE SKREEEEE SKREEEEE
AH-HH... NOW THERE IS A MOST SATISFYING SOUND!
SCANS SHOWING MORE THAN FIVE THOUSAND TRIBBLES DESTROYED, KOLOTH.
BUT THERE ARE STILL MORE THAN TWENTY THOUSAND ALIVE IN THIS IMMEDIATE AREA!
SIGNAL THE SHIP! CALL DOWN TEN ADDITIONAL TEAMS - EIGHT MEN EACH.
AND EXPAND THE EXTERMINATION ZONE. WE NEED TO COVER THE ENTIRE PLANET!
ORDERS RECEIVED. TEAMS IN TRANSIT.
BUT, CAPTAIN, WE ARE HAVING DIFFICULTY ISOLATING THE TRIBBLE POPULATIONS.
THEY SEEM TO BE LITERALLY EVERYWHERE!
SIR, IT SEEMS MOST OF THEM MAY BE UNDERGROUND!

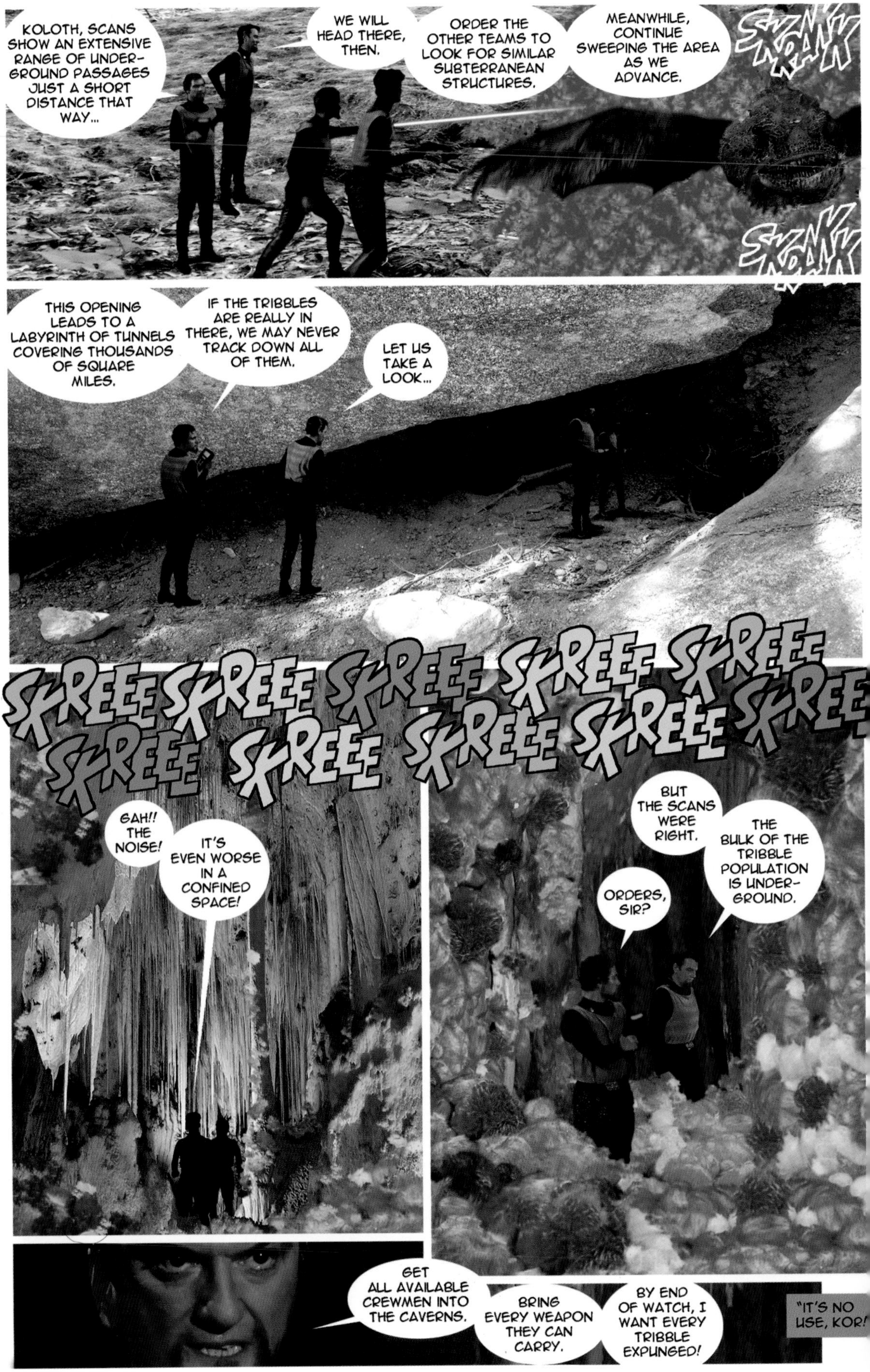

KOLOTH, SCANS SHOW AN EXTENSIVE RANGE OF UNDERGROUND PASSAGES JUST A SHORT DISTANCE THAT WAY...
WE WILL HEAD THERE, THEN.
ORDER THE OTHER TEAMS TO LOOK FOR SIMILAR SUBTERRANEAN STRUCTURES.
MEANWHILE, CONTINUE SWEEPING THE AREA AS WE ADVANCE.
SKRAAK
SKRAAK
THIS OPENING LEADS TO A LABYRINTH OF TUNNELS COVERING THOUSANDS OF SQUARE MILES.
IF THE TRIBBLES ARE REALLY IN THERE, WE MAY NEVER TRACK DOWN ALL OF THEM.
LET US TAKE A LOOK...
SKREEE SKREEE SKREEE SKREEE SKREEE
SKREEE SKREEE SKREEE SKREEE SKREEE
GAH!! THE NOISE!
IT'S EVEN WORSE IN A CONFINED SPACE!
BUT THE SCANS WERE RIGHT.
THE BULK OF THE TRIBBLE POPULATION IS UNDERGROUND.
ORDERS, SIR?
GET ALL AVAILABLE CREWMEN INTO THE CAVERNS.
BRING EVERY WEAPON THEY CAN CARRY.
BY END OF WATCH, I WANT EVERY TRIBBLE EXPUNGED!
"IT'S NO USE, KOR!

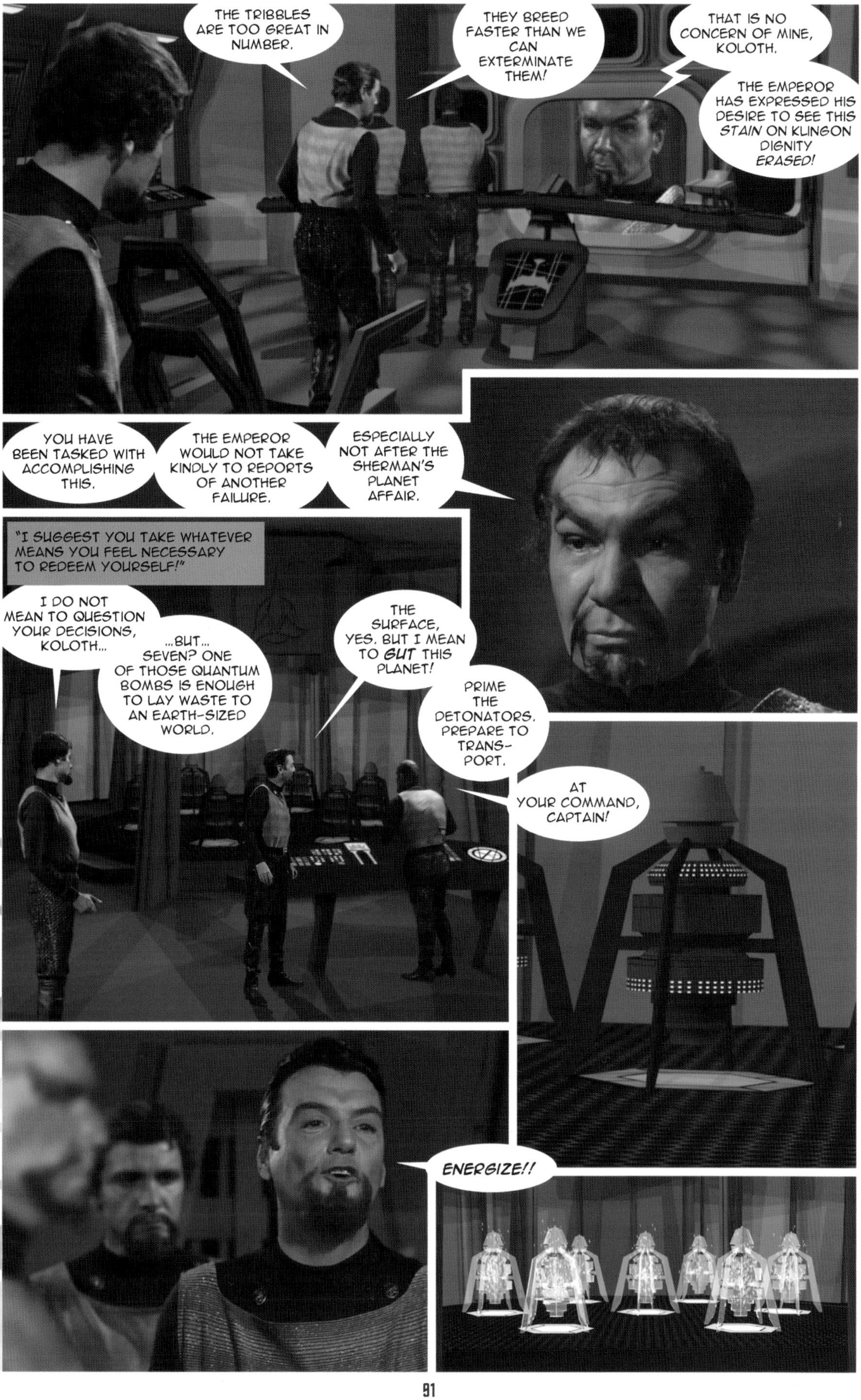

THE TRIBBLES ARE TOO GREAT IN NUMBER.
THEY BREED FASTER THAN WE CAN EXTERMINATE THEM!
THAT IS NO CONCERN OF MINE, KOLOTH.
THE EMPEROR HAS EXPRESSED HIS DESIRE TO SEE THIS STAIN ON KLINGON DIGNITY ERASED!
YOU HAVE BEEN TASKED WITH ACCOMPLISHING THIS.
THE EMPEROR WOULD NOT TAKE KINDLY TO REPORTS OF ANOTHER FAILURE.
ESPECIALLY NOT AFTER THE SHERMAN'S PLANET AFFAIR.
"I SUGGEST YOU TAKE WHATEVER MEANS YOU FEEL NECESSARY TO REDEEM YOURSELF!"
I DO NOT MEAN TO QUESTION YOUR DECISIONS, KOLOTH...
...BUT... SEVEN? ONE OF THOSE QUANTUM BOMBS IS ENOUGH TO LAY WASTE TO AN EARTH-SIZED WORLD.
THE SURFACE, YES. BUT I MEAN TO GUT THIS PLANET!
PRIME THE DETONATORS. PREPARE TO TRANS-PORT.
AT YOUR COMMAND, CAPTAIN!
ENERGIZE!!

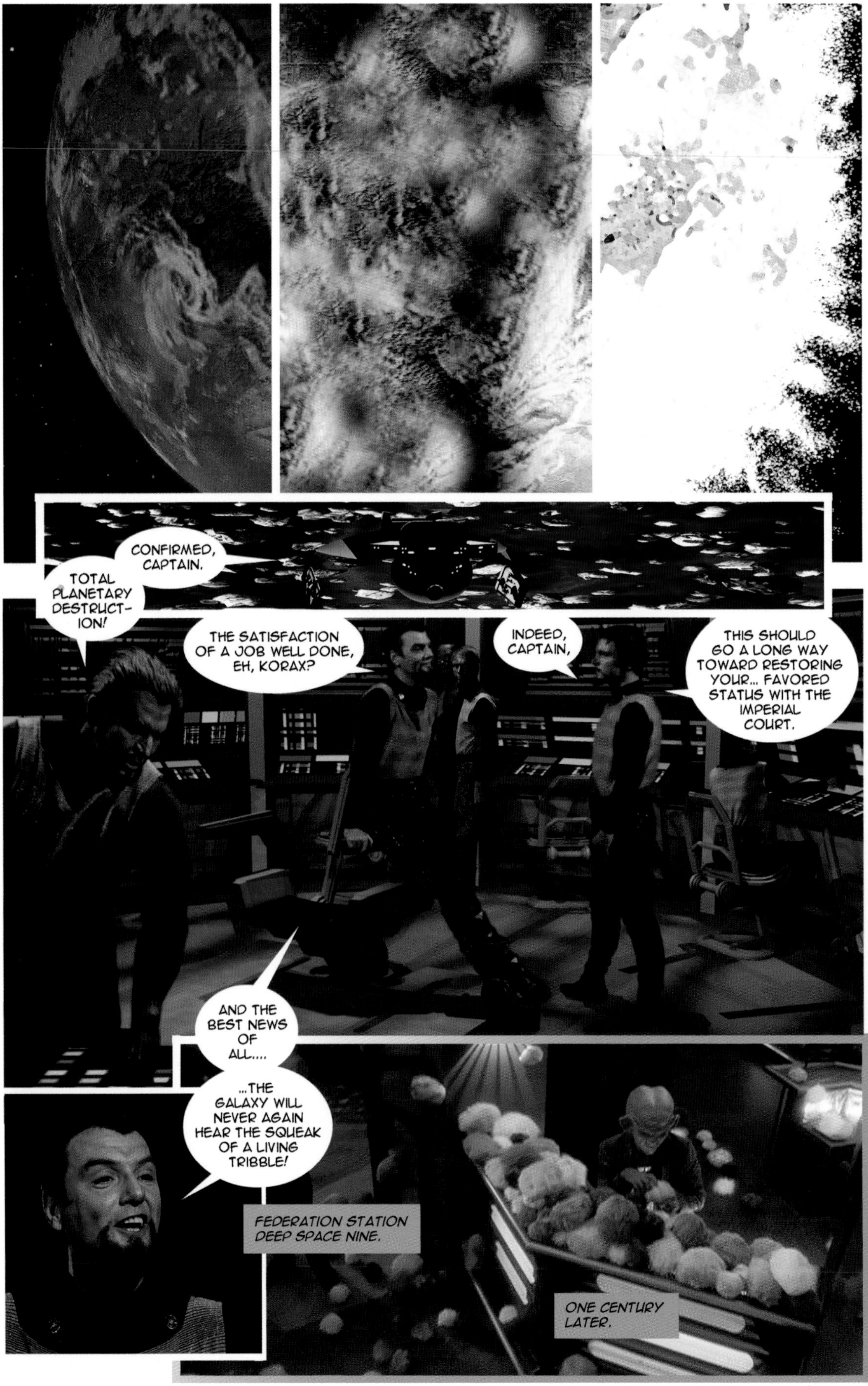

CONFIRMED, CAPTAIN.
TOTAL PLANETARY DESTRUCT-ION!
THE SATISFACTION OF A JOB WELL DONE, EH, KORAX?
INDEED, CAPTAIN,
THIS SHOULD GO A LONG WAY TOWARD RESTORING YOUR... FAVORED STATUS WITH THE IMPERIAL COURT.
AND THE BEST NEWS OF ALL....
...THE GALAXY WILL NEVER AGAIN HEAR THE SQUEAK OF A LIVING TRIBBLE!
FEDERATION STATION DEEP SPACE NINE.
ONE CENTURY LATER.

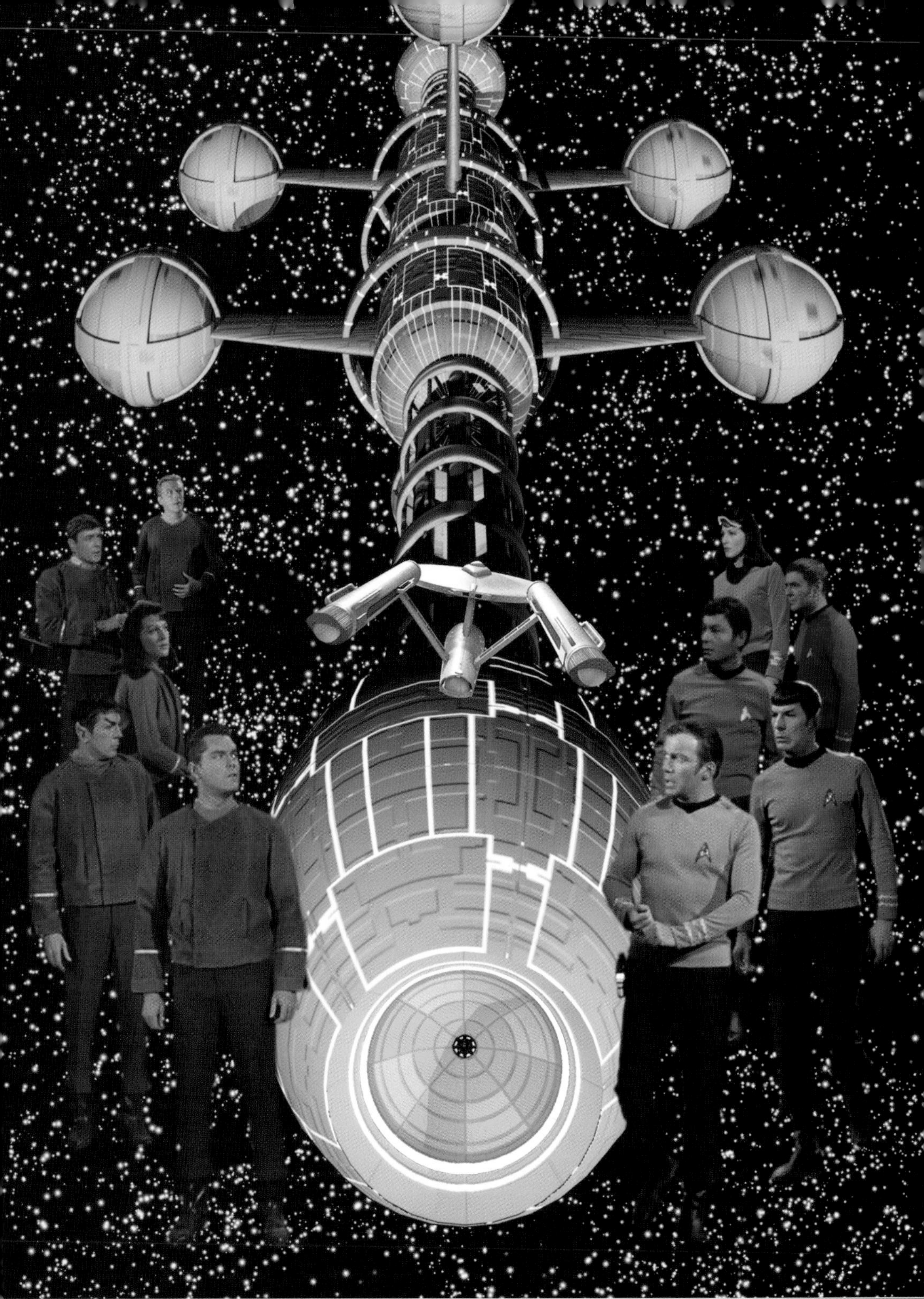

A SCENT OF GHOSTS

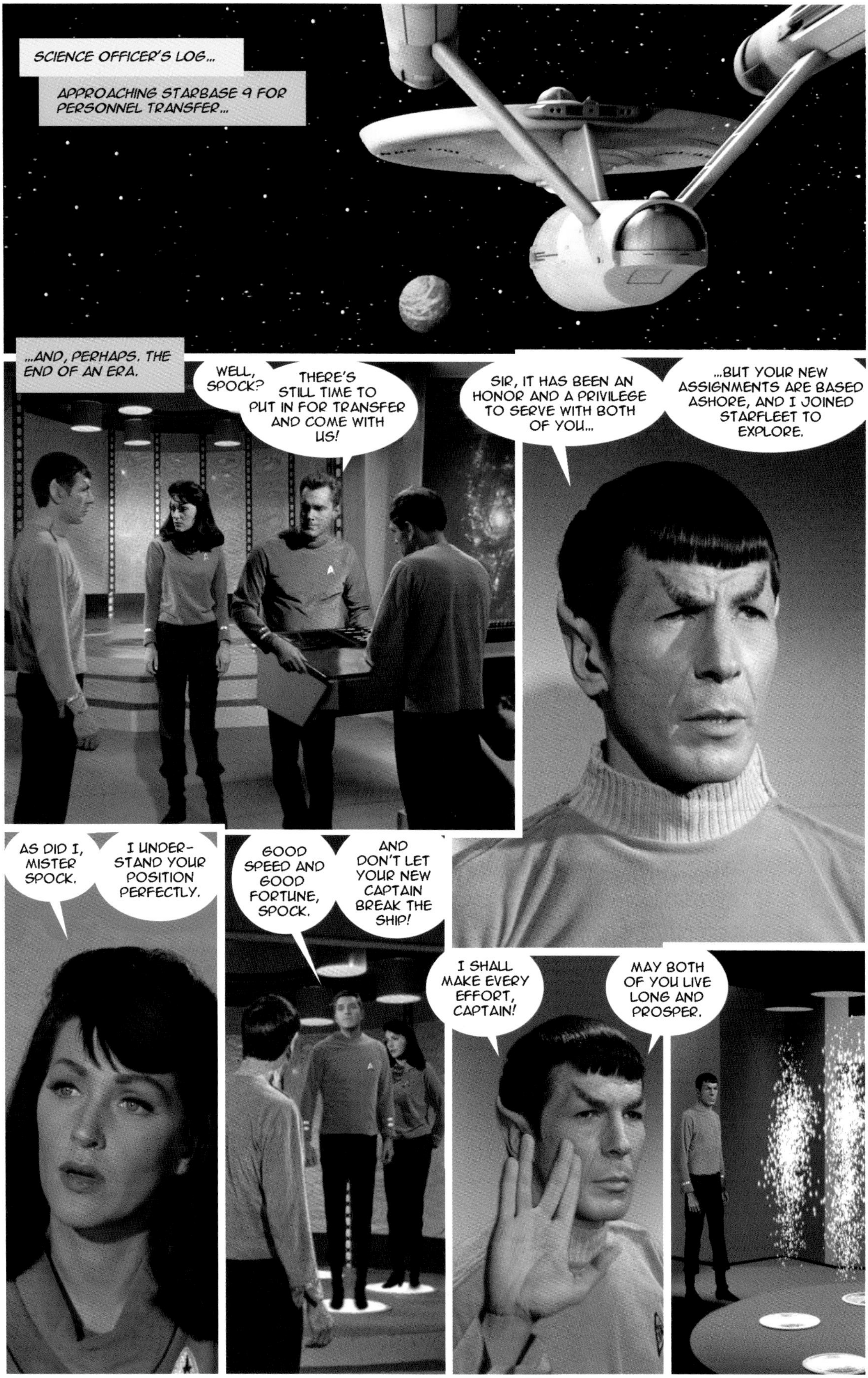

SCIENCE OFFICER'S LOG...
APPROACHING STARBASE 9 FOR PERSONNEL TRANSFER...
...AND, PERHAPS, THE END OF AN ERA.
WELL, SPOCK?
THERE'S STILL TIME TO PUT IN FOR TRANSFER AND COME WITH US!
SIR, IT HAS BEEN AN HONOR AND A PRIVILEGE TO SERVE WITH BOTH OF YOU...
...BUT YOUR NEW ASSIGNMENTS ARE BASED ASHORE, AND I JOINED STARFLEET TO EXPLORE.
AS DID I, MISTER SPOCK.
I UNDERSTAND YOUR POSITION PERFECTLY.
GOOD SPEED AND GOOD FORTUNE, SPOCK.
AND DON'T LET YOUR NEW CAPTAIN BREAK THE SHIP!
I SHALL MAKE EVERY EFFORT, CAPTAIN!
MAY BOTH OF YOU LIVE LONG AND PROSPER.

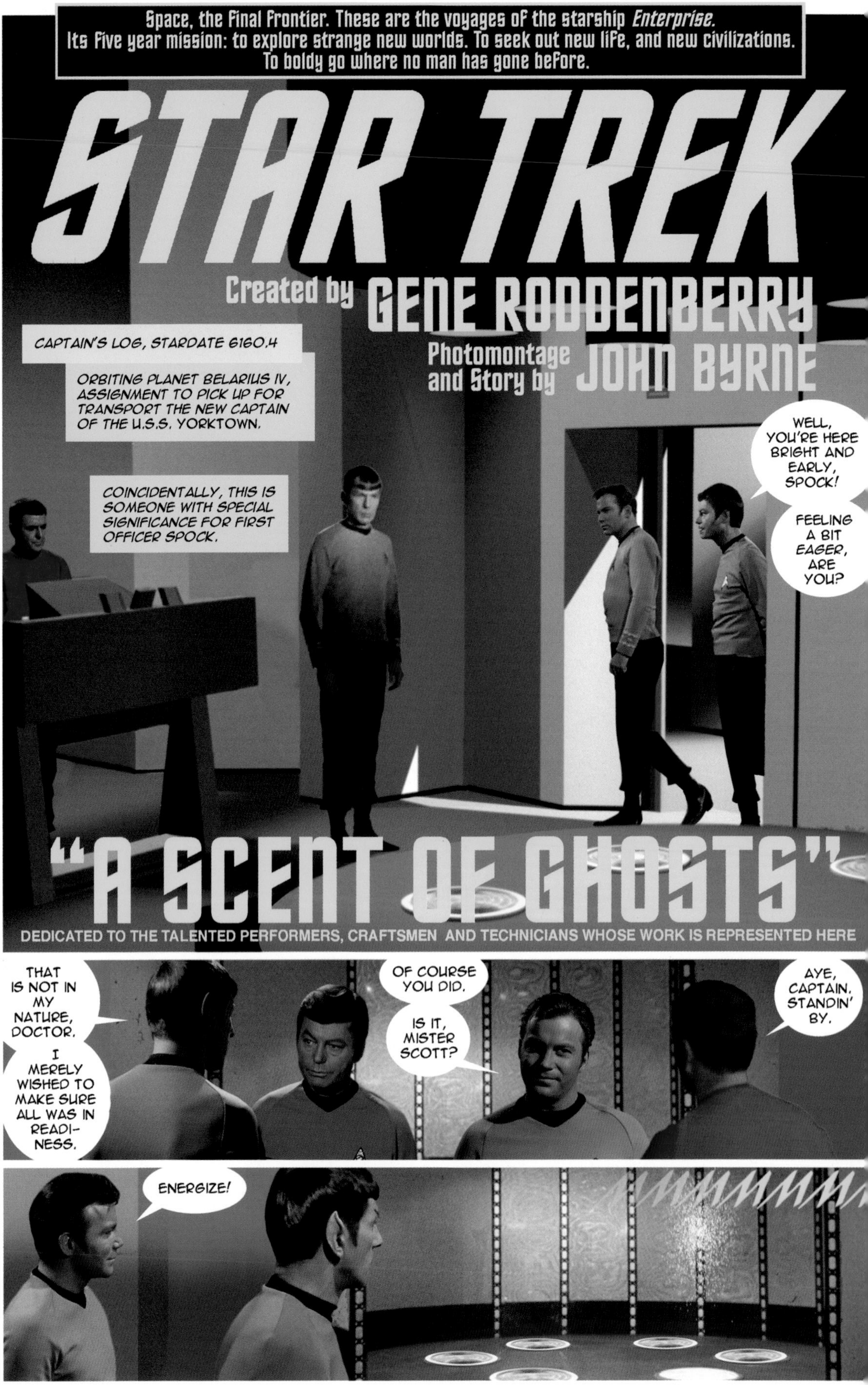
Space, the final frontier. These are the voyages of the starship Enterprise. Its five year mission: to explore strange new worlds. To seek out new life, and new civilizations. To boldy go where no man has gone before.
STAR TREK
Created by GENE RODDENBERRY
Photomontage and Story by JOHN BYRNE
CAPTAIN'S LOG, STARDATE 6160.4
ORBITING PLANET BELARIUS IV, ASSIGNMENT TO PICK UP FOR TRANSPORT THE NEW CAPTAIN OF THE U.S.S. YORKTOWN.
COINCIDENTALLY, THIS IS SOMEONE WITH SPECIAL SIGNIFICANCE FOR FIRST OFFICER SPOCK.
WELL, YOU'RE HERE BRIGHT AND EARLY, SPOCK!
FEELING A BIT EAGER, ARE YOU?
"A SCENT OF GHOSTS"
DEDICATED TO THE TALENTED PERFORMERS, CRAFTSMEN AND TECHNICIANS WHOSE WORK IS REPRESENTED HERE
THAT IS NOT IN MY NATURE, DOCTOR.
I MERELY WISHED TO MAKE SURE ALL WAS IN READI-NESS.
OF COURSE YOU DID.
IS IT, MISTER SCOTT?
AYE, CAPTAIN. STANDIN' BY.
ENERGIZE!

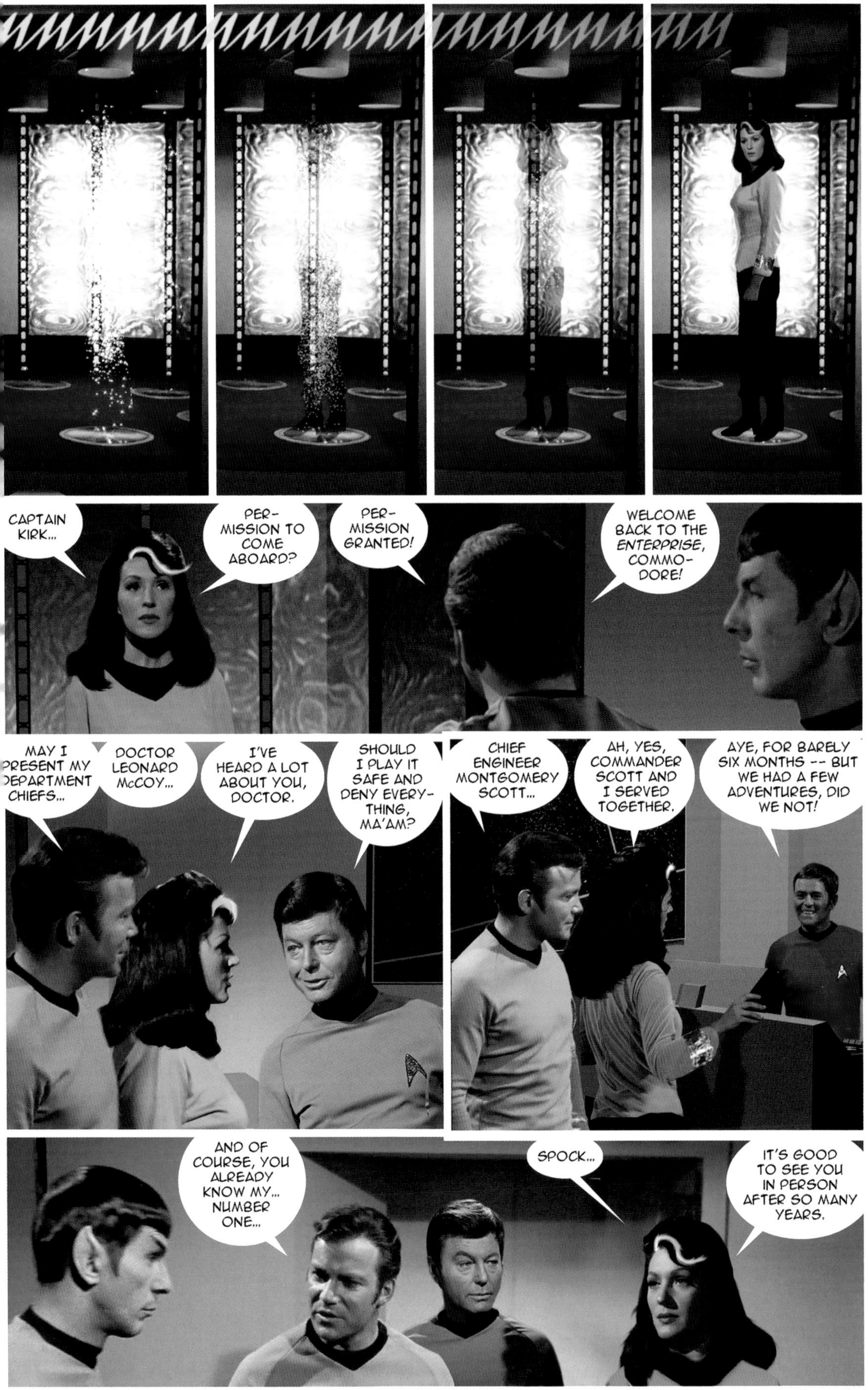
CAPTAIN KIRK...
PER-MISSION TO COME ABOARD?
PER-MISSION GRANTED!
WELCOME BACK TO THE *ENTERPRISE*, COMMO-DORE!
MAY I PRESENT MY DEPARTMENT CHIEFS...
DOCTOR LEONARD McCOY...
I'VE HEARD A LOT ABOUT YOU, DOCTOR.
SHOULD I PLAY IT SAFE AND DENY EVERY-THING, MA'AM?
CHIEF ENGINEER MONTGOMERY SCOTT...
AH, YES, COMMANDER SCOTT AND I SERVED TOGETHER.
AYE, FOR BARELY SIX MONTHS -- BUT WE HAD A FEW ADVENTURES, DID WE NOT!
AND OF COURSE, YOU ALREADY KNOW MY... NUMBER ONE...
SPOCK...
IT'S GOOD TO SEE YOU IN PERSON AFTER SO MANY YEARS.

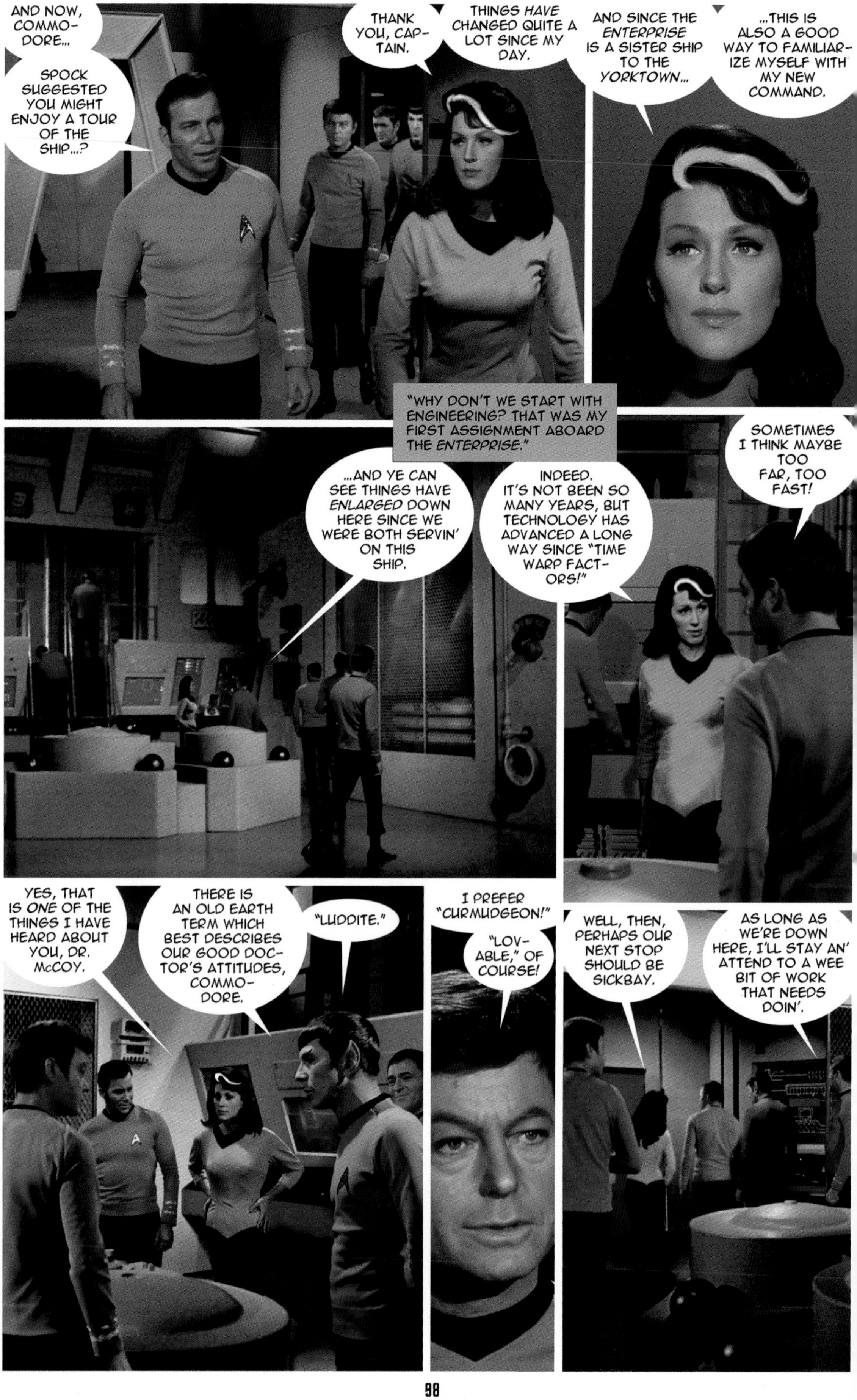
AND NOW, COMMODORE...
SPOCK SUGGESTED YOU MIGHT ENJOY A TOUR OF THE SHIP...?
THANK YOU, CAPTAIN.
THINGS *HAVE* CHANGED QUITE A LOT SINCE MY DAY.
AND SINCE THE *ENTERPRISE* IS A SISTER SHIP TO THE *YORKTOWN*...
...THIS IS ALSO A GOOD WAY TO FAMILIARIZE MYSELF WITH MY NEW COMMAND.
"WHY DON'T WE START WITH ENGINEERING? THAT WAS MY FIRST ASSIGNMENT ABOARD THE *ENTERPRISE*."
...AND YE CAN SEE THINGS HAVE *ENLARGED* DOWN HERE SINCE WE WERE BOTH SERVIN' ON THIS SHIP.
INDEED. IT'S NOT BEEN SO MANY YEARS, BUT TECHNOLOGY HAS ADVANCED A LONG WAY SINCE "TIME WARP FACTORS!"
SOMETIMES I THINK MAYBE TOO FAR, TOO FAST!
YES, THAT IS *ONE* OF THE THINGS I HAVE HEARD ABOUT YOU, DR. McCOY.
THERE IS AN OLD EARTH TERM WHICH BEST DESCRIBES OUR GOOD DOCTOR'S ATTITUDES, COMMODORE.
"LUDDITE."
I PREFER "CURMUDGEON!"
"LOVABLE," OF COURSE!
WELL, THEN, PERHAPS OUR NEXT STOP SHOULD BE SICKBAY.
AS LONG AS WE'RE DOWN HERE, I'LL STAY AN' ATTEND TO A WEE BIT OF WORK THAT NEEDS DOIN'.

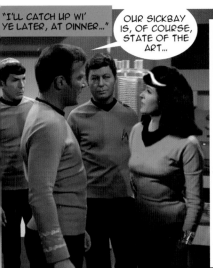

"I'LL CATCH UP WI' YE LATER, AT DINNER..."

OUR SICKBAY IS, OF COURSE, STATE OF THE ART...

...THOUGH DR. MCCOY HAS BEEN KNOWN TO HAVE A TRICK OR TWO OF HIS OWN.

A FEW!

I CAN'T BEGIN TO COUNT THE NUMBER OF LIVES HE'S SAVED.

IMPRESSIVE. BUT, DOCTOR, I DO NOT SEE ANY SCALPELS OR HACKSAWS...?

ONLY MY ANTIQUES, MA'AM.

ARE YOU SAYING I CONTRADICT MYSELF?

VERY WELL THEN I CONTRADICT MYSELF,

I AM LARGE, I CONTAIN MULTI-TUDES!

WELL DONE, DOCTOR!

I SURRENDER TO ANYONE WHO CAN CALL WALT WHITMAN TO HIS DEFENSE!

BRIDGE TO CAPTAIN KIRK.

KIRK HERE.

WHAT IS IT, LIEUTEN-ANT?

SIR, I'M PICKING UP A SHIP'S AUTOMATED EMERGENCY BEACON.

EMBEDDED REGISTRATION IDENTIFIES IT AS THE YORKTOWN.

KEPTIN... LONG RANGE SCANS CONFIRM IT IS THE YORKTOWN.

SHE IS UNDER POWER, BUT I AM DETECTING NO NAWIGATION BEAM.

SHE IS NOT TRANS-MITTING HER COURSE OR COVORDIN-ATES.

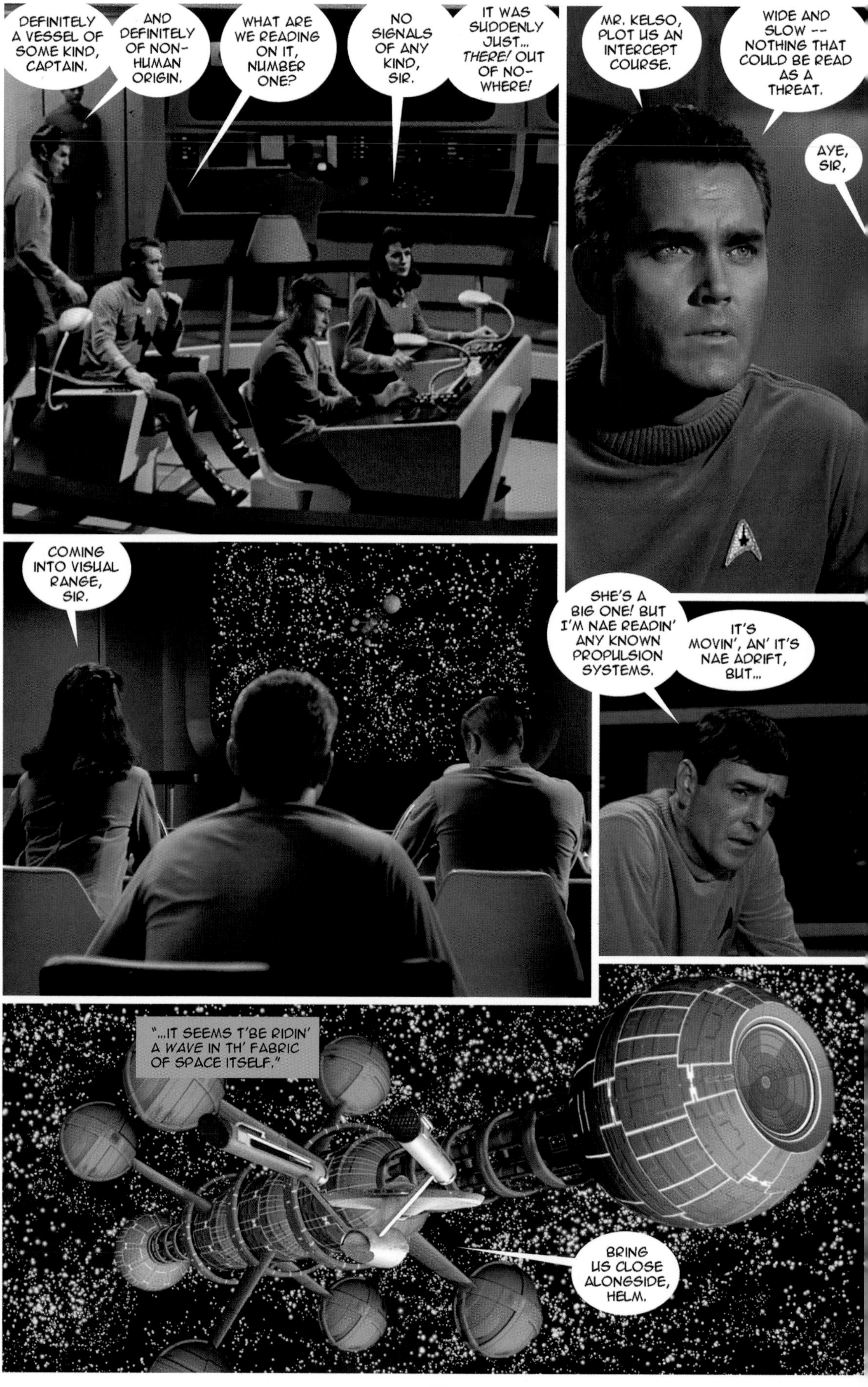
DEFINITELY A VESSEL OF SOME KIND, CAPTAIN.
AND DEFINITELY OF NON-HUMAN ORIGIN.
WHAT ARE WE READING ON IT, NUMBER ONE?
NO SIGNALS OF ANY KIND, SIR.
IT WAS SUDDENLY JUST... *THERE!* OUT OF NO-WHERE!
MR. KELSO, PLOT US AN INTERCEPT COURSE.
WIDE AND SLOW -- NOTHING THAT COULD BE READ AS A THREAT.
AYE, SIR,
COMING INTO VISUAL RANGE, SIR.
SHE'S A BIG ONE! BUT I'M NAE READIN' ANY KNOWN PROPULSION SYSTEMS.
IT'S MOVIN', AN' IT'S NAE ADRIFT, BUT...
"...IT SEEMS T'BE RIDIN' A *WAVE* IN TH' FABRIC OF SPACE ITSELF."
BRING US CLOSE ALONGSIDE, HELM.

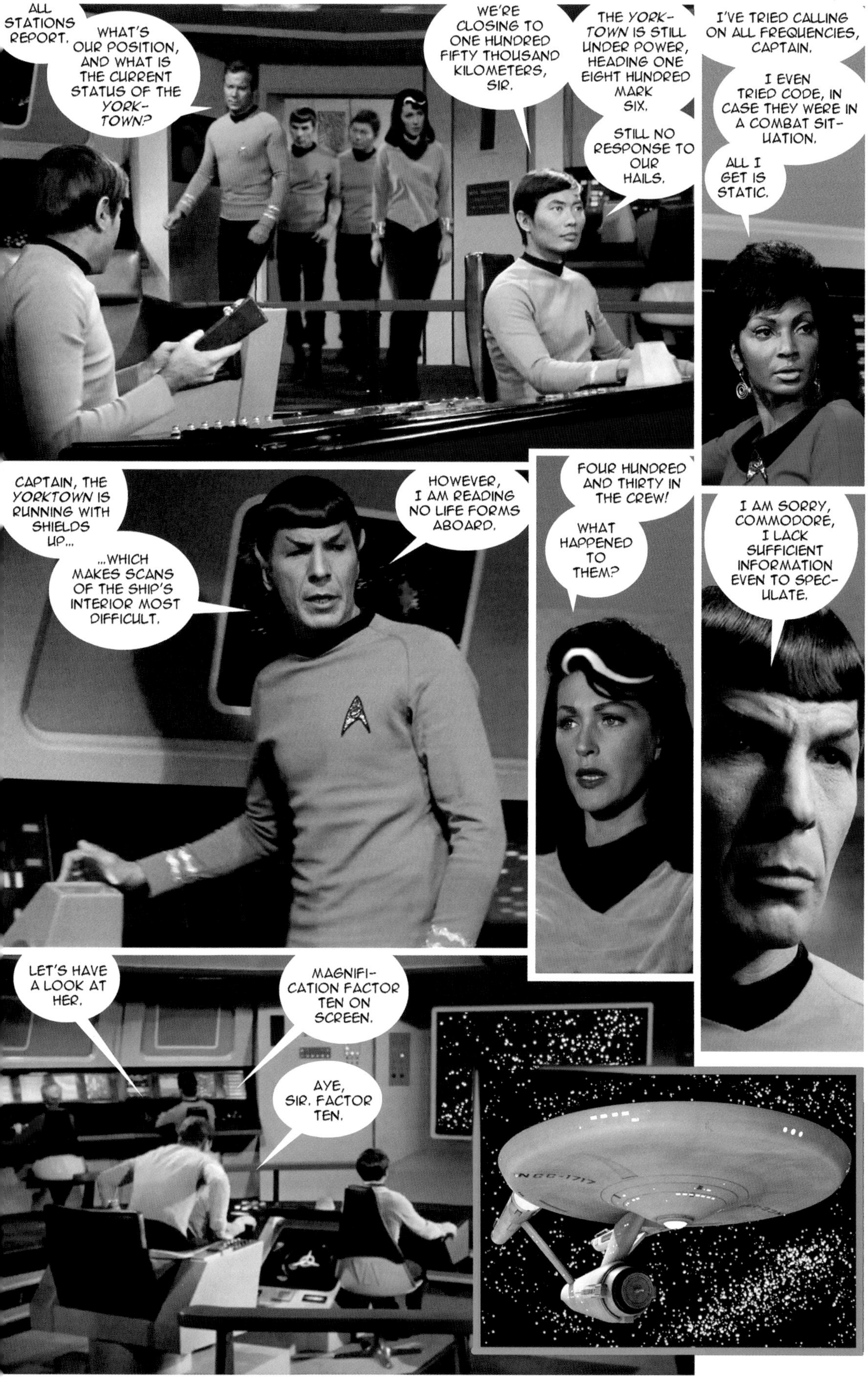
ALL STATIONS REPORT.
WHAT'S OUR POSITION, AND WHAT IS THE CURRENT STATUS OF THE *YORK-TOWN?*
WE'RE CLOSING TO ONE HUNDRED FIFTY THOUSAND KILOMETERS, SIR.
THE *YORK-TOWN* IS STILL UNDER POWER, HEADING ONE EIGHT HUNDRED MARK SIX.
STILL NO RESPONSE TO OUR HAILS.
I'VE TRIED CALLING ON ALL FREQUENCIES, CAPTAIN.
I EVEN TRIED CODE, IN CASE THEY WERE IN A COMBAT SIT-UATION.
ALL I GET IS STATIC.
CAPTAIN, THE *YORKTOWN* IS RUNNING WITH SHIELDS UP...
...WHICH MAKES SCANS OF THE SHIP'S INTERIOR MOST DIFFICULT.
HOWEVER, I AM READING NO LIFE FORMS ABOARD.
FOUR HUNDRED AND THIRTY IN THE CREW!
WHAT HAPPENED TO THEM?
I AM SORRY, COMMODORE, I LACK SUFFICIENT INFORMATION EVEN TO SPEC-ULATE.
LET'S HAVE A LOOK AT HER.
MAGNIFI-CATION FACTOR TEN ON SCREEN.
AYE, SIR. FACTOR TEN.

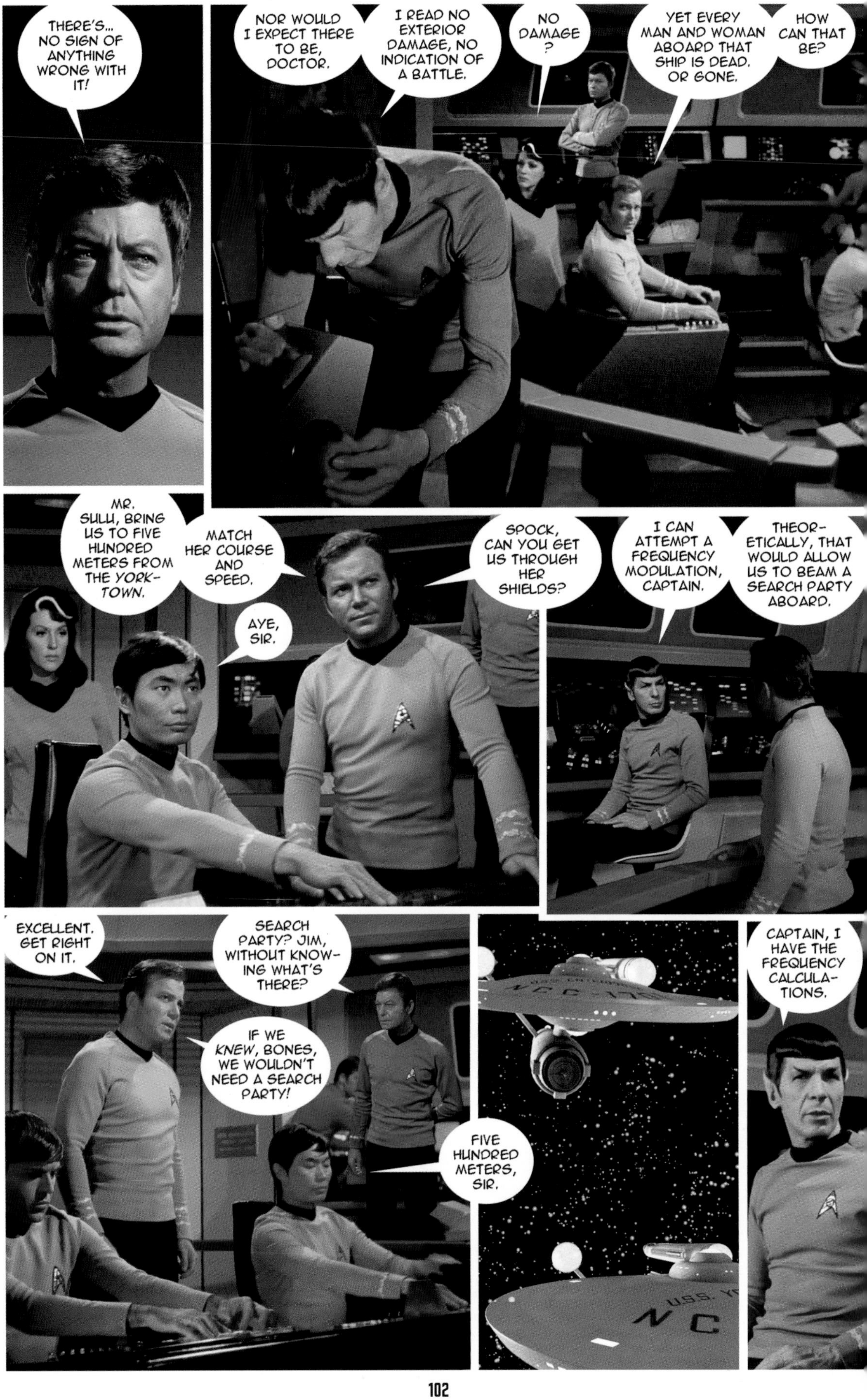
THERE'S... NO SIGN OF ANYTHING WRONG WITH IT!
NOR WOULD I EXPECT THERE TO BE, DOCTOR.
I READ NO EXTERIOR DAMAGE, NO INDICATION OF A BATTLE.
NO DAMAGE?
YET EVERY MAN AND WOMAN ABOARD THAT SHIP IS DEAD. OR GONE.
HOW CAN THAT BE?
MR. SULU, BRING US TO FIVE HUNDRED METERS FROM THE *YORK-TOWN.*
MATCH HER COURSE AND SPEED.
AYE, SIR.
SPOCK, CAN YOU GET US THROUGH HER SHIELDS?
I CAN ATTEMPT A FREQUENCY MODULATION, CAPTAIN.
THEOR-ETICALLY, THAT WOULD ALLOW US TO BEAM A SEARCH PARTY ABOARD.
EXCELLENT. GET RIGHT ON IT.
SEARCH PARTY? JIM, WITHOUT KNOW-ING WHAT'S THERE?
IF WE *KNEW*, BONES, WE WOULDN'T NEED A SEARCH PARTY!
FIVE HUNDRED METERS, SIR.
CAPTAIN, I HAVE THE FREQUENCY CALCULA-TIONS.

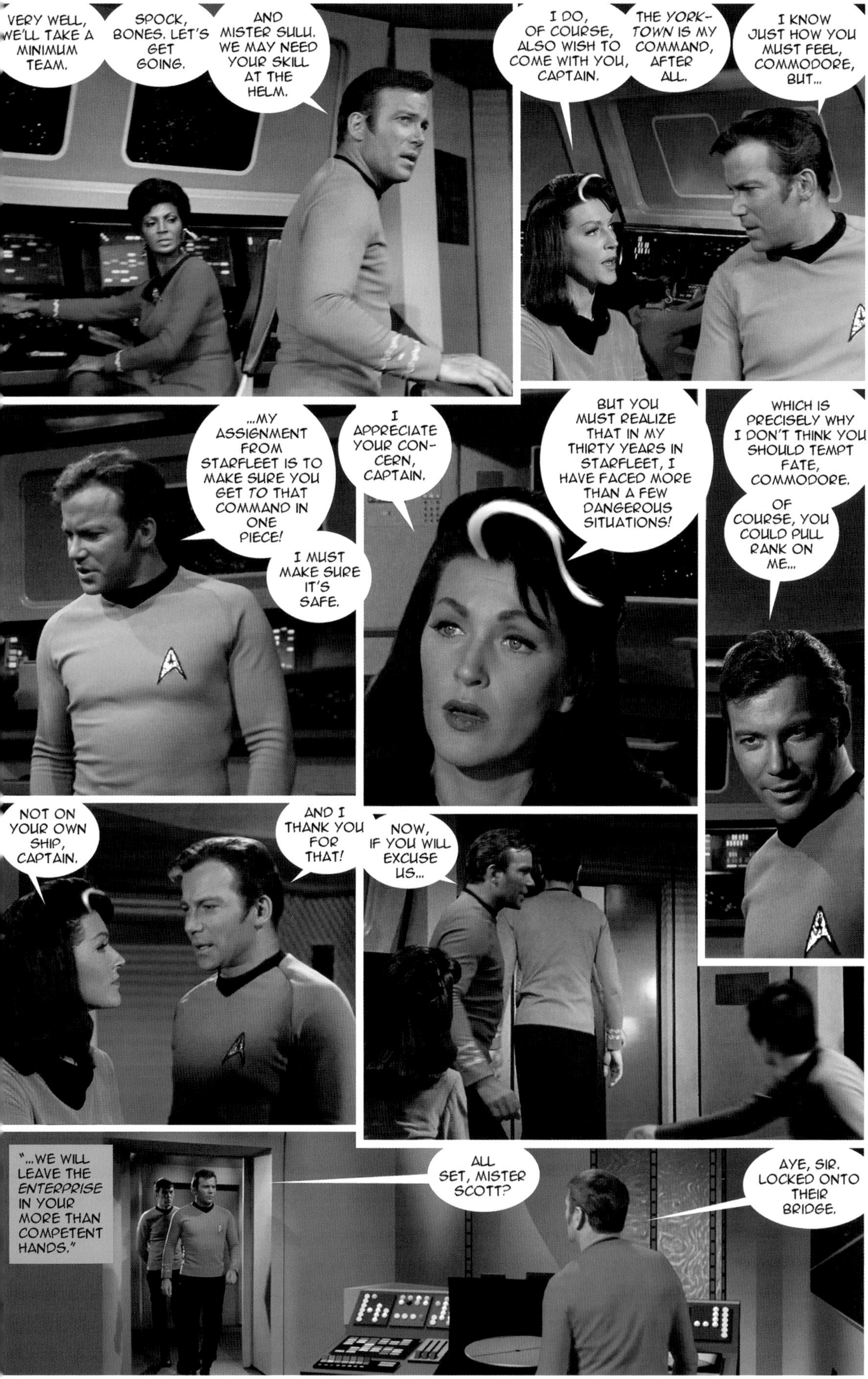

VERY WELL, WE'LL TAKE A MINIMUM TEAM.
SPOCK, BONES. LET'S GET GOING.
AND MISTER SULU. WE MAY NEED YOUR SKILL AT THE HELM.
I DO, OF COURSE, ALSO WISH TO COME WITH YOU, CAPTAIN.
THE *YORKTOWN* IS MY COMMAND, AFTER ALL.
I KNOW JUST HOW YOU MUST FEEL, COMMODORE, BUT...
...MY ASSIGNMENT FROM STARFLEET IS TO MAKE SURE YOU GET *TO* THAT COMMAND IN ONE PIECE!
I MUST MAKE SURE IT'S SAFE.
I APPRECIATE YOUR CONCERN, CAPTAIN.
BUT YOU MUST REALIZE THAT IN MY THIRTY YEARS IN STARFLEET, I HAVE FACED MORE THAN A FEW DANGEROUS SITUATIONS!
WHICH IS PRECISELY WHY I DON'T THINK YOU SHOULD TEMPT FATE, COMMODORE.
OF COURSE, YOU COULD PULL RANK ON ME...
NOT ON YOUR OWN SHIP, CAPTAIN.
AND I THANK YOU FOR THAT!
NOW, IF YOU WILL EXCUSE US...
"...WE WILL LEAVE THE *ENTERPRISE* IN YOUR MORE THAN COMPETENT HANDS."
ALL SET, MISTER SCOTT?
AYE, SIR. LOCKED ONTO THEIR BRIDGE.

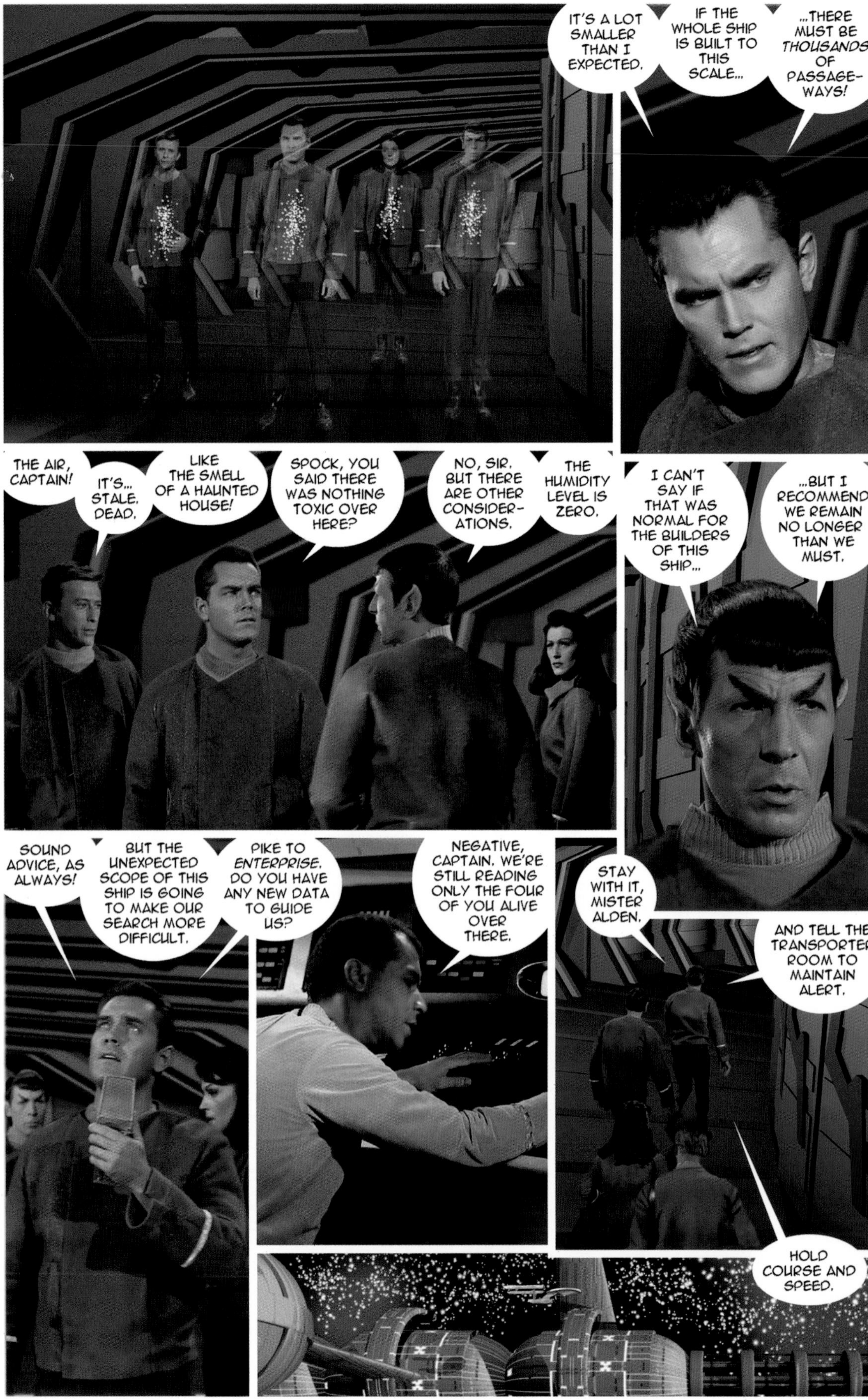

IT'S A LOT SMALLER THAN I EXPECTED.
IF THE WHOLE SHIP IS BUILT TO THIS SCALE...
...THERE MUST BE THOUSANDS OF PASSAGE-WAYS!
THE AIR, CAPTAIN!
IT'S... STALE. DEAD.
LIKE THE SMELL OF A HAUNTED HOUSE!
SPOCK, YOU SAID THERE WAS NOTHING TOXIC OVER HERE?
NO, SIR. BUT THERE ARE OTHER CONSIDER-ATIONS.
THE HUMIDITY LEVEL IS ZERO.
I CAN'T SAY IF THAT WAS NORMAL FOR THE BUILDERS OF THIS SHIP...
...BUT I RECOMMEND WE REMAIN NO LONGER THAN WE MUST.
SOUND ADVICE, AS ALWAYS!
BUT THE UNEXPECTED SCOPE OF THIS SHIP IS GOING TO MAKE OUR SEARCH MORE DIFFICULT.
PIKE TO ENTERPRISE. DO YOU HAVE ANY NEW DATA TO GUIDE US?
NEGATIVE, CAPTAIN. WE'RE STILL READING ONLY THE FOUR OF YOU ALIVE OVER THERE.
STAY WITH IT, MISTER ALDEN.
AND TELL THE TRANSPORTER ROOM TO MAINTAIN ALERT.
HOLD COURSE AND SPEED.

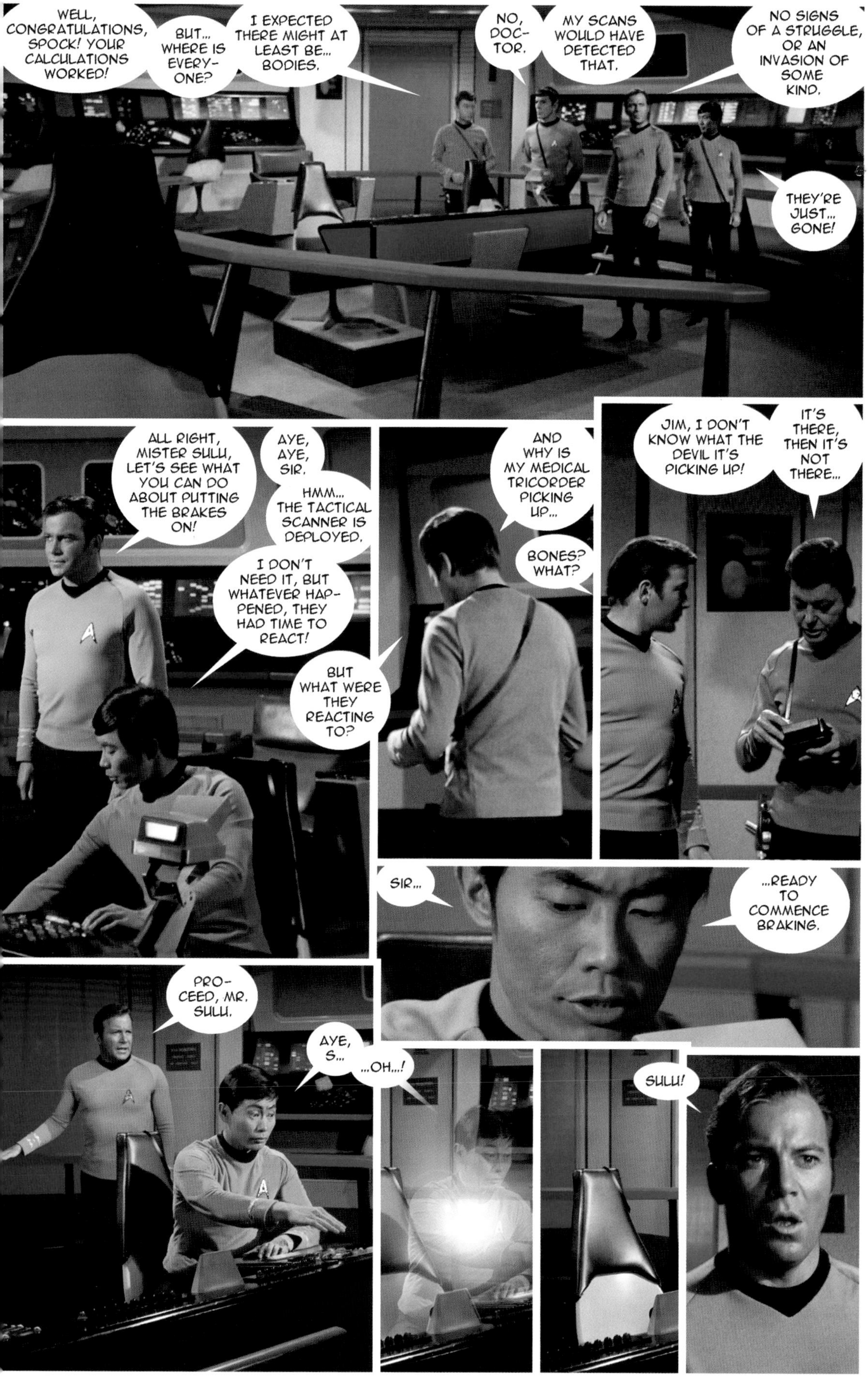
WELL, CONGRATULATIONS, SPOCK! YOUR CALCULATIONS WORKED!
BUT... WHERE IS EVERYONE?
I EXPECTED THERE MIGHT AT LEAST BE... BODIES.
NO, DOCTOR.
MY SCANS WOULD HAVE DETECTED THAT.
NO SIGNS OF A STRUGGLE, OR AN INVASION OF SOME KIND.
THEY'RE JUST... GONE!
ALL RIGHT, MISTER SULU, LET'S SEE WHAT YOU CAN DO ABOUT PUTTING THE BRAKES ON!
AYE, AYE, SIR.
HMM... THE TACTICAL SCANNER IS DEPLOYED.
I DON'T NEED IT, BUT WHATEVER HAPPENED, THEY HAD TIME TO REACT!
BUT WHAT WERE THEY REACTING TO?
AND WHY IS MY MEDICAL TRICORDER PICKING UP...
BONES? WHAT?
JIM, I DON'T KNOW WHAT THE DEVIL IT'S PICKING UP!
IT'S THERE, THEN IT'S NOT THERE...
SIR...
...READY TO COMMENCE BRAKING.
PROCEED, MR. SULU.
AYE, S...
...OH...!
SULU!

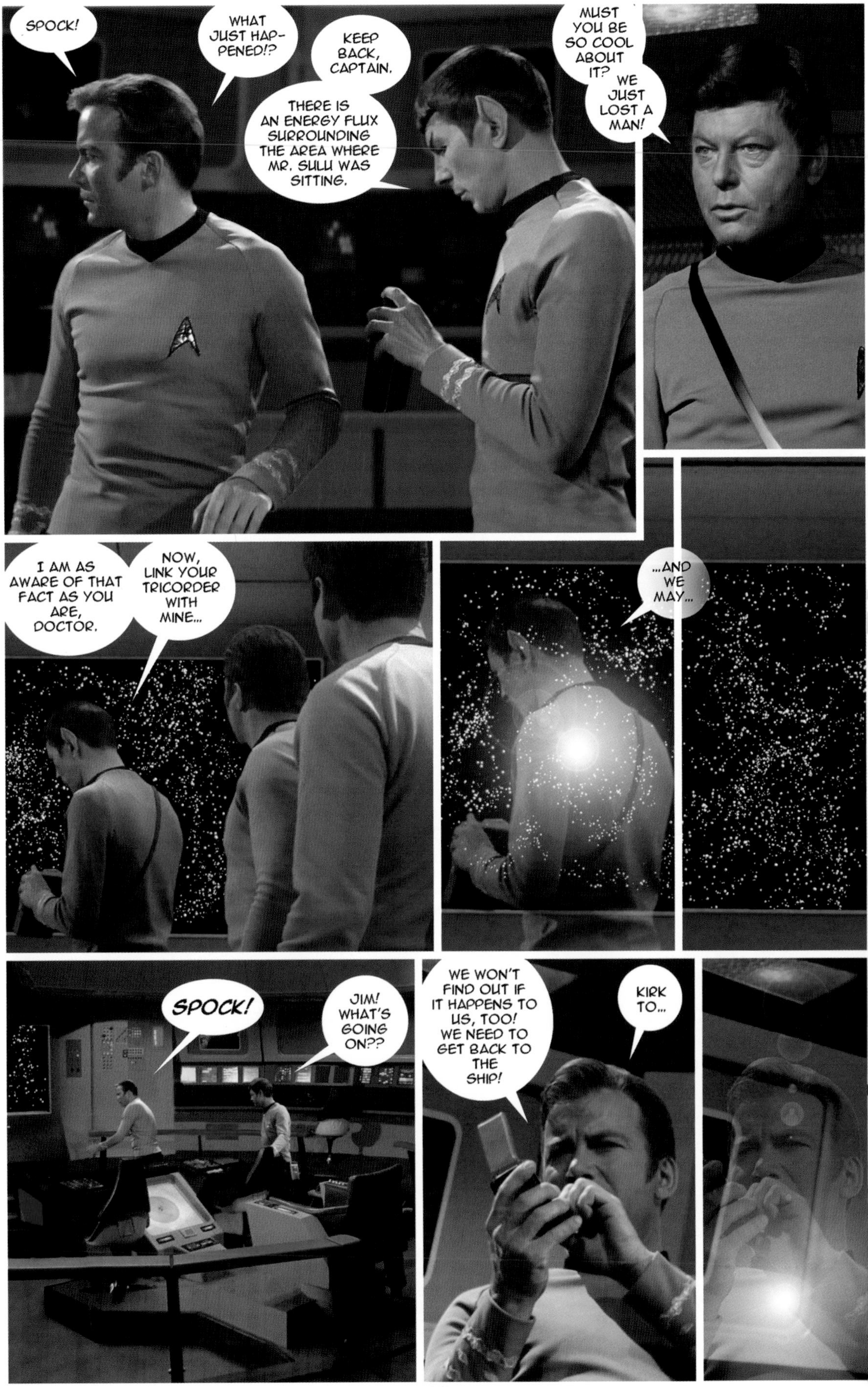

SPOCK!
WHAT JUST HAP-PENED!?
KEEP BACK, CAPTAIN.
THERE IS AN ENERGY FLUX SURROUNDING THE AREA WHERE MR. SULU WAS SITTING.
MUST YOU BE SO COOL ABOUT IT?
WE JUST LOST A MAN!
I AM AS AWARE OF THAT FACT AS YOU ARE, DOCTOR.
NOW, LINK YOUR TRICORDER WITH MINE...
...AND WE MAY...
SPOCK!
JIM! WHAT'S GOING ON??
WE WON'T FIND OUT IF IT HAPPENS TO US, TOO! WE NEED TO GET BACK TO THE SHIP!
KIRK TO...

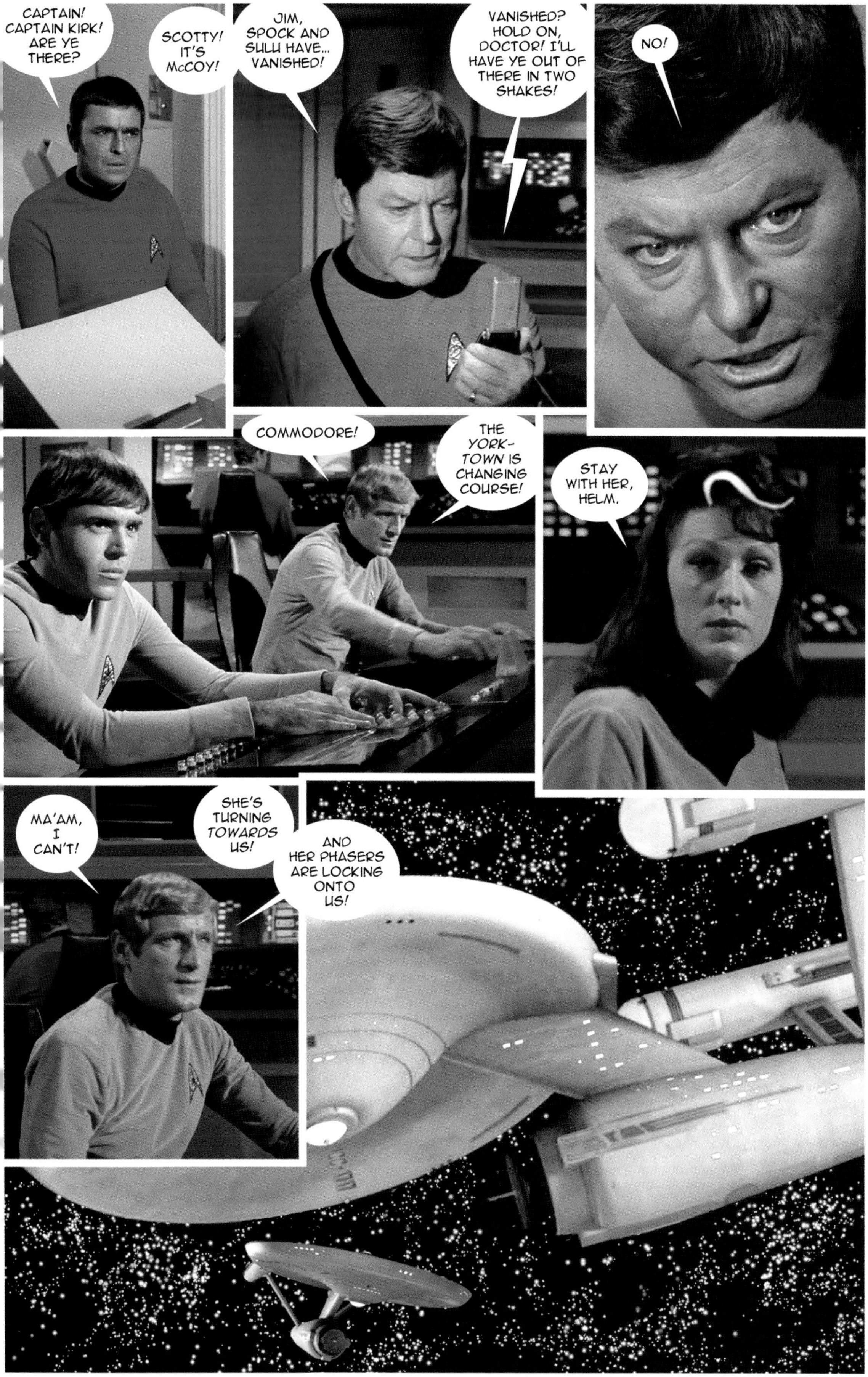
CAPTAIN! CAPTAIN KIRK! ARE YE THERE?
SCOTTY! IT'S McCOY!
JIM, SPOCK AND SULU HAVE... VANISHED!
VANISHED? HOLD ON, DOCTOR! I'LL HAVE YE OUT OF THERE IN TWO SHAKES!
NO!
COMMODORE!
THE *YORK-TOWN* IS CHANGING COURSE!
STAY WITH HER, HELM.
MA'AM, I CAN'T!
SHE'S TURNING *TOWARDS* US!
AND HER PHASERS ARE LOCKING ONTO US!

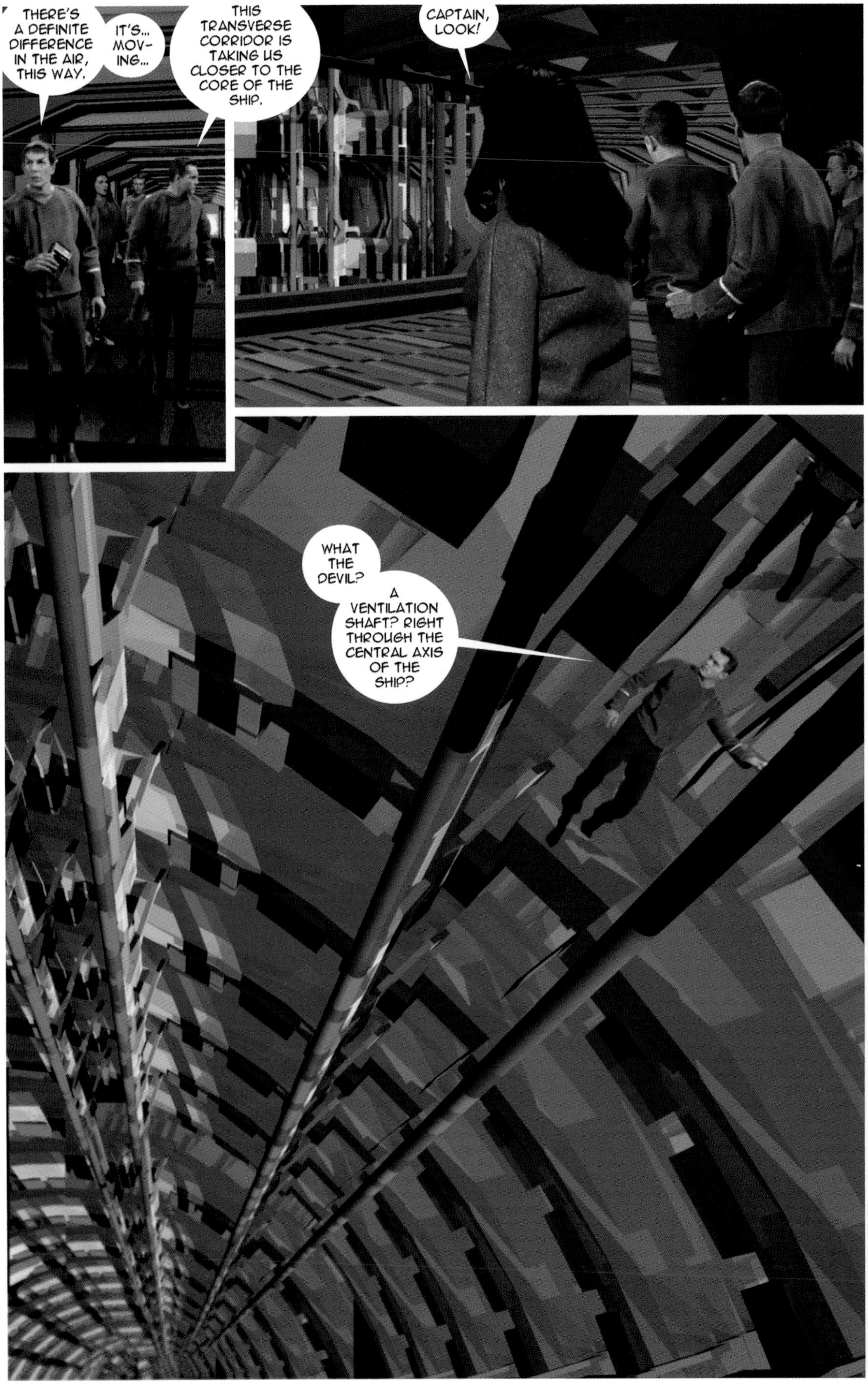
THERE'S A DEFINITE DIFFERENCE IN THE AIR, THIS WAY.
IT'S... MOV-ING...
THIS TRANSVERSE CORRIDOR IS TAKING US CLOSER TO THE CORE OF THE SHIP.
CAPTAIN, LOOK!
WHAT THE DEVIL?
A VENTILATION SHAFT? RIGHT THROUGH THE CENTRAL AXIS OF THE SHIP?

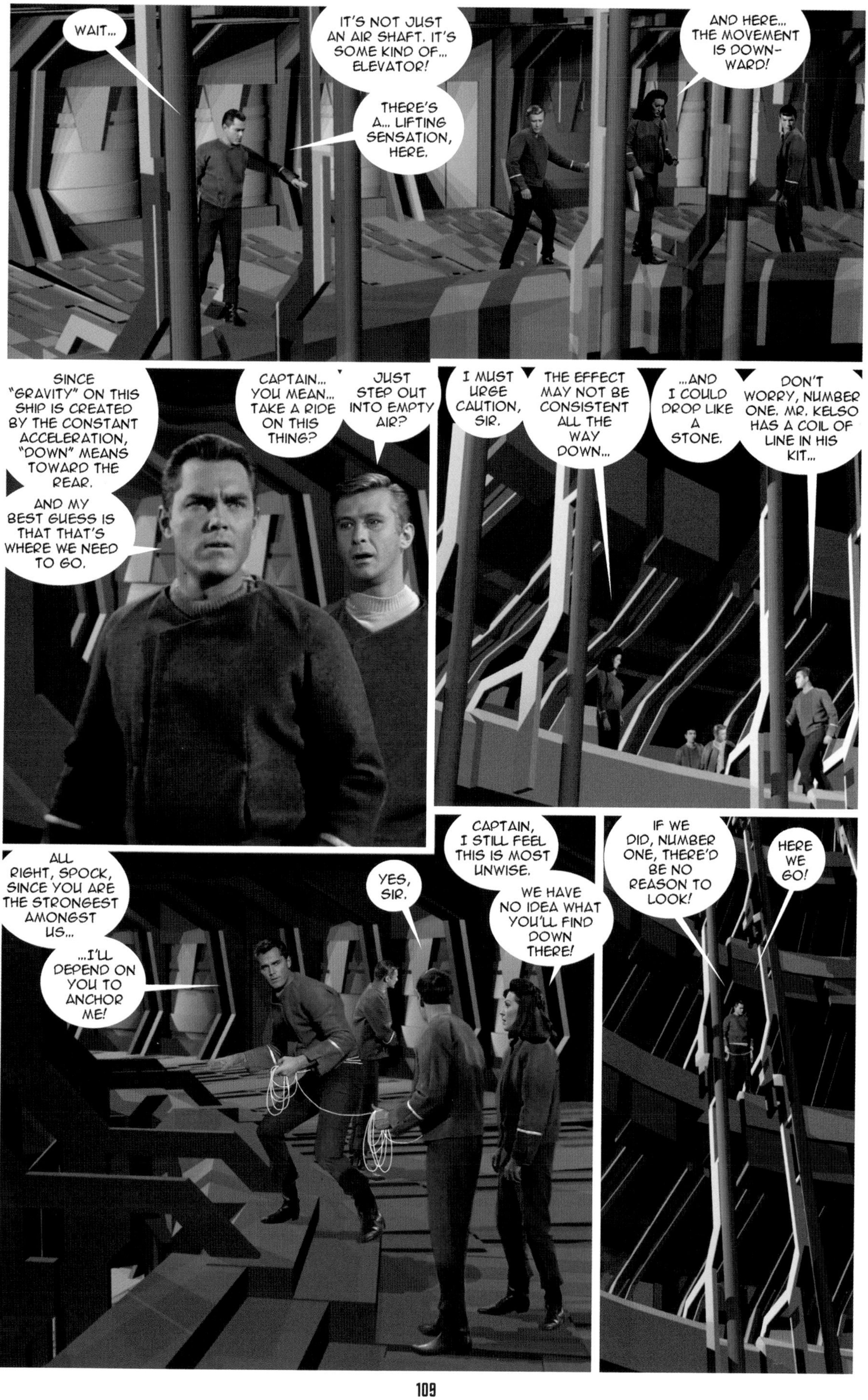
WAIT...
IT'S NOT JUST AN AIR SHAFT. IT'S SOME KIND OF... ELEVATOR!
THERE'S A... LIFTING SENSATION, HERE.
AND HERE... THE MOVEMENT IS DOWNWARD!
SINCE "GRAVITY" ON THIS SHIP IS CREATED BY THE CONSTANT ACCELERATION, "DOWN" MEANS TOWARD THE REAR.
AND MY BEST GUESS IS THAT THAT'S WHERE WE NEED TO GO.
CAPTAIN... YOU MEAN... TAKE A RIDE ON THIS THING?
JUST STEP OUT INTO EMPTY AIR?
I MUST URGE CAUTION, SIR.
THE EFFECT MAY NOT BE CONSISTENT ALL THE WAY DOWN...
...AND I COULD DROP LIKE A STONE.
DON'T WORRY, NUMBER ONE. MR. KELSO HAS A COIL OF LINE IN HIS KIT...
ALL RIGHT, SPOCK, SINCE YOU ARE THE STRONGEST AMONGST US...
...I'LL DEPEND ON YOU TO ANCHOR ME!
YES, SIR.
CAPTAIN, I STILL FEEL THIS IS MOST UNWISE.
WE HAVE NO IDEA WHAT YOU'LL FIND DOWN THERE!
IF WE DID, NUMBER ONE, THERE'D BE NO REASON TO LOOK!
HERE WE GO!

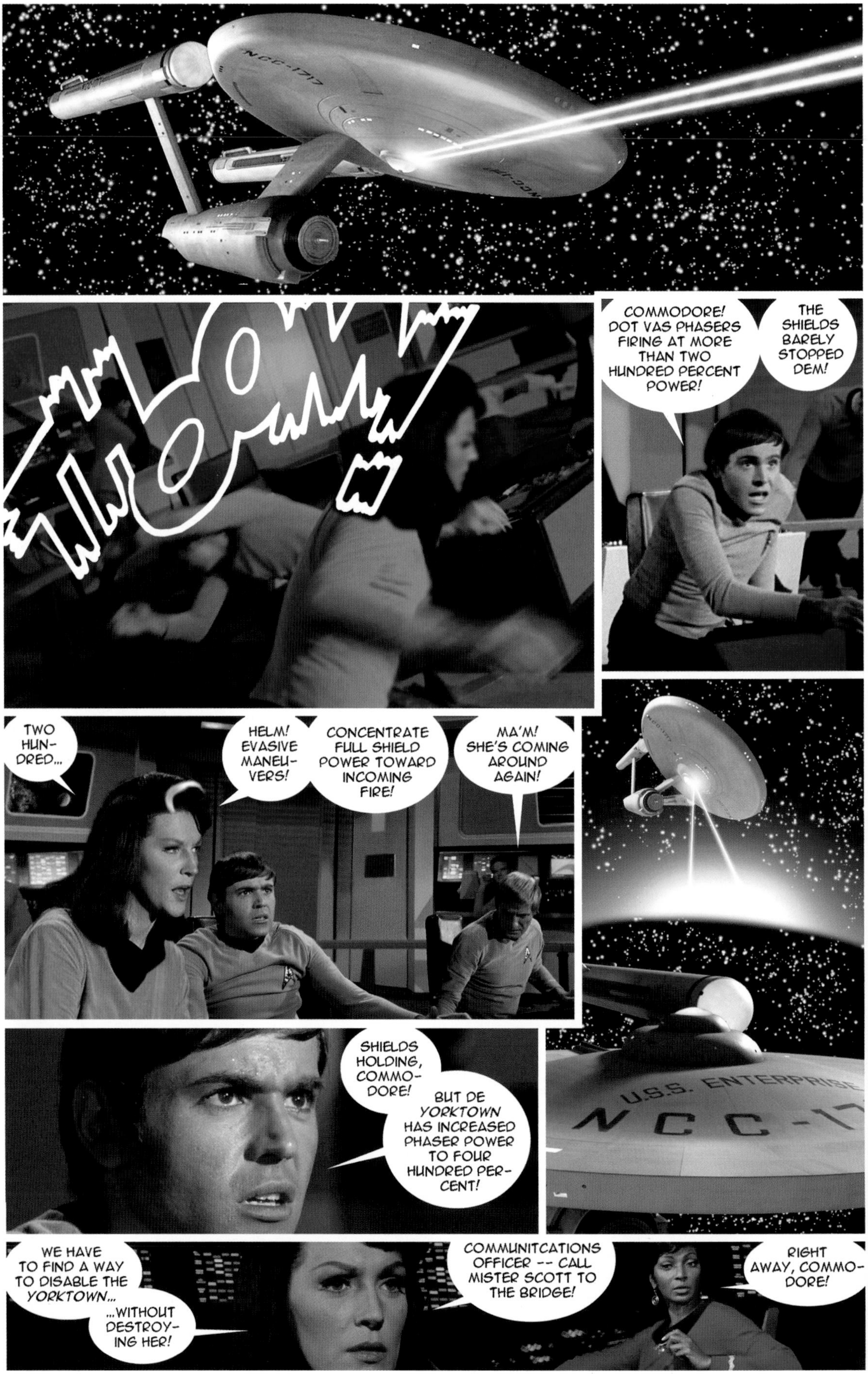
WHOOM!
COMMODORE! DOT VAS PHASERS FIRING AT MORE THAN TWO HUNDRED PERCENT POWER!
THE SHIELDS BARELY STOPPED DEM!
TWO HUN-DRED...
HELM! EVASIVE MANEU-VERS!
CONCENTRATE FULL SHIELD POWER TOWARD INCOMING FIRE!
MA'M! SHE'S COMING AROUND AGAIN!
U.S.S. ENTERPRISE
NCC-17
SHIELDS HOLDING, COMMO-DORE!
BUT DE YORKTOWN HAS INCREASED PHASER POWER TO FOUR HUNDRED PER-CENT!
WE HAVE TO FIND A WAY TO DISABLE THE YORKTOWN...
...WITHOUT DESTROY-ING HER!
COMMUNITCATIONS OFFICER -- CALL MISTER SCOTT TO THE BRIDGE!
RIGHT AWAY, COMMO-DORE!

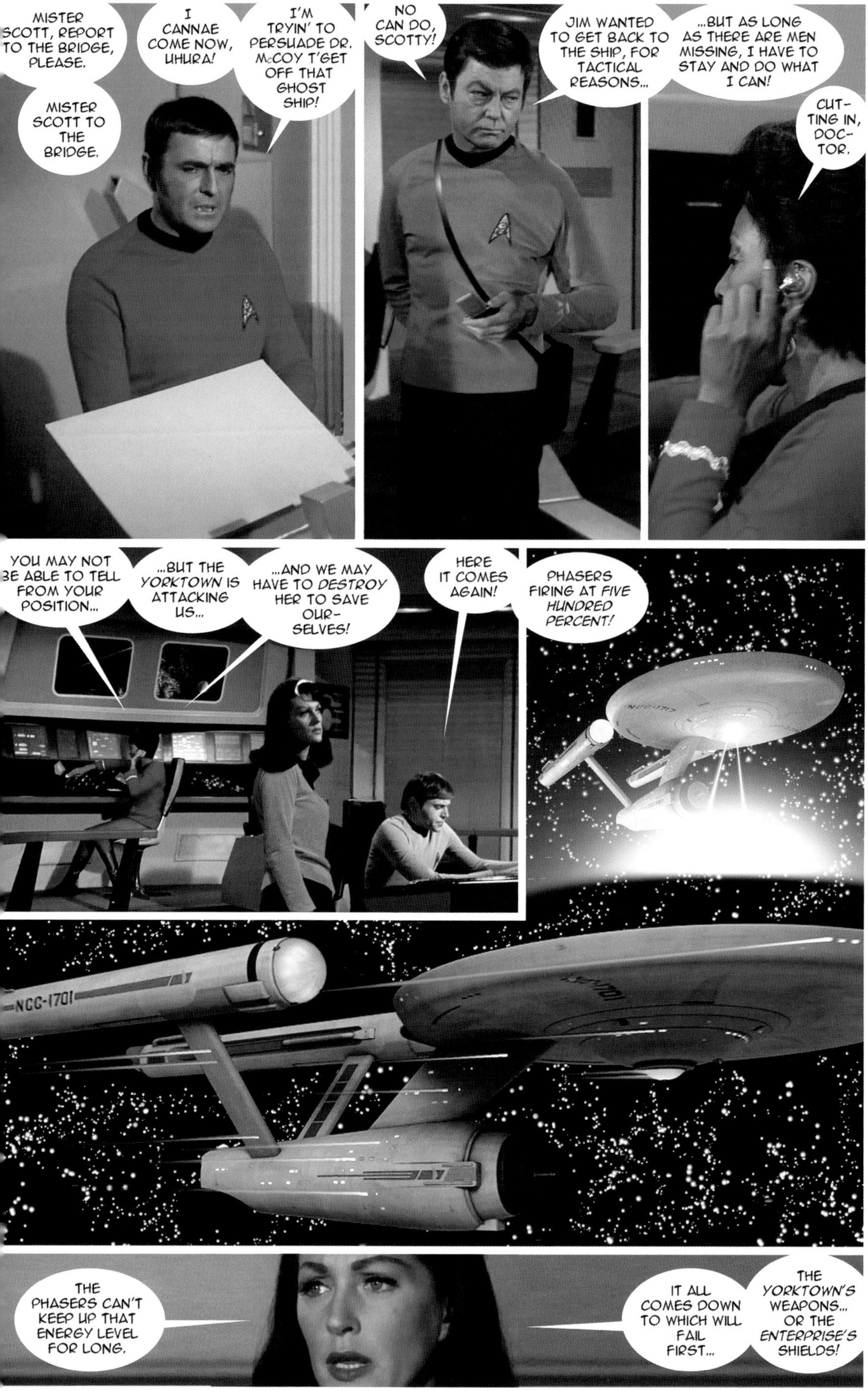

MISTER SCOTT, REPORT TO THE BRIDGE, PLEASE.
MISTER SCOTT TO THE BRIDGE.
I CANNAE COME NOW, UHURA!
I'M TRYIN' TO PERSUADE DR. McCOY T'GET OFF THAT GHOST SHIP!
NO CAN DO, SCOTTY!
JIM WANTED TO GET BACK TO THE SHIP, FOR TACTICAL REASONS...
...BUT AS LONG AS THERE ARE MEN MISSING, I HAVE TO STAY AND DO WHAT I CAN!
CUT-TING IN, DOC-TOR.
YOU MAY NOT BE ABLE TO TELL FROM YOUR POSITION...
...BUT THE YORKTOWN IS ATTACKING US...
...AND WE MAY HAVE TO DESTROY HER TO SAVE OUR-SELVES!
HERE IT COMES AGAIN!
PHASERS FIRING AT FIVE HUNDRED PERCENT!
NCC-1701
THE PHASERS CAN'T KEEP UP THAT ENERGY LEVEL FOR LONG.
IT ALL COMES DOWN TO WHICH WILL FAIL FIRST...
THE YORKTOWN'S WEAPONS... OR THE ENTERPRISE'S SHIELDS!

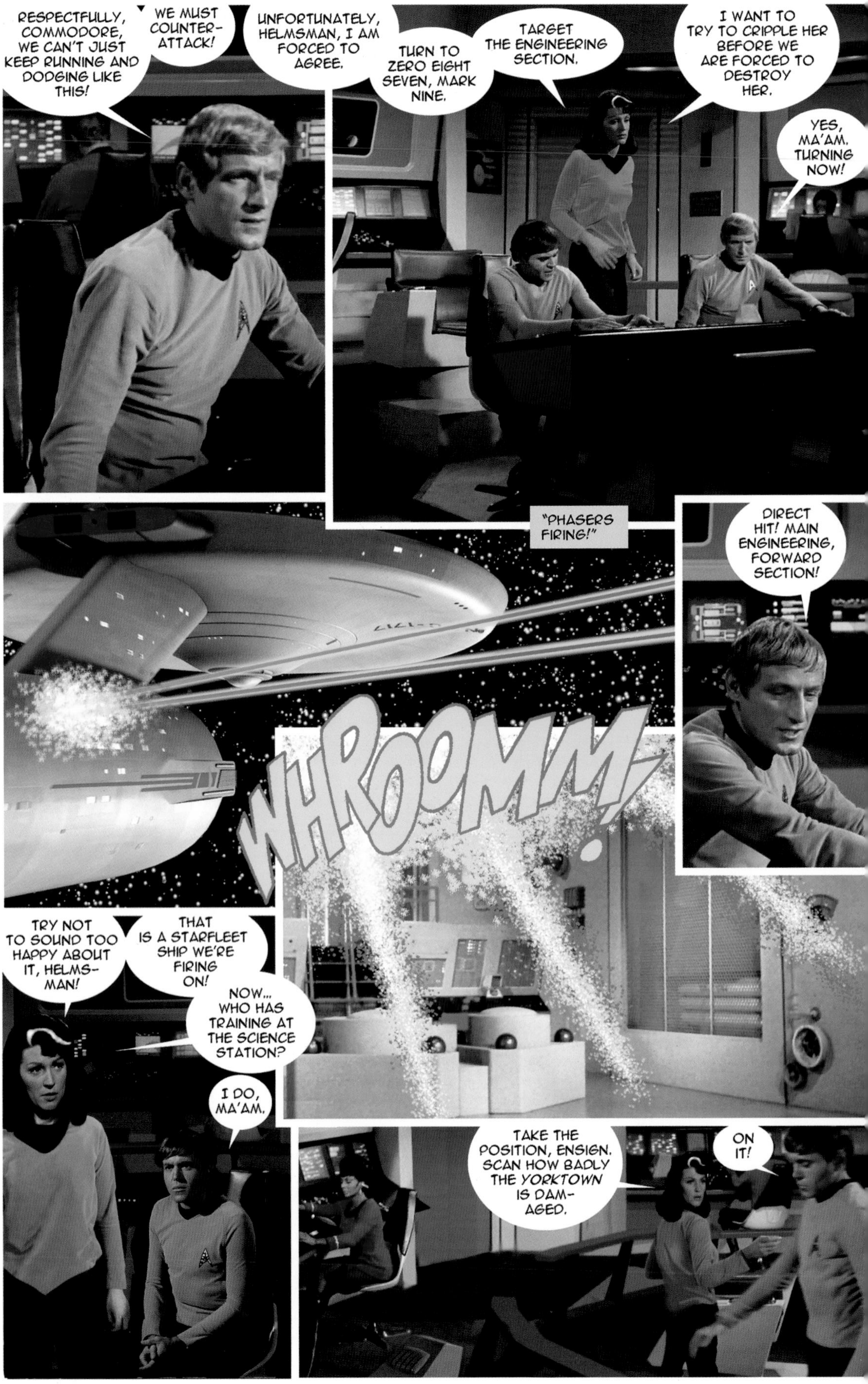

RESPECTFULLY, COMMODORE, WE CAN'T JUST KEEP RUNNING AND DODGING LIKE THIS!
WE MUST COUNTER-ATTACK!
UNFORTUNATELY, HELMSMAN, I AM FORCED TO AGREE.
TURN TO ZERO EIGHT SEVEN, MARK NINE.
TARGET THE ENGINEERING SECTION.
I WANT TO TRY TO CRIPPLE HER BEFORE WE ARE FORCED TO DESTROY HER.
YES, MA'AM. TURNING NOW!
"PHASERS FIRING!"
DIRECT HIT! MAIN ENGINEERING, FORWARD SECTION!
WHROOMM!
TRY NOT TO SOUND TOO HAPPY ABOUT IT, HELMS-MAN!
THAT IS A STARFLEET SHIP WE'RE FIRING ON!
NOW... WHO HAS TRAINING AT THE SCIENCE STATION?
I DO, MA'AM.
TAKE THE POSITION, ENSIGN. SCAN HOW BADLY THE *YORKTOWN* IS DAM-AGED.
ON IT!

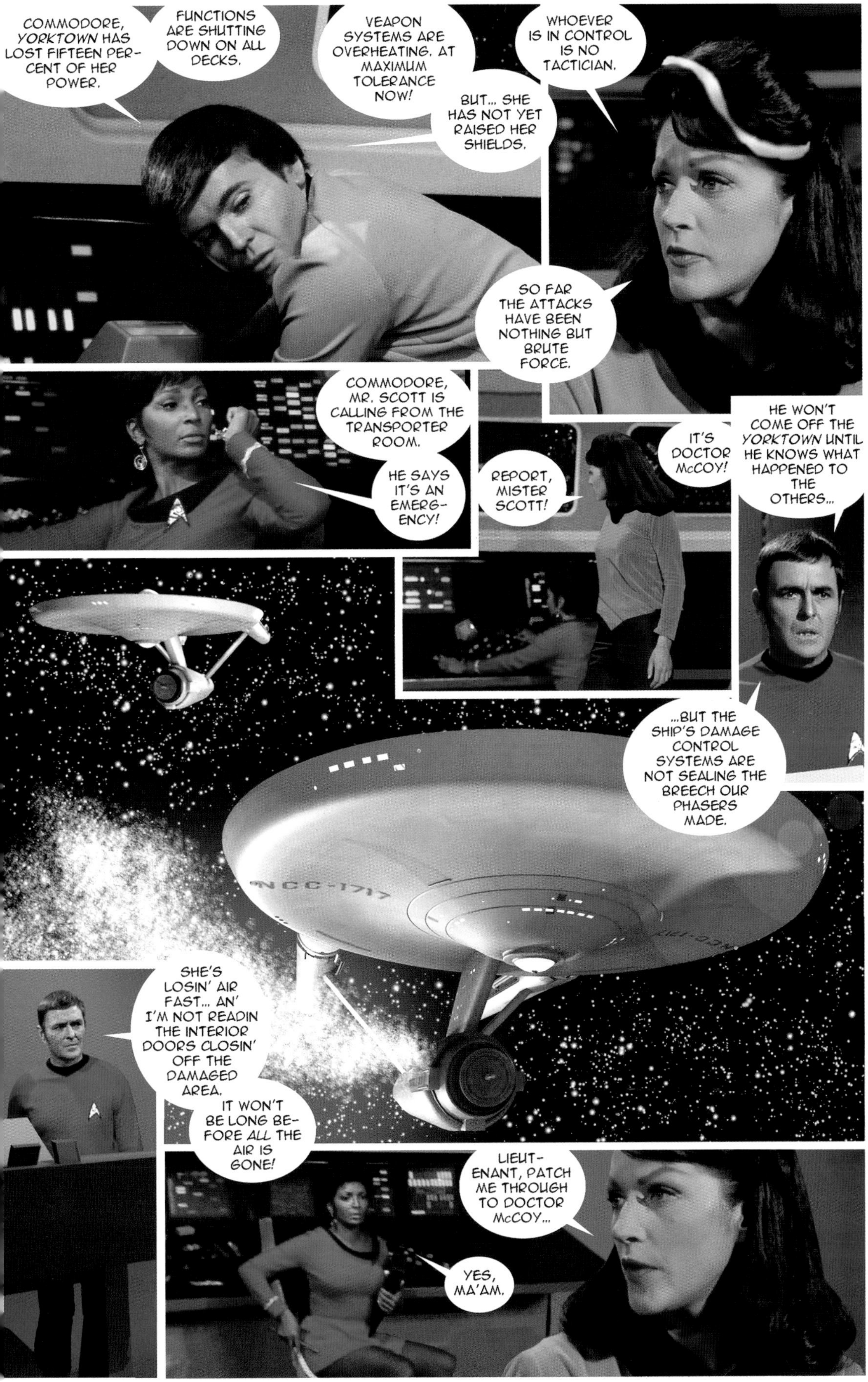
COMMODORE, YORKTOWN HAS LOST FIFTEEN PER-CENT OF HER POWER.
FUNCTIONS ARE SHUTTING DOWN ON ALL DECKS.
VEAPON SYSTEMS ARE OVERHEATING. AT MAXIMUM TOLERANCE NOW!
BUT... SHE HAS NOT YET RAISED HER SHIELDS.
WHOEVER IS IN CONTROL IS NO TACTICIAN.
SO FAR THE ATTACKS HAVE BEEN NOTHING BUT BRUTE FORCE.
COMMODORE, MR. SCOTT IS CALLING FROM THE TRANSPORTER ROOM.
HE SAYS IT'S AN EMERG-ENCY!
REPORT, MISTER SCOTT!
IT'S DOCTOR McCOY!
HE WON'T COME OFF THE YORKTOWN UNTIL HE KNOWS WHAT HAPPENED TO THE OTHERS...
...BUT THE SHIP'S DAMAGE CONTROL SYSTEMS ARE NOT SEALING THE BREECH OUR PHASERS MADE.
NCC-1717
SHE'S LOSIN' AIR FAST... AN' I'M NOT READIN THE INTERIOR DOORS CLOSIN' OFF THE DAMAGED AREA.
IT WON'T BE LONG BE-FORE ALL THE AIR IS GONE!
LIEUT-ENANT, PATCH ME THROUGH TO DOCTOR McCOY...
YES, MA'AM.

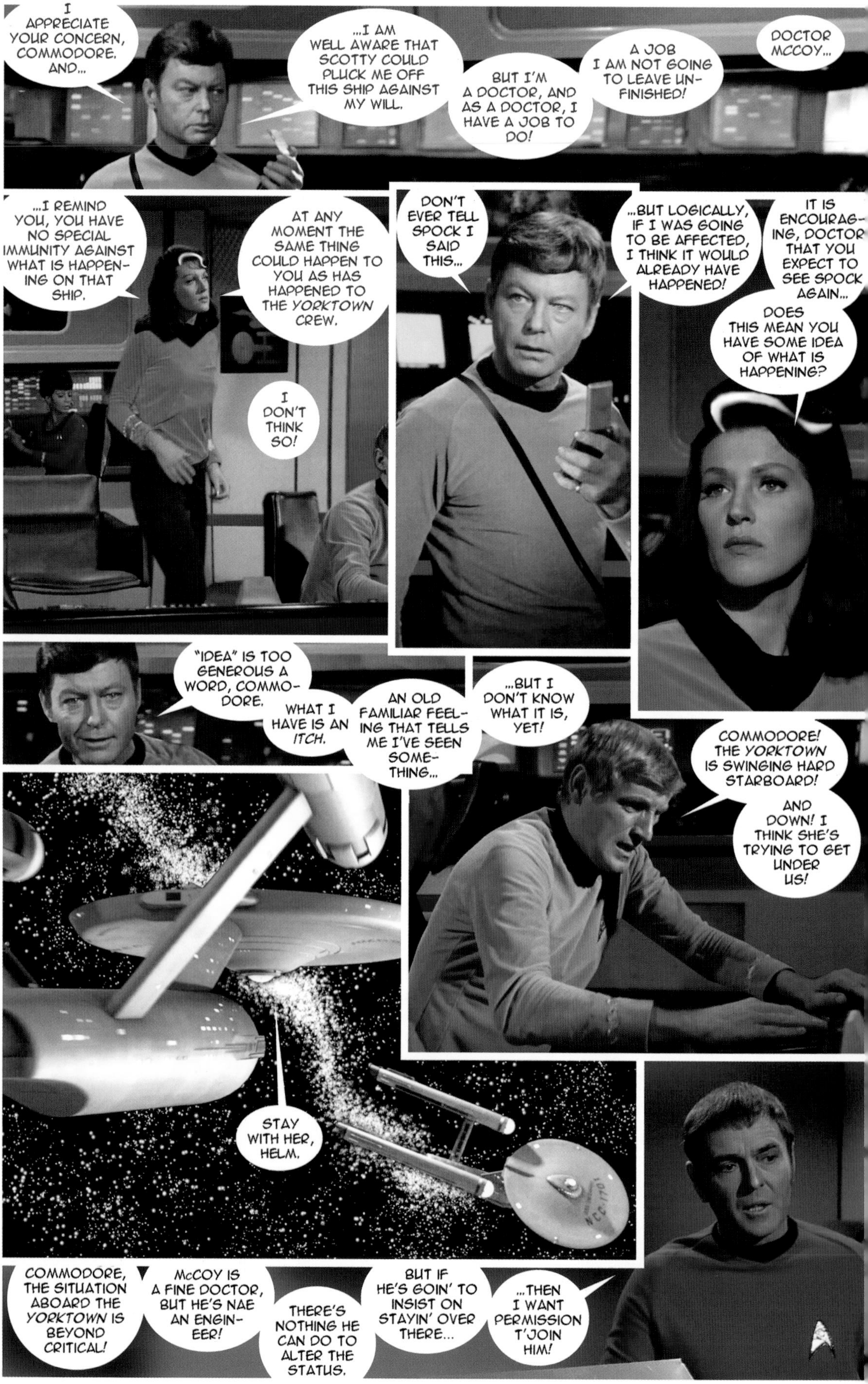

I APPRECIATE YOUR CONCERN, COMMODORE. AND...
...I AM WELL AWARE THAT SCOTTY COULD PLUCK ME OFF THIS SHIP AGAINST MY WILL.
BUT I'M A DOCTOR, AND AS A DOCTOR, I HAVE A JOB TO DO!
A JOB I AM NOT GOING TO LEAVE UN-FINISHED!
DOCTOR MCCOY...
...I REMIND YOU, YOU HAVE NO SPECIAL IMMUNITY AGAINST WHAT IS HAPPEN-ING ON THAT SHIP.
AT ANY MOMENT THE SAME THING COULD HAPPEN TO YOU AS HAS HAPPENED TO THE *YORKTOWN* CREW.
I DON'T THINK SO!
DON'T EVER TELL SPOCK I SAID THIS...
...BUT LOGICALLY, IF I WAS GOING TO BE AFFECTED, I THINK IT WOULD ALREADY HAVE HAPPENED!
IT IS ENCOURAG-ING, DOCTOR THAT YOU EXPECT TO SEE SPOCK AGAIN...
DOES THIS MEAN YOU HAVE SOME IDEA OF WHAT IS HAPPENING?
"IDEA" IS TOO GENEROUS A WORD, COMMO-DORE.
WHAT I HAVE IS AN *ITCH*.
AN OLD FAMILIAR FEEL-ING THAT TELLS ME I'VE SEEN SOME-THING...
...BUT I DON'T KNOW WHAT IT IS, YET!
COMMODORE! THE *YORKTOWN* IS SWINGING HARD STARBOARD!
AND DOWN! I THINK SHE'S TRYING TO GET UNDER US!
STAY WITH HER, HELM.
COMMODORE, THE SITUATION ABOARD THE *YORKTOWN* IS BEYOND CRITICAL!
McCOY IS A FINE DOCTOR, BUT HE'S NAE AN ENGIN-EER!
THERE'S NOTHING HE CAN DO TO ALTER THE STATUS.
BUT IF HE'S GOIN' TO INSIST ON STAYIN' OVER THERE...
...THEN I WANT PERMISSION T'JOIN HIM!

CAPTAIN, ARE YOU ALL RIGHT?

REPORT!

EVERYTHING IS FINE, NUMBER ONE.

I HALF EXPECTED TO BE BOBBING AROUND LIKE A BALLOON...

...BUT SO FAR IT'S AS STEADY AS A TURBOLIFT.

WHAT 'BOUT THE SHIP, CAPTAIN? HAVE YOU SPOTTED ANYTHING SIGNIFICANT?

SOME VERY MINOR VARIATIONS...

...BUT SO FAR EVERY DECK IS VIRTUALLY IDENTICAL.

MAYBE THERE'D BE GREATER DIFFERENCES IF I WAS SEEING THIS THROUGH ALIEN EYES.

ENTERPRISE TO CAPTAIN PIKE.

PIKE HERE. WHAT IS IT, MISTER SCOTT?

SIR, I STILL CANNAE FIGURE OUT WHAT MAKES THAT THING GO...

...BUT I'M READIN' CHANGES IN TH' WAVEFRONT IT'S RIDIN'.

I THINK IT MAY BE GETTIN' READY T'CHANGE COURSE...

...OR ACCELERATE!

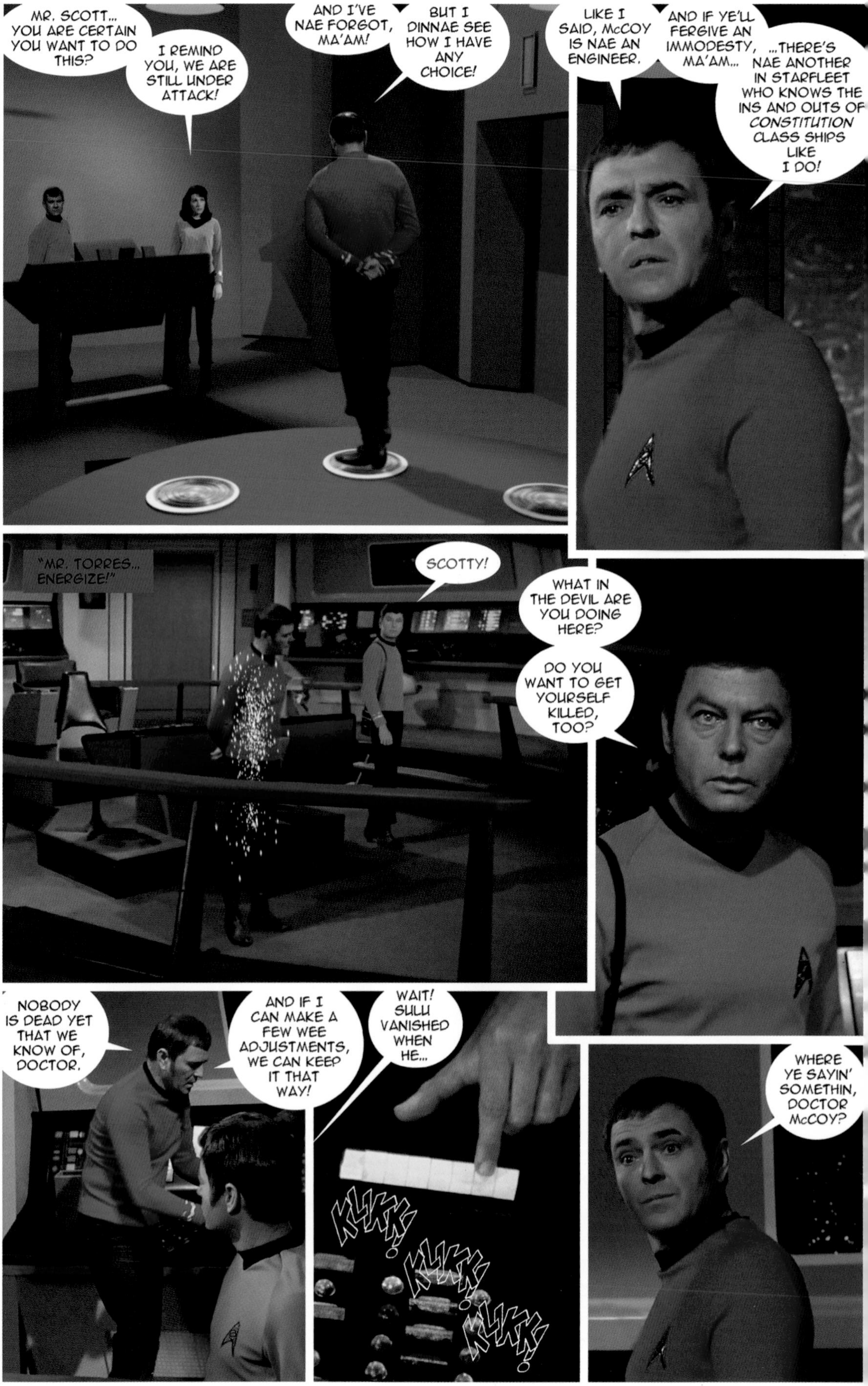
MR. SCOTT... YOU ARE CERTAIN YOU WANT TO DO THIS?
I REMIND YOU, WE ARE STILL UNDER ATTACK!
AND I'VE NAE FORGOT, MA'AM!
BUT I DINNAE SEE HOW I HAVE ANY CHOICE!
LIKE I SAID, McCOY IS NAE AN ENGINEER.
AND IF YE'LL FERGIVE AN IMMODESTY, MA'AM...
...THERE'S NAE ANOTHER IN STARFLEET WHO KNOWS THE INS AND OUTS OF *CONSTITUTION* CLASS SHIPS LIKE I DO!
"MR. TORRES... ENERGIZE!"
SCOTTY!
WHAT IN THE DEVIL ARE YOU DOING HERE?
DO YOU WANT TO GET YOURSELF KILLED, TOO?
NOBODY IS DEAD YET THAT WE KNOW OF, DOCTOR.
AND IF I CAN MAKE A FEW WEE ADJUSTMENTS, WE CAN KEEP IT THAT WAY!
WAIT! SULU VANISHED WHEN HE...
KLIKK!
KLIKK!
KLIKK!
WHERE YE SAYIN' SOMETHIN, DOCTOR McCOY?

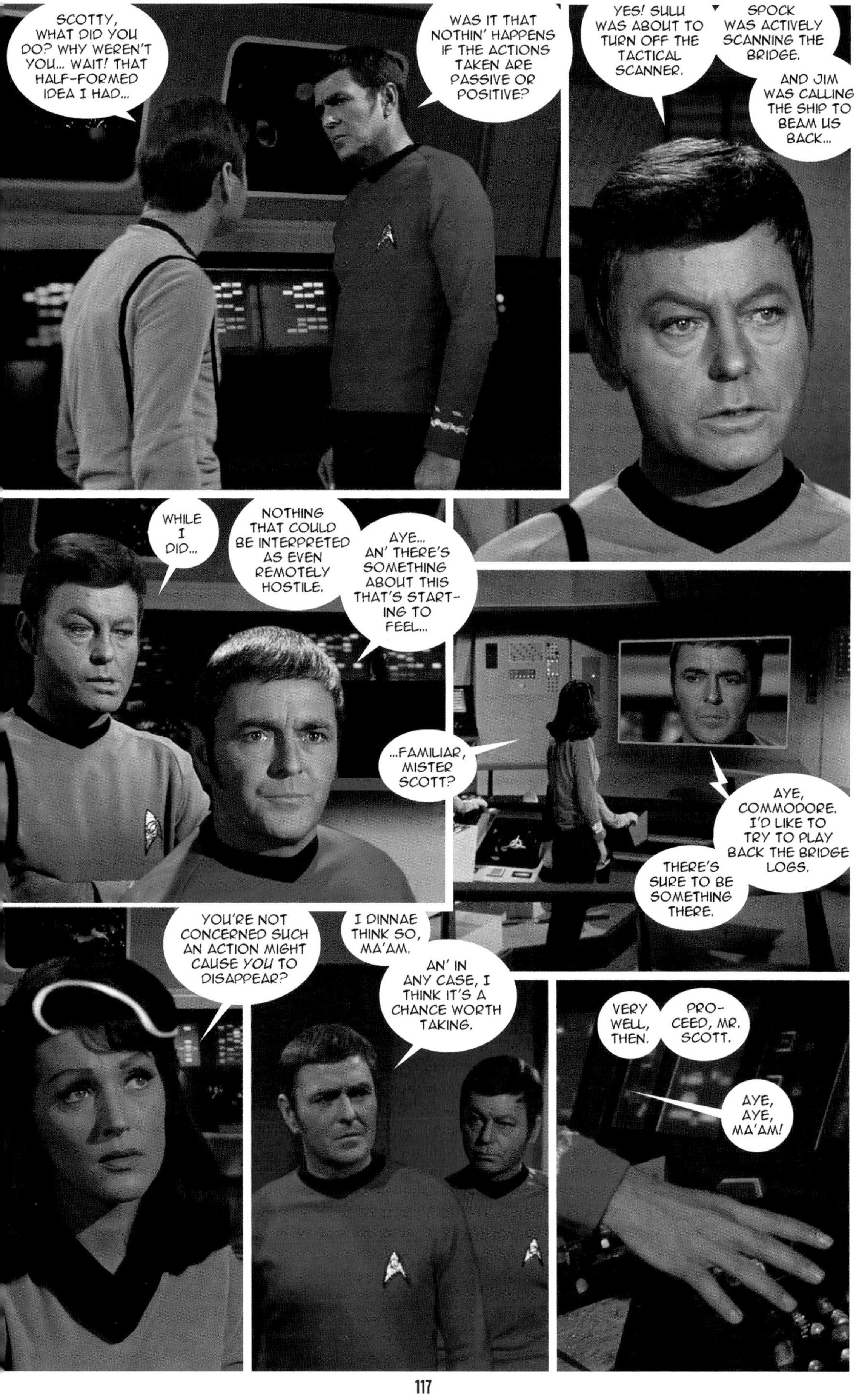
SCOTTY, WHAT DID YOU DO? WHY WEREN'T YOU... WAIT! THAT HALF-FORMED IDEA I HAD...
WAS IT THAT NOTHIN' HAPPENS IF THE ACTIONS TAKEN ARE PASSIVE OR POSITIVE?
YES! SULU WAS ABOUT TO TURN OFF THE TACTICAL SCANNER.
SPOCK WAS ACTIVELY SCANNING THE BRIDGE.
AND JIM WAS CALLING THE SHIP TO BEAM US BACK...
WHILE I DID...
NOTHING THAT COULD BE INTERPRETED AS EVEN REMOTELY HOSTILE.
AYE... AN' THERE'S SOMETHING ABOUT THIS THAT'S STARTING TO FEEL...
...FAMILIAR, MISTER SCOTT?
AYE, COMMODORE. I'D LIKE TO TRY TO PLAY BACK THE BRIDGE LOGS.
THERE'S SURE TO BE SOMETHING THERE.
YOU'RE NOT CONCERNED SUCH AN ACTION MIGHT CAUSE *YOU* TO DISAPPEAR?
I DINNAE THINK SO, MA'AM.
AN' IN ANY CASE, I THINK IT'S A CHANCE WORTH TAKING.
VERY WELL, THEN.
PRO-CEED, MR. SCOTT.
AYE, AYE, MA'AM!

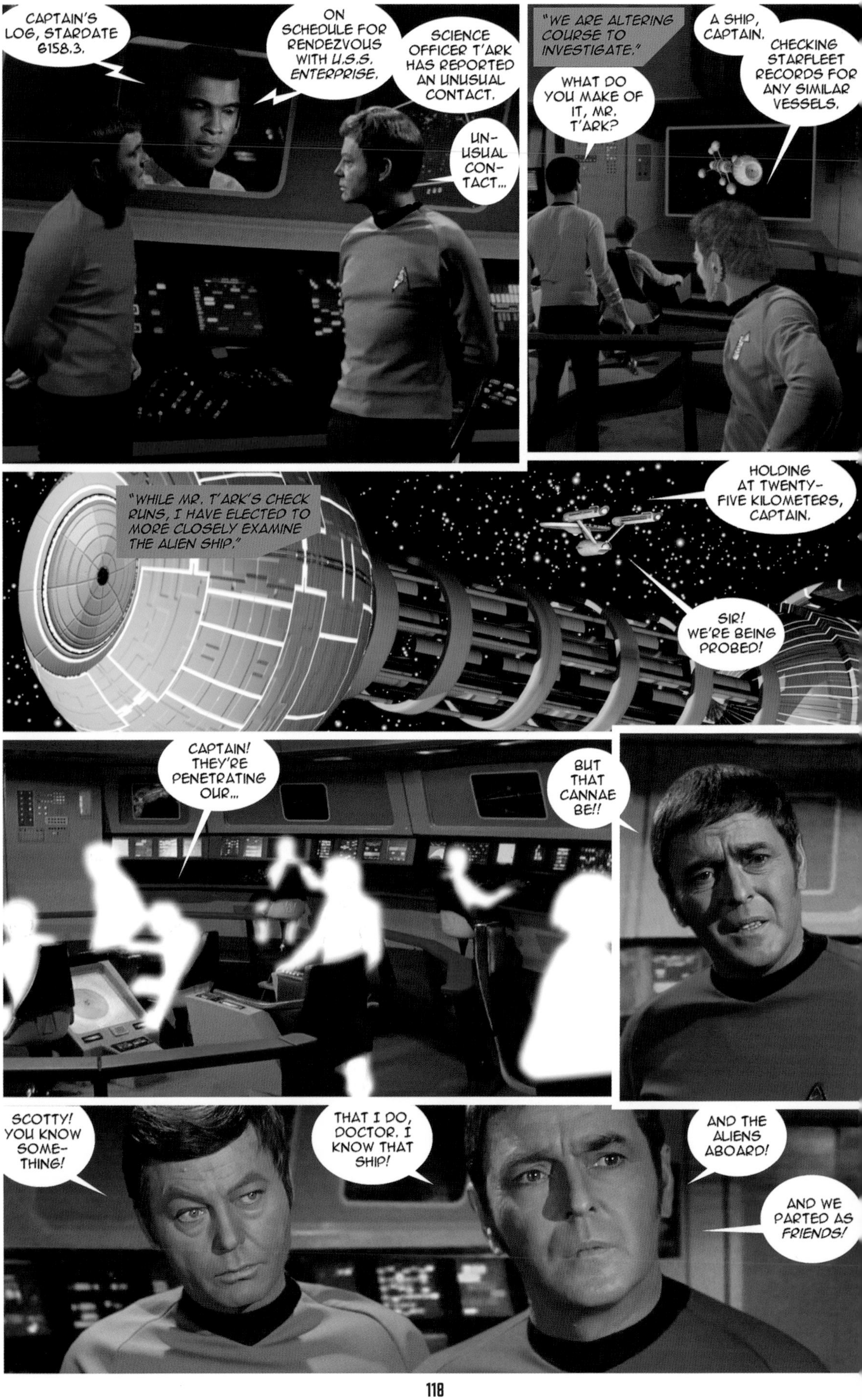
CAPTAIN'S LOG, STARDATE 6158.3.
ON SCHEDULE FOR RENDEZVOUS WITH U.S.S. ENTERPRISE.
SCIENCE OFFICER T'ARK HAS REPORTED AN UNUSUAL CONTACT.
UN-USUAL CON-TACT...
"WE ARE ALTERING COURSE TO INVESTIGATE."
WHAT DO YOU MAKE OF IT, MR. T'ARK?
A SHIP, CAPTAIN.
CHECKING STARFLEET RECORDS FOR ANY SIMILAR VESSELS.
"WHILE MR. T'ARK'S CHECK RUNS, I HAVE ELECTED TO MORE CLOSELY EXAMINE THE ALIEN SHIP."
HOLDING AT TWENTY-FIVE KILOMETERS, CAPTAIN.
SIR! WE'RE BEING PROBED!
CAPTAIN! THEY'RE PENETRATING OUR...
BUT THAT CANNAE BE!!
SCOTTY! YOU KNOW SOME-THING!
THAT I DO, DOCTOR. I KNOW THAT SHIP!
AND THE ALIENS ABOARD!
AND WE PARTED AS FRIENDS!

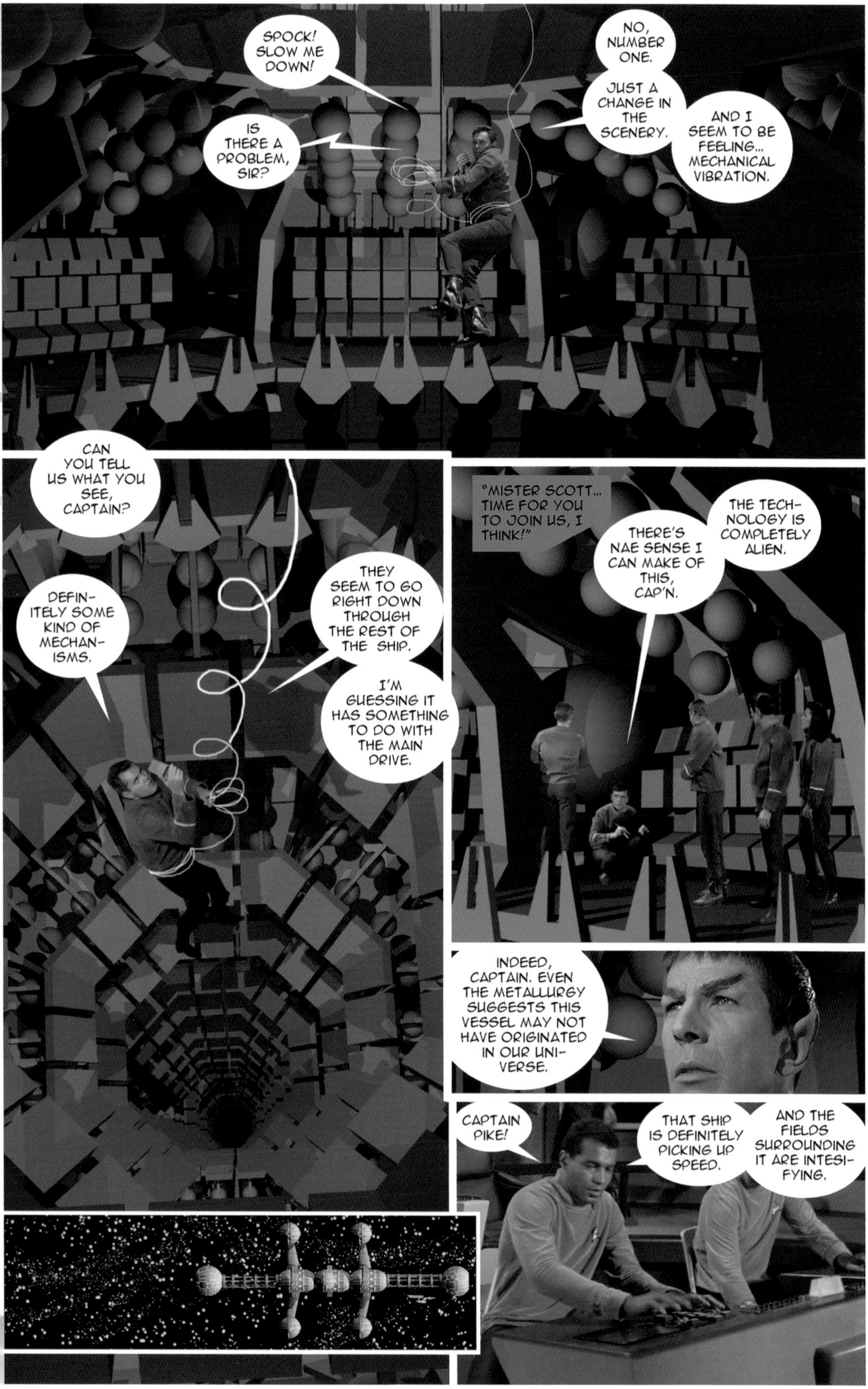
SPOCK! SLOW ME DOWN!
IS THERE A PROBLEM, SIR?
NO, NUMBER ONE.
JUST A CHANGE IN THE SCENERY.
AND I SEEM TO BE FEELING... MECHANICAL VIBRATION.
CAN YOU TELL US WHAT YOU SEE, CAPTAIN?
DEFIN-ITELY SOME KIND OF MECHAN-ISMS.
THEY SEEM TO GO RIGHT DOWN THROUGH THE REST OF THE SHIP.
I'M GUESSING IT HAS SOMETHING TO DO WITH THE MAIN DRIVE.
"MISTER SCOTT... TIME FOR YOU TO JOIN US, I THINK!"
THERE'S NAE SENSE I CAN MAKE OF THIS, CAP'N.
THE TECH-NOLOGY IS COMPLETELY ALIEN.
INDEED, CAPTAIN. EVEN THE METALLURGY SUGGESTS THIS VESSEL MAY NOT HAVE ORIGINATED IN OUR UNI-VERSE.
CAPTAIN PIKE!
THAT SHIP IS DEFINITELY PICKING UP SPEED.
AND THE FIELDS SURROUNDING IT ARE INTESI-FYING.

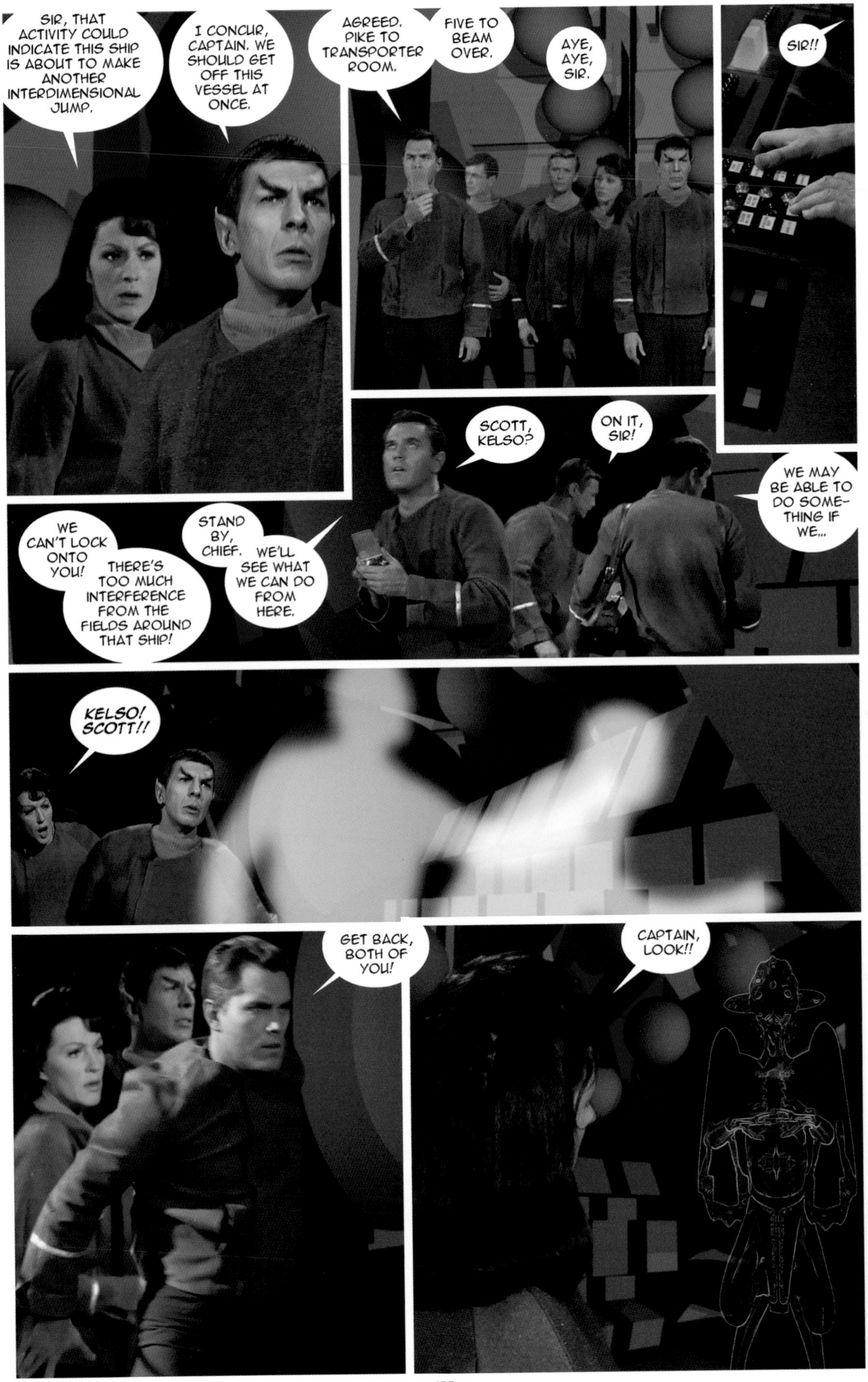
SIR, THAT ACTIVITY COULD INDICATE THIS SHIP IS ABOUT TO MAKE ANOTHER INTERDIMENSIONAL JUMP.
I CONCUR, CAPTAIN. WE SHOULD GET OFF THIS VESSEL AT ONCE.
AGREED. PIKE TO TRANSPORTER ROOM.
FIVE TO BEAM OVER.
AYE, AYE, SIR.
SIR!!
SCOTT, KELSO?
ON IT, SIR!
WE MAY BE ABLE TO DO SOME-THING IF WE...
WE CAN'T LOCK ONTO YOU!
THERE'S TOO MUCH INTERFERENCE FROM THE FIELDS AROUND THAT SHIP!
STAND BY, CHIEF.
WE'LL SEE WHAT WE CAN DO FROM HERE.
KELSO! SCOTT!!
GET BACK, BOTH OF YOU!
CAPTAIN, LOOK!!

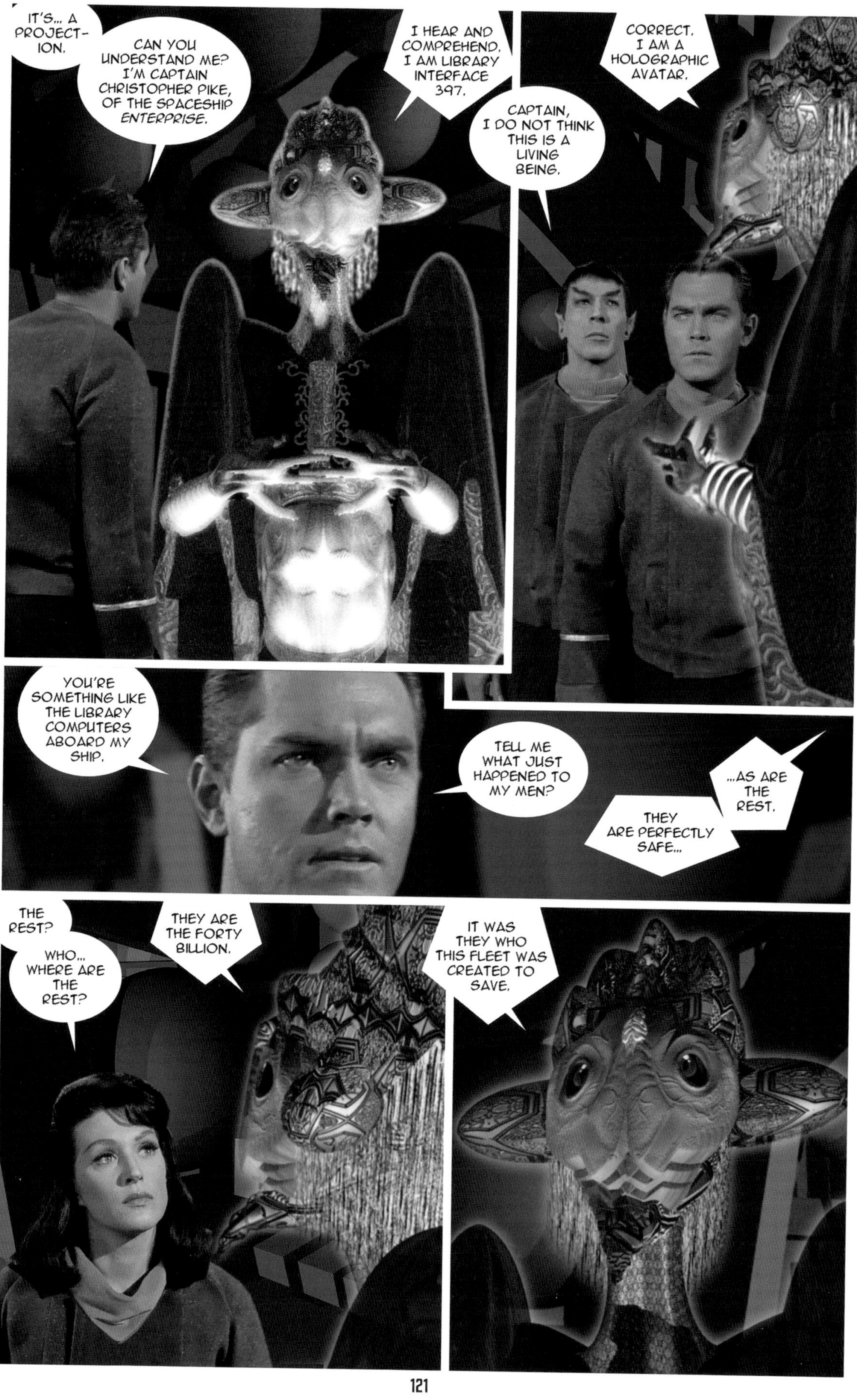
IT'S... A PROJECTION.
CAN YOU UNDERSTAND ME? I'M CAPTAIN CHRISTOPHER PIKE, OF THE SPACESHIP ENTERPRISE.
I HEAR AND COMPREHEND. I AM LIBRARY INTERFACE 397.
CORRECT. I AM A HOLOGRAPHIC AVATAR.
CAPTAIN, I DO NOT THINK THIS IS A LIVING BEING.
YOU'RE SOMETHING LIKE THE LIBRARY COMPUTERS ABOARD MY SHIP.
TELL ME WHAT JUST HAPPENED TO MY MEN?
THEY ARE PERFECTLY SAFE...
...AS ARE THE REST.
THE REST?
WHO... WHERE ARE THE REST?
THEY ARE THE FORTY BILLION.
IT WAS THEY WHO THIS FLEET WAS CREATED TO SAVE.

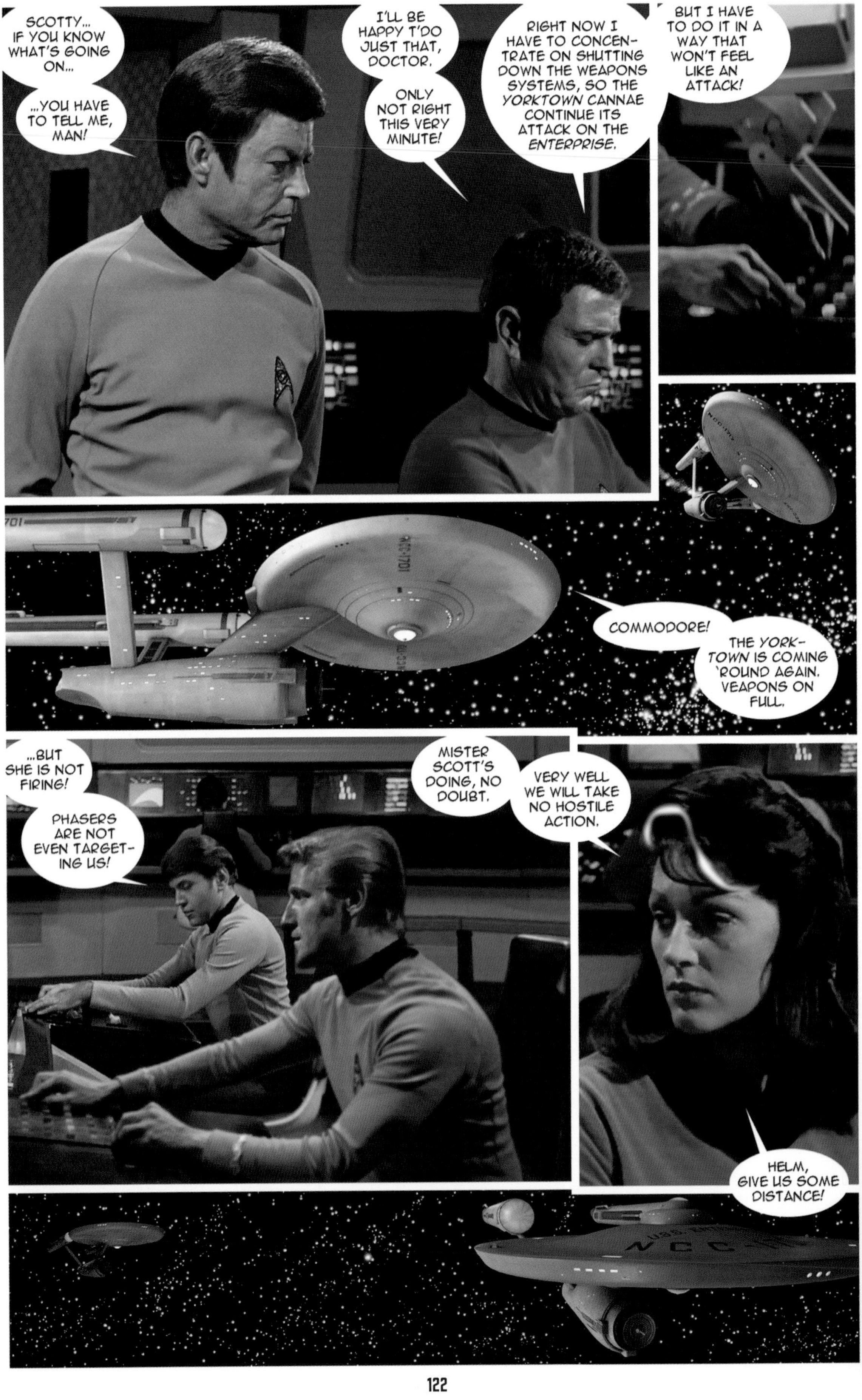
SCOTTY... IF YOU KNOW WHAT'S GOING ON...
...YOU HAVE TO TELL ME, MAN!
I'LL BE HAPPY T'DO JUST THAT, DOCTOR.
ONLY NOT RIGHT THIS VERY MINUTE!
RIGHT NOW I HAVE TO CONCEN-TRATE ON SHUTTING DOWN THE WEAPONS SYSTEMS, SO THE *YORKTOWN* CANNAE CONTINUE ITS ATTACK ON THE *ENTERPRISE*.
BUT I HAVE TO DO IT IN A WAY THAT WON'T FEEL LIKE AN ATTACK!
COMMODORE!
THE *YORK-TOWN* IS COMING 'ROUND AGAIN. WEAPONS ON FULL.
...BUT SHE IS NOT FIRING!
PHASERS ARE NOT EVEN TARGET-ING US!
MISTER SCOTT'S DOING, NO DOUBT.
VERY WELL WE WILL TAKE NO HOSTILE ACTION.
HELM, GIVE US SOME DISTANCE!

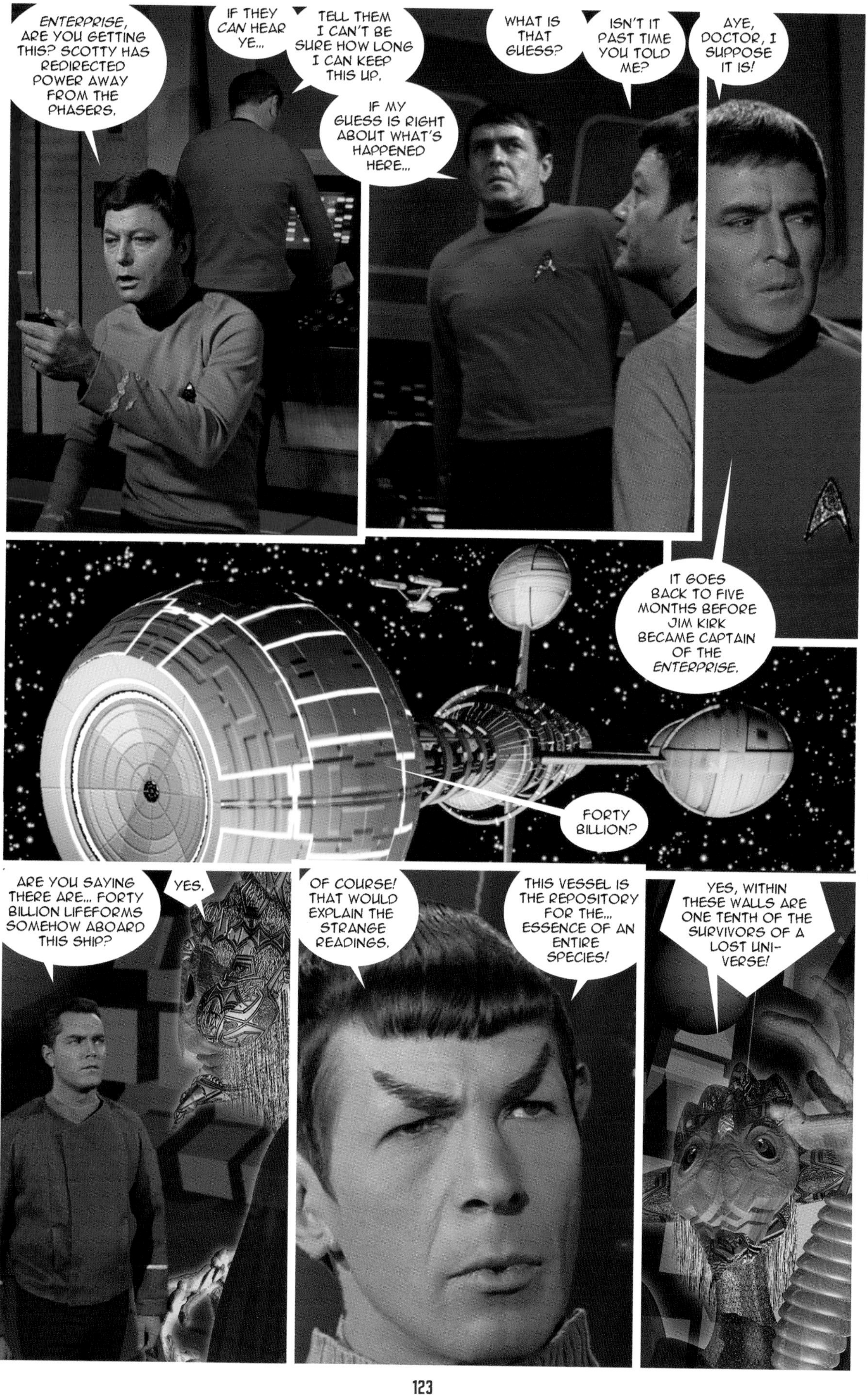
ENTERPRISE, ARE YOU GETTING THIS? SCOTTY HAS REDIRECTED POWER AWAY FROM THE PHASERS.
IF THEY CAN HEAR YE...
TELL THEM I CAN'T BE SURE HOW LONG I CAN KEEP THIS UP.
IF MY GUESS IS RIGHT ABOUT WHAT'S HAPPENED HERE...
WHAT IS THAT GUESS?
ISN'T IT PAST TIME YOU TOLD ME?
AYE, DOCTOR, I SUPPOSE IT IS!
IT GOES BACK TO FIVE MONTHS BEFORE JIM KIRK BECAME CAPTAIN OF THE ENTERPRISE.
FORTY BILLION?
ARE YOU SAYING THERE ARE... FORTY BILLION LIFEFORMS SOMEHOW ABOARD THIS SHIP?
YES.
OF COURSE! THAT WOULD EXPLAIN THE STRANGE READINGS.
THIS VESSEL IS THE REPOSITORY FOR THE... ESSENCE OF AN ENTIRE SPECIES!
YES, WITHIN THESE WALLS ARE ONE TENTH OF THE SURVIVORS OF A LOST UNI-VERSE!

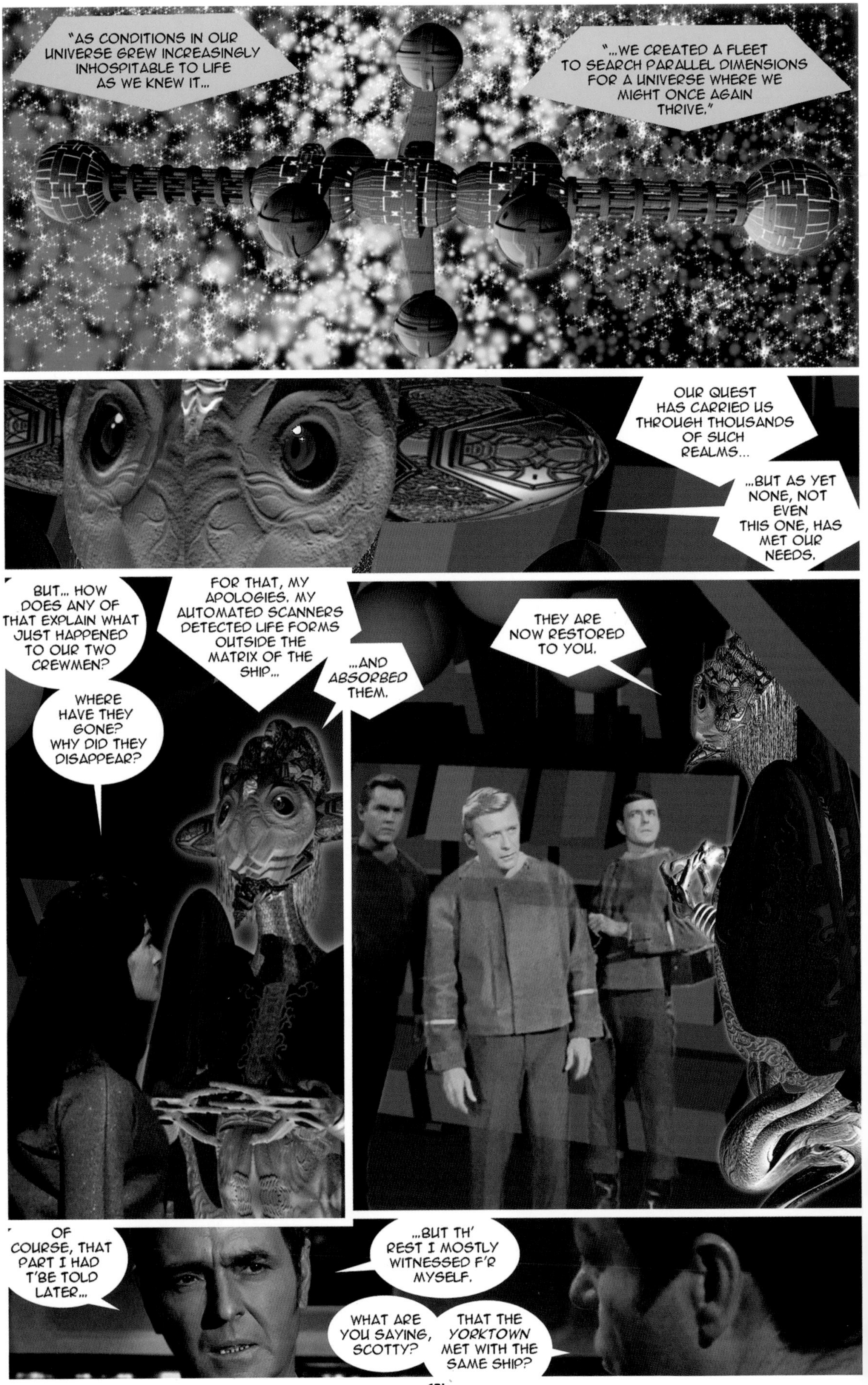
"AS CONDITIONS IN OUR UNIVERSE GREW INCREASINGLY INHOSPITABLE TO LIFE AS WE KNEW IT...
"...WE CREATED A FLEET TO SEARCH PARALLEL DIMENSIONS FOR A UNIVERSE WHERE WE MIGHT ONCE AGAIN THRIVE."
OUR QUEST HAS CARRIED US THROUGH THOUSANDS OF SUCH REALMS...
...BUT AS YET NONE, NOT EVEN THIS ONE, HAS MET OUR NEEDS.
BUT... HOW DOES ANY OF THAT EXPLAIN WHAT JUST HAPPENED TO OUR TWO CREWMEN?
WHERE HAVE THEY GONE? WHY DID THEY DISAPPEAR?
FOR THAT, MY APOLOGIES. MY AUTOMATED SCANNERS DETECTED LIFE FORMS OUTSIDE THE MATRIX OF THE SHIP...
...AND ABSORBED THEM.
THEY ARE NOW RESTORED TO YOU.
OF COURSE, THAT PART I HAD T'BE TOLD LATER...
...BUT TH' REST I MOSTLY WITNESSED F'R MYSELF.
WHAT ARE YOU SAYING, SCOTTY?
THAT THE *YORKTOWN* MET WITH THE SAME SHIP?

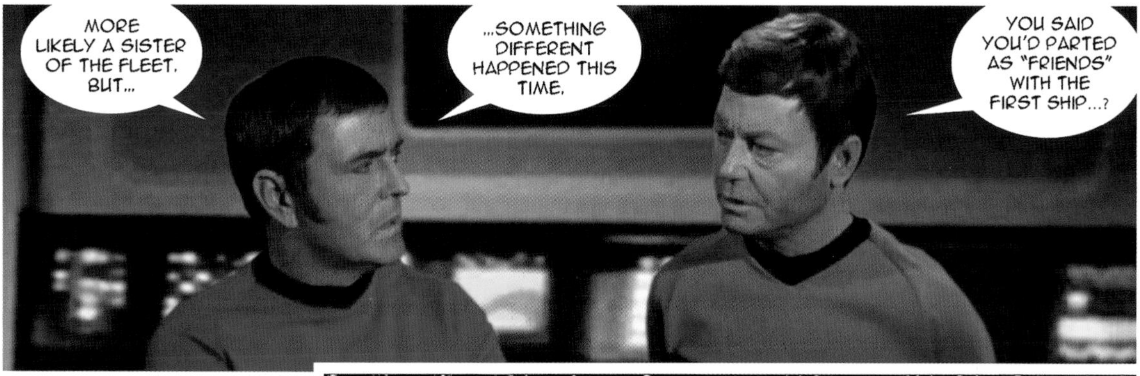
MORE LIKELY A SISTER OF THE FLEET. BUT...
...SOMETHING DIFFERENT HAPPENED THIS TIME.
YOU SAID YOU'D PARTED AS "FRIENDS" WITH THE FIRST SHIP...?

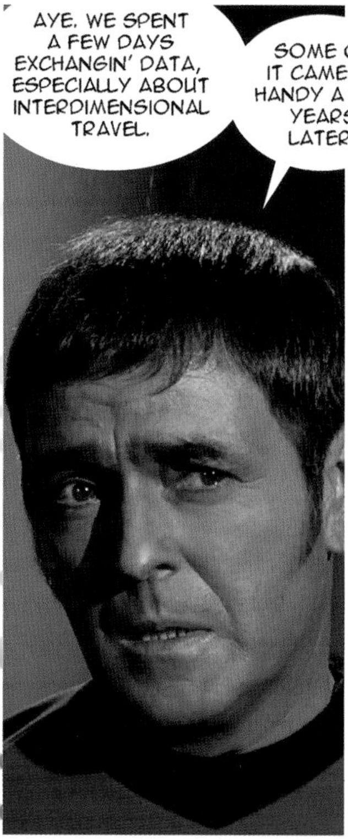
AYE. WE SPENT A FEW DAYS EXCHANGIN' DATA, ESPECIALLY ABOUT INTERDIMENSIONAL TRAVEL.
SOME OF IT CAME IN HANDY A FEW YEARS LATER!

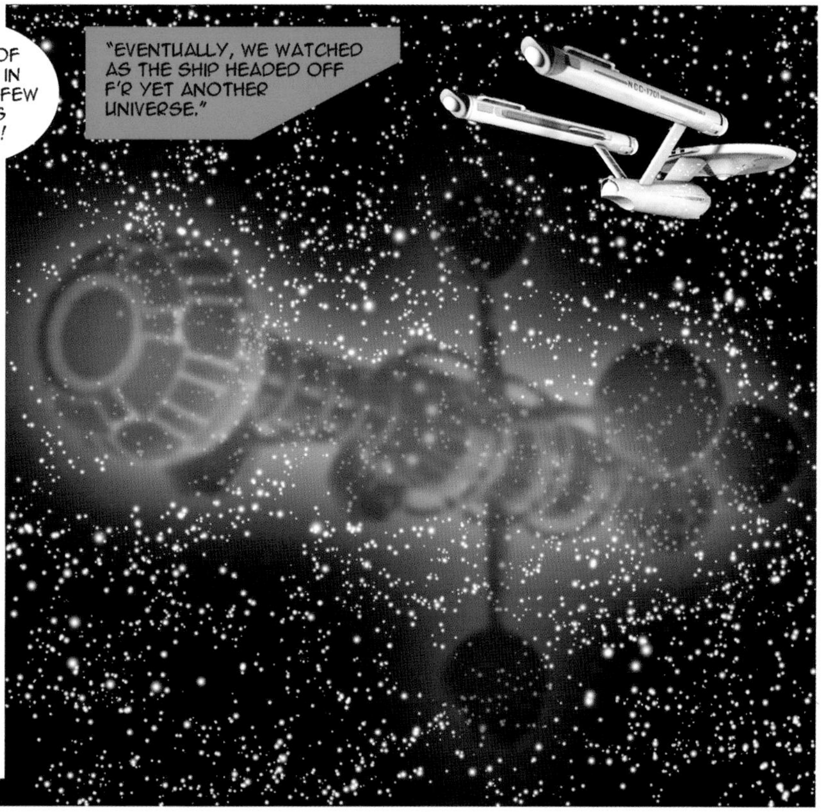
"EVENTUALLY, WE WATCHED AS THE SHIP HEADED OFF F'R YET ANOTHER UNIVERSE."
NCC-1701

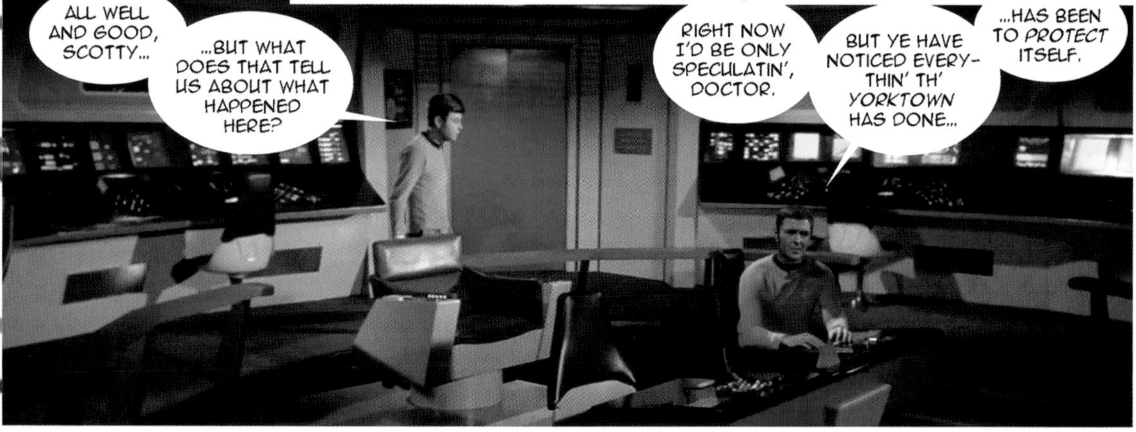
ALL WELL AND GOOD, SCOTTY...
...BUT WHAT DOES THAT TELL US ABOUT WHAT HAPPENED HERE?
RIGHT NOW I'D BE ONLY SPECULATIN', DOCTOR.
BUT YE HAVE NOTICED EVERY-THIN' TH' *YORKTOWN* HAS DONE...
...HAS BEEN TO *PROTECT* ITSELF.

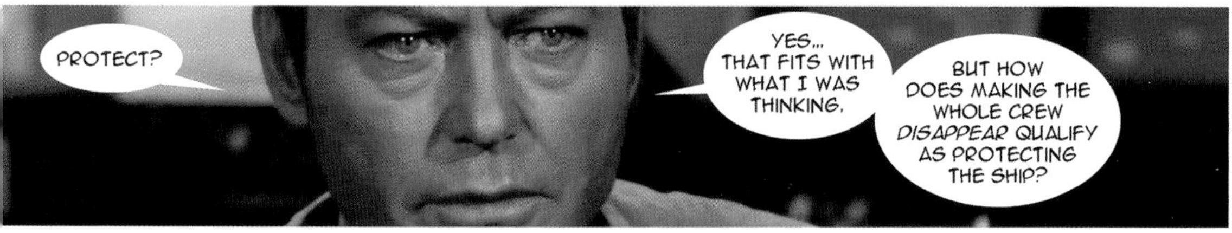
PROTECT?
YES... THAT FITS WITH WHAT I WAS THINKING.
BUT HOW DOES MAKING THE WHOLE CREW *DISAPPEAR* QUALIFY AS PROTECTING THE SHIP?

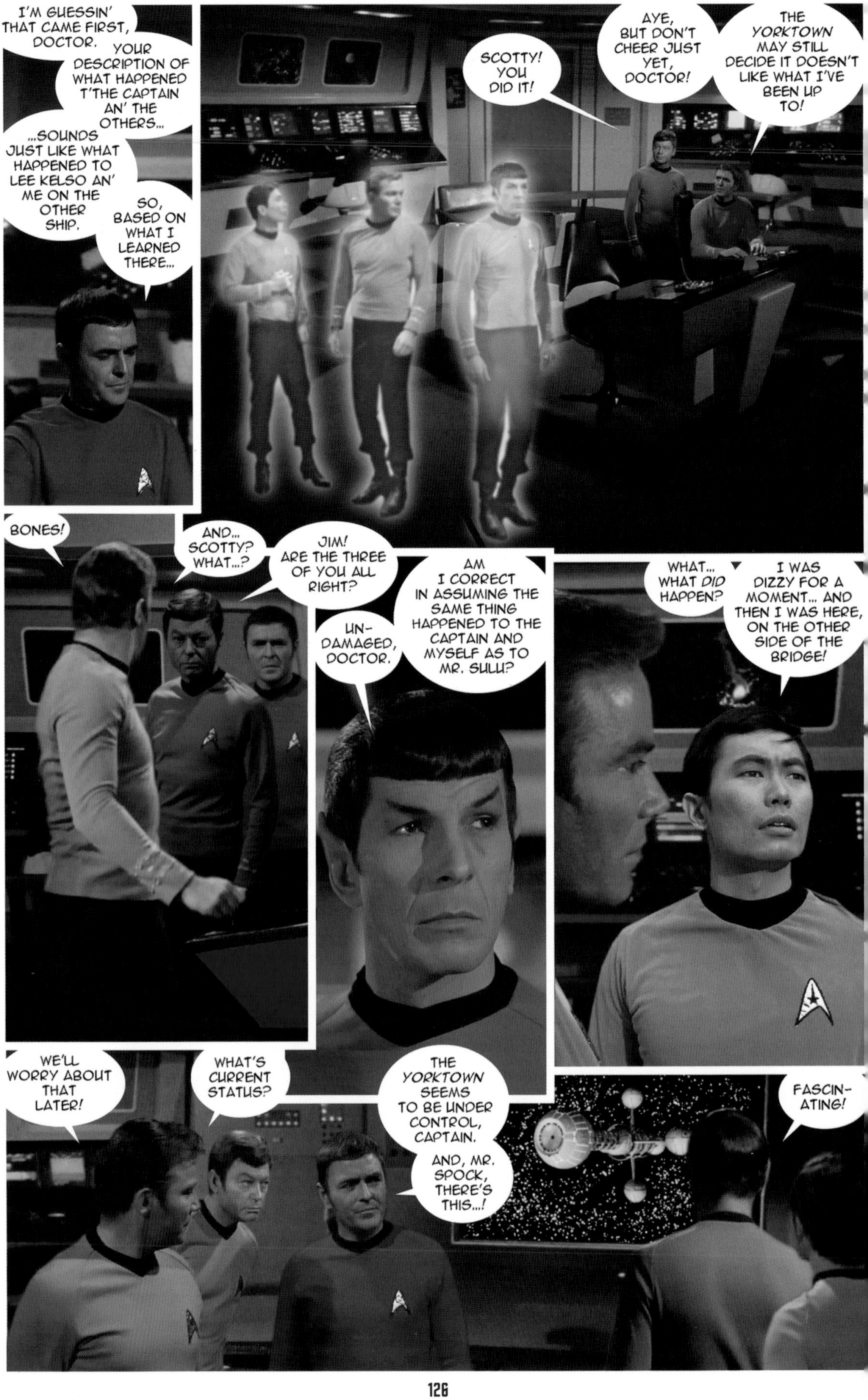
I'M GUESSIN' THAT CAME FIRST, DOCTOR.
YOUR DESCRIPTION OF WHAT HAPPENED T'THE CAPTAIN AN' THE OTHERS...
...SOUNDS JUST LIKE WHAT HAPPENED TO LEE KELSO AN' ME ON THE OTHER SHIP.
SO, BASED ON WHAT I LEARNED THERE...
SCOTTY! YOU DID IT!
AYE, BUT DON'T CHEER JUST YET, DOCTOR!
THE *YORKTOWN* MAY STILL DECIDE IT DOESN'T LIKE WHAT I'VE BEEN UP TO!
BONES!
AND... SCOTTY? WHAT...?
JIM! ARE THE THREE OF YOU ALL RIGHT?
UN-DAMAGED, DOCTOR.
AM I CORRECT IN ASSUMING THE SAME THING HAPPENED TO THE CAPTAIN AND MYSELF AS TO MR. SULU?
WHAT... WHAT *DID* HAPPEN?
I WAS DIZZY FOR A MOMENT... AND THEN I WAS HERE, ON THE OTHER SIDE OF THE BRIDGE!
WE'LL WORRY ABOUT THAT LATER!
WHAT'S CURRENT STATUS?
THE *YORKTOWN* SEEMS TO BE UNDER CONTROL, CAPTAIN.
AND, MR. SPOCK, THERE'S THIS...!
FASCIN-ATING!

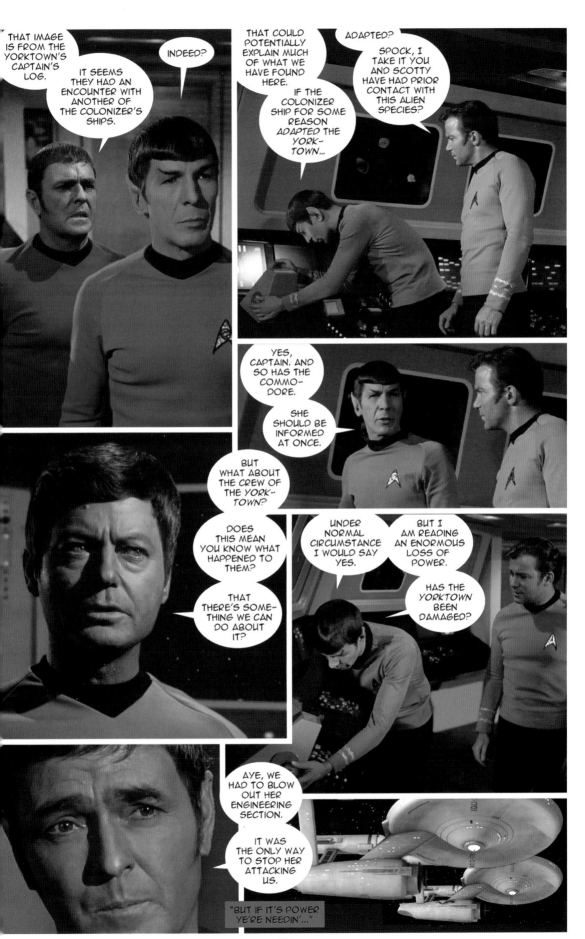

THAT IMAGE IS FROM THE YORKTOWN'S CAPTAIN'S LOG.

IT SEEMS THEY HAD AN ENCOUNTER WITH ANOTHER OF THE COLONIZER'S SHIPS.

INDEED?

THAT COULD POTENTIALLY EXPLAIN MUCH OF WHAT WE HAVE FOUND HERE.

IF THE COLONIZER SHIP FOR SOME REASON ADAPTED THE YORK-TOWN...

ADAPTED?

SPOCK, I TAKE IT YOU AND SCOTTY HAVE HAD PRIOR CONTACT WITH THIS ALIEN SPECIES?

YES, CAPTAIN. AND SO HAS THE COMMO-DORE.

SHE SHOULD BE INFORMED AT ONCE.

BUT WHAT ABOUT THE CREW OF THE YORK-TOWN?

DOES THIS MEAN YOU KNOW WHAT HAPPENED TO THEM?

THAT THERE'S SOME-THING WE CAN DO ABOUT IT?

UNDER NORMAL CIRCUMSTANCE I WOULD SAY YES.

BUT I AM READING AN ENORMOUS LOSS OF POWER.

HAS THE YORKTOWN BEEN DAMAGED?

AYE, WE HAD TO BLOW OUT HER ENGINEERING SECTION.

IT WAS THE ONLY WAY TO STOP HER ATTACKING US.

"BUT IF IT'S POWER YE'RE NEEDIN'..."

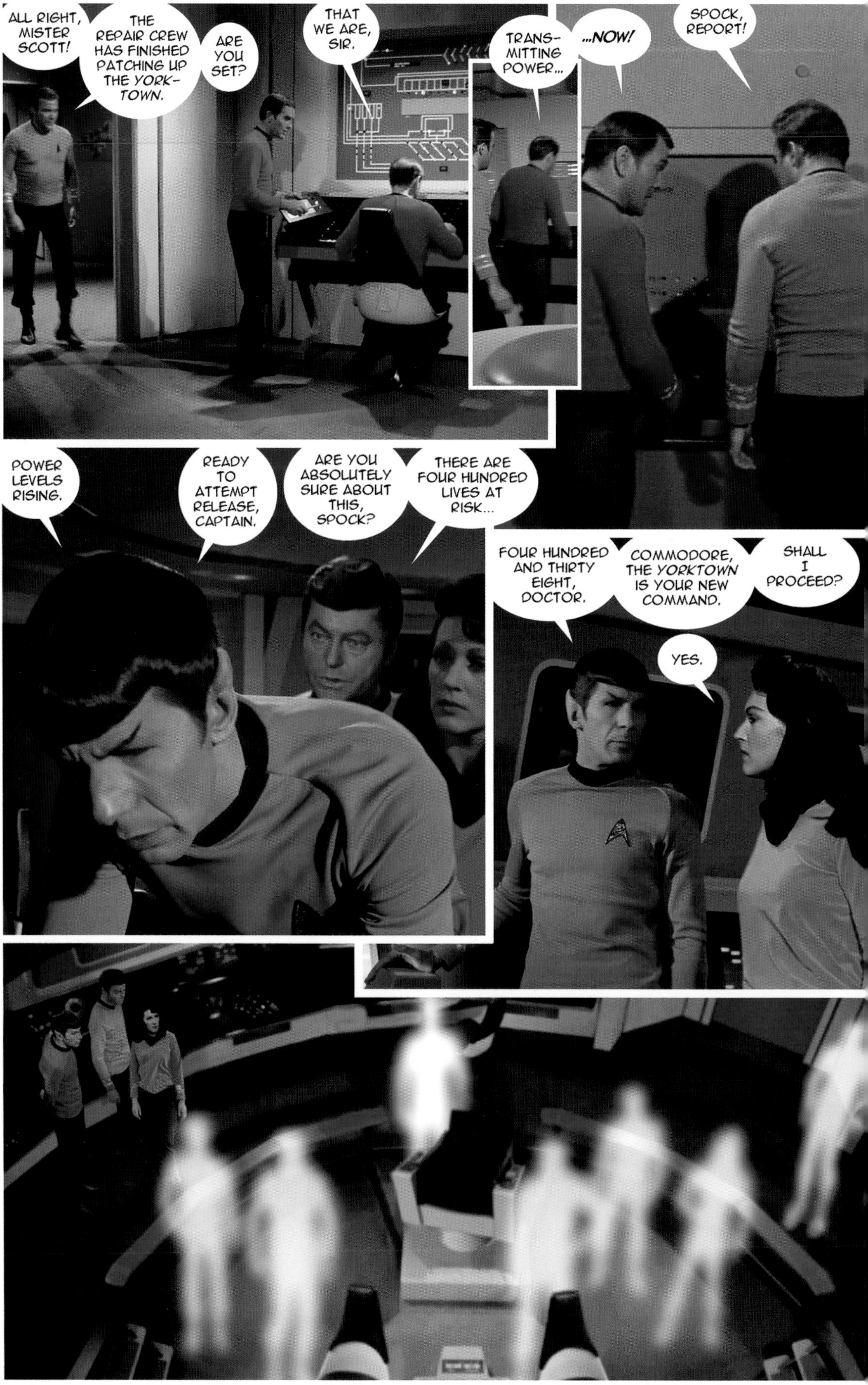
ALL RIGHT, MISTER SCOTT!
THE REPAIR CREW HAS FINISHED PATCHING UP THE *YORK-TOWN*.
ARE YOU SET?
THAT WE ARE, SIR.
TRANS-MITTING POWER...
...NOW!
SPOCK, REPORT!
POWER LEVELS RISING.
READY TO ATTEMPT RELEASE, CAPTAIN.
ARE YOU ABSOLUTELY SURE ABOUT THIS, SPOCK?
THERE ARE FOUR HUNDRED LIVES AT RISK...
FOUR HUNDRED AND THIRTY EIGHT, DOCTOR.
COMMODORE, THE *YORKTOWN* IS YOUR NEW COMMAND.
SHALL I PROCEED?
YES.

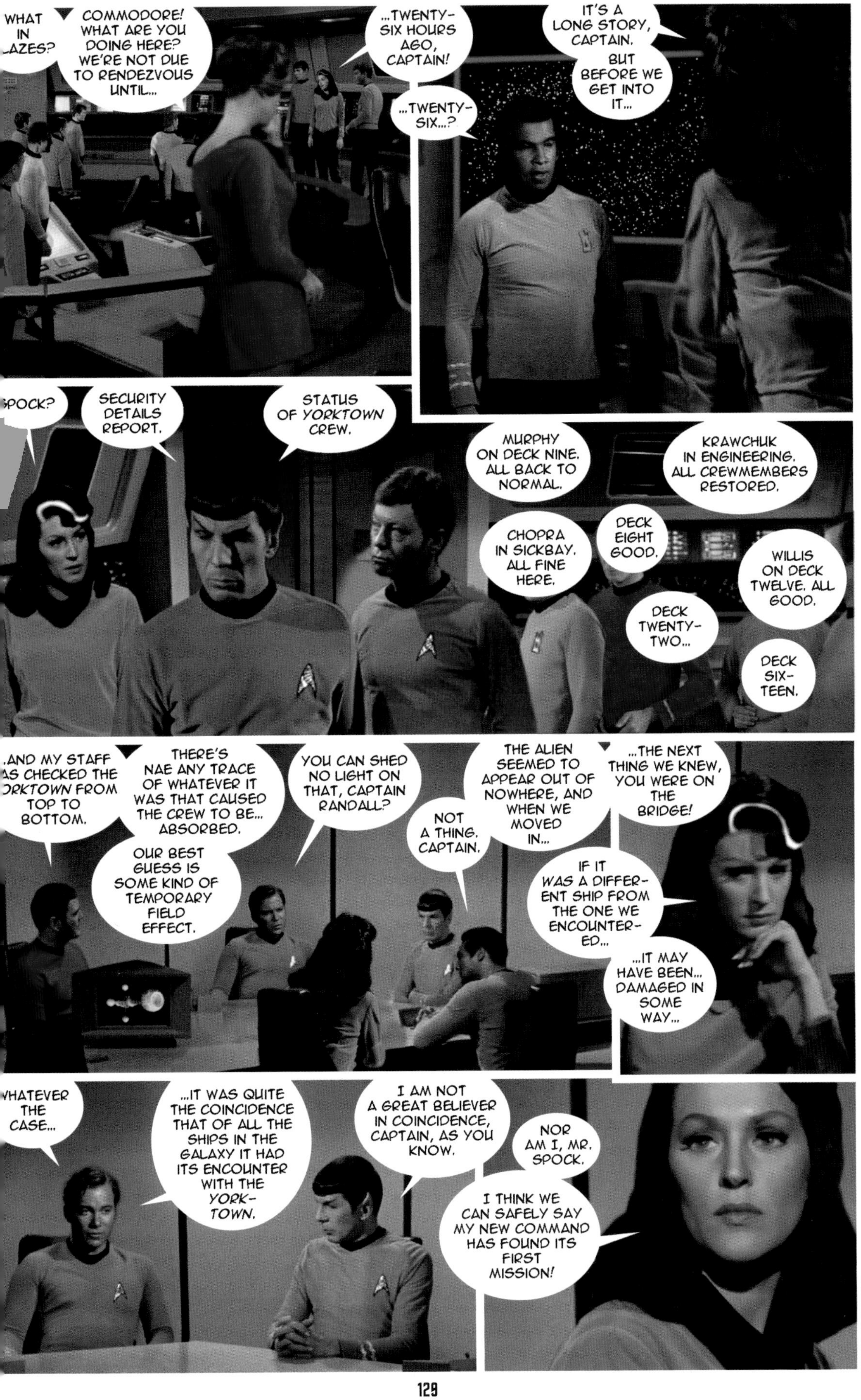
WHAT IN AZES?
COMMODORE! WHAT ARE YOU DOING HERE? WE'RE NOT DUE TO RENDEZVOUS UNTIL...
...TWENTY-SIX HOURS AGO, CAPTAIN!
...TWENTY-SIX...?
IT'S A LONG STORY, CAPTAIN.
BUT BEFORE WE GET INTO IT...
POCK?
SECURITY DETAILS REPORT.
STATUS OF *YORKTOWN* CREW.
MURPHY ON DECK NINE. ALL BACK TO NORMAL.
KRAWCHUK IN ENGINEERING. ALL CREWMEMBERS RESTORED.
CHOPRA IN SICKBAY. ALL FINE HERE.
DECK EIGHT GOOD.
WILLIS ON DECK TWELVE. ALL GOOD.
DECK TWENTY-TWO...
DECK SIX-TEEN.
AND MY STAFF AS CHECKED THE ORKTOWN FROM TOP TO BOTTOM.
THERE'S NAE ANY TRACE OF WHATEVER IT WAS THAT CAUSED THE CREW TO BE... ABSORBED.
OUR BEST GUESS IS SOME KIND OF TEMPORARY FIELD EFFECT.
YOU CAN SHED NO LIGHT ON THAT, CAPTAIN RANDALL?
NOT A THING, CAPTAIN.
THE ALIEN SEEMED TO APPEAR OUT OF NOWHERE, AND WHEN WE MOVED IN...
...THE NEXT THING WE KNEW, YOU WERE ON THE BRIDGE!
IF IT WAS A DIFFER-ENT SHIP FROM THE ONE WE ENCOUNTER-ED...
...IT MAY HAVE BEEN... DAMAGED IN SOME WAY...
HATEVER THE CASE...
...IT WAS QUITE THE COINCIDENCE THAT OF ALL THE SHIPS IN THE GALAXY IT HAD ITS ENCOUNTER WITH THE *YORK-TOWN*.
I AM NOT A GREAT BELIEVER IN COINCIDENCE, CAPTAIN, AS YOU KNOW.
NOR AM I, MR. SPOCK.
I THINK WE CAN SAFELY SAY MY NEW COMMAND HAS FOUND ITS FIRST MISSION!

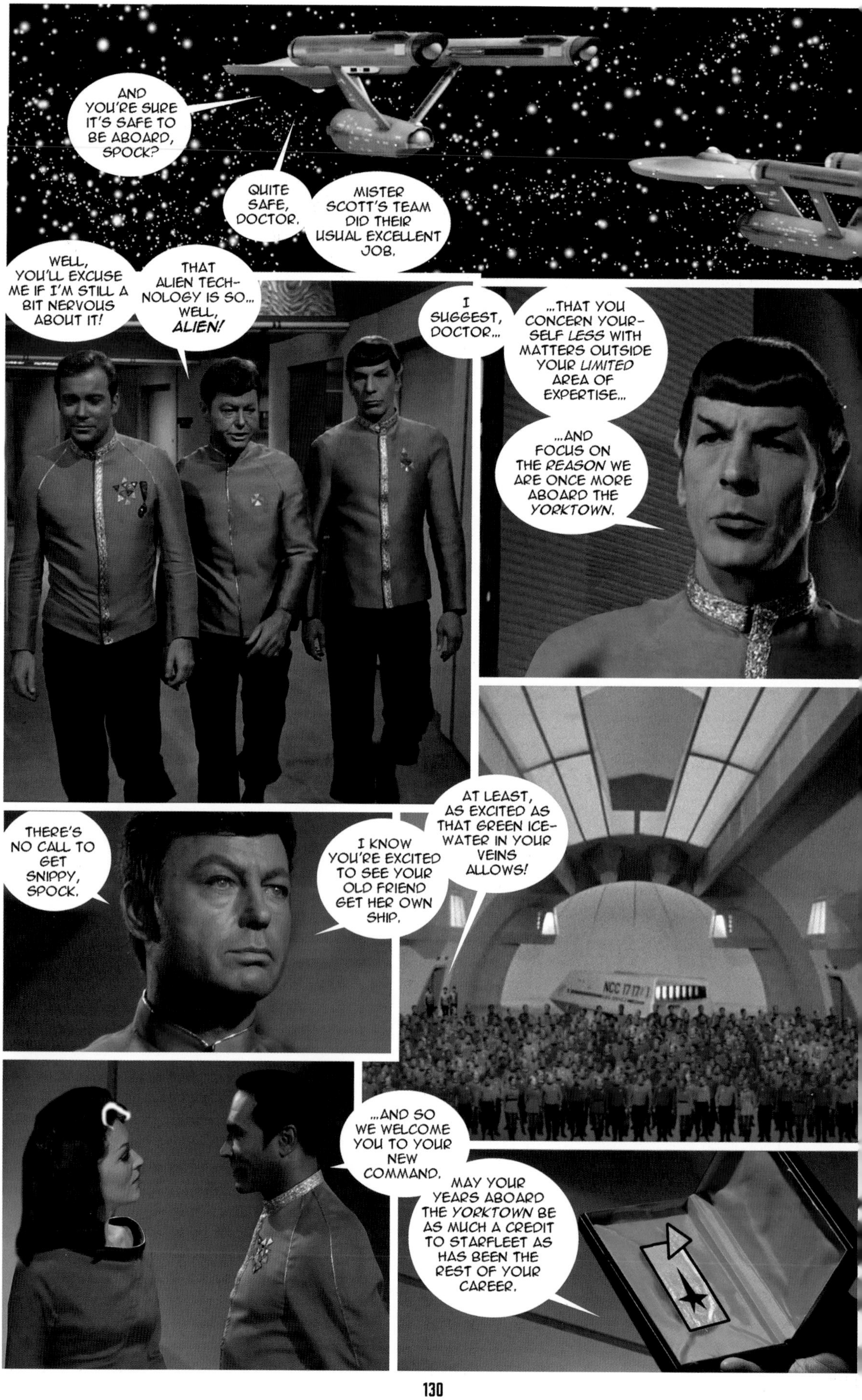
AND YOU'RE SURE IT'S SAFE TO BE ABOARD, SPOCK?
QUITE SAFE, DOCTOR.
MISTER SCOTT'S TEAM DID THEIR USUAL EXCELLENT JOB.
WELL, YOU'LL EXCUSE ME IF I'M STILL A BIT NERVOUS ABOUT IT!
THAT ALIEN TECH-NOLOGY IS SO... WELL, *ALIEN!*
I SUGGEST, DOCTOR...
...THAT YOU CONCERN YOUR-SELF *LESS* WITH MATTERS OUTSIDE YOUR *LIMITED* AREA OF EXPERTISE...
...AND FOCUS ON THE *REASON* WE ARE ONCE MORE ABOARD THE *YORKTOWN.*
THERE'S NO CALL TO GET SNIPPY, SPOCK.
I KNOW YOU'RE EXCITED TO SEE YOUR OLD FRIEND GET HER OWN SHIP.
AT LEAST, AS EXCITED AS THAT GREEN ICE-WATER IN YOUR VEINS ALLOWS!
NCC 1717
...AND SO WE WELCOME YOU TO YOUR NEW COMMAND.
MAY YOUR YEARS ABOARD THE *YORKTOWN* BE AS MUCH A CREDIT TO STARFLEET AS HAS BEEN THE REST OF YOUR CAREER.

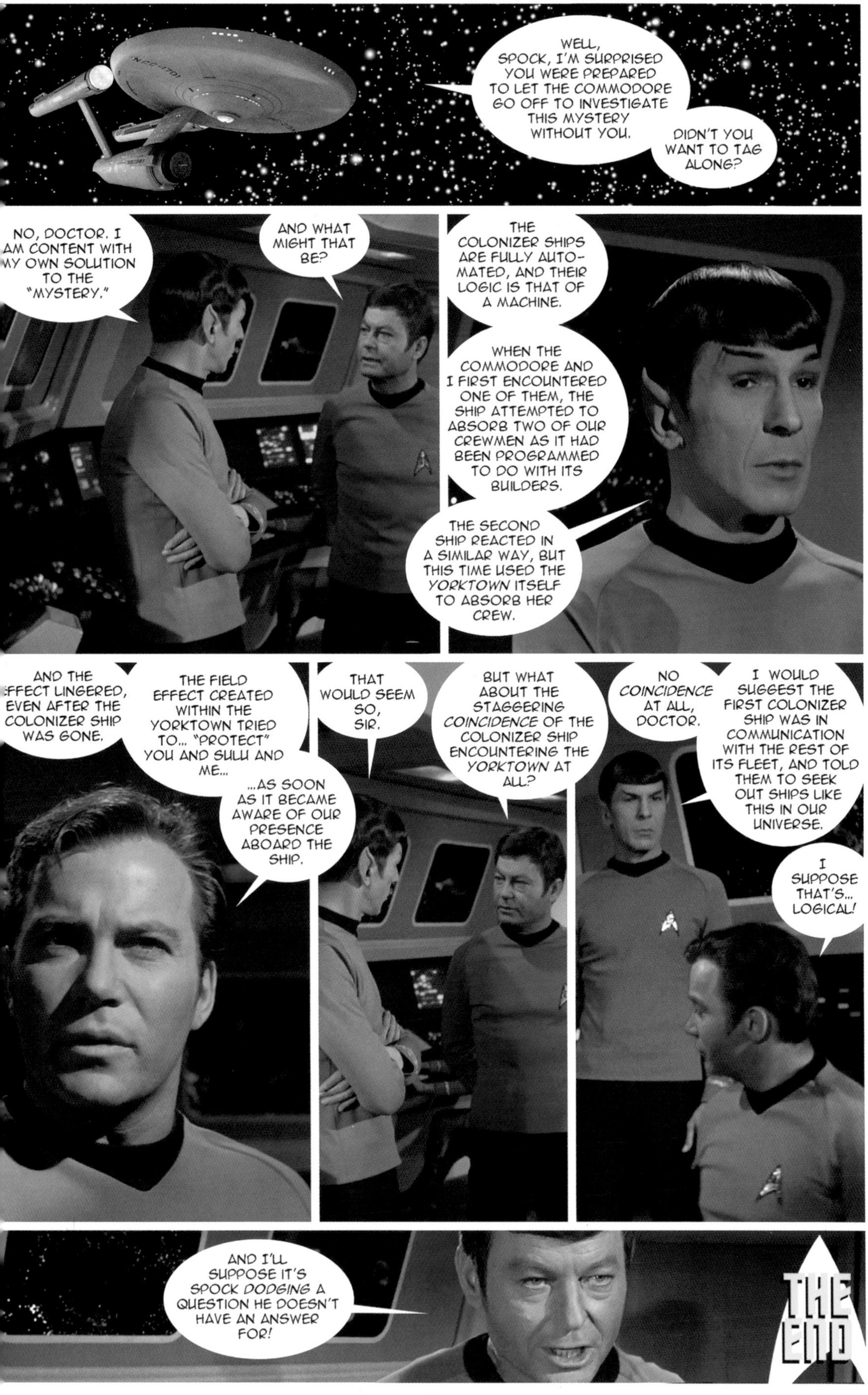
WELL, SPOCK, I'M SURPRISED YOU WERE PREPARED TO LET THE COMMODORE GO OFF TO INVESTIGATE THIS MYSTERY WITHOUT YOU.
DIDN'T YOU WANT TO TAG ALONG?
NO, DOCTOR. I AM CONTENT WITH MY OWN SOLUTION TO THE "MYSTERY."
AND WHAT MIGHT THAT BE?
THE COLONIZER SHIPS ARE FULLY AUTO-MATED, AND THEIR LOGIC IS THAT OF A MACHINE.
WHEN THE COMMODORE AND I FIRST ENCOUNTERED ONE OF THEM, THE SHIP ATTEMPTED TO ABSORB TWO OF OUR CREWMEN AS IT HAD BEEN PROGRAMMED TO DO WITH ITS BUILDERS.
THE SECOND SHIP REACTED IN A SIMILAR WAY, BUT THIS TIME USED THE *YORKTOWN* ITSELF TO ABSORB HER CREW.
AND THE EFFECT LINGERED, EVEN AFTER THE COLONIZER SHIP WAS GONE.
THE FIELD EFFECT CREATED WITHIN THE YORKTOWN TRIED TO... "PROTECT" YOU AND SULU AND ME...
...AS SOON AS IT BECAME AWARE OF OUR PRESENCE ABOARD THE SHIP.
THAT WOULD SEEM SO, SIR.
BUT WHAT ABOUT THE STAGGERING *COINCIDENCE* OF THE COLONIZER SHIP ENCOUNTERING THE *YORKTOWN* AT ALL?
NO *COINCIDENCE* AT ALL, DOCTOR.
I WOULD SUGGEST THE FIRST COLONIZER SHIP WAS IN COMMUNICATION WITH THE REST OF ITS FLEET, AND TOLD THEM TO SEEK OUT SHIPS LIKE THIS IN OUR UNIVERSE.
I SUPPOSE THAT'S... LOGICAL!
AND I'LL SUPPOSE IT'S SPOCK *DODGING* A QUESTION HE DOESN'T HAVE AN ANSWER FOR!
THE END

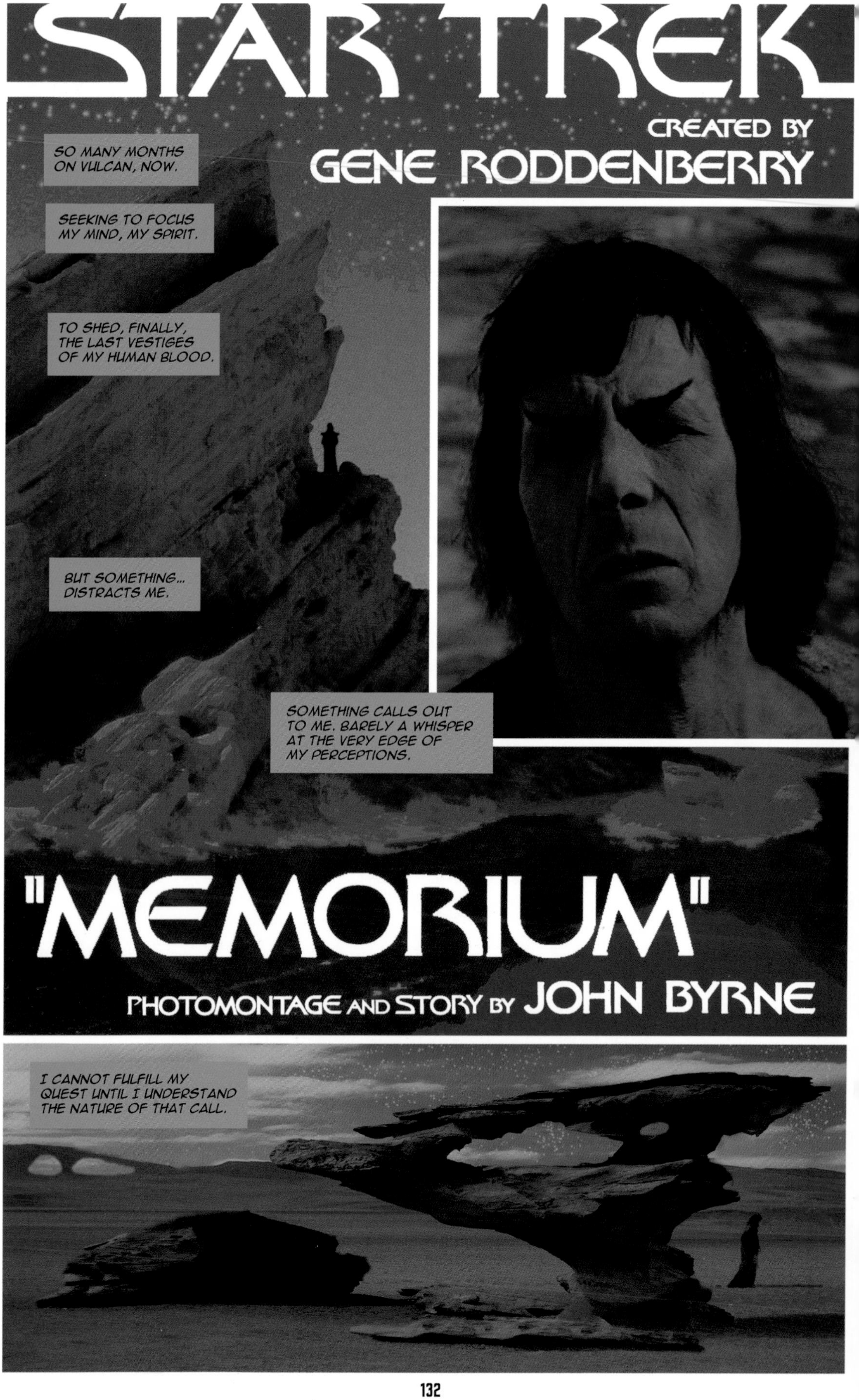
STAR TREK
CREATED BY
GENE RODDENBERRY
SO MANY MONTHS ON VULCAN, NOW.
SEEKING TO FOCUS MY MIND, MY SPIRIT.
TO SHED, FINALLY, THE LAST VESTIGES OF MY HUMAN BLOOD.
BUT SOMETHING... DISTRACTS ME.
SOMETHING CALLS OUT TO ME. BARELY A WHISPER AT THE VERY EDGE OF MY PERCEPTIONS.
"MEMORIUM"
PHOTOMONTAGE AND STORY BY JOHN BYRNE
I CANNOT FULFILL MY QUEST UNTIL I UNDERSTAND THE NATURE OF THAT CALL.

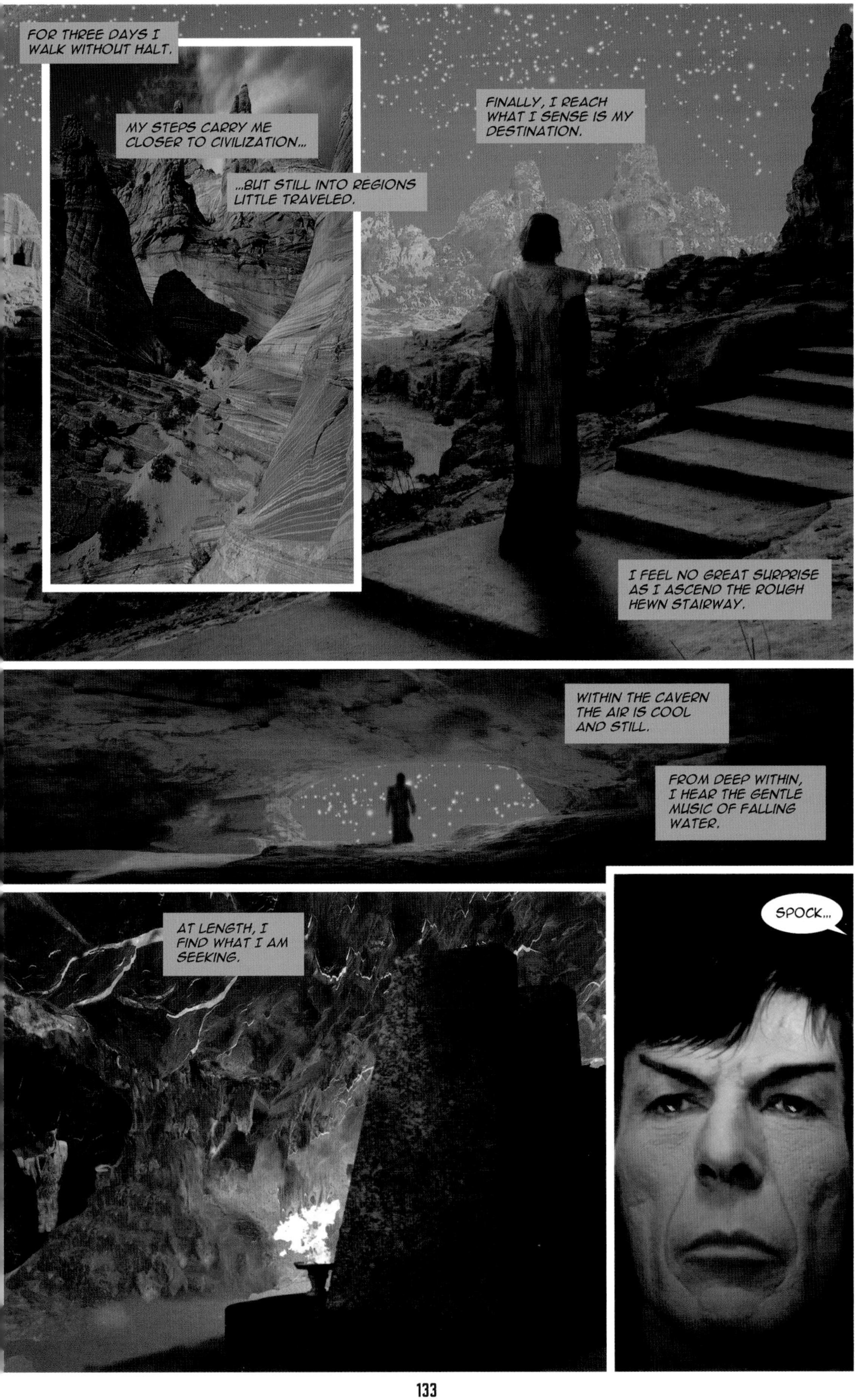
FOR THREE DAYS I WALK WITHOUT HALT.
MY STEPS CARRY ME CLOSER TO CIVILIZATION...
...BUT STILL INTO REGIONS LITTLE TRAVELED.
FINALLY, I REACH WHAT I SENSE IS MY DESTINATION.
I FEEL NO GREAT SURPRISE AS I ASCEND THE ROUGH HEWN STAIRWAY.
WITHIN THE CAVERN THE AIR IS COOL AND STILL.
FROM DEEP WITHIN, I HEAR THE GENTLE MUSIC OF FALLING WATER.
AT LENGTH, I FIND WHAT I AM SEEKING.
SPOCK...

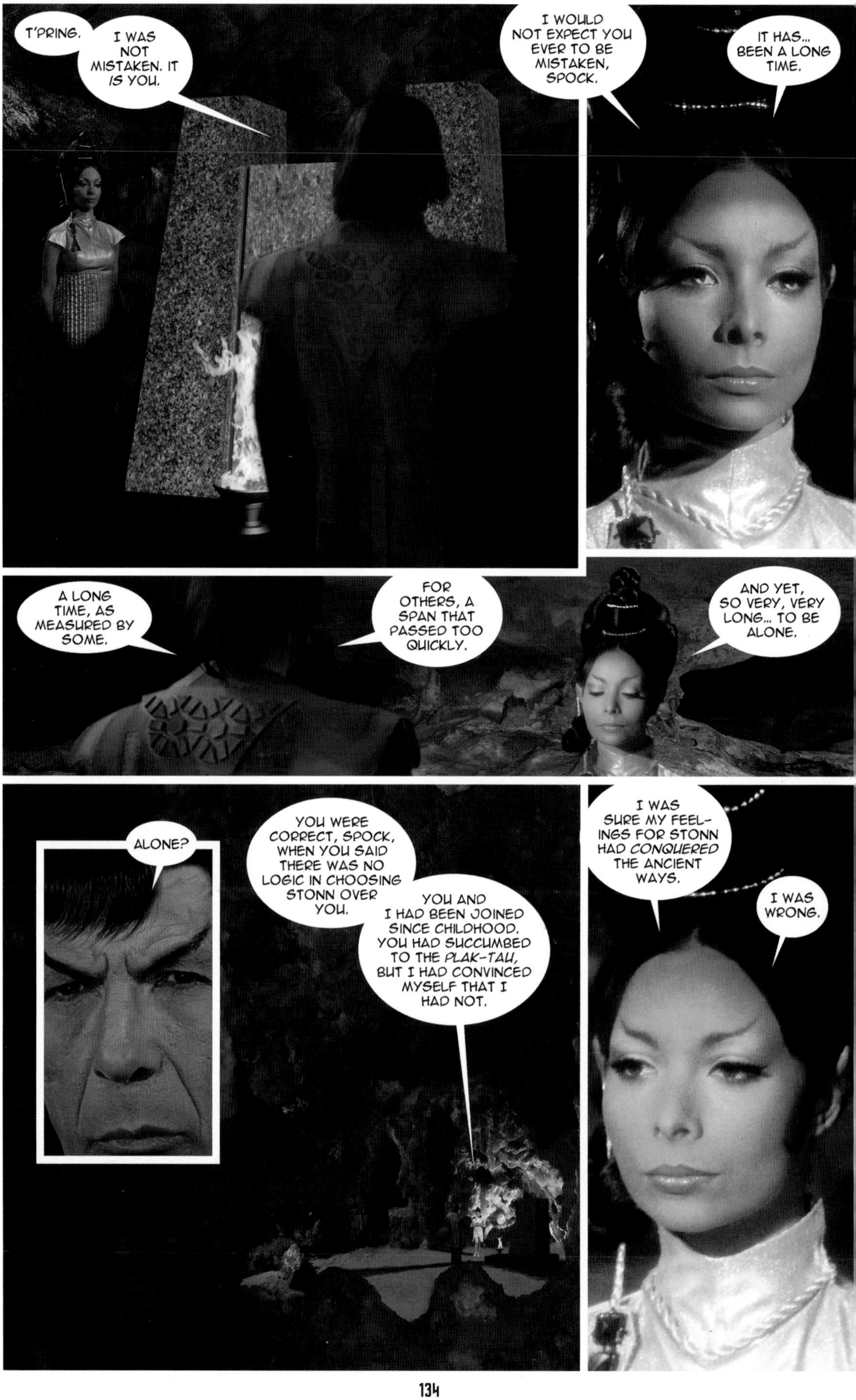

T'PRING.
I WAS NOT MISTAKEN. IT IS YOU.
I WOULD NOT EXPECT YOU EVER TO BE MISTAKEN, SPOCK.
IT HAS... BEEN A LONG TIME.
A LONG TIME, AS MEASURED BY SOME.
FOR OTHERS, A SPAN THAT PASSED TOO QUICKLY.
AND YET, SO VERY, VERY LONG... TO BE ALONE.
ALONE?
YOU WERE CORRECT, SPOCK, WHEN YOU SAID THERE WAS NO LOGIC IN CHOOSING STONN OVER YOU.
YOU AND I HAD BEEN JOINED SINCE CHILDHOOD. YOU HAD SUCCUMBED TO THE PLAK-TAU, BUT I HAD CONVINCED MYSELF THAT I HAD NOT.
I WAS SURE MY FEEL-INGS FOR STONN HAD CONQUERED THE ANCIENT WAYS.
I WAS WRONG.

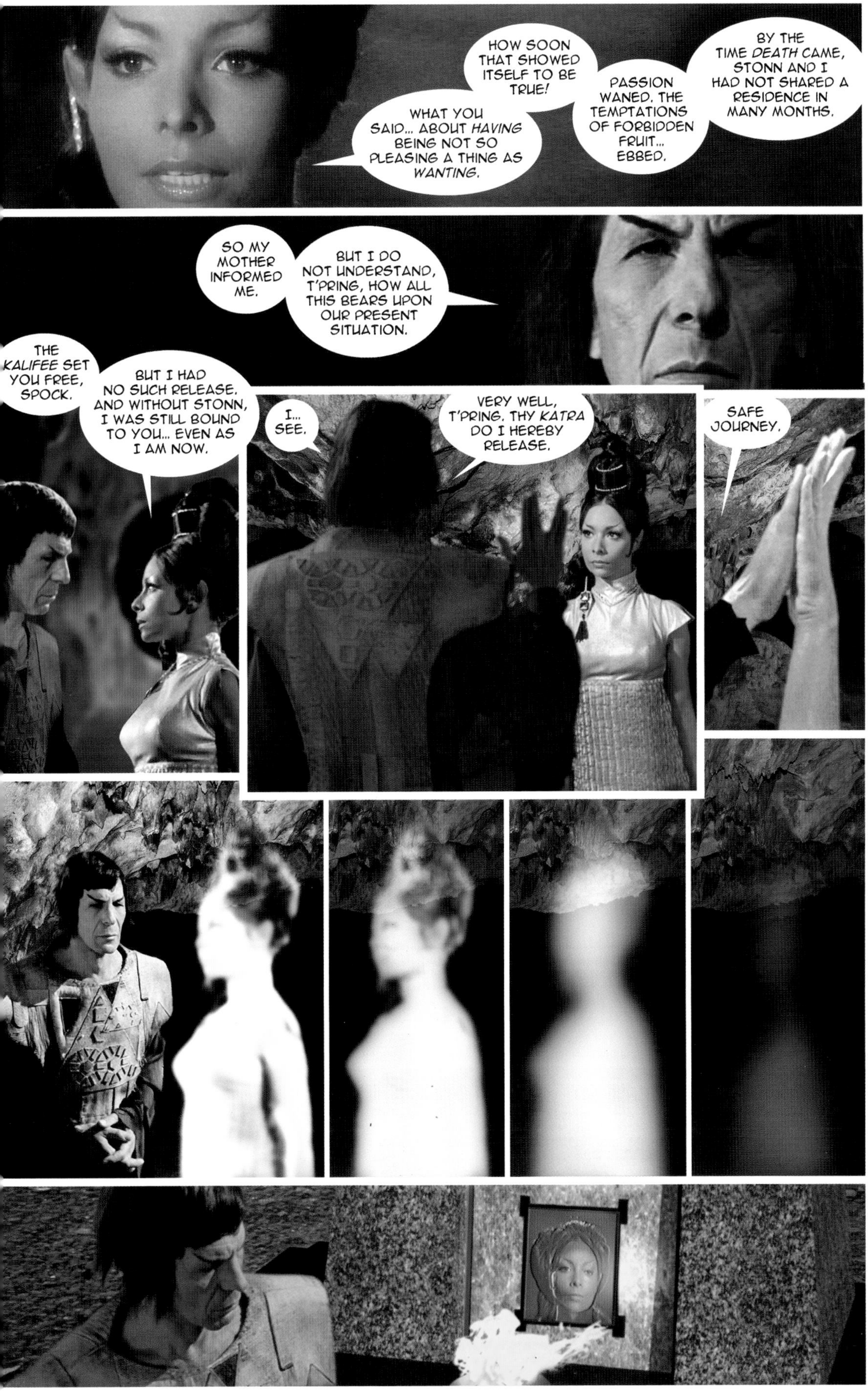
WHAT YOU SAID... ABOUT *HAVING* BEING NOT SO PLEASING A THING AS *WANTING*.
HOW SOON THAT SHOWED ITSELF TO BE TRUE!
PASSION WANED. THE TEMPTATIONS OF FORBIDDEN FRUIT... EBBED.
BY THE TIME *DEATH* CAME, STONN AND I HAD NOT SHARED A RESIDENCE IN MANY MONTHS.
SO MY MOTHER INFORMED ME.
BUT I DO NOT UNDERSTAND, T'PRING, HOW ALL THIS BEARS UPON OUR PRESENT SITUATION.
THE *KALIFEE* SET YOU FREE, SPOCK.
BUT I HAD NO SUCH RELEASE. AND WITHOUT STONN, I WAS STILL BOUND TO YOU... EVEN AS I AM NOW.
I... SEE.
VERY WELL, T'PRING. THY *KATRA* DO I HEREBY RELEASE.
SAFE JOURNEY.

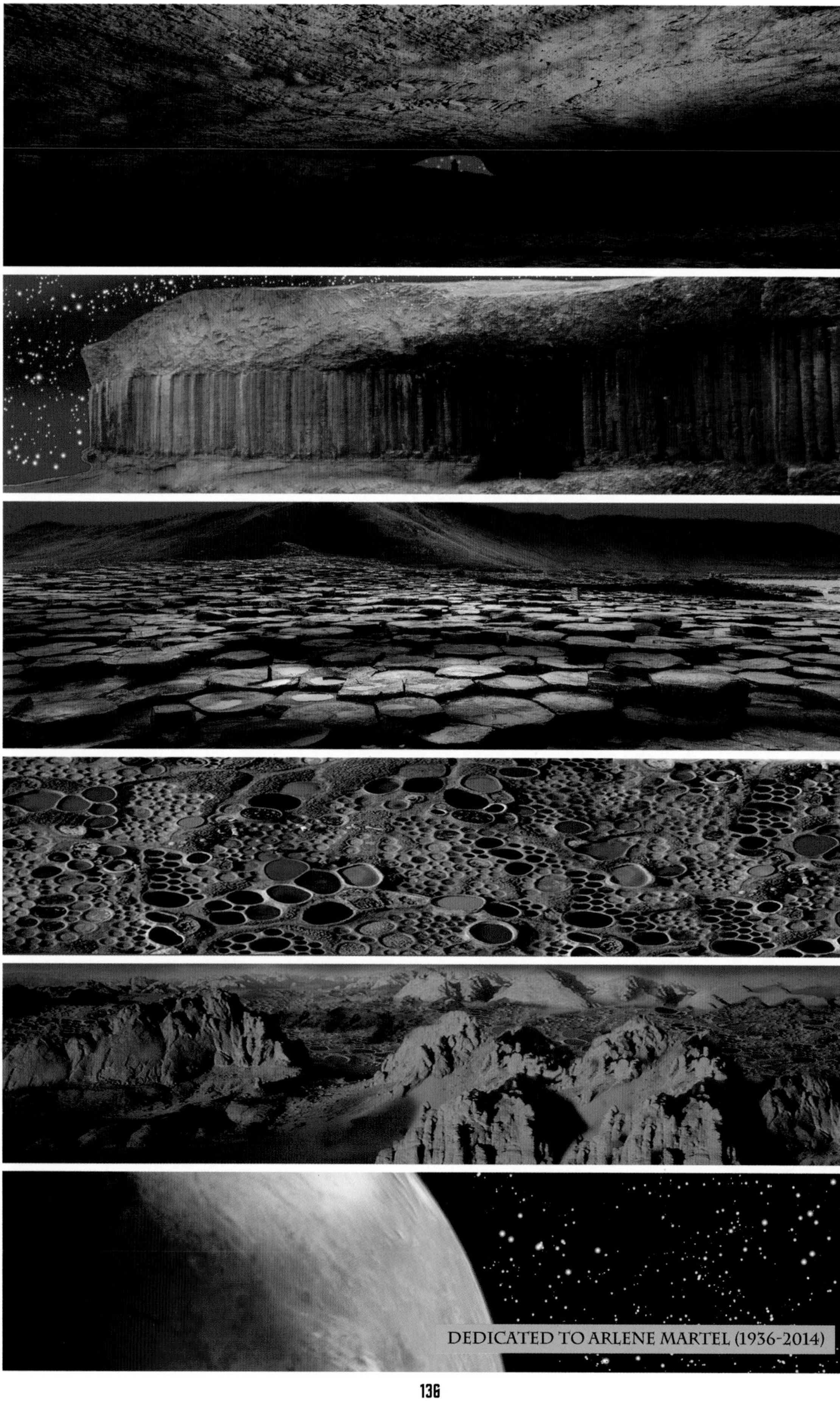
DEDICATED TO ARLENE MARTEL (1936-2014)

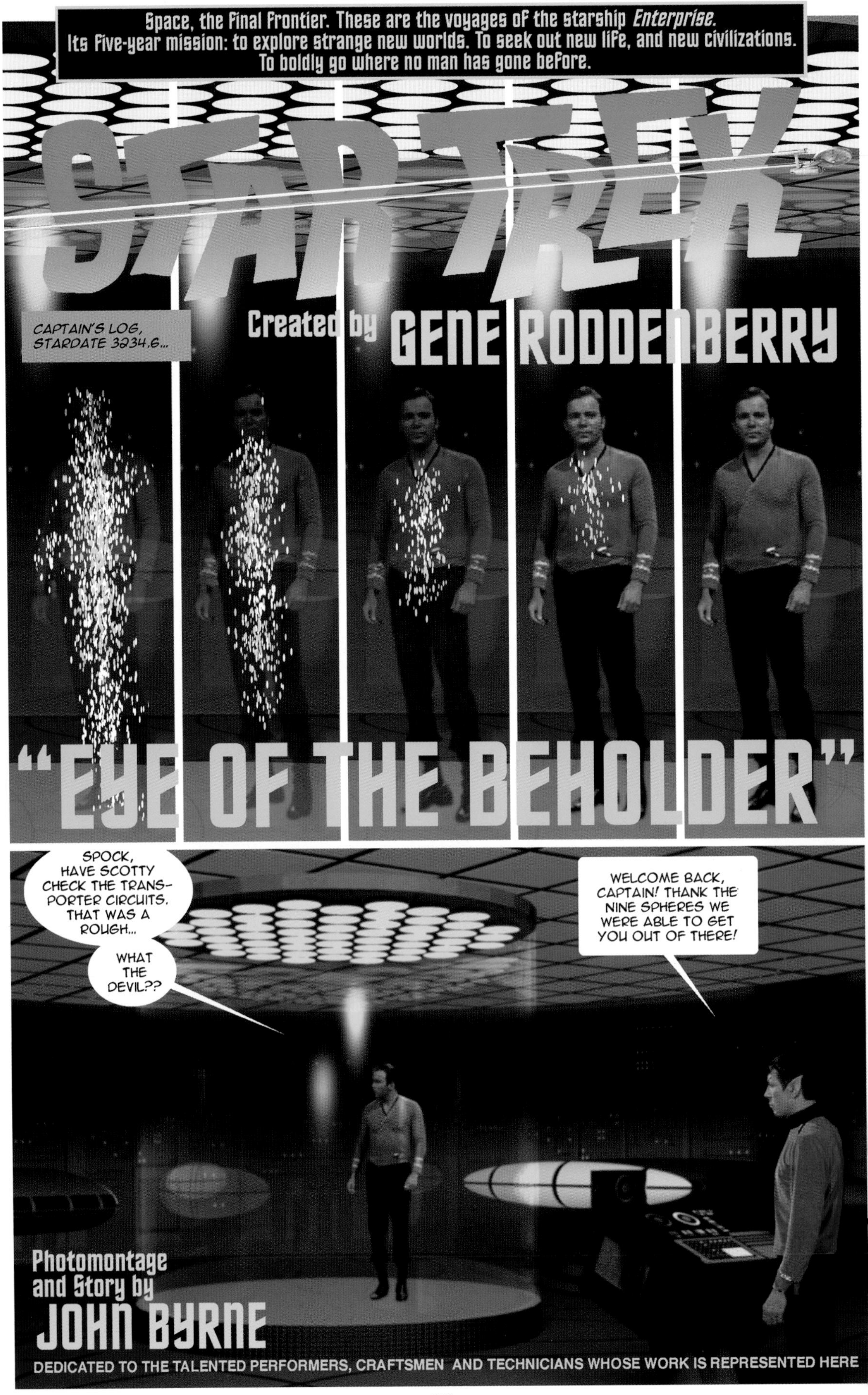
Space, the final frontier. These are the voyages of the starship *Enterprise*. Its five-year mission: to explore strange new worlds. To seek out new life, and new civilizations. To boldly go where no man has gone before.
STAR TREK
Created by GENE RODDENBERRY
CAPTAIN'S LOG, STARDATE 3234.6...
"EYE OF THE BEHOLDER"
SPOCK, HAVE SCOTTY CHECK THE TRANSPORTER CIRCUITS. THAT WAS A ROUGH...
WHAT THE DEVIL??
WELCOME BACK, CAPTAIN! THANK THE NINE SPHERES WE WERE ABLE TO GET YOU OUT OF THERE!
Photomontage and Story by JOHN BYRNE
DEDICATED TO THE TALENTED PERFORMERS, CRAFTSMEN AND TECHNICIANS WHOSE WORK IS REPRESENTED HERE

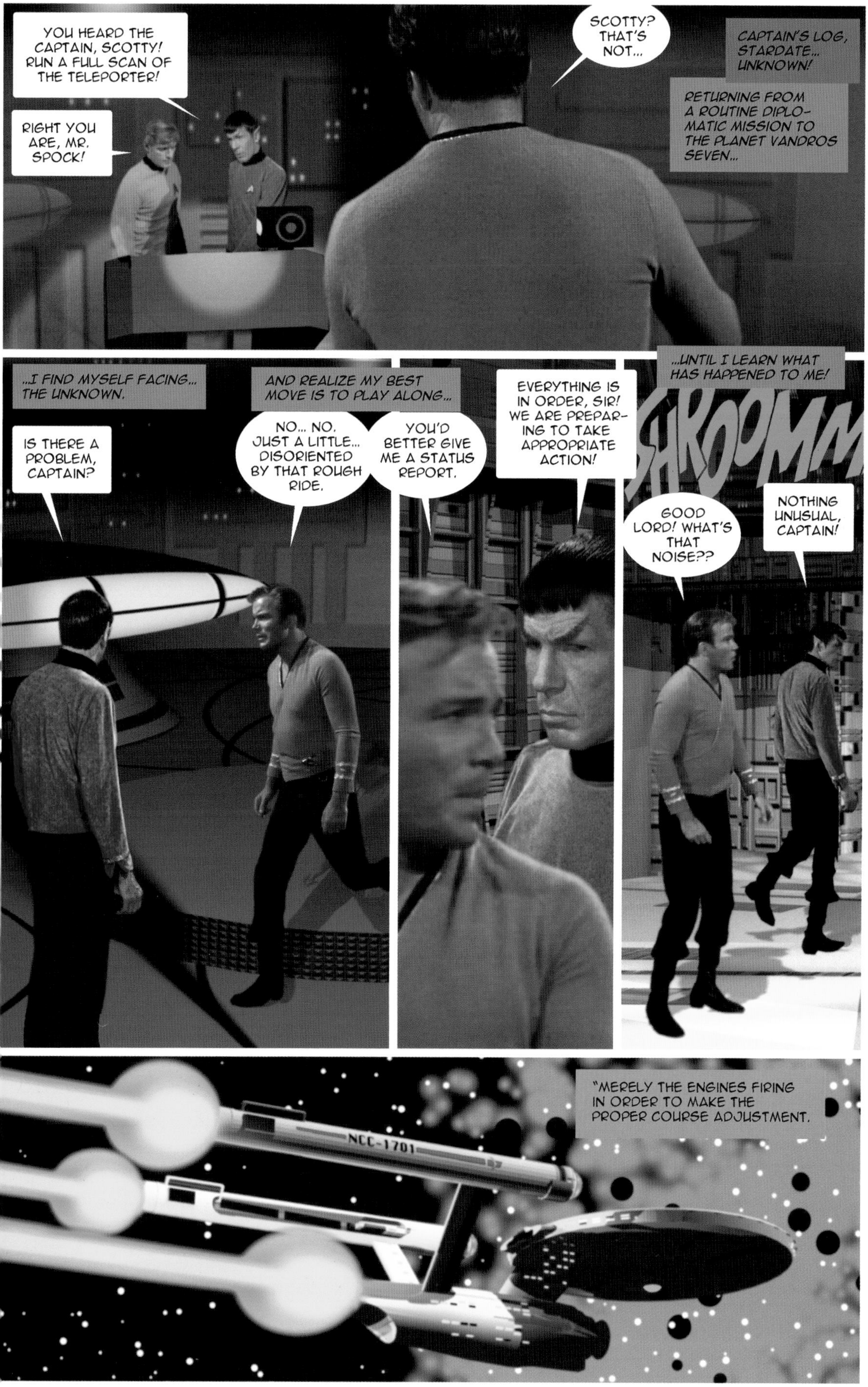
CAPTAIN'S LOG, STARDATE... UNKNOWN!
RETURNING FROM A ROUTINE DIPLOMATIC MISSION TO THE PLANET VANDROS SEVEN...
YOU HEARD THE CAPTAIN, SCOTTY! RUN A FULL SCAN OF THE TELEPORTER!
RIGHT YOU ARE, MR. SPOCK!
SCOTTY? THAT'S NOT...
...I FIND MYSELF FACING... THE UNKNOWN.
IS THERE A PROBLEM, CAPTAIN?
AND REALIZE MY BEST MOVE IS TO PLAY ALONG...
NO... NO. JUST A LITTLE... DISORIENTED BY THAT ROUGH RIDE.
YOU'D BETTER GIVE ME A STATUS REPORT.
EVERYTHING IS IN ORDER, SIR! WE ARE PREPARING TO TAKE APPROPRIATE ACTION!
...UNTIL I LEARN WHAT HAS HAPPENED TO ME!
SHROOMM
GOOD LORD! WHAT'S THAT NOISE??
NOTHING UNUSUAL, CAPTAIN!
"MERELY THE ENGINES FIRING IN ORDER TO MAKE THE PROPER COURSE ADJUSTMENT.
NCC-1701

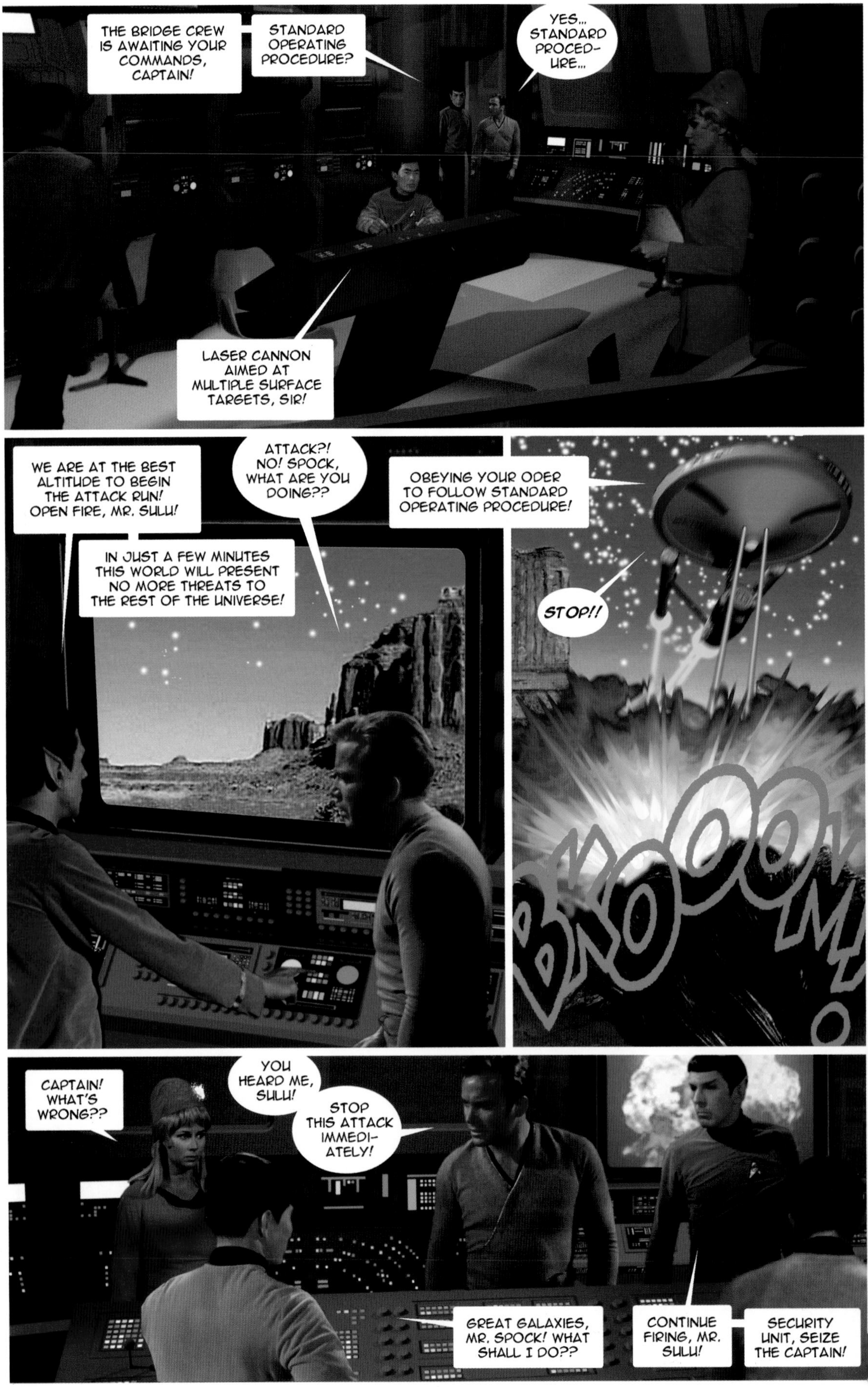
THE BRIDGE CREW IS AWAITING YOUR COMMANDS, CAPTAIN!
STANDARD OPERATING PROCEDURE?
YES... STANDARD PROCED-URE...
LASER CANNON AIMED AT MULTIPLE SURFACE TARGETS, SIR!
WE ARE AT THE BEST ALTITUDE TO BEGIN THE ATTACK RUN! OPEN FIRE, MR. SULU!
IN JUST A FEW MINUTES THIS WORLD WILL PRESENT NO MORE THREATS TO THE REST OF THE UNIVERSE!
ATTACK?! NO! SPOCK, WHAT ARE YOU DOING??
OBEYING YOUR ODER TO FOLLOW STANDARD OPERATING PROCEDURE!
STOP!!
BKOOOM
CAPTAIN! WHAT'S WRONG??
YOU HEARD ME, SULU!
STOP THIS ATTACK IMMEDI-ATELY!
GREAT GALAXIES, MR. SPOCK! WHAT SHALL I DO??
CONTINUE FIRING, MR. SULU!
SECURITY UNIT, SEIZE THE CAPTAIN!

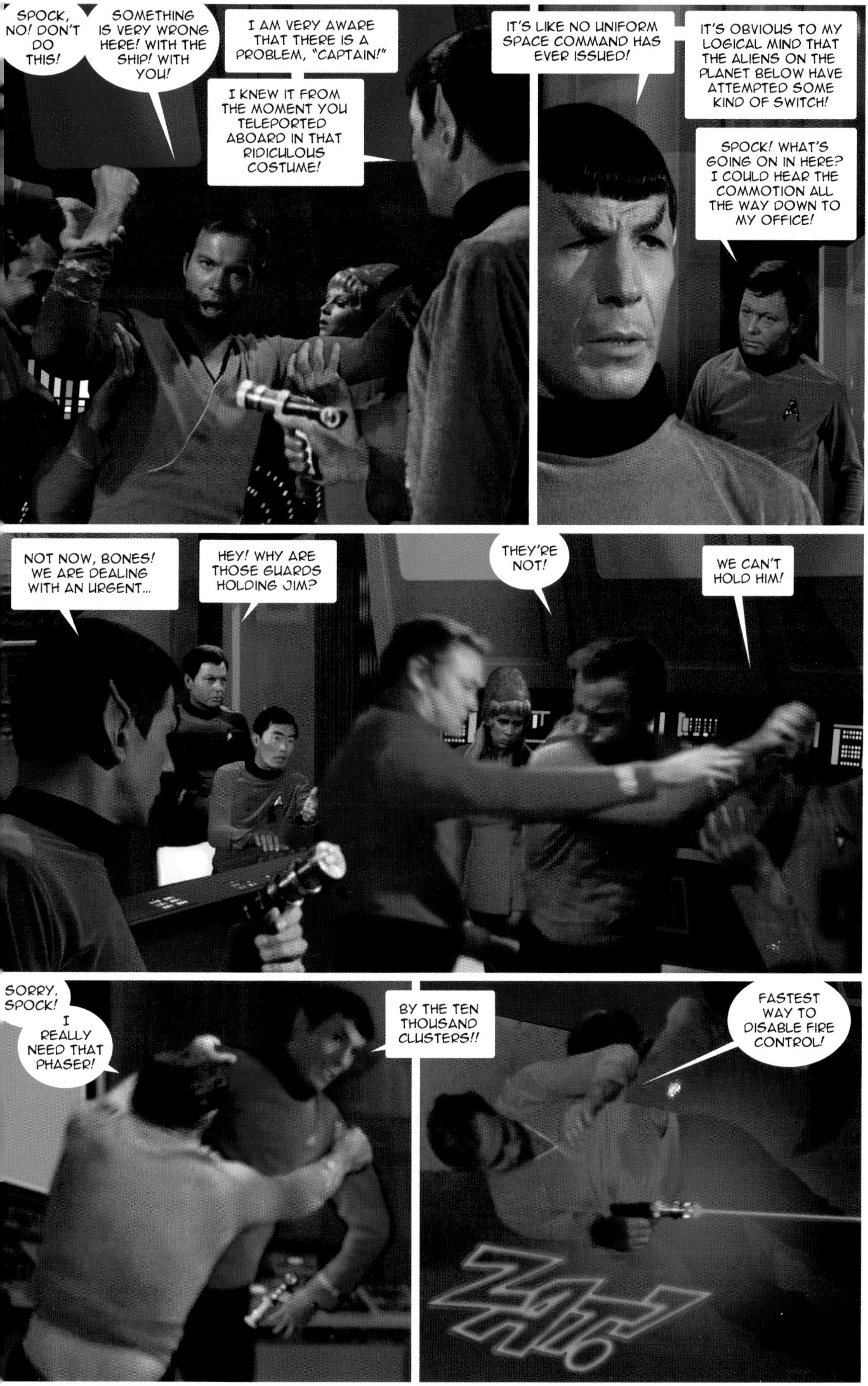
SPOCK, NO! DON'T DO THIS!
SOMETHING IS VERY WRONG HERE! WITH THE SHIP! WITH YOU!
I AM VERY AWARE THAT THERE IS A PROBLEM, "CAPTAIN!"
I KNEW IT FROM THE MOMENT YOU TELEPORTED ABOARD IN THAT RIDICULOUS COSTUME!
IT'S LIKE NO UNIFORM SPACE COMMAND HAS EVER ISSUED!
IT'S OBVIOUS TO MY LOGICAL MIND THAT THE ALIENS ON THE PLANET BELOW HAVE ATTEMPTED SOME KIND OF SWITCH!
SPOCK! WHAT'S GOING ON IN HERE? I COULD HEAR THE COMMOTION ALL THE WAY DOWN TO MY OFFICE!
NOT NOW, BONES! WE ARE DEALING WITH AN URGENT...
HEY! WHY ARE THOSE GUARDS HOLDING JIM?
THEY'RE NOT!
WE CAN'T HOLD HIM!
SORRY, SPOCK!
I REALLY NEED THAT PHASER!
BY THE TEN THOUSAND CLUSTERS!!
FASTEST WAY TO DISABLE FIRE CONTROL!
ZAP

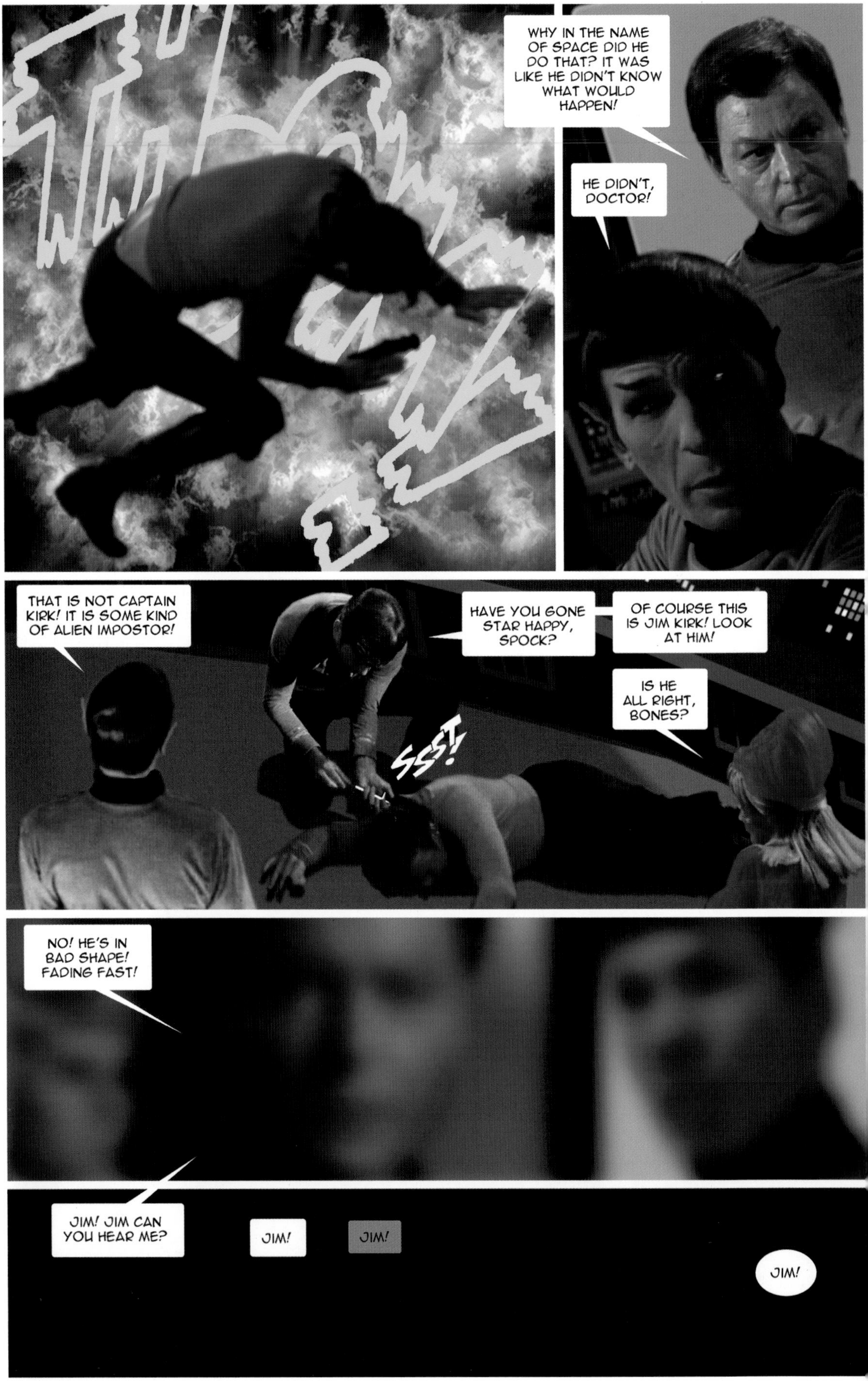
WHY IN THE NAME OF SPACE DID HE DO THAT? IT WAS LIKE HE DIDN'T KNOW WHAT WOULD HAPPEN!
HE DIDN'T, DOCTOR!
THAT IS NOT CAPTAIN KIRK! IT IS SOME KIND OF ALIEN IMPOSTOR!
HAVE YOU GONE STAR HAPPY, SPOCK?
OF COURSE THIS IS JIM KIRK! LOOK AT HIM!
IS HE ALL RIGHT, BONES?
SSST!
NO! HE'S IN BAD SHAPE! FADING FAST!
JIM! JIM CAN YOU HEAR ME?
JIM!
JIM!
JIM!

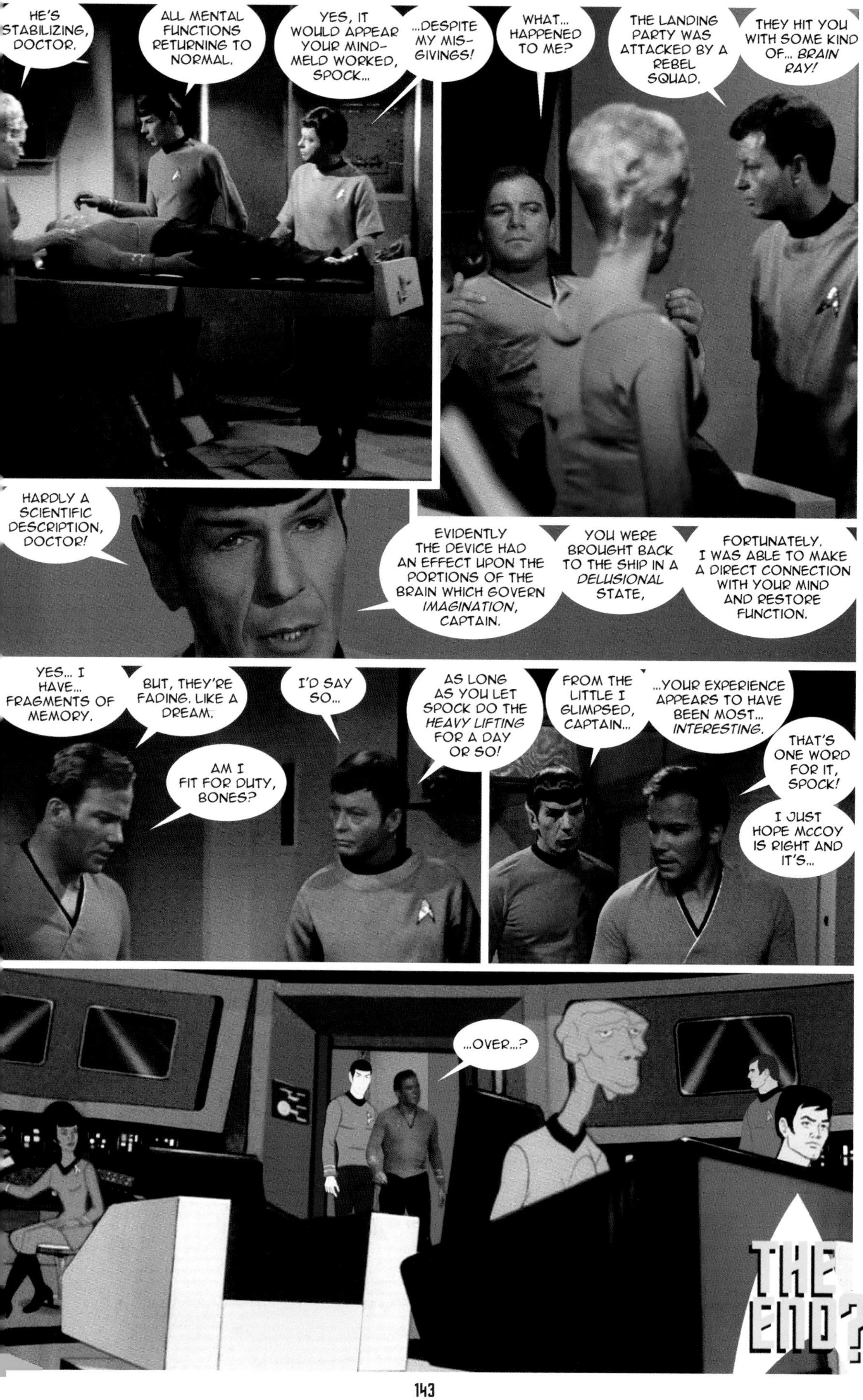
HE'S STABILIZING, DOCTOR.
ALL MENTAL FUNCTIONS RETURNING TO NORMAL.
YES, IT WOULD APPEAR YOUR MIND-MELD WORKED, SPOCK...
...DESPITE MY MIS-GIVINGS!
WHAT... HAPPENED TO ME?
THE LANDING PARTY WAS ATTACKED BY A REBEL SQUAD.
THEY HIT YOU WITH SOME KIND OF... *BRAIN RAY!*
HARDLY A SCIENTIFIC DESCRIPTION, DOCTOR!
EVIDENTLY THE DEVICE HAD AN EFFECT UPON THE PORTIONS OF THE BRAIN WHICH GOVERN *IMAGINATION,* CAPTAIN.
YOU WERE BROUGHT BACK TO THE SHIP IN A *DELUSIONAL* STATE.
FORTUNATELY, I WAS ABLE TO MAKE A DIRECT CONNECTION WITH YOUR MIND AND RESTORE FUNCTION.
YES... I HAVE... FRAGMENTS OF MEMORY.
BUT, THEY'RE FADING, LIKE A DREAM.
AM I FIT FOR DUTY, BONES?
I'D SAY SO...
AS LONG AS YOU LET SPOCK DO THE *HEAVY LIFTING* FOR A DAY OR SO!
FROM THE LITTLE I GLIMPSED, CAPTAIN...
...YOUR EXPERIENCE APPEARS TO HAVE BEEN MOST... *INTERESTING.*
THAT'S ONE WORD FOR IT, SPOCK!
I JUST HOPE McCOY IS RIGHT AND IT'S...
...OVER...?
THE END?

STAR TREK
NEW VISIONS